ARRIVALS AND DEPARTURES

Skeleton City sat poised like a silver filigree crown on the mountain foothills. Tall, narrow buildings rose forever, towering up to two thousand feet above the plain. Far above him, Mike saw dwarfed figures of people sauntering along thin crossways between the buildings.

Suddenly there was a cry of fear. Two men had carried a bound figure out onto one of the crosswalks about five hundred feet above the surface. Before the Traders knew what was happening, the body was swung outward and thrown clear. The scream of terror did not end until the woman's impact with the stone flags of the sidewalk.

Robin Songbird looked at Mike. "My apologies for the unfortunate timing. That execution was supposed to take place earlier today."

TRADER'S WORLD

Charles Sheffield

A Del Rey Book

BALLANTINE BOOKS • NEW YORK

For Victoria Jane

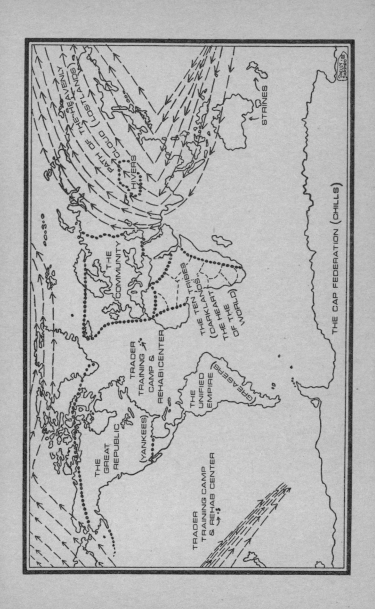

CHAPTER 1

At eighty thousand feet it was already dawn. A thin pink fingernail of solar disk had hooked the horizon and was clawing its way higher, pulling itself above a line of far-off clouds. In that early light, the slow-cruising Trader vehicle gleamed like a rosy pearl.

The woman of the crew had slept very little. Awake for the past two hours, she had been surveying the land far beneath through one of the image intensifiers in the forward cabin. Three times she pulled in overlays of surface radioactivity and soil maps, registered them to the image, and shook her head in dissatisfaction. Finally she removed the headset and went to sit quietly in the center compartment galley, drinking steaming cola tea and watching through the cabin window the broken line of daybreak as it crept westward. The vehicle she sat in was drifting in the opposite direction at a few miles an hour. They were too high for any sense of movement across the land, but the view beneath was imperceptibly changing.

"Morning, Lucia. Where are we?" The voice, which came from behind her, was thick with sleep.

She shook her head, not bothering to turn. "Nowhere. Nothing on the recent charts. I keyed into Daddy-O for the old overlays, and they show we're in an area that used to be called Dzungaria; but the modern maps have no names and no features, not even the Hive locations."

"See anything interesting down there?"

"Nothing to justify our presence. I'm starting to wonder why

1

Daddy-O gave us these coordinates. We could have been in Orklan by now."

"A statistical anomaly, that's all the briefing data said. You know Daddy-O, everything is statistics and probabilities."

"Well, there's no anomaly that I can find. No sign of strange landforms, no surface settlements, no water bodies, and our data base shows no Hive within three hundred miles."

"Radioactivity?"

"Not bad—hardly above general Lostlands background. But look at the landscape for yourself."

She picked up her cup, led the way into the forward cabin, and handed her companion the headset of the image intensifier. There was enough light now for the image to be clear without photon amplification, but Lyle Connery took the set anyway and fitted it across his forehead. After a few seconds he activated the zoom feature and did a slow high-magnification scan across the ground directly beneath the hovering craft.

At full magnification the footprint of the observing instrument was less than ten yards. With that resolution, Lyle Connery could have counted individual plants—even individual blades of grass. But there was not one to be counted. The ground beneath rolled in slow folds from north to south, in a series of shallow-sided hills and vales each three or four miles across. There were plenty of eroded paths showing the course of runoff of heavy rain, but no signs of vegetation. Connery could see dust devils swirling along the barren, dry creek beds and blowing across the cracked red subsoil; there was no other movement to catch his eye, no sign at all of life.

Lyle Connery sighed and requested a spectral analysis. When it appeared on the screen he shrugged his shoulders and removed the headset. "We're in the Lostlands all right. No humans, nothing alive. Not even bacteria."

He set the instrument to perform an automatic high-resolution scan of the whole area and to match composition against library signatures, then turned as far as he could toward Lucia Asparian. She was a big woman, but he was huge, and the two of them were crowded into a small forward compartment that had originally been designed for only one person. While they talked, their knees fought for space.

"Is it all like that?" Connery pointed to the screen where a low-resolution backup display ran continuously.

"So far, it is. I've been watching for hours. It's all like what you've seen. Barren substrate materials. No vegetation. Sandstones and hard clays. No organic content, and not a sign of topsoil."

"Then maybe we've got the location wrong." Connery rubbed his head and reached out absentmindedly to the mug of hot cola tea.

She casually smacked his hand away. "That's not possible, Lyle. I fed in the reference overlays, and everything in the data base matches what we're seeing. We're exactly where we are supposed to be. The only mystery is *why* we're here."

"So let's call back and ask Daddy O for details." Connery was already reaching for the console when a clear chime sounded through the cabin. Both of them looked up to the display screen. The automatic scan of the ground had ceased, leaving the observing instrument frozen on a view at nadir.

"See anything new?" Lucia Asparian sounded puzzled. "I don't."

"Neither do I. But that's a low-res screen. Take a look with—"

She was already moving. She had lifted the headset and was peering into it at the high-resolution image.

"There *is* something there," she said abruptly. "I see why we missed it until we were right overhead. It's a miniature valley. Steep sides on it—and deep—but there's topsoil showing at its bottom . . . and vegetation! It's tiny, though. It can't possibly hold a new Hive. The whole thing is less than a hundred yards long and thirty across."

Connery's sleepiness had vanished and he felt suddenly energetic and cheerful. "We weren't told to expect a Hive." As he spoke he was reaching for the controls to damp the ionization pad around the vehicle. The cushioning field diminished in range, and the craft began to drift lower in altitude, spiraling down toward the little valley in the center of the field of view.

"Even vegetation here is a surprise," he went on. "So people would be too much to hope for, because we're a long way from—Holy Greasers! Hold tight!"

His final words were a high-pitched shout of surprise and alarm. The screen showed a bursting plume of black smoke in the little valley beneath, followed by the bright orange-white flare of a rocket rushing up erratically toward their craft. Connery cut the ionization field completely to send the craft into free-fall, switched on the propulsion system to full throttle, and threw them into a sideways spiral. The Trader ship twisted and dropped like a broken-winged bird.

The rising rocket turned to follow their trajectory.

"Solid fuel—an antique, but not all that primitive—got targeting sensors on it!" Lyle Connery had wedged his legs under the console and was reaching across to the defense unit controls, while Lucia Asparian had been thrown back hard against the bulkhead. She struggled to sit upright.

"Heat-seekers?"

"Don't know." Connery hit a panel of switches. "Have to destroy it, even if it is an antique—an impact would do for us, even if the warhead's dead."

The pulse of radiation from the Trader vehicle had been released before he finished speaking. There was no sign of damage to the approaching rocket, but it veered away sharply and headed north with random changes in attitude. Its control electronics were dead. Lucia stared after it through the window until it hit the ground, then pulled herself slowly back into her seat.

She rubbed her head where it had thumped the cabin wall. "I guess that proves how much we know about what's going on in these parts. Taking us down?"

"Have to. Now we know there's something interesting on the ground."

"No heroics!"

"Trust me. I got that out of my system on my first mission." Connery feathered the craft into a gently descending curve, his full attention on the little valley. Lucia Asparian donned the headset again and turned the image to maximum magnification.

"Crops," she said at last. "I can see them now. All along the west side. Pretty ragged growth, but there must be a decent depth of topsoil there and not too much radioactivity. I can see the launcher, too, standing next to a hole in the other side of the valley. Looks absolutely ancient, even older than Daddy-O. Living quarters have to be back inside that hole. Catchment basin next to it, to collect rainwater runoff. Looks pretty full, must be used for irrigation as well as drinking. No sign of another rocket. We ought to be safe enough."

"Got my fingers crossed."

"Looks like they're growing Yankee barley and corn." Lucia Asparian gave the crop area a few more seconds of detailed inspection. "Delaunay variant varieties. That's Yankee technology. Wonder where they got the seed?"

"Keep watching the launch site," Connery grunted. "I won't

hold it against you if you don't learn any more about the crop species."

As they descended he was steadily slanting their path farther away from the valley, to present an increasingly oblique target for a ground-to-air defensive system. "I'm going to put us down a couple of miles away," he said. "Then we'll go in slow and steady, on the ground."

"Think they'll have a surface defense system?"

"With that small a living area, it wouldn't make much sense. But I wouldn't have expected any defenses at all, so maybe I'm going to be surprised again. We'd better go in bulletproof."

The Trader survey craft touched down on a gray-red inclined plain of exposed rock. Connery and Asparian pulled on Kevlar-14 coveralls with fitted face masks, slid open the door, and stepped cautiously out onto the rubble-strewn slope. The valley was completely hidden from this angle. It did not become visible again until they were on the brink of the final slope downward.

"We're right on top of it, and still you'd never know there's a fertile spot here," Lucia Asparian said softly. "Good topsoil, no Hives anywhere near, invisible a mile away on the ground, almost invisible from the air—great place for a hideaway."

"But *who's* hiding here? And why?" Connery, for all his bulk, was moving light-footed onto the final steep slope, leading the way into the narrow north end of the valley. The whole depression was visible to them now. There was no sign of life anywhere in it. Green corn, four feet high, waved gently in the southern breeze, and the temperature was noticeably higher. Lyle Connery was sweating profusely inside his flak suit.

"No way anyone could hide here," Lucia said, "unless they went underground or lay down in the middle of the crops. I can't see any trails leading that way. And there's no way they could have left without us seeing." She gestured to the dark opening carved into the valley's steep eastern side. "They have to be in there."

"Then it's your turn to cover me." Lyle Connery moved down to the valley floor and approached the entrance. He looked at it with disfavor. It was small and narrow, no more than four feet high and three feet across, and it was elevated a couple of feet above the smooth soil of the valley bottom.

"Not sure I can fit in there," he said after a moment. "Makes me claustrophobic just looking at it. It's meant for Hivers, that's for certain." He walked a few paces nearer and shone a flashlight into the aperture. "Blocked off with a door, just the way you'd expect. Must get pretty cold here at night. Looks like pre-War plastic, but I can't be sure. Well, we've come this far, better keep going. Don't come any nearer—I'm heading in."

He was moving forward as he spoke, stepping upward and then crouching to fit into the cramped opening. Lucia saw him reach out, saw the door swing open, then heard a sudden startled cry. Lyle Connery was in the middle of a blizzard of dark snowflakes, swirling all around him. She raised her weapon but there was no definite target other than Connery himself.

"Lyle! What's happening?"

"I'm all right." There was a gasp, then a shaky laugh. "But I'll bet my hair's turned white. They were all over me in a second. They're *hornets*—a whole nest of them! The door was booby-trapped, and when I opened it I pulled the whole lot down on my head. If I hadn't been wearing the flak suit and helmet . . . Hell and damnation!" He was suddenly beating at his neck, then capering around in the front of the door. "One of 'em stung me—must have got in at the neck join."

"Stand still." Lucia raised her weapon and bathed Connery in low power thermal flux. There was a louder hum of fury for a couple of seconds, then the whole swarm rose into the air and buzzed off to the south end of the valley. "Now, stop the dance practice and get right inside before they come back."

Connery grunted, swore, and squeezed into the narrow doorway.

"Little tunnel here, goes back a couple of yards," he said after a few seconds. His voice was breathless through the radio. "Then opens up. Dirt walls, pile of hay on the floor—must be a bed. Some dried food around—rotten looking stuff, I wouldn't want to touch it. No sign of a fireplace, must do all their cooking outside. Batch of sharp knives hanging on the wall, and a spare warhead for that surface-to-air missile. And somewhere there has to be . . ." There was a long pause. "But there isn't. There's no sign of any other way out."

"Concealed, maybe? Look for a hidden tunnel."

"Lucia, there's just no space for it in here. Come on, see for yourself."

Lucia took a quick look around the quiet valley. Nothing stirred. After a few moments she hurried forward and went in through the little door.

The room was no more than ten feet square, with a ceiling too low for her to stand up. She looked around carefully, then went across and moved the pile of hay to one side. Behind it lay nothing but a faceless dirt wall. Small ventilation holes, each no more than three inches across, had been cut in the forward wall. She went across and put her eye to one, and found she was looking out onto the floor of the valley.

She walked across to another one and peered into it briefly. "It's just the sort of mud hole the Hivers would choose to live in. The floor rises so they can never be flooded out, and the airholes run downward. So it *must* be Hivers—but where are they?"

Connery shrugged and led the way outside. The pair stood for a minute or two, gazing all around them.

"You stay right here and cover me," Lucia said at last. "Don't argue about it. I know I'm overweight, but I'm still a smaller target than you. If you have to talk, use radio contact— and whisper." She moved faster and went ahead on the final slope.

The hornet sting was itching intolerably. Connery removed the gloves of his suit and scratched furiously at his sore neck. He watched in silence while Lucia walked the full length of the valley, turning to look around her every few paces. Finally she began to retrace her steps.

"Nothing?" Connery asked.

"Nothing." After a few more moments she went across to the little pond of the water catchment and stood staring at it. It was built into the side of the valley and stood with its clay and stone retaining wall waist high from the main valley floor. She walked slowly around its semicircle, staring at the base.

"This is the surprise," she said. "You've seen more Hiver communities than I have. How many of them have ponds like this to catch rainwater?"

"None of 'em. Every Hiver I've met has been too scared of being trapped underground by water. That's why they build the Hives the way they do, to make it impossible. Hell, most of 'em hate water so bad they won't even wash."

"Right. So the last thing that any Hiver would ever do is this." As Lucia spoke she was bending down by the foot of the catchment wall, pulling at a rectangular stone in the base.

"You'll empty the whole thing over you if you're not care-ful," Connery began; but as he was speaking, the big stone came free to reveal that it was no more than a facing lamina of thin rock. Lucia crouched down toward the dark hole that lay behind it. She was still at half-stoop when a small, mud-smeared figure sprang out, dived between her legs, and ran away madly around the catchment pond.

"Grab him!"

It was a skinny, naked boy, moving as fast as a startled bird. Connery was already responding to Lucia's cry. He made a dive and grabbed the fleeing figure as it tried to swerve past him.

"I've got him. Ouch!" Connery had released his hold, and the boy was off and running again. He shook his hand violently. "The little bugger bit me on the thumb. Come on, let's get him!"

The youngster was heading right up the steep side of the valley. He ascended the slope at twice the speed that Connery could manage, but once on the flatter surface above he had no chance. Connery's long legs ate up the ground and caught him within fifty strides. There was a brief struggle, then Connery had lifted the boy off the ground and was holding him with one arm around his neck and the other pinioning his arms.

The captive went on fighting desperately. When Lucia Asparian caught up with them she found herself staring at a purpling, half-strangled face and a pair of terrified and angry eyes. She looked at the boy in silence for a few moments, then shook her head.

"He was the only one in there?" Connery asked.

She nodded. "He was. I took a good look. I'm not sure what we should do next, but I think we can go back to the Surveyor now. Daddy-O wanted us to find an anomaly. I guess we've got one."

CHAPTER 2

The boy was undersized, emaciated, and feral, with black hair shoulder length at the back and chopped crudely short over his ears and forehead. His age could have been anywhere between ten and sixteen years. Connery waited, inspecting his injured thumb and glowering at the boy, while Lucia went on a cautious walk through the growing crops.

She took her time, systematically exploring every row of vegetation. A thorough search of the valley revealed no sign of other people. Connery kept one eye on her progress, and one on the boy. All his attempts to ask questions were totally ignored. Finally he abandoned the effort.

Lucia Asparian rejoined Connery and they began to head back to the airship. "Do you think he understands *anything* you've been saying to him?" Lucia asked. She had switched from the less-familiar Hiver dialect to standard Trader.

Connery still held the youth in a tight grip. His thumb had stopped bleeding from the bite, but he was not risking another one. He looked at his captive's angry profile and skin-and-bone rib cage. "I don't know. Could be he's playing dumb and looking for another chance to run for it. Or he could be a true wild boy, somebody who's never been exposed to language before; but if he is, then where the devil did he learn to launch that missile? Here now—" Connery tightened his grip further, but his voice took on its first trace of sympathy. At the sight of the aircar as they breasted the slope, the youth had groaned in dismay and was struggling to free himself. "Take it easy, young fellow, we won't eat you."

9

He had to drag the boy the rest of the way to the ship, and began to lift him bodily into the cabin. He grimaced as his face came close to the lad's dark head. It was alive with lice, crawling through the mud-spattered and matted hair.

"Lucia, give me a hand here. We can't question him in this condition. He needs cleaning, and he needs clothes—and I'd guess he's long overdue for a decent meal. I'm going to dump him into the cleanser and let it wash him, but he'll probably be scared of it and fight like a demon. I think we ought to put him right out."

"Agreed. And as soon as he wakes up, maybe we'll find out a bit more about him." Lucia climbed into the vehicle ahead of Connery. She administered the painless spray injection while the boy was being lifted in. He had no time to struggle. Within a few seconds he was lying unconscious on the cabin floor. While Connery strapped their find into the automatic cleansing unit, she prepared the on-board interrogation system.

The cleansing unit opened two minutes later to show the boy soaped, rinsed, and disinfected from head to toe. His stick-thin limbs showed the sores and ulcers of severe malnutrition.

Lucia was ready for him. She picked up the unconscious body, wrapped a warm towel around him, and laid him gently on a bunk. While she strapped him down and attached the terminals and headset that put them into three-way communication with Daddy-O, Lyle Connery sat frowning on the other bunk.

"We're ready to go home," he said, "but what are we going to do with *him*? We can't put him back in the valley, living like that. You saw the food supply—he must have been scraping along close to starvation. Can we drop him off at one of the Hives?"

"If we can find out where he came from originally. Maybe he was abandoned, or maybe others will be coming back to the valley any time now. He'll be awake in a minute or two. I'll see what I can find. Why don't you get some food ready while I'm doing it? I think he's more scared of you."

She remained quietly by the boy's side. He was alert and struggling as soon as his dark eyes opened. Lucia Asparian smiled at him, kept her voice soft, and said in Hiver local dialect, "Don't be afraid, we are not going to hurt you. What is your name?"

He looked terrified, rolled his eyes sideways to try to follow the line of the terminals attached to his temples and throat, and clenched his teeth tight.

Daddy-O's interrogation circuits back in the Azores caught the prisoner's brain patterns and the subvocalized word, and provided the local inputs to Lucia Asparian. *"His name is Mikal,"* said the voice in her headset. There was a fraction of a second delay while the information passed through the Chipponese satellite relays, then Daddy-O added, *"A high level of fear beyond what can be explained by his surroundings. I think he is disturbed by direct input. He understands Hiver, and it will be better if we restrict ourselves to that as his signal from you. But I will tap his visual and emotional codes, so that you can see his responses. He will be unaware of that operation."*

Lucia nodded. "Mikal," she said, and the boy's eyes bulged. "Mikal, do you have another name?"

The jaw clenched tighter for a moment, then there was an imperceptible shake of his head.

"He does not think of himself as having any other name," Daddy-O said. *"If he ever lived in the Hives, he left there before puberty. That is their time for caste naming. There is no strong associated visual signal for your question."*

Lucia again tried to guess the age of the youth on the bunk. Certainly no less than ten, and probably no more than fifteen. "You live down there in the valley," she said. "Do other people live with you?"

There was another imperceptible shake of the head.

"They no longer live there," Daddy-O said. *"One moment. We have visuals."*

A clear image of two people's faces appeared to Lucia, apparently hovering above the bunk. Daddy-O had a direct feed through her optic nerve. Both the people she was looking at were male. One of them was perhaps a couple of years older than Mikal, the other seemed to be in his late twenties.

"Your two friends in the valley," Lucia asked. "What happened to them, Mikal? Where are they now? Are they hiding from us?"

This time there was a gabble of Hiver words. "Why do you pretend you don't know? You took them, you *destroyed* them." And within a second came a sharp sequence of images: the side of the valley . . . six bulky figures with grotesquely enlarged and boxlike heads rushing down the steep slope . . . hand weapons at the ready. As they came closer Lucia saw that they wore protective Hive-armor. The "heads" were ribbed and padded helmets, with holes for eyes and mouth. As the scene ended, Mikal's two companions were seized and thrown to the ground.

"Destroyed them." Mikal shivered, and closed his eyes.

"Possible, but unlikely." Daddy-O's electronic voice in her ears was as calm as ever. *"You know the customs of the larger Hives."*

Lucia reached forward and took her captive by the hand. "Mikal, we are not Hivers. Open your eyes, and take a good look at me, and see for yourself. Did you ever see a Hive warrior who looked anything like us?"

The dark eyes opened. He stared hard at Lucia, and some of the fear drained from his expression. "No." His voice was perplexed. "Warriors cannot be women, and the man with you does not look right. But you have a machine that flies in the air—just like the one that took away Gregor and Pallast."

"There are many machines like ours, Mikal, in many places. We came from far away, beyond all the Hives." She was pleased at the change in him. At least he sounded rational now. "But how did you escape capture?"

"They didn't see me at first. I was up at the far end of the valley. I dropped down and hid in the corn until they were all gone." His voice was bitter with self-reproach. "I was afraid—too afraid to help."

Daddy-O provided another image: two struggling figures beaten to the ground, dragged back up the slope. The view of the scene was not clear, screened by tall stalks of ripe wheat.

"One full year, and they never came back," Mikal continued. "I am ashamed." He turned his head to one side, and would not look at her. There was a long silence while Lucia waited for visual signals from Daddy-O that never came.

"They never came back," she prompted at last. "But why do you say your friends were destroyed? The people who came here were warriors from a southern Hive—and they do not kill prisoners."

"Not killed dead. I did not mean that. We were not supposed to be killed dead. Destroyed. It was already planned for Gregor and me, if we had stayed one more month. To serve as Royal Suppliers to the Hive-Lord, and ensure his immortality. They were going to . . ."

This time the images from Daddy-O formed a long, kaleidoscopic thought sequence, a progression that flickered on through time and space but returned again and again to a single intolerable moment.

Lucia saw the inside of a Hive.

. . . narrow chambers and corridors, scarcely tall enough to

stand in, burrowed deep into red sandstone . . . the central chamber, lit by the green glow of fluorescents, a group of women wearing the full cowl of Hive-Lord servants. Along one wall stood the rusting rows of ancient weapons, the anti-tank guns, radar units, power lasers, and flamethrowers. Opposite them sat the Royal Suppliers, huge, soft-skinned, smiling.

"*. . . a great honor, Gregor. You and Mikal have been called to the service of the King . . .*"

. . . glowing red lamps, flickering red torches, the long wooden table in the central chamber, the ritual gold knife held ready . . .

. . . his two companions at his side, laden with as much food and water as they dared carry, creeping out of the least-used entrance to the Hive and heading north beneath the open night sky, running and running, covering themselves at dawn with red-gray gravel, crouching all day at the bottom of the dry gulch . . .

. . . the knife had been sharpened against a grinding stone. It must never touch base metal.

The chief of the warriors, bending low over the boy strapped to the table until the eyes were visible, glittering through the eye slits, red reflections of the torchlights . . .

"*. . . a life wholly dedicated to the service of the Great King, the body of the new Supplier must be prepared . . .*"

The line of Royal Suppliers sat nodding in their endless dreams, pale and motionless. They were fed constantly, Strine synthetics spooned into soft, red-lipped mouths dwarfed by vast cheeks and bloated jowls. The mouths smiled, on and on.

. . . the knife coming slowly down, the serving women standing by.

. . . the three were staggering along, water supply close to gone, food running low, longing looks at the precious seedcorn. They passed a hundred old settlements, derelict buildings, rubble of houses long since plundered for glass, wood, and metal, rank grass growing along old streets, missile defenses all crumbled and useless. Onward . . . seeking the hidden place, the legendary land of plenty that lay beyond the farthest Hive, location and distance known not even to the Hive-Lord . . . peering again and again through dust-blurred eyes, scanning hopelessly the northern horizon . . .

A shower of rain, unexpected and life-saving, sent flash floods rushing dangerously through the gravel-bottomed arroyos. Drinking to capacity, filling every water bottle, walking on to meet the Pole Star...

"... drink deep, and repeat these words ..."

The service of dedication was almost over; the final cup was being held to the boy's lips as he lay silent on the table. His place among the Suppliers had already been prepared, a new padded dais designed to accommodate endlessly increasing bulk, tap lines ready to be inserted at spleen and pancreas and running to the fungal growth vats.

... the first sight of the valley, its springing wild greenery, the astonishing sight of the ancient rocket launcher, rusted and menacing on the south end of the valley floor...

The knife was sweeping down with a ceremonial flourish, down to the naked belly of the youth, closing with the flesh. The drink had been drugged, but not enough. The cry when the knife sliced into his scrotum and removed his testicles was weak and high pitched, quivering through the quiet chamber. The woman bent to cauterize the wound with smoking pitch... the scream became full throated and agonized. The boy was carried fainting to his place in the line of Suppliers...

This was to be Gregor, to be me...

Mikal was writhing on the table, and Lucia Asparian was shaking. She jerked the terminals from her head and walked blindly through to the rear cabin of the Trader craft.

The woman had gone, leaving him alone and still strapped to the bunk. For a few moments Mikal lay shivering. The old memories were so strong; a year had done nothing to dim them, and the woman's questions had brought them again into full focus. Now, suddenly, he knew that Gregor and Pallast would never be coming back.

Ever since his two friends were taken he had kept things going in their valley home in makeshift fashion, marking time, hoping, doing little more than surviving, waiting for some new event. Now that was over. Talking to the big woman had finally taught him the truth: they were gone, gone forever. He had to act on his own.

Mikal craned his head up, peering toward the rear cabin. He could hear voices, but could not see anyone through the narrow doorway.

What were they going to do with him? Surely they would return him to the Hive. The chief of the warriors had told him that was his destiny, to be a Supplier to the Hive-Lord. He imagined again the placid line of Royal Suppliers, and the whole room seemed to shake and shiver around him. He began to struggle with the bonds that held him down.

This time he was more systematic. The straps had been designed to restrain a semiconscious man, not to imprison a thin-limbed and determined boy. In a few seconds he had worked one wrist free. At once he reached up and yanked off the thin snakes of wire that led to terminals and headset. He wriggled free of the other straps, working in total silence. His own breath sounded loud enough to alert his capturers in the next room.

Mikal eased off the bunk and stood for a moment on the room's swaying floor. He sniffed at his hand and forearm. It made him uneasy. Instead of his own comforting and familiar smell, he was covered with a flowery, musky scent, like the perfume of a Hive-Lord serving maiden. Now he realized that the man who had caught him and the big woman who talked to him had smelled the same.

He stole across to the cabin door. If he could open it quietly enough and find a hiding-place before they knew he had gone . . .

With his hand touching the door, he stopped. He could see out of the window, and now he understood why the room had seemed to be shaking around him. The whole cabin had risen high into the air. Looking down, he could see the whole valley stretched out below, as though he sat at the top of an incredibly high and steep hill. There was nothing but air beneath them, nothing for hundreds and hundreds of yards.

Mikal pulled back from the chasm, aware of an endless drop just beneath his bare feet. He grabbed for the support of a bunk. At the edge of panic, he remembered Pallast's lesson, drilled into him as they struggled across the Lostlands. *When you are in trouble, blind fear will never get you out. You have to think, use whatever tools you have.*

Logic imposed itself. The man and the woman were still there; he could hear voices. They would not expose themselves to great danger. This was a flying machine, fully controlled, rising or falling as they wanted it to. He was not in immediate danger.

But how could he possibly escape when they flew high in the air?

Again, logic told him the answer: he could not escape, not until they returned to the ground. What could he do?

Mikal sat down on the bunk. The woman had said they were

not Hivers. He believed her. They did not look like Hivers, and he had never seen a Hiver woman so tall. But that did not mean that he was not in terrible trouble. He covered his eyes with hands that felt oddly soft and smooth.

What could he do?

Listen; watch; wait. He could do that, and until they landed, that was all he could do. Very well. Mikal fought the butterflies in his stomach, stood up, and stole quietly back toward the rear cabin.

They were still talking. There might be one thing more that he could do. It was hard to explain, but he did not feel frightened of the big woman. She spoke Hiver, and her voice had been warm and gentle. He would do what she asked and try to make her a friend. If only he had not bitten the man! But it was too late to do anything about that.

Mikal crouched down by the door and peeped past it to the other cabin.

Lyle Connery was busy preparing food, but he stood up at once when he saw her face. "Lucia! What happened in there— you look terrible."

"I feel terrible." She sat down abruptly. "Lyle, go back in there and untie him. And let's get out of here."

"But what about him?"

"He's going with us. I'm not leaving him behind. Poor little devil, he's survived in this place for a full year, all alone. Now he's friendless and hopeless—he's even *nameless*. We have to take him with us."

"But we—"

"No arguments."

"Did you discuss it with Daddy-O?" Connery could see her intensity, but not the reason for it. "For Shannon's sake, Lucia, he might be dangerous—we still don't know how he was able to throw that missile at us, single-handed. And we're supposed to go on to Orklan and discuss Hiver secretions with the Strines! You know the rules. We can't do that with a passenger present —a complete stranger who doesn't know the first thing about being a Trader."

"I don't care. We're taking him." Lucia Asparian stood up again. "You stay here and carry on with the meal. I'll go back and untie him myself. And damn what Daddy-O says. If I have to, I'll invoke Prime Rule. We're human beings first, and Traders second."

"The invoking of Prime Rule will be unnecessary." Daddy-O had been monitoring with interest the activities in both cabins, especially the actions of the captive. *"A low-probability event has occurred. You have found exactly what I hoped might be there. Proceed to Orklan. A Trader vehicle will be on hand to transport your captive to the Azores."*

"What are you going to do with him?" Lucia Asparian was still defiant and defensive. "He's not to be harmed, or turned back to the Hivers."

"We will do to him no worse than was done to you, Lucia Asparian." There was simulated amusement in the electronic voice. *"First he will be given a name—and plenty of food. He is twenty kilos below optimum weight. Then he will begin to learn to speak standard Trader."*

"And then?"

"Can you not guess for yourself?" Daddy-O was diverting resources to other areas, ready to close off the connection. *"Once he is fully healthy, he will be tested for his potential—as a Trader trainee."*

The computer's voice circuits could not in principle synthesize a pleased tone, nor could Daddy-O feel such an emotion as pleasure, but something in those final words had an undeniable ring of self-satisfaction.

Nothing in the universe offered more promise of interesting complexity than a low-probability event.

CHAPTER 3

During the night the wind had veered to the southwest, bringing with it moister and milder weather. Hard showers of rain were mixed with bright, gusty spells.

The classrooms were a good way up the hilly slopes of Pico Mountain, a few hundred meters higher than the sea-level dormitories and dining rooms. The trainees had watched the squalls whipping in from the sea and tried to time their run from the dining room to coincide with one of the sunny patches. As class time came closer the weather worsened. By five minutes to eight a mixed crowd of damp and dry trainees stood looking out of the classroom windows, jeering and cheering a last group running desperately uphill in a squall of warm, driving rain.

The last person in was a tall youth, fair haired and thick limbed. The eight o'clock siren was ringing out across Pico Island when he reached the gentler entrance slope. He sprinted the final thirty yards and arrived gasping, face gleaming with rainwater. Two others were waiting for him at the door as the siren ceased.

"We thought you weren't going to make it." The speaker was a pink-cheeked young woman, a blond teenager plump in her arms and legs. "Come on, Cesar, hurry up. Me and Jake saved you a place."

"Why'd you leave it so late?" asked the dark-skinned, angry-looking youth leading the way in front of her. "Today's the worst day—you could lose points before you've even started."

Cesar Famares had run half a mile uphill in less than three

18

minutes. He was too winded to reply. He allowed himself to be steered through the long ranks of desks to his place, then leaned forward across the desk, panting hard and dripping water from his hair onto the smooth gray surface. "Tell you later, Jake," he said at last. "Found out a lot from my brother. Bad news."

"Are we going to be assigned to separate groups?" the girl asked.

"No. Worse than that, Melly."

"I don't see how anything could be—"

The girl received a hard nudge from the other youth before she could finish the sentence. "Melinda! Shhh." She dropped into her chair and spun around to face the front of the classroom.

A tall, broad man wearing the sleeveless tunic of a senior instructor had appeared from the inner classroom and was standing in front of the central control panel. By his side, dominating the room, was a great Earth-globe. It was nearly six feet across and slowly rotating. Every five minutes the continents swept by, each one marked by bright points of illumination on the surface of the sphere.

For a couple of minutes the man did not speak. As his gaze ran along the ranks of trainees, the sound level in the room gradually faded. He waited until all the coughs and shuffling of feet had ended.

"Good morning," he said at last. "And welcome to the Azores' training camp. You are going to see a lot of me in the next couple of years—if you're lucky—so let me introduce myself. My name is Lyle Connery. I will be the main instructor for this group, until you either qualify for Final Trial, or flunk out. Previous statistics show you have about a fifty-fifty chance of making it. I'm going to talk to you for one hour or so now, and then we'll have a short break. When that break time comes, I want you all to get up from your seats and take a look at the side walls of this room." He lifted a muscular arm and waved to left and right. "You'll find pictures there of the most successful Traders in our history. And when the going here gets rough— and you have my word for it, it's going to get rough—I have one piece of advice for all of you to fix in your heads. Just remember, everyone on those walls, including the Master Traders, was once sitting right where you are. They didn't know any more about being a Trader than you do."

He stared at the ranks of young people in front of him and allowed himself a trace of a smile. "Or maybe they knew a bit *less*, and maybe that helped. When I was in your shoes, ten years ago, I found it wasn't the things I didn't know that got in my way. It was all the things I knew about the Traders and the regions that weren't so. I'm sure that some of you have brothers and sisters and parents who've been through this course." To Cesar Famares, Jake Kallario, and Melinda Turak, Connery's eyes seemed to pick them out and focus on them exclusively. "I'm sure they've told you all sorts of things, and you've picked up all sorts of others from the rumor mills on your way here. Well, early on we're going to *unlearn* most of what you think you know. First, though, we'll have a roll call. There are forty-four of you. If you want to know how good a Trader you are—today, without training—then try to remember everyone's name as you hear it. I know, it sounds impossible. But you'll have to be able to do that—and a lot more—before you'll pass Trader training." He pointed. "From the far right. First name, last name."

The roll call got off to a shaky-voiced start, then passed smoothly along the rows of desks. Except for the person speaking, the room was silent with total concentration. Some people were scribbling notes, others mouthed each name as it was given.

"Judith Brindel."

"Simone Agnus."

"Brendan Lausanne."

The names rolled on, until they finally reached the front row.

"Tomas Liviano."

"Carlos Oyonarte."

"Mikal Asparian."

Cesar Famares gave a little grunt at that name and nudged Melinda Turak below desk level. She raised her eyebrows at him. He shook his head.

"Tell you later." He breathed the words so she could only just hear him. But Melinda thought she also picked up an increased interest on the part of the instructor when that one name was given.

The youth in question was two rows in front of her and four seats to her left. She stared at him. He was certainly not promising in appearance. Judged in sitting position he was below average height, with a thin face and a long, stringy neck. She could see only a rear half profile, but his nose looked flat and his browridges prominent. His skin was sallow, almost yellowish. And the hair! It was dark and lank, cut in the farthest thing from Trader fashion that she could imagine. He wore a dark long-sleeved shirt of some coarse-grained material, an outfit that neither Jake nor Cesar—nor anyone who was anyone in the Trader families—would be seen dead in.

And yet he was an Asparian—a top Trader family! That didn't make much sense. Melinda looked again at Cesar Famares, but he was staring toward the front of the classroom. The roll call was ending.

"Good." Lyle Connery was leaning against the front wall, bare arms crossed. "Anyone here think they remember everyone's name?"

The trainees looked at each other. No one spoke.

"*Very* good." Connery nodded. "Chances are, a few of you could make a fair shot at most names, even before you've been trained—you were pretty well screened before you got here, and you're supposed to be smart. But if you *could* name names, you all had the sense to keep quiet about it. You're going to find that advice in the Traders' Rule Book: 'Always know more than you reveal.' Now, I don't want you to apply that rule right now, so let's have some honest answers. How many of you have already seen a Traders' Rule Book?"

The trainees were looking around at one another. After a few seconds Cesar Famares lifted his hand. His two friends did the same, and finally twenty or so hands were raised.

Connery nodded. "All right. So you people are going to have a little advantage—for a few days. The rest of you, you'll find a stack of Rule Books waiting for you on the table by the window at the back of the room. I want each of you to take one. And I want everyone *word perfect* on every rule one week from today. You won't *understand* many of them, that comes later—for some of them, a lot later. But if you learn nothing else in the next seven days, I want you to learn those rules. You'll hear a lot about an *informal* book of rules, too—find out about that for yourselves. That's going to be free-time work, for your evenings. Now, let's do a little classwork."

He turned to the slowly rotating globe and tapped a continent of the southern hemisphere. "You're all supposed to come here with some idea of geography. So I assume you all recognize this region. Know what the people from this part of the world are called by the Traders?"

There were a few chuckles, and lots of knowing grins. A number of the trainees had been told by their relatives how training began. No one spoke. Finally Connery pointed at a woman two seats in front of Cesar Famares. Cesar recognized her from earlier school days—she was from a family distantly related to his own.

"If no one wants to talk, I'll have to find a volunteer. You—Valeria Constantin. Do you know the answer?"

"Yes, sir."

"Well?"

"The Traders call them Greasers, sir."

"Quite right. We call them Greasers." Connery shook his head. "And I'm afraid we'll probably continue to call them Greasers. But here's your first piece of unlearning. You're going to hear that name, Greasers, a thousand times, all over this camp. You'll even hear it from me. But it's Trader talk, and you have to train yourselves not to say it to non-Traders. If you ever use 'Greaserland' when you are talking with a member of the Unified Empire, you won't be a Trader there for long. Not only that, you'll be lucky if you escape with your lights intact. Get it? Not Greaserland—the Unified Empire. Not Chill Central—Cap City. And not the Darklands—they call it the Heart of the World. Call them what I *tell* you to call them—and not what I may call them myself, or you hear 'em called in other regions."

He turned again to the globe, which had rolled on around its axis through a slow sixty degrees. "All right, let's try another one. What do Traders call the people who live *here*?" He tapped the globe and pointed to a startled youth in the back row. "You, Ferenc Skassy, how'd you like to give me an answer on that?"

"Er—I've usually heard them called 'Strines,' sir."

"Very good. And what do they call themselves?"

The boy hesitated, then shook his head. "I don't know."

"Any offers?" Connery waited a few moments, then shrugged. "All right, so it was a trick question. They call themselves Strines, too—the only group that are pleased with their own nickname. You're safe enough with that one. Just a couple more questions, then we'll make a systematic review of your training for the next few months. Look at this. There's a big blank area on the globe here, northwest of the Strine territories. No Trader lights showing, which means we have no negotiations going on there at the moment. Who lives there?"

He pointed at a redheaded girl in the middle of the room, who blushed. "Nobody," she said. "That's all part of the Lostlands."

"It is. But that doesn't mean nobody *lives* there. Anyone else want to answer the question? Speak up, don't wait for me to point at you."

Half a dozen voices spoke at once.

"The Hives."

"Hivers."

"Hiver colonies."

"Quite right. They're wild, and they're all independent, and they're not an organized power group with their own full weapons arsenal; but they're real enough, and someday you might have to go and negotiate with them. We can't afford to neglect them. Here's another question for you. There's an old story that the Hivers practice a secret ritual for prolonging life, and some of them are a couple of hundred years old. True or false?"

"False, sir." There was a chorus of answers this time, from many more of the audience. "It's false."

Connery shook his head. "Sorry, that was another trick question. The best answer for a Trader was no answer. You see, I asked you two different questions at once, something that will happen to you all the time in negotiations. It's a Traders' Rule, *anything* can be a negotiation technique. Question one was: Do the Hivers practice a ritualistic form of life prolongation? Answer: Yes, that's quite true. We don't know if it works or not, but there's some pretty persuasive evidence that it may. Question two: Are some of the Hivers a couple of hundred years old? Answer: No, of course that's false—it couldn't possibly be true, they've only been using the rituals since the Lostlands war, and that's less than fifty years."

He pressed the control panel, and the globe silently moved back into a broad recess in the wall. "You'll learn. Before you're through here the right answers to questions like this will be second nature. We're going to take a break now, but before we do it, let's talk one more piece of geography. Here's where we are now." A touch of the control panel brought a map into position on the display screen. "No surprise. This is Pico Island. We're right here, on the southwest side of the mountain. If you go up to the top of Mount Pico—try it this afternoon, if you like, after the classes are through—and look northeast, you'll see this other island, St. George."

A long, thin island, twenty miles in length but only three or four across, was highlighted on the screen.

"Now so far as you are concerned, that island isn't going to be 'St. George' for the next few months. I don't want you even to think of the name. It's going to be the Great Republic—I'll bet my uniform some of you were calling it Yankeeland until today. Don't do it. The natives there *hate* to be called Yankees, even more than the Unified Empire people object to Greaserland. We'll be making a field trip to that island in a month or two. The whole place is a simulated Great Republic environment: language, people, manners, morals, and lifestyle. The only thing we can't do much about is the climate. When you're ready for it, you'll be going over there solo, for practice negotiations in a Great Republic community."

The pattern of highlights was moving again, drifting up the display screen. "Same over the whole group of islands," Connery said. "Here's Cap City—Chill Central, if you've been muddying up your mind with Trader slang. You won't find snow and ice there, the way you would at the South Pole, but you'll see most of the other things that the Cap Federation pride themselves on. And over there is the Economic Community, and way up to the north you've got a simulated Lostland. Before you are done you're going to visit and negotiate in every one of them. You're not likely to die in those simulation areas, but you can easily fail, and for a lot of you that will seem almost as bad when it happens. One failure in the simulations, and you're out. It sounds harsh, but it's not. Because after the simulations you'll be going on to real test missions. And you can die very easily there, with a single, small failure. Any questions?"

A hand was raised over on the right, a thickset youth with bright, fair hair and a ruddy complexion. "What about the Chips—the Chipponese, sir? How do you simulate their environment?"

"Not very well, I'm afraid. We've set up one of the islands to use the Chipponese language and mimic the customs, but it hasn't been a great success. And of course, they live in zero gee or one-sixth gee, and we can't simulate that down here. You won't get much useful experience in advance for Chipponese negotiation—that's why negotiating up on the Geosynch Ring is such a challenge. And no Trader has ever yet been allowed as far as the Chipponese lunar settlements. Maybe one of you will be the first. Don't worry, though, it won't happen for quite a while. The Chipponese and the Lostlands only come when you're fully trained—if ever."

He looked to the back of the room, where the windows were showing another bright spell. "All right, let's take that break now. Grab a copy of the Rule Book, have a look around the walls here, go outside if you want to. We'll start again in twenty minutes—and this time, you'll have to do more than just sit and be entertained by me."

While most of the other trainees went at once to the back of the room, Cesar Famares and his two friends stayed at their desks. They had seen the Rule Book long ago in a pirated copy from Cesar's brother; already they knew it by heart.

"So where on earth is Cissy?" Jake Kallario asked. "First she didn't arrive two days ago, then she didn't come yesterday. She told me she had a few things to take care of back home, but if she's not careful she'll miss some of the real training. What's keeping her?"

"That's part of the bad news," Cesar said. "Cissy won't be coming. She didn't make the final cut."

"What!" Kallario was open-mouthed. "She said she had the whole thing fixed—that it was a certainty."

"I know." Cesar bit at his thumbnail and shook his head. "I'm really sorry, Jake. I thought that you and Cissy were— well, you know. It seems there's less certainties here than we realized."

"She can appeal it, can't she?" Melinda asked. "Sure she can. She'll get in later."

Famares looked at her unhappily. "You know, Melly, my brother understands the Admin system here inside out. I asked Davy if there was any way Cissy could appeal, or get a second chance." He shook his head. "He said even if she tries again and makes it, the next batch will go to the Cook Islands training camp instead."

"But that's terrible!" Melinda flopped back down into her seat. "They can't do that to us. We've been a *team*, all these years—ever since First Application. To break us up now, when we know each other so well—"

"And we'll have to have a fourth person for the combined trials," Jake interrupted. "They're always performed as a quartet. If we don't have Cissy, we might get some real loser."

"That's another bit of bad news." Cesar Famares turned to face the back of the classroom and gestured unobtrusively toward the right wall. "We're not supposed to know them yet, but the preliminary groupings have already been decided, based on the test scores. The three of us will be together, just the way we expected. But we'll be getting *him* as partner."

Melinda followed the jerky gesture of his arm. "Which one? The tall one, or the little one?"

"The runt."

Melinda looked, and recognized the ill-fitting jacket and untidy hair. "Him! Mikal Asparian. I noticed him at roll call."

"So did I." Jake was staring with contempt at Asparian. "Don't joke me, Cesar—you mean we'll be working with him?"

Melinda was taking a longer and closer look at their proposed partner. "Well, if we're stuck with him we'll have to make the best of it. He seems harmless enough. But he's a funny-looking bird, isn't he? Look at his hair! At least he's an Asparian—that's a good Trader family, not some dogsbody from a Pacific school. I wonder why we've never seen him around?"

"That's the third piece of bad news." Cesar shook his head. "I was late getting here because I hung around while Davy ran a check on backgrounds. He's not an Asparian at all! He was *given* that name by Daddy-O, only four years ago."

"By *Daddy-O*," Jake said. "Nobody gets their name from Daddy-O."

"He did. Before that he was an outsider. A Hiver, would you believe?"

"On *our* team? I won't stand for it."

"Steady on, Jake." Melinda had seen the color rising in his face. "He can't help being what he is, can he?"

"A Hiver! They don't even wash; he'll be a stinker, as well."

"He couldn't have got into this training program without being smart and reasonably presentable," Cesar said. "Calm down, Jake—it's bad news, but it's not the end of the world."

"He probably eats mud. What sort of screwup assigned him to *us*? I'm telling you, for Cissy to lose her place to some moron Hiver from the Lostlands—I won't take it."

"Calm down, Jake." Cesar gripped his friend's arm. "We can't do a thing about it."

"Can't we?" Jake Kallario's face had gone from red to white. "We'll see about that. I'm going to the instructor, to protest."

"No, you're not." Melinda took the other arm. "Remember, we're not even supposed to know anything about the teaming. All you'll do is get Cesar and Davy into trouble."

"And it wouldn't do any good complaining to Connery, even if the teams were officially known." Cesar Famares looked at Kallario's face, then slowly released his hold on his arm.

"There's one other thing you don't know about Mikal Asparian. Connery is the one who brought him out of the Lostlands. Asparian is going to be his special pet, you can count on it. All you'll do if you complain is get on the wrong side of your senior instructor."

Jake Kallario shook his arm free of Melinda's hand and rubbed at the place where she had been holding him. "I don't understand you two. You seem all ready to put your arms round him and welcome him—just as though he were really from a Trader family. Well, I'm not. You know we compete for places. If it weren't for *him*, damn it, Cissy could be here with us." He stared at Mikal Asparian, who was still wandering along past the display of Trader photographs and souvenirs that covered the side walls. "Maybe you're right, it's useless protesting if he's Connery's private pet. But I won't work with a stinking Hiver. Just wait and see."

"Here, Jake, don't get any crazy ideas." Melinda put her hand on his shoulder. "Cesar and I came here to learn how to be Traders—we're not going to stand by and encourage you, while you spoil all our chances just because you're mad at Asparian."

"Don't worry, I'm not going to sabotage you." Kallario's face was grim. "I want to be a Trader, too, as much as you do. But I bet you Mikal Asparian thinks he's God's gift to the Traders, someone really special. Well, I intend to find out just how good he is. I'm going to get through this training as fast as I know how, and I'm going to test him all the way." He turned again to stare at Asparian as the trainees began to wander back to their places in the classroom. "Then let's see if he can stay the course."

And you may never know it, Melly, he thought, but if I get a chance I'll find a way to fix him properly.

"Trainee Asparian!"

Mikal froze at the low-voiced call from behind him. He had deliberately hung back when the others left, very aware that they were forming cheerful, chattering groups of three or four people. Everyone seemed to know everyone else. They had all arrived just a couple of days ago, but already most of them walked about Pico Island as though they owned it.

And while he felt confused, they apparently knew exactly what was going on. He had taken a copy of the Rule Book, but some of the trainees hadn't even bothered; they already had copies, and they acted as though they knew everything that was in there. He had done no more than glance at his own book, and he still had no idea where he was supposed to find that "informal" Rule Book.

Mikal turned to face the senior instructor. Everyone else had left. Was it forbidden to do what he had been doing, staying to look at the pictures on the classroom walls? He looked nervously at the man on the dais.

"Yes, sir?"

"Relax, Trainee. We're out of class now." Lyle Connery had eyed Mikal in the classroom with never a glint of recognition. It was as though they had never met—still less that Connery had rescued Mikal from the Lostlands. Now a trace of a smile appeared on the instructor's face, and Mikal found it hard to hide his relief.

"There's someone who wants to meet you," Connery went on. "Come on." He turned and walked through the inner door of the classroom. After a second's hesitation Mikal followed.

Connery led the way deep into the mountain, along corridors that Mikal had not known existed. They wound round and down for hundreds of yards, past a score of branching corridors and through a hundred closed and color-coded doors. Finally, when Mikal no longer had any idea of direction, Connery paused in front of a pea-green door and gestured Mikal to go on through.

The room was a small one, furnished with just a table, a wheeled trolley, and four chairs. A woman sat in the room alone, facing the door. She stood up as Mikal entered. He looked at her open mouthed. It had been nearly four years since he last saw Lucia Asparian, and he still thought of her as huge, towering over him. Now they were about eye-to-eye, and she was much younger than he remembered her.

"Yes, it's me," she said. The door slammed shut. Lyle Connery had gone, leaving just the two of them. "What's wrong?" she continued. "Don't you remember me?"

"Of course I remember you. I'll always remember you. If it weren't for you and Instructor Connery, and what you did . . ." The rush of words petered out. All he could do was stand there looking at her.

She stepped forward, put her hands on his shoulders, and stared right back at him. "All right, Mikal *Asparian*." She placed great stress on the second word. "You've made it this far. Now stand right there and let me take a good look at you."

She surveyed his face and clothing for a few seconds, shaking her head, and then used her hold on his shoulders to move him slowly through a full turn. She ran one hand across the back of his head, tugged at the shoulders of his jacket, and put one finger inside his collar.

"You've grown a lot," she said at last. "And I think you'll grow a good deal more before you're finished. Lyle tells me that the school gave you a bit of education. We'll see. Let's sit down."

Mikal had stood uneasily through her inspection. "What am I doing here?" he blurted out as she stepped away from him.

"Doing?" Lucia raised one dark, pencilled eyebrow. "Well, take a look over there and see if you can guess." She gestured to the table, set for two people, with closed dishes of food already waiting on the trolley. "We're going to have dinner. And we're going to talk. All right?"

"Yes." Mikal gestured at the door. "But what about Instructor Connery?"

"Lyle? He'll be back later to pick you up. He's a stickler for the rules, and a senior instructor doesn't single out one trainee and have dinner with him on the first day of training. Me, I'm not an instructor. I've been away on long-term assignment, so I couldn't visit you when you were in school. But I can do what I like while I'm here." She gestured to the serving trolley. "How would you like to help me and you to some food."

"You mean, serve both of us?"

"That's what I said." She watched closely as he ladled out two bowls of thick mushroom soup, then shook her head as he fumbled with the cork in a bottle of wine. She held out a hand without speaking. Mikal, feeling all thumbs, looked on sheepishly as she took the corkscrew and opened the bottle with a couple of quick turns of her wrist.

"See that?" she said. "You asked me what you are doing here. *That's* what you're doing here. You're going to get a crash course on taking corks out of wine bottles, and serving food without spilling it all over."

Surely she wasn't serious. "But *why?*" Mikal couldn't help asking. "I don't even drink wine."

"You will, if you get to be a Trader. You'll learn to drink anything you are given—that's part of negotiation. As to why you have to do things well, good Traders do everything well. And there's an even better reason." She lifted her glass of wine and stared critically through the pale liquid at the overhead light. "You're not just going to be a Trader," she said without looking at him. "You're going to be an *Asparian*. Don't you ever forget that, Mike. I'm not going to have somebody using my name unless he's the best he can be. You have to make the family *proud* of you." She leaned forward to study him, her head cocked to one side. "I'll be leaving in a couple of days for the Cook Islands training center, and who knows when I'll be back here. So after I'm gone you'll have to work by yourself. You have to work on *everything*. How to make social conversation, how to meet people, how to dress, who to trust, when to talk, and when to listen. Did you ever have a girl friend?"

Mikal shook his head.

"Thought not. Here's rule number one: don't ever get a haircut like that again. Who did it?"

Mikal touched his hand self-consciously to his temple. "Well . . . I did it myself."

"Self-inflicted. I should have guessed. And you made your own clothes? Those trousers, and that horrible coat?"

"No. Of course not." Mikal looked indignantly down at his jacket. It had seemed just fine to him. "This was supplied at the trainee stores."

"I believe you. And tomorrow, you go right back there, and you make them give you a shirt that's a size larger at the collar, and a jacket that's a lot tighter across the shoulders, and trousers two inches longer in the legs." She shook her head. "I'm always amazed, the things they *don't* teach you in school. Did you like it there?"

"I thought it was wonderful." Mikal felt easy in his answer for the first time. "Plenty of food, my own room, and interesting work. No crops to grow, no worries about defending yourself. Wonderful."

"Hmm. Make many friends?"

"I thought I had." Mikal looked surprised. "But I haven't heard from any of them since I got here."

"I believe it. This is a fast track. Not many get invited here, and some resent people who do. You'll have to make your friends among the trainees. Got any enemies?"

Mikal hesitated. He was all ready to say no, but during the classroom break he had studied every face, matching them with names and working hard at storing them away in his memory. All the other trainees were strangers to him, and their looks mostly skated right past him as though he were a photograph on the wall. But he had seen open and surprising hostility on the face of one of them, Jake Kallario, a dark-haired youth with angry eyes. "Maybe I've got an enemy," he said at last. "But I don't know why. I never saw him before today."

"Then that's going to be one test of how good a Trader you're going to be. You have to find out why he doesn't like you." Lucia Asparian was watching Mikal critically as he cut meat and speared it on his fork. "Then you have to try to change his mind. When you're a Trader you have to know how to turn an enemy to a friend. And you have to learn that some people won't be a friend, no matter what you do with them. Those, you have to learn to work around, push them out of the way if they won't budge. And when I say *work*, I mean it. These things aren't easy." She pushed her plate out of the way. "All right, we don't have much time. First, I'm going to talk about how you learn to work with the other trainees. Any questions before we begin?"

"You say I have to work at everything. How will I know if I'm doing well?" Mikal was feeling very self-conscious, but at the same time he was full of a warm sensation that he had never experienced before. It was strange to have someone *worried* over him, caring how he looked and acted. Was this what being a Trader meant, that other people were concerned about you? If so, it was the finest world he could imagine.

"Lyle Connery will tell you how you're doing," Lucia said. "He'll tell me, too. And I promise you this: the Asparian family owns a vacation lodge in the Economic Community, high in the Alps. It's the nicest place left on Earth. The day you become a full-fledged Trader, you'll get your own key to it. Visit it any-time. How does that sound?"

"It sounds wonderful. Too good to be true." Mikal could not resist adding his other thought. "But *why*? Why are you doing all this for me?"

"Because Lyle Connery and I probably saved your life when we brought you out of the Lostlands." Lucia sighed. "You'll understand that statement better in a few more years. Come on now, let's get to work. I don't have much time tonight. We'll start with something simple: eating. When you take a forkful, the object of the exercise is not to see how much food you can get in your mouth in one go. Watch me."

The sky was overcast and completely dark when Mikal walked back down the hill. It was a steep descent, and he kept his eyes on the guiding line of lights.

Near the cluster of buildings at the bottom, he paused. The dormitory was set apart from the other structures, half hidden from them by a great rock outcrop. A stone-flagged pathway curved down to it. A second path ran off to the right, to the dining hall, library, gymnasium, and recreation rooms.

Mikal had intended to go directly to the dormitory. He was conscious of the fact that he had yet to look at more than the first page of the Rule Book under his arm, and all his natural inclinations urged him to go to his room and study.

Yesterday he would have done it. But he could see that there were still lights in the recreation room, and he could hear the chatter of voices. Late as it was, some of the trainees were up. It was an opportunity for informal meetings.

What would Lucia Asparian want him to do?

He sighed. If there was anything he hated, it was meeting strangers. So how did he have the nerve to imagine he might make a good Trader? He steeled himself and headed for the recreation hall.

The Rule Book would have to wait. He had something to live up to now: his name.

CHAPTER 4

It was no day for an outdoor climb. Lyle Connery walked the long corridors to the innermost chambers of the mountain, then rode the elevator to the peak. The communication center on top was shaking in the grip of a midwinter sou'westerly, with the wind at full gale force. In the center's topmost room, seventy-five hundred feet above the foaming waters of the Atlantic, Connery sat down at a terminal and dialed an audio-video link to Daddy-O.

The computer responded at once. It checked the ID of the incoming signal, and compared it with the video signal. *"Wild weather. Problems, Lyle Connery?"*

"I don't know. Not with most of the group—they're coming along as well as I could ask. But I'm still uneasy about the Kallario team."

"Their full reports are in the databanks. They have completed three sample negotiations, in record time and with fine results. An outstanding performance. No sign of difficulties is reported."

"That's true on the face of it. But I'm particularly worried about Mikal Asparian."

"Ah. Now you become more honest."

Connery stared gloomily out of the glass-faced chamber at the racing clouds. Their dark face matched his mood. "I'm not sure we know what we're doing with Mike Asparian. But I think we may be ruining one damned good Trader."

"Indeed? That possibility must be evaluated. One moment." Daddy-O switched additional computing capacity from an Ice-

33

land facility in preparation for a possible extra load. *"He seems to have performed impeccably. As well as anyone else in the whole training group, perhaps better."*

"I'm not talking about negotiation skills, or test scores. They look superb; I know that as well as anyone. But I'm worried about the boy himself. I'm afraid that he's still an outsider—not just with the other three members of his team, though I sense a lot of animosity there. Kallario had been their leader and he believes that Asparian is challenging him. I feel sure it's their competition that's pushing all four of them along so fast—they're months ahead of any other quartet. But it's not helping Asparian, personally. He's trying desperately hard, but he's still like an alien among all the other trainees."

"Be specific."

"All right, I will. For a start, he didn't come from the usual Trader trainee background. We got him from a region which has *never* provided us with a recruit before. Most of the other candidates here are preselected by the time they are twelve years old, and they have a good idea even before then that they may become Traders. They belong to related families. Lots of them already know each other before they arrive here. Asparian didn't get out of the Lostlands until he was fourteen, and he had to be schooled privately because he couldn't speak Trader. Then he was pulled out of normal schooling a year early."

"He was as old as most trainees."

"Perhaps, but in my opinion he wasn't psychologically ready. That was your decision. He didn't know anyone well when he came here to start training."

"His profiles showed that he was more than ready for Trader Training."

"Sure—*mentally* he's fine, smart as they come. But he's smaller than most of the others, and he still isn't totally comfortable with the language. He has a bit of a Hiver accent, can't pronounce 'th' correctly. I've caught some of the others laughing at him behind his back, imitating the way he pronounces things. 'Zis is mine, zat is yours.'"

"His accent is a good deal less pronounced than it was when he began with you, four months ago. It will not be a problem for much longer."

"Maybe not. But he still won't fit in. He just doesn't know the ropes. This will be hard for you to comprehend, but there's a *network* that precedes entry to formal Trader training. If you've not been part of it—and he wasn't—then you make social blunders. He has learned an enormous amount, but some things come hard. He was completely tongue-tied the other day when he had to talk to a Master Trader who was meeting with his group. All the other trainees were smooth as could be, and he could hardly manage a word. I'm sure it was just that he was overwhelmed—he thinks Master Traders are like gods—but it was hard on him. If only he had a bit more self-confidence. I've seen how his minds works, and that goes beyond anything we can measure on the tests. He doesn't have any idea of his own potential. Look, I know some people around here think I'm biased in his favor, just because Lucia and I found him. And maybe I am. But I think Mike Asparian could be something very special. Even another Max Dalzell."

Daddy-O remained silent.

"Well, maybe I'm going overboard when I say he could be like Big Max," Connery went on after a few more seconds. "But that's how well I think of him. And I don't like what's happening."

"One moment." Daddy-O was silent again, for so long that Connery wondered if they had lost the circuit. Nothing they were discussing should need that much computation. *"Your notes and the student records suggest that you have not yet arrived at your main concerns,"* Daddy-O said at last. *"You are still worried, are you not, by the remaining scheduled visits to the simulation facilities on the other islands?"*

"Of course I am. But it's the same problem. The other three of that quartet are all from long-established Trader families. They have *relatives* in the simulation facilities. Asparian doesn't. He'll be at a big disadvantage."

"True, if we restrict our thoughts to simulations. But that will become his advantage in the real world, and a possible disadvantage for the others. No one has helpful relatives in other regions. Asparian will not look for sympathy or under-standing where there is none; the others may. But I take your point, and it is consistent with conclusions that can be drawn readily from available data, without reference to emotional considerations. We are ready for the next step. A real training test."

"It's too early for that."

"Not for this particular mission. In fact, we will be permit-ted to send only inexperienced trainees."

"Trainees only? I've never heard of such a mission. Where is it?"

"A unique opportunity has arisen to send a junior group to

the Darklands. The Kallario quartet is the obvious choice."

Connery swung to face the camera eye. "Be reasonable—Traders are hardly allowed into the Darklands, even for big negotiations. A trainee group wouldn't get past the port of entry—and if they did, we wouldn't know how to brief them properly! We don't have data. And the Darklands bought a Chill system for radio jamming, so we couldn't provide a Mentor. Why not a Hive environment, if we're going to be ridiculous? A Hive would be no worse than the Darklands for a trainee—and Asparian would have some advantage there."

"You are joking. A Hiver mission would not be consistent with our goals. But my proposal is serious. Also, the primary mission is one of quite negligible risk."

"In the Darklands? I don't believe it."

"Nonetheless, it is true. Listen to me, and see if you change your mind. The role of our group would merely be to serve as invited guests to a formal ceremony. The Ten Tribes are ready to crown a new emperor. The man who will ascend to the throne, Rasool Ilunga, has decided that his crowning will be an event unprecedented in Darklands history. He plans an elaborate coronation, putting on display the wealth of the Darklands. And to observe those ceremonies, with their jewel-encrusted robes and jeweled and priceless emblems of office, and also to be witness to his imperial greatness, Ilunga has invited representatives from every region; even a Chipponese party has been asked to descend from the Moon to Coronation City and attend the event. But the Ten Tribes have traditionally been highly suspicious of Traders, and Ilunga's condition on our presence is that children or trainees be invited, not qualified Traders. The Kallario group qualifies. The mission has no danger that I am able to identify." There was a substantial pause. *"Of course, one could entertain a speculation that might lead to a possible second agenda: the Chipponese are looking for a permanent equatorial launch and landing franchise. The central part of Rasool Ilunga's Darklands empire is ideally located. It is tempting to correlate those facts and explore the implications. But it would be at the Fourth Level of difficulty."*

"For Shannon's sake, you *are* trying to get them killed. You can't let them even look at Fourth Level—we'd never see them again!"

"With this trainee group, there is evidence to suggest otherwise. However, that is not a point to be profitably pursued at this moment. To ease your fears, I promise this: the quartet will

not be charged with any second agenda. May we leave the situation thus? We both believe that the remaining scheduled visits to the Azores' simulation facilities are likely to be of limited use to the Kallario group. We will therefore cancel them. Also, the opportunity of the Darklands visit is something that requires further consideration. Let me attend to that, and prepare the necessary briefing documents."

"Don't you think—"

Connery paused. The circuit light had begun to blink, indicating that the terminal would remain open but that minimal computing capabilities would be linked into it. For all practical purposes, Daddy-O was saying good-bye.

A few more moments, and Lyle Connery was left staring out at the bleak Atlantic winter. The whole structure he sat in was shaking and swaying with the force of the wind. He stood up, wondering as he often did after a session with Daddy-O whether they had achieved any worthwhile communication at all.

CHAPTER 5

"**H**ello. On behalf of Rasool Ilunga, let me welcome you to the Heart of the World, home of the Ten Tribes."

The words were spoken the moment the four passengers stepped out of the Trader aircar. They peered around them. The Mach Six trip from midwinter at the Azores to tropical noon had left them with transit shock. They blinked, shielded their eyes against the glare of the equatorial sun, and squinted at the speaker. The temperature was in the middle nineties. Reflected sunlight flared from a thousand places on the baked ground.

The man standing in front of them was an albino, skeletally thin and frail looking. He was wearing a suit of white silk, white shoes, and a broad coolie hat that extended across his head and shoulders. Blue-tinted glasses covered his eyes. His features were fine-boned, with a thin, chiseled nose. He was extending a cotton-gloved hand as he continued in excellent Trader: "You have come a long way to be here, but I am sure that you will not find it a wasted journey. There are exciting times ahead for you."

Jake stepped forward and took the man's hand in both of his, Darklands fashion. "It is a pleasure to be here. I am Jake Kallario, leader of our group. Allow me to compliment you on your command of the Trader language, and permit me to ask your name."

"I am Inongo Kiri, principal negotiator for the Ten Tribes. And your companions?"

"Of course. This is Melinda Turak . . ."

Mikal Asparian had been last off the plane. Now he stood a

38

pace to the rear of the other three and stared around him. Sub-consciously he had noted and approved of Kallario's opening remarks. Straight from the Trader book of rules. *Rule Number 44: Give praise; it is free.* And *Rule Number 64: Get everything else wrong if you have to, but get their names right.*

His eyes had adjusted to the bright sunlight. Now he took advantage of the other trainees' introductions to perform a more thorough visual exploration.

The plane had landed six hundred miles inland at a fork in a great river. To the south of the landing point, where the branches merged, a sluggish expanse of gray-brown water was visible, over two miles across. The land toward the river was marshy and covered with tall reeds, but the airfield itself stood on a cleared plain. Mike looked down, expecting concrete, and saw a vast tiling of baked clay bricks. There must have been tens of millions of them. A dozen ground vehicles waited at the edge of the field, each surrounded by a score or more of brightly dressed black people. Beyond them—unless the bright light was playing tricks with his eyes—stood two of the legendary animals of this continent.

Huge, bulky, improbable. *Elephants.*

Two hundred years ago, according to Daddy-O's data bases, this had been deep, rich jungle and broad plains, teeming with wild animals. Now it seemed as tired and eroded as the Lostlands, the forest gone, the fertile game plains diminished, the animals vanished. What had happened here? The Lostlands War had not reached this region.

". . . Mikal Asparian."

At the sound of his own name, he jolted back to his immediate surroundings.

The thin albino was holding out his gloved hand and smiling a pink-gummed smile. "Delighted to meet you. Since this is the first visit for all of you, Mikal, and since we have a full day free before the coronation ceremonies begin, I have arranged for you to be given a tour of the region and a boat trip along the Great River. First, however, let us proceed to your living quarters and make you comfortable there. And then we will have a brief audience with Rasool Ilunga himself. Two days from now, he will of course be known only as Emperor, the Light of the World, the Lord of the Ten Tribes." He beamed at the four trainees. "But today, it is still all right to call him Rasool Ilunga."

The man speaks Trader superbly, Mikal thought. Probably

better than I do! He shook Inongo Kiri's hand and felt the bones beneath the cotton glove. He had never met a man so thin. They began to walk slowly toward the parked ground vehicles. As usual, Jake and Melinda took the lead. Mike still trailed along behind, gaping at everything and somehow excluded from the group.

The relationship among the four team members had been tense for months. Only the common and powerful desire to become Traders had held them together. Things had taken a turn for the worse just before they left the Azores. Lyle Connery had briefed them, but had made it clear that they had a decision to make, and that it was one he could not make for them.

"You can work as a team if you want to." The Trader plane was already waiting for them. "If you do, you'll be pooling everything that you learn and reporting back as a group. That's the way to generate the most information. Or you can each use this as training for an *individual* mission. If you do that, you will each gather whatever information you can get, and keep it to yourself. When you arrive back here, you will file four individual reports. That has advantages, too, because when you qualify as Traders many of your missions will be conducted solo, without even a Mentor. So. How do you want to handle this mission? It's up to you."

He surveyed the intent young faces. "Well?"

Melinda spoke first. "Solo."

"No, Melly." Cesar shook his head at her. "I think we get more benefit working together."

Connery looked at Asparian.

"I agree with Cesar. We should cooperate."

"And you, Jake?"

Kallario looked at each of the others. His gaze lingered on Mike. I'll work with you when I have to, Asparian, it seemed to say. But not if I have a choice. "I say, we work solo."

"Two for each." Connery shrugged. "In that case, Kallario as senior member of the group breaks a tie vote. So you'll all be working solo. Remember what that means: you can each tell any of the others your thoughts or your findings, but you are not obliged to; and no one is required to reciprocate. Now, let's get you on your way."

The atmosphere in the plane during the Darklands flight had been unmistakably unpleasant. Mike knew that Jake was still furious with him, and Cesar was annoyed with Jake. Cesar was convinced they ought to be working together. Only Melinda had

tried to smooth things over, speculating about the coronation
ceremony.

"Spears and gold robes and ostrich plume hats, that's what
I'm betting on."

"What have you been reading? Ancient history?" Cesar
handed her a fat volume of briefing materials prepared by
Daddy-O. "Here, Melly. Take a look at this, and bring yourself
up to date. Rasool Ilunga wants the Ten Tribes to become more
technological. He's already started to build a weapons arsenal."

"I don't call *weapons* technology. I'd rather he went in for
gold and feathers."

"Well, Ilunga disagrees, and he owns the place—or he will,
in two more days. Anyway, ostriches are extinct. They haven't
been around this continent for half a century."

"More's the pity."

But now, walking across the scorching ground to the waiting
cars, Mike saw to his delight that half a dozen of the waiting
people were carrying long spears—and wearing headdresses
decorated with the gorgeous plumage of ostrich tail feathers. He
reached out to tug Melinda's sleeve. "It's red robes, not gold,"
he said softly. "Otherwise you hit it exactly."

Inongo Kiri had somehow heard him—the albino must have
ears like a cat. He turned his head as he led the way. "Wait until
the coronation, Mikal Asparian. You'll see your gold then—and
a lot of other things you will like."

They had reached the leading car. Inongo Kiri made no attempt to introduce them to any of the standing natives. He
ushered them into the enormous and antique vehicle, two in
front and two behind, then took the driver's seat himself. After
two minutes of fiddling with a control on the dashboard, he
turned a long copper key, started the engine, and drove off at a
sedate pace to the north, following the riverbank. The car's
motor coughed and choked. The exhaust spat out clouds of blue
smoke behind them. To the surprise of the trainees, a couple of
dozen of the people around the other cars, still ceremonially
clad in their long robes, began to run along behind.

Mike Asparian and Melinda Turak were sitting together in
the rear. She turned her head and watched the struggling runners. "A technological society!" she shouted to Mike.

With the racket from the engine, there was no chance that
she would be overheard by anyone, no matter how good their
ears. Mike could scarcely hear her himself, with her mouth only

a few inches away from his head. "That's what the briefing materials said," he called back.

"Well, a bit of technology is long overdue." She banged the battered side of the car. "This is a mobile junk heap. Do you know, I believe it has a gasoline engine. Where are they getting the fuel?"

Mike merely shook his head. The reek of those exhaust fumes was poisonous—it was alarming to think what it must be doing to those running behind. The car was traveling at only a few miles an hour, and a great cloud of blue-black smoke marked their progress all the way from the airfield.

A cluster of new buildings was creeping into view, all taller than the one- or two-story constructions that stood on the airport's perimeter. The car chugged steadily along until it came to the biggest, a seven-story structure built of white stone. There Inongo Kiri again turned the copper key, and the car's engine expired with a final spluttering cough. They stepped out into a huge open square, its sides flanked by palm trees.

They had driven perhaps five miles. The plumed and robed attendants were now spread out all the way back to the airfield. Kiri gave them a casual glance. The nearest was a mile or more away.

"They will all be here eventually, but it is not worth waiting for them." He laughed. "Come along. By the time we return from your rooms they will be waiting for us. You will have them as an honor guard when you meet the future emperor."

"But where will we meet him?" Kallario asked. He had been expecting a grand imperial palace. The white stone building was big, but it did not match his mental image.

"Right here. Up on the topmost floor. Ah, I see—you find this building a little drab to be *his* home. Do not worry. You will see his future palace tomorrow, when we make a trip north of here. The castle will be finished in time for the coronation—or else." He chuckled. "For the moment, Rasool Ilunga is content to live a simpler life-style. Come, let us move upstairs."

The four third-floor bedrooms assigned to the trainees were small, hot, identical, and simply furnished. Blown air, circulating from the wall vents, felt no cooler than room temperature on Mike's hand. He dropped his little traveling case on the bed. *Rule 68: Everything you need for a negotiation should be small enough to fit inside your head.* He was ready to leave at once, but instead he went across to the window.

His room looked north across a level, parched plain. There was no attempt to irrigate the soil with river water. The buildings below petered out after another half-dozen structures, and a white-topped road, parallel to the river, led across a desolate landscape to the northern horizon. On that horizon, barely visible in the heat haze, twinkled a glint of silver.

Mike went to his satchel, took out a tiny Chill-fabricated spyglass, and looked again. The silver glint resolved to a set of half a dozen steeples. They rose high above the plain, each one ending in a needle point of light. Even at maximum magnification Mike could pick out no details. While he was still peering north he heard a footstep behind him.

Cesar Famares was standing in the doorway. "Look here." He paused, then made up his mind. "Look, Mike, if you and Jake want to fight, that's up to you. But count me and Melly out of it. I know you think the three of us are lined up against you, and maybe we were when we started. But we're not now. Melly and I have been talking, and we're agreed, we're not going to take Jake's side. Or yours, either. If he—or you—does anything to hurt our chances of becoming Traders, we'll chop you to pieces. All right?"

Mike looked at him for a moment, face startled. Then he smiled. "All right. Better than all right. You know, Cesar, I've been trying hard. I really have. I'm not the one who's been looking for trouble. I want to be a successful Trader, maybe even more than you do. If it doesn't work out for you and Melly and Jake, so what? You'll all go back to your families. But until I make it as a Trader, I'm a *fake* Asparian. If I don't have this, I have nothing."

"You do now." Cesar walked forward and took Mike's hand. "You've got friends. Come on, let's go and see what the Light of the World eats for lunch."

At the head of the stairs Melinda Turak stood waiting. She glanced inquiringly from Cesar to Mike and back. Cesar nodded, and she laughed in relief. "That's great. Let's get a move on. Jake and Inongo Kiri have already gone up there to organize our ceremonial bodyguard. How does it feel to rate a thirty-man escort?"

The elevators in the building were all slow and creaking. Rather than wait for them again, Melinda led the way up the stairs. At the entrance to the top floor they were met by four semi-naked guards and crossed spears.

"Oh, come on now." Kiri's amused voice came from somewhere ahead of them. "That's really quite unnecessary." He spoke a few words in the Darklands tongue, too fast for the trainees to follow. No one else said anything, but the spears were turned at once to a vertical position. Melinda led the way uneasily past the guards and on down the middle of a corridor lined with men and women in ceremonial red robes. Some of them were still panting and leaning in exhaustion on their spears.

Inongo Kiri and Jake were waiting outside a pair of massive black doors armored with iron studs.

"Actually, all these fripperies are unnecessary, in my humble opinion," Kiri said softly in Trader. "But Rasool Ilunga insists we must have it this way, and most of the people would agree with him. So there's no point in discussion. Come on. Just the five of us. We leave the pomp and circumstance on the outside."

No signal seemed to be given, but at Kiri's words the doors creaked open. The trainees went through into a small, window-less room without furnishings. In front of them stood a second pair of double doors. As the first set closed behind them, the ones ahead opened. Kiri led the way into a large, well-lit room with windows of tinted glass. The furniture was simple: half a dozen chairs, a small conference table, and a long desk over in one corner. Next to the desk, sound asleep, lay a monstrous catlike animal.

The man who stood up from the desk was short and squat—no taller than Mike Asparian, but twice his width. He wore simple native costume decorated with Darklands motifs, and black thong sandals of woven Darklands leather. A Chill translation unit on his wrist was the only evidence of other regions.

"Welcome. You are the first visitors to arrive." He waved them to chairs at the conference table. "I expect representatives of the Unified Empire, the Strines, and the Community later today, and everyone else either tonight or tomorrow."

As Kiri began the formal introductions, Mike thought back to the briefing. Rasool Ilunga supposedly was fluent in the tongues of all Earth's Regions—even including Hiver. But he was speaking only the Darklands language, choosing to rely upon the translation unit and Inongo Kiri to be his interpreters. Why?

Mike found himself unable to look anywhere but at Rasool Ilunga's face. The man was not old, probably no more than thirty-five; but that face was lined and battered, as broad and black and seamed as a shield of ancient leather. The eyes alone redeemed his ugliness: glittering out of deep-set sockets, they were a clear and surprising gray. And they were as intelligent as any that Mike had ever seen.

"Our lands extend north to the Great Sand Sea," Ilunga said as soon as his guests were comfortably settled. Refreshments had been offered, and cups of powerful distilled liquor distributed. "To the west, we govern where the Father of Waters meets the ocean; to the east, as far as the land of Little Devils; to the south, until the Heart of the World meets the End of the World."

The trainees were automatically converting Ilunga's flowery speech to more familiar terms. The borders of the Darklands ran to the northern desert that spanned the African continent, west to where the Zaire River flowed into the Atlantic Ocean, and south to the African Cape. The eastern plateau remained uninhabitable; sand-fly fever, malaria, and rift valley fever discouraged all settlement there.

"We have great lands," Ilunga continued, "but unfortunately we do not yet have great wealth. That will come. The Heart of the World is changing. In the past the Ten Tribes have shunned relationships with other regions. But no longer. We will move from being a poor and technically backward society, to one that will lead the world." He stopped and peered at each trainee's face in turn. "Ah. I perceive that you do not believe me. That is not unreasonable. One should judge by deeds, not words. Wait and see. In less than ten years, I promise you that we will have negotiated major partnership treaties. And who knows? Perhaps one of you will become our principal negotiator."

He placed his untouched cup of liquor on the table and stood up. "Unfortunately, time runs. I must now return to other duties. The final preparations for the coronation are in process. I am afraid I cannot be the one to show you the glories of the Ten Tribes. But Kiri will accompany you wherever you wish to go. Or, if you prefer to do your own sightseeing tomorrow, there will be cars available for your use—to drive where you choose. Everyone has been ordered to assist you in every way. Do you have questions, any requests that you would like to make of me?"

Jake Kallario looked at his companions, then shook his head. "No, sir. And if we do not see you before the coronation, let me express our appreciation for all your hospitality."

"I am delighted to welcome your presence here." Ilunga laughed. "You may enjoy the ceremony much more than I will.

Kiri will show you the site for the coronation itself, and you will see my formal robes at the coronation. The imperial garments weigh as much as I do. Let us hope for cooler weather."

His polite speech did not hide the fact that the audience had ended. No one spoke as they filed again past the double line of bedecked guards and on down the stairs. At the third floor Inongo Kiri paused. "You are completely free until the formal dinner at eight o'clock," he said. "By that time I hope at least three other regions will be represented."

As he left, the Trader group lingered in the corridor. No one welcomed the idea of returning to those hot rooms.

"I'm going to take a walk outside," Melinda announced after a few moments. "I want to see if the cars he mentioned are in working order. If we decide to take a drive by ourselves tomorrow, I don't want to have to walk back."

"I'll come with you." Mike hesitated, then looked at Jake. For Cesar and Melinda's sake, he ought at least to offer the olive branch. "Before we go, do you think we ought to take a few minutes to compare notes? We're in a pretty odd position here. All of us probably have different insights."

Everyone turned to Jake. He stared down at the ground and would not meet Mike's look. "I think you are forgetting what we agreed to before we came here," he said at last. "We're going solo. I certainly don't propose to spoon-feed anyone with information." He hurried on down the corridor and went at once into his room. After a moment Cesar followed him.

Melinda shrugged at Mike. "Well, you tried. Jake's not a bad guy, but he's still furious because his girlfriend didn't make it to training camp, and you did."

"I know. Cesar told me." Mike started on down the stairs. "That's why he wanted to work the mission solo. I'm sure if I were not with you, everyone would be comparing notes. I'd still prefer it that way. You don't have to tell me anything if you don't want to, but I'll gladly tell you what I think so far."

"If you're anything like me, you're pretty puzzled. Rasool Ilunga doesn't fit the typical Darklander profile."

"Not in the slightest. I expected this to be a primitive society, all the briefings told us that. The cars, buildings, and people support the idea, and a gigantic, flashy coronation fits right in with it. But Ilunga?" Mike shook his head. "He seems no more interested in elaborate rituals and pompous ceremonies than Daddy-O would be. I think he meant what he said about moving the Darklands towards advanced technology. But I don't see what he has to offer a partner."

"And did you notice his clothes? They were *simpler* than anyone else's." Melinda paused as they reached street level. "Now you've met him, can you believe he's conceited enough to want representatives of every group here on Earth here to marvel at his coronation—and pay to ensure their presence?"

Mike stared at her. "*Did* he pay for us to come?"

"That's what Jake told me. Paid a lot. So there's another mystery. What do we do next?"

"Rule Eighteen: 'Collect as much data as you can get—' "

" '—and remember it may not be enough.' All right, Kiri said the cars for us are parked just around the side of the building." Melinda stepped out into the afternoon glare. "Let's see if they'll fall apart under us. That will be a data point of a sort—though it's hard to see what use it might be."

Twenty-four hours later Mike was beginning to wonder how much data was enough. Nothing would form a sensible pattern. It had started with the ground vehicles reserved for use by the Trader trainees. Instead of ancient, fume-belching limousines, he and Melinda had been shown four smart electric runabouts. They were new, expensive, and obviously imported from the Great Republic. With their balloon tires, air/oil suspension, and topside solar panels, they could carry a single passenger a hundred miles at night without recharging, and half again as much in daytime. Mike and Melly had taken a car on a trial run and found it comfortable, silent, and simple to drive.

Dinner had been another paradox. Traditional Darklands food, side by side with the most modern Chill service robots; flickering rush and palm-oil lamps next to bioluminescent globes straight from the Strine Interior.

The invited guests offered the same contrast of old and new. The trainees had found their dinner companions to be an average of fifty years older than they were. Mike had been seated next to an oldster from the Chipponese lunar mines, a wizened woman who knew, or admitted to knowing, not a word of Trader or Darklands languages. Jake Kallario was partnered with a graybeard Yankeeland cityboss; Cesar Famares sat with a drooling aristocratic wreck from the Economic Community, who offered him a free sample of a recent—and totally addictive—Greaserland drug.

Melinda felt she was the lucky one, with a personable companion in her late thirties—until the Strine bigmomma made a hard and open pass at her.

The four trainees beat a retreat as early as possible, pleading a long day ahead. But as Mike was going into his room, Melinda lingered on the doorstep. She was still quivering. "That woman! Did you see what she *did* to me?" Her gray eyes were open even wider than usual with the shock.

Mike shrugged. "I don't know what she did below table level, but above it she whispered in your ear and rubbed your breasts. I'm not well up on the habits of the Strine Interior. For all I know that's a neat social compliment. Better get used to it, Melly, worse things will happen when you get out there in real negotiations."

"Then I'm not sure I'll ever make Trader. It's easy enough for you, Mike. You're such a cool fish, these things roll right off you. Nothing gets you upset."

"Sure. Someday let me tell you about my life in a Hive." Mike hesitated, then opened the door to his room. "Come on in for a minute. I have to ask you something."

"What is it?" Melinda was inside before he had finished speaking.

Mike made sure the door was firmly closed before he answered. "If you're willing, I want to share a piece of information with you. I asked the Chipponese woman I was sitting next to at dinner if she would be going with us on our sightseeing tour of the area north of here. She looked at me as though the translation unit was making rude noises at her. I wondered if your bigmomma talked at all about *her* plans, before she decided your body was more interesting."

"Not really. But she did ask me if we were going to the precoronation Trade Fair. It's in the two-story building, west of where we're staying. Kiri hasn't mentioned any fair, so I assume we're not invited. But why do you care? Surely you'd rather see the Darklands than watch their publicity campaign?"

"I certainly would. But doesn't it strike you as a little odd that everyone else who's visiting seems to be staying here, and the four of us—*just* the four of us—will be wandering around the Darklands countryside?"

"It does if you put it that way. What does it mean?"

Mike had shrugged. "To me, not one thing. Maybe it will make more sense tomorrow."

* * *

But it didn't. Kiri had met the four of them after an early breakfast. This time he commandeered a smaller and more modern car for his use. Not long after sunup they were on their way.

They headed north along the white-graveled road, following the riverbank. Within three or four miles the bare plain gave way to head-high scrub and tall, spiky grasses. The road headed inland at that point and cut straight through the dusty vegetation. Mike looked ahead with increasing anticipation as they approached the area of the silver spires; he was beginning for the first time to have some idea of their size. But while the car was still three or four miles away from them it came to a barrier of thornbush and wire. Inongo Kiri followed the curving road on a great semicircular detour.

"An area it is not permitted to enter," he said blandly, in reply to Cesar Famares's question. "As Rasool Ilunga told you, the Ten Tribes are moving into a new era of technology. He wishes to protect the commercial value of our work."

Melinda was again sitting in the rear, next to Mike. She caught his eye, and mouthed a question. *Rockets?*

Mike nodded and settled back in his seat. Five hundred feet high? Six hundred? It was difficult to make a good assessment, with no reference objects available and no accurate idea of distance. But they were enormous.

Most of the tour, for all its advance advertising by Inongo Kiri, proved a tantalizing disappointment. They followed the river for nearly a hundred miles, pausing to look at a Darklands agricultural station, where a hundred strange fruits and vegetables had been developed, then moving farther inland to walk through a high-pressure plant. Their visits to both facilities were no more than quick walk-throughs.

"Of course, it is nothing like it will be in ten years." Inongo Kiri was keeping up a continuous and light-hearted commentary. He waved a white-gloved hand at the compressors and solar array. "This is only the beginning. We wish to be leaders in biology and exotic materials, to rival the Strines and the Chipponese in their own fields."

"And the rockets?" Cesar asked. He had been brooding on the denied area ever since they had been diverted from it.

"The—ah—rockets?" Kiri seemed taken aback by the sudden question.

"They *were* rockets, weren't they? How do the Chipponese feel about that?"

"Well—as a matter of fact . . . yes, they were rockets." Kiri had lost his composure. "Of course, as I said, that is a sensitive issue. We do not wish to reveal our capabilities prematurely. As soon as the time comes . . ."

They drove on. But Inongo Kiri's flow of chatter had been stemmed. On the return journey he answered their questions but contributed little himself. The drive back to Coronation City was a quiet and thoughtful one.

When they arrived the sun was on the western horizon, but the Trade Fair was still in full swing. They had time to tour the displays and observe that technology development was the big pitch. Biological developments were emphasized, along with pressure products. They saw synthetic gemstones, half an inch across, of unique color and purity. The visitors from the Unified Empire and the Economic Community were drooling over them. But the most interesting item was the one that was missing. At least half of the Darklands products would need a substantial capability to move materials to and from space. That aspect of operations was never mentioned.

Cesar Famares had been standing in front of a diagram of an ultracentrifuge for a long time when Mike joined him. Cesar shook his head. "Look at those rotation rates. Better than anything you can buy from the Community or the Chips. I don't see how they could fabricate the bearings unless they do it in orbit."

"You're apparently not the only people who think so." Mike moved his head to indicate a tight-knot of four Chipponese guests, all talking excitedly. A few paces behind them, watching the group with equal attentiveness, stood Jake Kallario. When he saw Mike and Cesar looking at him he turned and sidled away into the crowd of visitors and Darklanders.

By seven o'clock it was totally dark. The Trade Fair was closing. People began to move to the open square in front of the building. At eight o'clock the outdoor events would begin, a feast cooked on open fires and accompanied by native displays of acrobatics, fire-eating, and dancing. Vats of iced punch were being moved into position by serving men. Their size and composition suggested that Rasool Ilunga wanted his coronation to be remembered for spectacular intoxication.

Mike stood on the edge of the square and watched the crowds. He could not get the image of those brilliant synthetic gemstones out of his head, and their memory tugged at something else, some elusive part of the briefing they had all received before they left the Azores. He leaned against a pillar, stared into darkness, and reviewed everything that had happened since they stepped off the aircar. He had little bits and pieces of an overall picture—but he would never see the whole thing here, at the coronation party.

By 8:15 he knew what he needed to do. He slipped away alone, passing quietly through the crowd and walking in darkness back to their own building. The road was deserted. With the Chill spyglass in his pocket he climbed into an electric ground car and headed north.

The tropical moon was half-full, and there was no sign of other traffic. Mike needed no lights—and wanted none. He increased the current. The car hummed the miles away, flitting like a black ghost along the gravel road. Within twenty minutes Mike had reached the thornbush barricade, supported by its wire fence.

He ran the car off the road and parked in a thicket of dark shrubs. As he walked back to the barricade he examined it closely. Was it protected by some form of electronic surveillance? That was an unavoidable risk.

When he came to the road he lay down flat. He parted a pair of wire strands on the fence and wriggled through. The bushes carried formidable thorns, and by the time he emerged from the other side he had bleeding scratches on face and hands; but there was no sign of an alarm.

Most of the scrubby growth had been cleared on this side of the barrier. He stood up and walked slowly forward across an uneven surface covered with tough sawtooth grasses. There were plenty of lights ahead, clustered around the silver steeples. When he was still half a mile away, his progress was halted again. It was another fence, and the transformers along its top were an ominous sign. Mike grounded one strand of wire with a long stem of sawtooth grass. There was a puff of smoke, and the cindered grass fell to the ground.

He retreated fifty yards to a hollow in the ground, lay down in it, and took out the spyglass. Its light-intensifiers provided an excellent image of the whole area beyond the electrified fence.

He was looking at a rocket test facility. Over on the left were the structures to permit static firing tests, and on the right were the gantries for launches. There was considerable activity in both areas, with uniformed men and women bustling to and fro.

The night insects had discovered Mike's exposed head and arms. He lay there, spyglass held to his eye, and did his best to ignore the bites. The activity in front of him was becoming more focused, concentrating around the facility for static firing. He could see covers being pulled back from a monster rocket, thirty yards across at its base.

There was a sudden noise from behind him. Mike froze. Someone was hurrying past him, no more than twenty yards from where he lay. They went on until they encountered the second fence, testing it as he had done, and halting there. Mike was about to train his spyglass on them when he heard a second noise. Another man dressed in native costume was snaking past. Mike lay motionless again, trying not to breathe, while the second stranger eased forward and stopped not far behind the first.

Any sound at all would betray Mike's presence. He lay motionless for many minutes. He could feel the insects on his exposed skin, crawling on his ears and eyelids. Finally a thunderous rumble sounded from far in front. The moonlight paled before an orange-white glare of rocket engines.

Mike flattened himself closer to the ground. The flare of burning rocket fuel lit up everything for miles. The light came from the static firing facility, and it was bright enough to allow Mike to see every detail of the test—and of the two people in front of him. One was Jake Kallario; the other, crouched down and watching Jake, was a stranger in soot-black tribal dress.

The covering darkness had vanished. If either one chose to turn and look this way...

Mike placed his face flat on the earth. There was fire all along the base of the giant rocket now. He could smell the smoke and feel the vibrations of the combustion through his cheekbone and skull and all the way along his spine.

Two minutes. Five minutes. Then the glare faded and the thunder ceased. The night became pitch black and graveyard quiet.

Mike lay motionless, waiting for night vision to return and for his overloaded ears to recover their sensitivity. After a couple of minutes he could see the stars and hear again the soft ripple of night wind across the dried grass. Five minutes more, and Jake was hurrying back toward the outer fence. He made a good deal of noise. His black-clad shadow followed soon after, slipping as silently as ever through the grass.

Mike did not move. He had taken up his spyglass and was again directing it at the facilities beyond the electrified fence. Workers were moving there, pulling covers over the base of the

squat rocket. Then the lights began to go out, one by one, and
the level of activity slowly dwindled.

Mike stood up and looked all around him. There was no sign
of anyone, and no point in worrying anymore about possible
discovery. He ran to the thorn fence and wriggled through.
Then he was back in the electric car and driving fast toward
Coronation City.

Amazingly, the party was still going strong when he got
there. Mike looked at his watch and found to his surprise that it
was not yet midnight. Groups of people stood talking, eating,
and drinking on the borders of the square, and the middle area
around the fountain was filled with dancers—solos, couples,
and groups. Visitors and natives were one jumble of bodies.

Mike was starving. He went to a table loaded with food,
grabbed a spoon, and filled a deep bowl with fermented bean
curd and steaming rice. Then he began to make the rounds,
gobbling food as he went. Within fifteen minutes he had said a
few friendly sentences to fifty strangers. Halfway along the second side of the square he met Melinda.

"Where have *you* been?" She frowned. "If you and Jake—"

She was interrupted by cheers and whistles from the crowd
of dancers. They were applauding a figure, giant mug of liquor
in hand, who had climbed the fountain and was now standing
dizzily on top of it. He drank deeply from the vessel, gave a
shout of triumph, and fell backward. There was a roar of approval from the dancers, followed by screams as gallons of
water splashed out over those nearest.

"That's *Jake*!" Melly said in disbelieving tones. "Come on."
She left Mike and ran forward to the fountain. He followed
more slowly. By the time he got there a group of laughing
dancers had lifted Jake out of the fountain and was holding him
upright. He was smiling foolishly, and still held the empty mug.

"We'll take him," Melly was saying. "He's all right, isn't
he?"

"Wonderfully all right," Jake said. He beamed at her,
grunted, and slid toward the ground.

"Give me a hand." Melly turned to Mike. "I can't believe
this—he's drunk as a Greaser's monkey, and he's supposed to
be the leader of our group! Let's get him out of here."

With Mike holding one arm and Melinda the other they led
Jake away through the cheering crowd. Mugs were raised,
dancers reached out to slap Jake on the back, and the drums
played a long accompanying roll. Finally they reached the dark

region at the edge of the square. There Jake paused, straightened, and turned to the other two.

"That's fine." His voice was sober. "Thank you. And now, I'm going to bed."

He walked quickly away, heading for their sleeping quarters. Melinda stared after him. "He's not drunk."

"No, he's not," Mike said. "But he has the right idea."

"You mean, falling in the fountain?"

"No. I mean going to bed. Good night." Without another word, Mike walked away after Jake Kallario.

The insect bites had seemed no more than an annoyance when they happened. Mike had been far too busy looking at the rocket facility to pay much attention to them.

It was a mistake he would never make again. While he slept, an inch-wide region around each bite had become itchy, puffy, and red. Looking into a mirror the next morning Mike saw an unfamiliar bloated landscape, red and blotchy, with narrow slits for eyes.

He cursed his own stupidity. He should have swallowed an anti-inflammatory before going to bed. He could make excuses easily enough—other thoughts had pushed worry about his own condition and comfort into the background. But they didn't help. How was he going to explain his peculiar appearance at the coronation ceremony? Dark sunglasses would disguise the effects a bit. Maybe no one would realize that his eyes were swollen almost shut.

Mike smeared on ointment, swallowed a pill—better late than never—and headed downstairs. It was not until he was in the bright sunlight outside the building that he realized he had nothing to worry about. The previous night's party had apparently been a tremendous success. Standing by the building and leaning on it for support stood a Strine bigmomma. Her face was a bilious yellow-green—even the lips were pale—and her body sagged as though unfamiliar with gravity. She carried a broad white parasol and wore the biggest and darkest sunglasses that Mike had ever seen.

"Good morning."

The bigmomma turned slowly at Mike's words. "Gawd. It might be good for you, honey. Not for me." She didn't even look at his face.

"Are you sick?"

"Sick? I'm shattered. That bloody Darklands booze! Here,

sweetie, gimme a hand to the car. Got to get to the ceremony. But I feel ready to puke all over Rasool Ilunga."

Mike decided he would go with her. By comparison, he looked the picture of health.

The coronation ceremony had supposedly been two years in preparation, but it was still chaos. Half the stands on the far side were incomplete. Mike was shown to a third-row seat, right in the middle of a native group who had obviously been celebrating all night long. They were still drinking, but they were beginning to slump in their seats. By the time that Rasool Ilunga, muffled and unrecognizable in a two-foot crown and thick vestments of gold and purple, was carried forward in a great sedan chair, half of Mike's neighbors had nodded off. The Strine bigmomma, sitting a row in front of him, was snoring audibly.

He could barely see her anyway. Despite the medication, his insect bites had continued to swell. He was peering at the world through slitted eyes, their lids puffy and inflamed. After a while he gave up the battle and closed his eyes completely. If anyone asked Mike about the great coronation of Rasool Ilunga, Emperor of the Darklands, Light of the World, Lord of the Ten Tribes, he would tell them: heat, dust, brass fanfares, drums, speeches, and a parade of weapons. It would be as good as any analysis offered by his suffering neighbors; and a fair description, he thought wearily, of most coronations in history.

At only one point in the proceedings, when Rasool Ilunga appeared in full regalia for the actual crowning, did Mike open his suffering eyes as far as he could and observe closely. Heavy gold cloth robes, gold and ivory orb and scepter, solid gold crown. They provided the missing element in Mike's mental picture.

He closed his aching eyes and allowed his head to sag forward onto his chest. In the sunlit square below, the ceremony dragged on and on.

Instead of improving, Mike's condition worsened. By the time they said good-bye to Inongo Kiri he was hot and aching. The albino's smiling face swam in and out of focus, and it was an effort to shake his gloved hand. When the Trader plane took off for the Azores, Mike was shivering and sweating. The whole ride back was a fever dream.

Lyle Connery took one look at Mike and put him in sick bay for twenty-four hours.

"Malaria, sleeping sickness, dengue—or all three. What the devil have you been doing to yourself? Look at your face. Joints ache?"

"All over."

"Could be anything. But a couple of shots will fix you."

"What about my report?"

Connery smiled. "If I were you, I'd write it in the hospital. If we don't like the results, you can always claim you were delirious."

But he was not smiling the next day when Mike Asparian and Jake Kallario were ordered to his office. Mike still felt terrible, weak and feverish, but he had to hear how his report had been received. He struggled out of bed, dressed himself, and walked the hundred yards from sick bay. It took him over ten minutes.

When they were all seated Connery nodded at the monitor. "Daddy-O read your reports and is online. We have a rare situation here. Four trainees go on a straightforward mission to attend a coronation. Four trainees, four reports—all with different statements on what was seen, heard, and done." He tapped the four documents sitting on his desk. "You can't all be right. I'm starting with you two, because you had the complicated stories. Jake, here's a direct question: did you drink any alcohol the night before the coronation?"

"No, sir."

"But you don't deny that you climbed up the fountain and fell into the water, as Melinda and Mike here claim? It was not in your report."

"I don't deny it." Jake looked very comfortable. "I omitted it from my report, true; but I climbed the fountain for a purpose."

"To make Traders look like buffoons?"

"No, sir. To make everyone remember that I had been at the feast on the night before the coronation, and not somewhere else." Jake gave Mike a smug look. "And they did think that, all of them. I pretended to be drunk for the same reason. You see, sir, when we were given our tour it was obvious that something big was being hidden from us. The Darklanders have a space program that they didn't want us to see. Transportation, *and* manufacturing—there were synthetic gemstones on display at the Trade Fair, wonderful ones, so big and pure they could only be made in a zero-gee environment. That's when I decided I had to take a close look at their main facility north of the town. When it was dark, I left the other three at the feast and drove out to the space center. And I saw a static test firing, of a rocket as big as anything used by the Chipponese. The Ten Tribes have come farther and faster than anyone dreamed. I concluded that they are now a powerful region, with a spacegoing capability."

"Which is just what you reported." Daddy-O's voice entered the conversation. *"Did you two compare notes during the mission?"* Both youths shook their heads. *"So you, Jake Kallario, did not know that according to Mikal Asparian you were shadowed on that nighttime trip? By a Darklander?"*

Jake stared, first at Connery and then at Mike. "I'm sure I wasn't." He paused. "At least, I don't think I was—and how could he possibly know?"

"Because he also visited that facility on the same evening. He saw you, and your shadow. Mikal Asparian, please give your report."

Despite the medical treatment, Mike was still in bad shape. He tried to stop his teeth from chattering as he began to talk. "I feel sure we were *both* shadowed, though I didn't ever see the person trailing me. When we returned from the sightseeing tour I felt, as Jake Kallario did, that there were things we hadn't been allowed to see. But my reaction was a bit different from his. If you want to keep a secret, you simply don't allow people to get anywhere near it. The *last* thing you do is tempt them with a quick look, then make sure they have the time and opportunity to come back for a good look later. But that's what was done with us. And we—the Trader trainees—were the *only* people given that sneak look at the space facility, plus easy access to ground vehicles. So far as I can tell, the other visitors didn't leave Coronation City. I decided we were being set up for something. Rasool Ilunga and Inongo Kiri *wanted* us to go back for a second look."

"That makes no sense." Jake was shaking his head. "If they wanted us to see it, they could have shown it to us."

"That's what puzzled me." Mike shivered and turned to Lyle Connery. "Why did they want us to sneak in? And why did they make sure we could only do it at night? I didn't know—until I saw their test firing. That was impressive, lots of sound and fury, the static test of a gigantic new rocket. It was deafening. It would have been heard easily in Coronation City—unless there happened to be a mighty party going on there at the time, with everyone talking and singing, and the bands playing. So the night test seemed to make sense, if you wanted to keep it secret.

But when I thought about it some more, I realized it still didn't *have* to be what it seemed. Jake and I were a fair distance away, outside the fence. The test could just as well have been the firing of old solid rockets, lots of them; old weapons, all clustered together. They didn't have to *do* anything, except look enough like a test to fool us. No Darklands 'space program,' just an elaborate illusion of one. And why at night, on this particular night? *Because that's when we could be there to see it.* We were manipulated perfectly. The people shadowing us must have signaled the facility when it was time to start the show."

¹ Mike paused. He wished he were back in bed. His logic had seemed ironclad when he was in Coronation City; now it sounded weak. Jake Kallario was staring at him in disbelief, and Lyle Connery's expression was unreadable.

"But why you?" Connery said softly. "Why would Rasool Ilunga and Inongo Kiri want to fool four Trader trainees? Why not the Chipponese, or the Strines? In fact, why *anyone*?"

"It's preposterous," Jake said. His face was pale. "You're suggesting that the Darklanders were faking a space capability. *Why should they?*"

"*Well, Mikal Asparian?*" Daddy-O said. "*Those are good questions. Do you have answers?*"

"Yes." Mike forced himself to sit up straighter and looked into the camera eye. "I have answers. You gave them to us yourself. In the briefing materials for the mission, you said that the Chipponese were looking to the Darklands as a possible equatorial launch and landing site. Correct?"

"*Quite correct. They have been considering it for some time. They need a permanent Earth-based facility.*"

"All right. Ilunga wanted that agreement. Traders' Rule: 'Anything can be a negotiation technique.' Rasool Ilunga controls a primitive region, and he seemed to have little to offer the Chipponese. But he's very intelligent, and I think he's also devious."

"*Rasool Ilunga participates in the Chess Network. My assessment is that he occupies fourth place among Earth's human players, just above Max Dalzell.*"

"So we can assume his actions won't always have their face value. Very good. Everything we saw in the Darklands, and everything that happened to us there, makes sense if it is regarded as *preliminaries to a negotiation between the Ten Tribes and the Chipponese*. Ilunga was maneuvering for an opening position, and he wanted us as some of his pawns."

Mike was leaning forward, talking fast. His head was reeling. He had to get it all out quickly, before he collapsed. "Here's another Traders' Rule: 'Never show that you need what is being offered.' Ilunga wants a treaty with the Chipponese desperately. But he pretends he has no need for one. He wants us to tell the Chipponese that he has been developing a big space program of his own—we saw it with our own eyes. If Traders say something is so, other groups usually believe it. And the Chipponese representatives at Coronation City will support the idea. They saw artifacts—the gemstones—that required either an unmatched Earth-based technology, or a space manufacturing capability. Of course, Ilunga couldn't let the Chipponese visit his 'space test center' for themselves—they would see through it in a picosecond. But four gullible Trader trainees, who could be steered where he wanted them, like little children, and be made to watch things from a suitable distance . . ."

Mike shivered and swayed on his chair. Lyle Connery reached out and took his arm, supporting him. "Steady now. God help us, you're burning up again. You should be back in the hospital. Why didn't you tell me you were feeling so bad? Kallario, give me a hand."

Mike allowed himself to be lifted from the chair. "I'm all right. I had to come here and explain why I did what I did."

"Well, you're leaving now."

"I can walk."

"I'll help you." Kallario's face had mirrored his feelings while Mike was talking. He had been incredulous, uneasy, and finally resentful. "But if you're right about all this, the rest of us are idiots." His voice was bitter as he helped Mike to stand up. "That's the hardest thing for me to accept. Come on. I'll take you back to the hospital."

With Mike's arm across his shoulders, they headed out of the room. At the doorway Jake paused. "Wait a minute. Maybe they were faking the rocket test. But what about the synthetic gemstones? Everyone agrees they couldn't be fabricated without hi-tech programs and space operations. Isn't that true, Daddy-O?"

"Quite true. I know of no technique for such synthesis without a space environment."

Everyone looked at Mike.

He nodded. "That worried me. And then I realized that we had also been given the answer to that in our original briefing.

But I couldn't confirm it until I saw the actual coronation ceremony. There was something in the briefing material about the fabulous jewels that Rasool Ilunga would be wearing—can you quote it for us?"

" '...He plans an elaborate coronation,' " Daddy-O's voice began with no perceptible delay, " 'putting on display the wealth of the Darklands. And to observe those ceremonies, with their jewel-encrusted robes and jeweled and priceless emblems of office, and also to be witness to his imperial greatness, Ilunga has invited representatives from every region.' Is that the statement to which you are referring?"

"Exactly. I watched closely. At the ceremony there were miles of gold cloth, and a solid gold crown. Everyone else must have seen what I did. But apparently no one else wondered, where were the jewels?"

Connery looked at Jake, who thought for a moment, then nodded reluctantly. "He's right. I saw no jewels."

"So where were they?" Mike drooped against Kallario. "I'll tell you. They were in the Trade Fair. We were told 'synthetics' —the sign said as much—so we thought synthetics. It never occurred to anyone that what we might be seeing were natural gems, the finest in the Darklands—and that means the finest in the world. Rasool Ilunga stole from his own coronation to bamboozle his visitors. It was his most delicate touch. And it worked."

"Not quite," Daddy-O said. "But it came close. Go now, and rest."

Supported on Jake Kallario's shoulder, Mike tottered out. Lyle Connery watched until they were out of sight, then turned back to the terminal.

"Those two seem friendly now," Daddy-O said. "Do you think that is the case?"

Connery shook his head. "Jake Kallario will be a good Trader. He did well on this mission, and he's already learned how to hide his feelings. But it's my guess that he hates Mike Asparian more than he ever hated him."

"Unfortunately, that is my perception also. It is a problem that must be addressed at some time, but not now. For the moment, this mission confirms my earlier suspicion. The quartet is ready to be disbanded. They should move to solo missions."

"So soon? Are you saying that you believe Mike Asparian's analysis?"

"Of course." If an electronic voice could sound surprised,

this one did. *"No other interpretation of the events at Coronation City is remotely plausible. The amazing thing is only that
Asparian reached it. It was not a task for a trainee."*

"You said he was lacking confidence. Do you think he has it
now?"

"In an acceptable amount."

"Then he's going to be one hell of a Trader. He has it all."

*"No. One day he may, but I am able to identify in him nine
critical areas that still need development."*

"I can't imagine what they are."

*"Then we must discuss them, and plan the future. They are
as follows."* Daddy-O produced a near-human sigh as he ini-
tiated a data transfer to Connery's display screen and closed the
mission file. *"It was a near-perfect result, from a long-shot
mission."*

"You're too critical. I would have said, quite perfect. What
was wrong with it?"

Daddy-O paused. *"Nothing that affects these Trader
trainees. But old computers are allowed their dreams. I cannot
help wondering: what could we not do if we had Rasool Ilunga
working for us? A perfect mission would somehow have
achieved that result . . ."*

Nine critical areas of Asparian that need development; and a
tenth that cannot be mentioned. Daddy-O did not transmit that
thought. At the same time as the computer was talking to Lyle
Connery, a second transfer was taking place to an internal data
file. It had no outside pointers, and access came only through
Daddy-O's own operating systems.

By its nature, the computer had near-infinite speed and infinite patience. For two human generations, Daddy-O had
waited. Now the hidden file showed that a far-off and ancient
objective had moved one step closer.

CHAPTER 6

*R*ule 20: *Hang in there; help is on the way.*

And if a Trader trainee didn't believe it, Daddy-O would cite the case of Jack "Lover-boy" Lester. He had caused the Strines some minor annoyance and, worse than that, he wouldn't tell them the nature of his secret mission.

They had showed their irritation in a practical way. When a Trader Smash finally rescued him, he was not in good shape. He was armless and legless. The Strines had removed his penis and his scrotum, then carved out his eyes. When he still would not reveal his mission, they had become quite annoyed. They had flayed him, cut off his lips, burst his eardrums, pulled all his teeth, and cut out his tongue. They had of course done this slowly, a little at a time to cause maximum anguish, with full use of their life prolongation techniques to make sure he did not die before his time. Finally they had removed his heart, liver, lungs, and kidneys, and put him in a tank. This was sheer bitchiness, of course, since those operations were not even painful.

The Smash unit had rescued Lover-boy Lester, flown him back to the Azores camp, and hooked his brain in to Daddy-O. His first words were, "What kept you?"

Trader trainees inclined to be skeptical of the story were given one inarguable proof: they could go and see him. Jack Lester was alive, in the training camp hospital.

He was tremendously cheerful. He had frequent visitors. And he told all of them that the only thing that had kept him going in the Strine Interior was the knowledge that help was on the way.

"What can we do for you?" asked the more caring—or the less sensitive—visitors.

"Maybe a pepperoni pizza?" Jack said. *"Or if you're feeling super-energetic, there used to be an enormous big Greaser whore down in Punta Arenas. I bet she's still there. Her name is Little Suzie. I always wondered what it would feel like to jump on top of her. 'Course, she has sixteen sorts of pox, but if you'll go there and take a wallow, then come back here and tell me all about it, I'll pay you out of my pension."*

Of course, Jack Lester, what was left of him, was clinically insane. His conversation proved it. But he was still the Traders' best proof that help was always on the way.

Lover-boy Lester was far from Mike Asparian's thoughts as he sat in Lyle Connery's office. He had more immediate things to worry about. This was going to be the big one, the ultimate test that decided whether or not he would become a full-fledged Trader.

"Final Trial, so of course you're entitled to help from a Mentor," Lyle Connery was saying. "But I'm afraid we're having Mentor communication problems in Strine territory. Probably a Chill jammer in there. If you lose contact, you'll have to use the old-fashioned back-up system. This is a Trader recording disk. We used them as standard operating procedure before we had the Mentors. This one replaces your top shirt button."

Mike looked dubiously at the training director, then at the tiny disk on the table in front of them. It was about a quarter inch across and made of a white pearly material.

"Don't worry, it's unobtrusive and it works." Connery reached out a muscular bare arm and held the disk on edge between thumb and forefinger. "Audio and visuals. Not as good as a Mentor, but pretty good quality. All you have to do is make sure you give it a clear field of view. Just be sure you bring it back—swallow it, if you have to."

"But suppose it's—what if I—"

"Excrete it?"

"Yes."

"You won't. When the disk senses the composition of digestive juices, it extrudes hook attachments and stays put. It will be in your stomach until we take it out."

Mike looked again at Lyle Connery's expressionless face. This was the final test. According to camp rumors, any trick in the book could be thrown at a trainee. But surely there were limits. "Suppose the Strines take it out first?"

"That's a danger. But you can decrease the chances of that. Tell them you're part black. That way they'll be less likely to do any fancy cutting up on you. They save their most elaborate interrogations for white people. Illogical, but it's built into their prejudices."

"According to the gene codings, I *am* partly black."

Connery consulted the screen in front of him. "So you are. Then you ought to be convincing." The disk came rolling on its edge across the table toward Mike. "One other thing: has anyone talked to you about your Mentor assignment?"

"No. The Medlab people said they were waiting for Daddy-O's assignment of somebody with the right Strineland experience."

Connery frowned. "That should be easy enough. Let me find out what Daddy-O has been up to. You'll need a day or two to adjust to the presence of the Mentor, and your flight to Orklan is scheduled forty-eight hours from now. We don't have much time. You need to go and get an equipment check, and then you'll need a time-zone and a seasickness shot. You can get all those at the clinic. Might as well do it now."

Mike was dismissed. Lyle Connery waited until he was gone, then shook his head in perplexity. He called for a Daddy-O voice and video connection.

"Are you sure you want to do this?" he said as soon as the connect light came on. "I have to believe you know what you are doing—but in five years as an instructor, I've never seen a trainee treated this way."

"State your objections."

"You're not being fair to Asparian. This is his first solo mission. We usually pick out something simple as the entry test for full Trader status. But this mission profile would scare a Trader with twenty years' experience. It's too tough for him."

"Need I remind you that you are the one who has constantly lauded Asparian's superior talents and potential?"

"I believe he has them. But he's still only a trainee, for Crock's sake. Do you *want* him to fail?"

"I certainly do not." Daddy-O's voice sounded cold and casual. *"But my analyses convince me that a traditional Trader approach to the Strines would be useless for this problem. And you know that I, too, am interested in testing Asparian's potential. A conventional mission would fail to do that."*

"Fine, test him by all means—but give him some help! It would be a real shame to lose him. I hope that you've at least picked out a first-rate Mentor."

"The best there is."

"Good. That's something. Then I'd better help Asparian get ready." Lyle Connery had cut the circuit when he had second thoughts. The best Mentor—for the Strine Interior? He reconnected to Daddy-O. "Toto Larsen is on other assignment. Who will Asparian's Mentor be?"

"Who else?" The voice circuit sounded weary. *"Jack Lester knows more about the Strine psychology than Toto Larsen or any three other Traders."*

"Lover-boy! How are you going to explain *that* choice to Mike Asparian?"

"I'm not." There was a slight pause while Daddy-O diverted part of his network to handle conversion of a large incoming data base. *"You are."*

CHAPTER 7

An experienced Trader had three ways to reach the Strine mainland. If he had been there before and been well-received, he could go direct by air to Swales and BigSyd. Or he could go by sea, to one of the trading ports around the Strine south coast. And "he" meant *he*: the Strine mommas would not accept female Traders on the mainland.

If he was mad and quite desperate, there was the north approach. A Trader could go in by any damn fool way he liked through the northern badlands, where the southern fringe of the fallout had swept east. No one watched that coastline. Things still grew peculiarly there, even by Strine standards. And they acted worse than they grew.

Mike had looked at the northern approach for about five seconds, shuddered, and abandoned it. Get through the badlands, and then what? He would be carved up by the Interior tribes, unless he were very lucky or very skillful, before he got to Berra or BigSyd or anywhere else that counted.

As a neophyte on his first full mission, Mike decided he had no real choice. He had to take the second option of the southern sea-route. He would fly to Orklan, then go west by surface vessel to enter at BigSyd on the east coast. From there it would be a tough overland trek into the worst part of the Interior— only a few hundred miles south of the badlands.

And *after* he reached the Interior, the hard part would begin. According to Connery, the Strines were "expecting him." Instead of being reassuring, that somehow sounded ominous.

The flight to Orklan in a Trader transport was dull but comfortable. Mike spent the time taking a last look at briefing documents. The Strine penchant for swords and knives didn't sound promising. Mike had not seen a sword since he left the Darklands, and he certainly didn't know how to handle one. Nor did he intend to try.

Orklan was small and sleepy. The real culture shock began when he was dropped off at the jetty and went aboard the Strine ship waiting at the quayside. Although the three-funneled, broad-hulled vessel appeared to be totally deserted, within two minutes of his arrival the engines had started and they were maneuvering their way out of Orklan harbor.

"The crew—where are they?" Mike subvocalized the question deep in his throat. It went to the organic converter in his cerebellum, generated the hyperfrequency pulse, and sent a directional signal. Mike waited the necessary fraction of a second while the message went up to synchronous orbit, through a Chipponese relay satellite, down to the Azores, and back.

"*Probably asleep.*" The thread of Jack Lester's voice came amused to Mike's left ear. "*And there should only be one crew member. Read your briefing notes, matie. Don't worry, we'll find him once we're well on our way. Make yourself at home here. These ships can run on full automatic—the Strines use the best microcircuits that Cap City can provide. The only reason for a crew at all is probably to keep an eye on you. Take a good look round, would you? It's too long since I've seen this part of the world.*"

Mike dutifully took a tour of the deck, looking out now and again across the dark swells of the open sea. He did it slowly, waiting for Lester's acknowledgment at each stage before moving on. The ship was traveling at high speed. Orklan was already out of sight behind him.

"*Ah! Smell that air!*" The Mentor's voice was an ecstatic whisper. "*Take a good sniff for me, boyo. There's nothing like that anywhere else in the world. Dust and euclypts and mulgas. That west wind comes here right out of the middle of the Strine mainland; after it passes over Orklan it won't hit land again until the Greaserland coast—seven thousand miles of open sea!*"

Mike looked around and felt far from ecstatic. They were well out of sight of land, heading across endless gray water. The brisk wind in his face was blowing the surface of the sea into long, sullen swells, and the ship was plunging straight into them. The black metal deck had begun to pitch and roll in an alarming way. Spray from the bows was blowing back to wet his face.

Suddenly Mike had the feeling that they were cutting through dark hills of thick oil, the rendered fat of some primitive and gigantic beast. He could taste it on his lips. He held tight to a deck derrick, and wondered why the Medlab had bothered to give him a seasickness shot that didn't work.

"Three days before we reach BigSyd. Is it going to be like this all the way?"

"Like this? Nah." Lester giggled in his ear. *"This is a flat calm. We're in the Roaring Forties, where the winds blow right around the world and hardly see land. When we're farther out, we might get a real blow. Cheer up, boyo, you'll be all right once you get your sea legs. You'll be up and looking for trouble. Your problem is, you don't have enough to do, so you stand around and think about your innards. Why don't you go forward and look for the skipper? I've been wondering if I might know him from other trips."*

Mike stared around him, belched queasily, and shook his head. Lover-boy Lester might be right, and his conditioning would no doubt eventually take over. But there was no sign of it yet. He clutched his midriff, lurched down a dimly lit companionway to his quarters, and felt his way to a bunk.

"Here, what are you doing? You're not supposed to goof off before you even start."

Mike lay down and tongued the control that cut Lester out of contact. He had been told to do that only when he slept, but the hell with it. The Mentor was more than he could take at the moment. Mike closed his eyes and tried to concentrate on his mission. He had been briefed often enough about what he ought to do when he reached the Strine mainland, but no one had thought it worthwhile to mention how sick he was going to feel before he even got there. What else had they not bothered to tell him? And how many little surprises did the Traders deliberately put in their final test for admission? And whose idea was it to inflict Lover-boy Lester on him as his Mentor? And as for that damned clumsy recording disk . . .

Mike allowed himself five minutes of silent general misery— *Rule 39: Don't be ashamed of self-pity; it is the only sort you are likely to get*—then he forced his mind back to the present situation.

The mission. If he kept his mind on the mission, he wouldn't have time to think about being sick. He would lay out the bare facts and see if anything new came to mind. Think positive, he told himself. We've passed Orklan and are on our way.

Mission profile. It had sounded simple enough; but then, almost everything did, when Lyle Connery explained it. Three months ago, a Strine bigmomma had died of a sex-drug overdose in Ree-o-dee. All the expensive hotel rooms in the Unified Empire pleasure towns were bugged as a matter of course, so within five minutes the hired male consort had been decoupled and whisked away. The room was made ready for a new occupant. The bigmomma's body would be returned to Strineland, assuming suitable payment, or disposed of locally.

No problem. A neat, standard Greaser operation, something that happened ten times a day somewhere in the continent, handled with the efficiency that had made the Unified Empire the world center for illicit sex and drugs. The situation became more complicated when a Trader agent had the opportunity to search the momma's body before anyone else. He had found and removed a small package of yellow berries from a secret compartment of the momma's spiked bootheel. They were smuggled back to a Trader analysis lab, and there the mystery grew. Daddy-O had nothing like them in the data bases—and Lyle Connery assured Mike that if Daddy-O didn't have it, *nobody* did. It was a new plant species, genetically modified. Daddy-O had produced a couple of useful pointers: the berries seemed to be the fruit of some form of Strine euclypt; and the bigmomma had come to Ree-o-dce from The Musgrave, smack in the middle of the Strine Interior. Also she had let it be known in Ree-o-dee that she had something special with her that she might sell for the right price. Add in the Strine biolabs' skills in bioengineering, and the picture was clear. Some Strine lab had developed a new plant species.

"We thought that might be the end of it," Lyle Connery had said, "but it turned out to be the beginning. Our first set of tests on the berries showed that they contained a complex alkaloid, one that we couldn't identify. We weren't sure what we had, and we wanted the most complete analysis we could get. So we let the other regions bribe us a little. That way they could each get their hands on a few berries from our supply."

"Why let *them* into it?" Mike asked. "Aren't our labs as good as theirs? Seems to me they'd try and screw us if they found anything good."

Lyle Connery shook his head. "Our equipment may be as good, but we won't experiment on human 'volunteers' the way that some of them will. And even if they found the berries were valuable, they would still have to deal with us—because we are the only ones who know where the berries come from. The

Strines aren't talking. Anyway, about a month ago the agent grapevine began to pass along test results. They were quite something. Look at this video. It's the recent sprint final from the Unified Empire Games."

He called a video onto the display screen. It showed a group of eight runners lined up in starting blocks. At the electronic signal one woman burst off the mark well ahead of the others. She increased her lead all the way to the finish line and won by more than ten yards.

"That's a Chill competitor," Connery said. "Trudi Snorresen, from Cap City. There's no way she should have won. According to Daddy-O's records, before she ran in these games her best time for one hundred meters was about nine point seven. You've just seen her running eight point eight. Rumors from the southern ice cap say that Snorresen was holding herself back all the way in that race—in training, she is supposed to run the distance in just over five seconds."

Connery flicked off the display. "Those berries are something special. Apparently the alkaloid we discovered in them totally changes synapse speed and reaction times. The Chills call the active component 'Velocil,' and that's not a bad name. When a human being gets ten milligrams or so into the system, the only limit on speed of movement seems to be simple tissue-tearing stresses. We've heard reports from the Great Republic of a Yankee woman catching swallows out of the air with her bare hands, and a man grasping a rattlesnake safely by the head while it was striking at him. The Ten Tribes have a movie of a hunter running down an antelope in full flight, and from up in orbit there's a rumor of a Chipponese woman picking a bullet out of the air—though we're still skeptical about that one. But the rest are quite enough. Those berries are a unique new resource."

"But who wants them?" Mike had been dazzled by the speed and grace of the runner, but it was hard to see why improved reaction time was so valuable. "Isn't everything that needs really fast speed computer-controlled anyway?"

Connery smiled. "Most of the serious things are. But the Unified Empire would like to see Velocil completely under their control. Think what unlimited use of it would do to their businesses. It could screw up horse races, athletic contests, card games—everything that the visitors to the Unified Empire bet on. With a dose of Velocil, a card player could change a jack to a king so fast that no one would see anything happen. Cock-fights and bullfights and horse racing would be completely unpredictable. I suppose the Greasers could drug-test everything and everyone, but that would be a terrific hassle. Far better to control it at the source."

"But why not let them buy the rights from us?"

"Two reasons. First, we don't *have* the rights—though we haven't told anyone that. The other regions assume they can deal with us. Second, the Yankeeland farmers are also interested in the berries, as a Great Republic agricultural crop. Remove the alkaloid, and in what's left you have the highest vegetable protein per gram anyone has ever seen."

"Then why not just negotiate with the Great Republic and the Unified Empire—and the Chills and Chipponese, too, for that matter. I assume they're all interested."

"They are." Connery sighed. "And we can't. We have to work with the Strines—because someone else is at least as smart as we are. Those berries have seeds in them, but they are *sterile*. They were exposed to a big dose of radiation before we got our hands on them. Someone has to go to the Strine Interior and confirm the source of the Velocil berries. We need solid facts on their growth and production. That's your mission, and that's what they're expecting from you. After that we will have to strike some kind of deal for a guaranteed supply, but we're not asking you to do that. You don't have the experience for it. All clear to you?"

Mike nodded. "Information, not final negotiation. I'll remember."

"Good. One other thing before you go. Rule Four."

Mike cleared his throat. Rule Four was the kicker that could kill a Trader. "Sure. 'Anyone who isn't working two agendas at once should give up being a Trader.'"

"Right. We don't apply that to trainees, so there's no *official* second item. But here's something unofficial. A few weeks ago we had a rumor of something else in the Strineland Interior— something that might be a lot more important than Velocil. Did you ever hear of the Dulcinel Protocol?"

Mike stared at Lyle Connery and racked his brains. The Dulcinel Protocol. Something that had been a passing reference, near the beginning of Trader training. Where did it fit? Back at the very beginning of the Lostlands War, before the Chipponese went to space.

"Wasn't that a Strine development, too?" he said at last. "A long time ago. Something to do with the abo teams?"

"Not bad." Lyle Connery nodded approval. "It's nice to know

that some of the lessons stick. The original Dulcinel Protocol was used with the first haploid abo killing teams, forty years ago. It's a lymphocyte change to permit rapid self-healing after wounds— part of the reason the abos were so effective against the Chippon-ese. We thought we knew the whole story on it. But now we hear reports of a major new development. This time the Protocol is more general. It can be applied to anyone, not just haploid abos. And it does many more things: rapid healing, resistance to dis-ease, shrinking of malignant growths, tissue restoration, lessened need for sleep, and greater endurance. But there's a problem: the Strines are telling us that the new Dulcinel Protocol doesn't exist, so there's nothing to discuss. And it's not the usual situation, where they keep something close to their chests just to get a better deal. This time they don't want anyone to have it—period. We hear they'll kill anyone who tries to get it."

Mike swallowed. "And you want me to get—to try to—"

"No." Connery smiled. "It's fifteen years too soon for you. The final trainee test may be unreasonable, but it's not *that* unreasonable. We wonder if the new Dulcinel Protocol and Ve-locil are related. All we want you to do is keep your eyes and ears open. If you notice anything strange, make sure that Jack Lester gets a look at it, too. He's sometimes crazy, but he has the experience you're missing. If you get communication black-out with him, put it on the recording disk. And remember, dead heroes make bad Traders. The modified Protocol is a job for a very experienced operator. You concentrate on the Velocil ber-ries as your priority. Anything you pick up on the Protocol will be a nice bonus, but you're not to let it distract you."

"Yessir."

Mike had wondered, with a little bemusement, why Lyle Connery would tell him all about the Dulcinel Protocol, then instruct him not to think about it. Connery's instructions abso-lutely guaranteed that Mike would be distracted by thoughts of the Protocol. Now, lying on his bunk heading for a landing at BigSyd, he thought he understood. Connery was telling him to explore the Protocol as a *private* sideline. If he succeeded, the Traders would benefit; if he fell on his face, they could tell the Strines that it was all his idea—because he had been specifi-cally told not to meddle.

What was Jack Lester supposed to do if Mike began to ex-plore the Protocol? Assist him, or stop him?

Mike opened his eyes, all ready to tongue in a circuit to Lester. Then he became suddenly aware of two factors. First, his conditioning had at last come into operation. He could feel the ship's motion, and it was much greater than before. But now it was no longer unpleasant. That was good.

Less good was the fact that someone was standing at the end of the bunk, quietly watching him. And in the gloom he could see that the stranger was holding a long and wicked-looking blade of glittering steel. It was lined up on his unprotected abdomen.

Mike lifted his head slowly and carefully to face the intruder. He found he was looking at a woman of about thirty, a short-haired, strongly built blonde with tanned arms and legs. She wore a blue sleeveless blouse, tight pants cut off at knee level, and thick-soled sandals. Mike completed the tongue movement that should bring Jack Lester back into communication, then nodded at the woman.

"Hello," he said softly.

She lowered the blade so that it almost touched his belly. Mike felt the muscles there tighten up, independently of any conscious act on his part. He had a flash of memory of a descending knife, and of the ritual castration planned for him back in the Hives.

"You're a Trader, ain'tcher?" she said conversationally. "Where you come from, I hear men and women are equal. But not here. You know I could carve your guts out this minute, and no Strine would give a damn?" Her voice was husky and low-pitched, and it somehow matched the sun-tanned body and open-air look of her.

"I know that." Mike kept his voice as casual as hers had been. "But I'm not sure why you'd want to. Seems to me that my guts don't have much value to anybody—except me, of course. I value them highly."

As Mike spoke he heard a little hiss in his left ear. Jack Lester was back. The woman in front of him chuckled and lowered the blade.

"Maybe you'll do." She came forward along the bunk and stood just a foot from Mike. "Not like the lily-livered Yankee I had to deal with back in Orklan. All he did was scream and sob and beg me not to cut his balls off." She sheathed the blade and held out her hand. "My name is Lavengro. Fathom Five Lavengro."

"Don't touch her hand!" Lester said urgently in Mike's head. *"Let her take yours, if she wants to. Men don't touch women here first."*

"I know that." Mike subvocalized an impatient response. *"I*

have been briefed, you know." He held his hand out where Fathom Lavengro could take it if she wished.

"I guess you're the captain of the ship," he said aloud. "I'm Mike Asparian. And you're quite right, I'm a Trader." Or I will be, if I can just pass this test—so I hope you're going to help me, ma'am.

Fathom grabbed Mike's hands and helped him to swing to an upright position. She smiled at him, and he had his first good look at her face. She was a gray-eyed blonde, with a wide, pale mouth and two strange parallel vertical incisions between that and her chin.

"See the marks?" Lester hissed. *"She's a bigmomma—from the Interior! Better be careful, the Interior mommas are holy terrors; they control all the abo killing teams. Only way to get their respect is to beat 'em and fool 'em. Then you'll do a deal. But she's two thousand miles from home. What's she doing in Orklan?"*

Mike had been asking himself the same question, while the woman gave him a leisurely and careful inspection.

"Lordy. Bit young, ain'tcher?"

Mike flushed and pulled his hands out of her grasp. "I'm twenty-one years old."

"Thought so. Twenty-one. Don't know what's coming to you Traders, you get younger all the time. I like that. Did Daddy-O pick out a honey mouse, just for me?"

"She likes you!" Lester said. *"Great. Remember now, let her make the moves—and if it gets exciting, don't you dare cut me out of the circuit. I'm getting full sensory inputs back here. It's been a long time!"*

"For God's sake—calm down, Lester. This is business! How does she know about Daddy-O?" Mike took a step closer to the blond woman. *"Lavengro is a Strine Interior name, isn't it? Tommy Lavengro used to be chief of the Interior."*

That earned him a respectful nod. "Long time ago. I see you've done some homework. My Pops, old Tommy was. I don't know his reputation with the Traders, but he was a man who made a deal as easy as breathing. I'm his daughter, and I make deals, too. Try me."

"Tommy Lavengro," Lester whispered to Mike. *"The only man who could hold his own with the bigmommas. I knew him. Biggest liar in Strineland. Far as I know, he never told the truth in his whole life. Two children: Jessica, better known as Fathom Five—this one; and Jinjer, the mystery one that no-*

*body knows much about. Usually called Cinder-feller—had
some terrible deforming accident in a fire a few years ago. Got
the name there, but I don't have any details. Both big bosses in
the Strine Interior. Wonder if they take after their daddy."*

"We might find out if you'd just shut up for a minute." Mike
nodded at Fathom. "If you'll make deals, so will I. For a start,
how would you like to trade some information?"

Fathom looked at him shrewdly. "Could be—if you have
any. What makes you think you know anything I'd give a
kangy's cooch about?"

"I'm sure I do. But I don't want to talk down here." *Traders'
Rule: Try to see your opponent's home environment; it may tell
you what they need.* "I haven't eaten in fourteen hours, and I
need some fresh air. There's no food here. Can we go forward
to your quarters to eat and talk?"

She shrugged, turned without speaking, and led the way up
to the deck.

"Remember, don't trust her an inch," Jack Lester said urgently. *"She'll act all sweet and kind, then when you're no
more use to her she'll turn on you in a second. Make a pass at
her that she doesn't want, and she'll cut your throat. Coo-ee.
Might be worth it, though. Take a look at the wiggle on that
rear end! Makes you want to reach out and grab a handful."*

Mike sighed. Trader's luck. Of all the Mentors available, he
had been assigned the only disembodied lunatic would-be rapist
in the whole organization. *"Get your mind off sex for a minute,
Jack. Take a look in Daddy-O's data banks, and find something
we can use to trade for information. We need to know a lot
more about the Interior."*

Mike ignored his Mentor's protests and lagged behind on the
steep stairway, so that Fathom's posterior undulations were less
intimately revealed to them. He was finally beginning to understand the reason for Jack Lester's nickname.

When Mike came on deck he had to bend almost double to
make his way forward. The ship was scudding along fast into a
howling west wind. It was very cold and nearly dark. Invisible
salt spindrift broke over the bow with a roaring hiss and
drenched everything on deck with a freezing spray.

Fathom Lavengro, sure of her sea legs, had darted on ahead
of him. He saw her disappear suddenly from view. He followed
slowly after and descended another dark hatchway. The door at
the bottom had closed automatically, and the companionway

was unlit. Mike groped his way down, hand on the rail, until the door at the bottom sensed his presence and swung open. He found himself in a suite of rooms that contrasted sharply with his own quarters. Underfoot was the vivid blue-green of euclypt carpet, growing from wall to wall. The end of the room was one long serving area and autochef. As he stepped inside and looked around him, Fathom came through the low door on his left. She had removed blouse, pants, and sandals, and was naked except for a curious bracelet of linked metal tablets. She was toweling vigorously at her damp hair.

As he stared at her she nodded casually. "Damp out there, eh? Take your clothes off, grab a towel, and make yourself comfortable. I'll order us a couple of beers and some food."

Mike gaped at her, then went through the door she was pointing at. He came to a bedroom with a bathroom at one end and half the remaining space taken up by a broad floor mattress.

"I said she liked the look of you," Jack said triumphantly in his ear. *"Starkers! Stripped bare before you even come in the door."*

Mike picked up a big towel and thoughtfully began to remove his clothes. *"Nobody told me people went around naked in the middle of Strineland."*

"Some of 'em do, mostly the abos. It's not unusual here— but she sure as hell knows that Traders don't go around bare assed. That's why I'm sure she has a letch for you."

Mike shook his head, dried himself, and stood motionless for a moment. *"What's the Strine penalty if a man makes a pass at a momma—one she didn't invite?"*

"Anything she wants—chopped to bits, staked out in the sun, skinned alive." The Mentor sounded remarkably pleased by the thought. *"But there's no risk of that now—get in there."*

"Quite right. There isn't." Mike headed for the door, still naked and carrying the towel with him. He was leaving the recording disk behind him, on his shirt, but suddenly he felt very comfortable. He knew what Fathom was doing. It had been drilled in on Day One, as Lyle Connery covered the basic principles. 'Basic negotiation techniques: get a psychological advantage. Throw the opposition off balance. If they expect you to be angry, stay calm. If they negotiate only by moonlight, try to get them to do it at midday, in the full sun. If they hate to fly, hold the talks on board a plane. If nudity shocks them, take your pants off. And never forget: they'll be trying to do the same thing to you. 'Rule Twelve: Anything can be a negotiation technique.' "

Mike went back into the other room, walked across to the

autochef, and took the flask of beer that waited there. He looked Fathom calmly over from sun-bleached hair to sinewy bare feet, aware of the fact that she was giving him the same objective scrutiny, then nodded toward the table. "If you'd care to sit down, I'll be happy to bring the food over as soon as we get the signal."

He was pleased to see her frown in surprise before she nodded and went across to sit on a high stool at the table.

"You're cooler than I thought, sweetheart. All right, over to you. What do you know that you think I want?"

End of Round One, Mike thought. He sat down opposite her. He could feel a tingly sense of excitement in his stomach. This was the real thing, something he had been rehearsing for years: the first shot at negotiation. He tongued Jack Lester to low volume, so the Mentor could distract him only in an emergency. And he tried to ignore Fathom's suntanned breasts, a couple of feet away from him.

"We have to feel our way into this," he said. "Otherwise whoever speaks first will be afraid of giving too much away. I suggest we tell each other initially only what we *think* we know. Then each of us can make corrections. That way you won't really be telling me something I don't already know, and it will be the same for me."

She looked at him for a moment, her head on one side. "Why shouldn't I just wait until we get to the mainland, and then have whatever you know beaten out of you?"

Mike said nothing. If she was here, she needed him as much as he needed her. After a second she shrugged. "Oh, all right. Let's try it. But you go first."

"Careful what you tell her!" Lester's voice was a distant screech in his ear. Mike frowned and wondered if he was about to go too far. The information was Trader Confidential—but the chance that Fathom Lavengro already knew most of it was good. Why else would she travel to Orklan and have first contact with him, if she didn't have an idea of his mission?

"Stop me when I go wrong," he began, "but I believe a modified euclypt has been developed in the Strine Interior, somewhere near The Musgrave. And we already know what it can do." He gave her a summary of everything that had happened, from the moment of the dead bigmomma's discovery in Ree-o-dee until his arrival on board the ship in Orklan.

"Naturally, we're interested in acting as Trader negotiators for any sales of rights to Velocil," he concluded. "And as a first step, we need to know who controls the supply of the berries in Strine territory. From your appearance here, so far away from home, I assume you have more than a casual interest yourself. In fact, my first guess was that you were the key individual. Now I'm not so sure. If you were in control, you could have sat tight up in The Musgrave and waited for me to come to you. You know I'd have found my way to the right place eventually."

Fathom had listened to him in complete silence. Now she shook her head. "Smart little bugger, ain'tcher? You're quite right—I don't control the Candlemass Berries. And I'm not from the Musgrave. I'm from Alice, north of there. But I still have to put you right on a few things. First, you'll not be able to make a deal with the main producers of the berries. They want to work direct with the Unified Empire. That would cut you out of it, and me, too. The berries that have been shipped out of The Musgrave are *all* sterile, not just the ones you know about; so you need to get your hands on a supply of fertile ones. I think I can help you on that—if the deal is right. First, though, we have to worry about your side of the bargain. You promised information for me. You never told me the subject."

Mike nodded. "I will. From the way you've been behaving so far, the thing you need is correct information about Traders: how we're trained, how we operate. You don't have much idea about that—if you did, you'd never have tried that corny bit with the sword." He looked at her exposed body and shook his head. "And other things, too. Tell me what you think you know, and I'll take it from there. Even if the two of us can't make a deal this time, you'll need accurate data on the Traders for future deals."

"Fair enough." Fathom frowned, her gray eyes shadowed by thick blond eyebrows. "Let's start at the beginning. I guess that means with the Lostlands War? That's when the Strines got pretty isolated."

As she spoke the autochef chimed its message. Mike stood up and brought over the dish. It was barbecued mutton on a platter of cultivated saltbush seeds. Mike quietly swallowed a detox pill, then began to eat. The food was alien and quite unpleasant, but his Trader training allowed him to work his way through it and smile while he did so. He should probably count himself lucky—Jack Lester had told him horror stories of the roasted 'tremes offered as food—bills, feet, and all—in some parts of the Strine Interior.

Fathom ate her portion with obvious relish. While she did so she gave Mike a fascinating and strangely distorted version of world history. According to Fathom, it was the passage of fallout across northern Strineland that stimulated the rate of new species development and caused the growth of the secret biolabs in the Interior. All the other regions had been ruined then, but the Traders had taken unfair advantage of the general world chaos.

"You saw your chance and you jumped in," she said, pushing her empty plate aside. "You had that old, puritanical, moralistic society of yours, and you argued moral authority to become negotiators between all the regions." She paused, disconcerted, when Mike laughed out loud. "What's so funny?"

"I've heard the Traders called a lot of things—but puritanical and moralistic are new ones to me. Is that why we're sitting here with no clothes on, so I'll be too shocked to think straight? Fathom, you've got the whole thing backward. We're *Traders*, in the game for what we can get out of it. Commercial, yes. Immoral, if you insist on it. But *puritanical*, forget it—I'll tell you Trader yarns that would make your hair curl." There was a delighted cackle of *"Right on, boyo,"* in Mike's ear. "I'll sit bare as long as you want to. But you have to learn one central fact about us Traders: when we strike a deal, we stay bought. And what we're told under Trader Oath never goes any farther. Never, ever. Not even if people try to torture it out of us. Our conditioning would make us die before we talk against our will. We're Traders; and we make deals. And so—"

Mike finally pushed away his own plate and stared directly into Fathom Lavengro's eyes. "—I'm a Trader. Do you want to make a deal?"

She sat staring at him for a moment, her cheeks flushed. Finally she nodded. "I guess I do. Let me tell you what I can do for you, then you do some thinking about how much that's worth. I'll tell you now, I won't do it cheap."

"Whoo-ee! There you go, partner. She's hooked." Jack's voice was an excited shout in Mike's ear. *"But watch your step when you try to haul her in. If I know the Strine mommas, she's angling for some agenda of her own—we have to find out what it is."*

"I know, Jack. I'll do some thinking about that later." He nodded at Fathom. "Tell me your deal."

"Here's what I can do for you." She leaned close, her face only a foot away from his. "I can get you to the right place in the Interior—fast, safe, and easy. No entry to BigSyd and long trek overland for us. We'll put the ship on auto and take the hydrofoil launch. That'll bring us along the coast to Eucla, down on the Nullarbor Plain. I have an aircraft there, and we can fly straight up to The Musgrave. Second, I'll introduce you to the momma who controls the Candlemass Berries. All that ought to be worth a lot."

Mike nodded. "Agreed. I'll have to think about our terms, but don't worry. It's one of the Traders' basic rules, a deal that's not good for both sides should never be signed. Let me do some figuring tonight, and we'll nail down the details in the morning."

He rose to his feet and began to move back to the bedroom to collect his clothes. To his surprise Fathom at once stood up and followed him. She put her arms around his waist and moved into close contact with him, rubbing herself gently against his back.

"You need to learn Strine customs. If we're going to work as a team, we might as well operate as one." She spoke softly in Mike's ear, her hair fine spun on his neck and cheek. "I don't know Trader ways, and I doubt you know Strine ones. It's time we both learned."

Mike heard Jack's wild cackle of triumph in his ear. *"I knew it! I told you she fancied yer—get in there. Remember, though, let her make the moves. And bigmomma on top!"*

Mike turned to look at Fathom, her eyes wide and pale in the dim light. Intimate contact, with running commentary from Lover-boy Lester? No way. *"Good night, Jack,"* he whispered, deep in his throat. *"Maybe some other time, but not now."*

As he tongued to sever the Mentor connection he heard Jack's howl of rage and supplication. *"No, Mike, don't cut me off. We're a team! For God's sake, we're in this together—"*

"There it is, sweet baby," Fathom said softly. "Doesn't that feel nice? Come to momma."

"—partners! Mike, we're partners—"

The cabin was warm and dark. The ship surged west through rising seas.

Fathom Lavengro kept her part of the deal. In return for Mike's guarantee that she would be the Strine agent in any Trader deal for Velocil or anything else involving the Candlemass Berries, she moved them to the mainland through the Eucla port. Entry to Strineland was both quick and simple. Within twenty-four hours, Mike was heading for the Interior. Soon after that he had his first meeting with a killer Strine.

The aircraft was on course for The Musgrave when Fathom called back to Mike from the pilot's seat.

"Hold tight. Brickfielder up ahead." Without another word

she put on her headset and plunged them down from fifteen thousand feet in a fast landing pattern.

"What's she talking about, 'brickfielder'?" Mike whispered.

"Dust storm," said Jack Lester's scratchy voice, after a moment's silence. It had taken him half a day to forgive Mike for cutting him out of sensory contact, but now his natural cheerfulness was reasserting itself.

"This time of year," he went on, *"you get brickfielders around here—hot, dry, dust storms out of the Strine Interior. We ought to be able to fly above it to Alice and her territory, or go through it on instruments. I don't know why she brought you down. So keep your guard up—there might be a trap here. We're a long way south of The Musgrave, and farther still from Fathom's base."* Lester's voice had a strange, dry crackle to it, as though it were being filtered during transmission.

"Is it the brickfielder that's interfering with signal reception?" Mike asked. *"I'm having trouble hearing you."*

"No. We can handle any natural interference. What you're seeing is the first signs of the signal blackout. We knew it was coming. This part of the Strine Interior is covered by a Chill jamming system. Daddy-O will hold signal as long as possible."

"How long are we going to be stuck here on the ground?"

"No idea." Jack Lester's voice was a shade weaker and less clear. *"Storm could last a few days."*

They had finally halted in the middle of a single dirt runway. While Fathom was busy in the cabin with radio communications, Mike climbed down from the plane and wandered off to the edge of the landing field, to stare at the flat ochres and purples of the worn surrounding hills. Jack Lester had been quite right when he described the Strine Interior as battered. There was a primitive feel to the land, a timelessness that could not be expressed through any training sessions, and it had nothing to do with its current inhabitants. The surface rocks in this area were the oldest on Earth.

As Mike was looking around him, a silent file of dark figures came trotting around the landing field perimeter. They were all males, each no more than four feet tall, with thin legs and powerful torsoes. "Haploid abos!" Jack said. Mike nodded. The men were hairless, with impassive, unlined faces and dusty black skin. Every one was deformed in some way, with ugly tumors, missing digits, or deep abscesses on body and limbs. They each wore a light one-piece garment of fine metallic mesh and carried a silver-black attack tube. Though they passed within fifteen yards of Mike, they appeared to take no notice of his presence.

It was hard to believe that these squat, sick-looking little men were the most formidable fighters that the planet had ever known. But Mike knew it was true. Back in training camp, he and his fellow trainees had seen and marvelled at Chipponese high-resolution videos of abos in action. In one display, an un-armed haploid abo had tackled a pair of trained attack dogs and killed them both bare handed in twenty seconds; in another, an unarmed abo swimming offshore north of Strine mainland had been attacked by an eighteen-foot white shark. The naked abo had lost a foot and three fingers, but within fifteen minutes the disemboweled shark was thrashing helplessly in a widening cloud of its own blood.

"See how light they travel," Jack said faintly. *"Wish us Traders were as efficient. The abos never carry food or water, and they can live off the land anywhere in the world . . ."*

His voice faded to a thread of sound, and there was a sudden burst of random noise in Mike's ear. He listened intently for a signal from the Mentor. *"Jack, I've lost you."*

There was another crackle of static, from which a recogniz-able tone finally emerged. *"Same at this end."* Jack's voice had taken on a bizarre mechanical quality. *"We've hit the jamming system. Daddy-O's jockeying frequencies and filters to try to keep us in touch, but we're losing it . . ."* The voice in Mike's ear faded, then came back weaker than ever. *". . . in real time and feeding it to me and Daddy-O. Use your recording disk now, I'm losing you. The images I'm getting from your optic chiasma aren't in color any more, we're right at the edge of acceptable signal-to-noise ratio. Good luck . . ."*

There was a series of clicking burps, followed by a buzz of white noise. Mike sat at the edge of the landing field, listening hard and staring straight ahead of him. *No Mentor!* Several times since the mission began he had cursed the authorities who had assigned Lover-boy Lester to him. Now, without that jaunty and irrepressible voice in his ear, he realized how reassuring Jack's hidden presence had been.

Mike squinted down at the recording disk on his shirt. He was beginning to realize its one great disadvantage: it could *take* information, but unlike Jack Lester it couldn't *give* it. Even if it worked perfectly, it wouldn't help on this mission—only for planning future ones.

Mike checked to make sure that the disk was recording.

Trader Rule: make a good mission record. Even at that intense emotional moment with Fathom when he cut Jack out of the circuit, Mike had been conscious of the disk in his abandoned shirt, still making its audio and infrared recordings. He had remained aware of its presence for at least the first few minutes of what followed. But if that knowledge had affected him, Fathom apparently found no cause for complaint.

The recording disk was set now for wide-angle coverage. Off to Mike's left, the haploid abos were trotting single file toward the horizon—or what should have been the horizon. As Mike looked, he realized that the far distance was a single, endless wall of dull, rust-red haze. Land and sky merged seamlessly together.

"I guess Fathom Lavengro isn't lying about the brickfielder, whatever else she's lying to me about," Mike said softly to the recording disk. He began to hurry back toward the plane.

Did the abos know what they were doing, running directly at a storm?

Those low, flat foreheads and that dwarfed cranial capacity supported the figure of sixty-five for the average IQ usually assigned to the haploid abos. But their uncanny skill in combat, plus the ability to draw food and water from the most unpromising environment, suggested that their intelligence was not measureable by the usual methods. If a haploid abo could survive on the Chill ice cap without clothing or weapons, in the Grand Erg Oriental without water, and in the Strine northern badlands without radiation treatment or protection—all circumstances that would mean certain death to Mike—who should be assigned the higher intelligence? Mike climbed back into the plane and closed the door securely behind him. Although it was only midafternoon, the sun had disappeared and the northern sky had darkened to an ominous dried-blood red. At the front of the cabin Fathom was still crouched over the commset, ignoring Mike completely.

He went to sit quietly in the back of the aircraft. If she was not worrying about the coming storm, then what *was* she doing so busily? Mike could not produce even a plausible guess. Jack Lester insisted that some deep Strine plan was being worked out, something that Mike and the Traders knew nothing about; but he had been unable to make any suggestion as to what it might be, and Mike was equally baffled. According to Daddy-O, their destination, The Musgrave, did indeed have a big-momma boss—but it was Cinder-feller, Fathom's sister, rather than Fathom herself. So was Cinder-feller the momma who controlled the Candlemass Berries and, therefore, the source of Velocil? Or was there some other game being played between the two Lavengro sisters?

Daddy-O's data base, according to Jack, showed that the two bigmommas were deadly rivals, enemies who would rather feud than cooperate on anything. They would normally not even enter the other's territory. And according to Jack Lester, Cinder-feller had been so hideously mutilated by her accident that she refused meetings with anyone outside her immediate circle of servants and advisors. So why fly Mike to her territory?

Rule 30 from the Traders' informal Rule Book: *Assume everyone is lying for his own reason—including me.*

Was *anyone* telling Mike the whole truth?

Not Fathom, that was certain. Last night, when she believed Mike to be sound asleep, she had risen and moved across to his scattered heap of belongings. What she found there apparently satisfied her. She had returned to his side after a few minutes. The detox pill that Mike had taken before they ate, as a precaution against drugging or poisoning, was highly effective, but it produced a side effect of insomnia. He had remained fully awake, wondering. Other than the recording disk, he was carrying nothing to interest anyone; and the messages on that were unreadable to anyone except the Traders.

Mike thought back now to the abos he had just seen, and wondered again about the new Dulcinel Protocol. If it had been developed and used in the Strine Interior, it was not being used in this area. Lyle Connery had told of a technique that would shrink malignant growths and regrow tissues; but the abos' disfiguring tumors had been obvious, and many were missing fingers and toes.

Fathom had finally finished with her intent exchange of messages. She stood up and came to the rear of the cabin, where Mike was sitting in deep thought.

He looked up at her. It occurred to him how little, despite all the briefings and study, he knew of Strine culture. What was their music, their dance, their literature? What were their motives and ambitions in life? He had little idea. But how could he be an effective Trader if he didn't know what the group he was dealing with most wanted out of life? Back in Trader Headquarters, it was easy to say "Strine" and imagine that the single noun described the whole group. But now it was obvious that the Strines were many groups, fiercely independent and competitive with one another. And it was only in the face of a greater threat—from some other region—that the Strines would combine their arsenals and behave as a unit.

Fathom squatted easily in front of him. She smiled and shook her ash-blond head. "Bad news. I've been on the blower to the stations north of here. The brickfielder extends a long way, right past The Musgrave."

"Can't we fly right over it? What's the altitude limit on the aircraft?"

"Ninety thousand feet. Sure, we can fly *over* it easily enough—so long as we don't try to land. But I can't bring us down in The Musgrave without ruining my plane's engines. You don't know this dust—it's like grinding powder on machined surfaces."

Mike stared out of the window. The red wall was nearer, towering from ground to heaven just a few miles away. "So what do we do? Wait here—or head north on foot, like the abo warriors?"

Fathom smiled again and reached out to rub her hand along his cheek. "Wouldn't mind waiting here with you, sweetie-pie. But I can't spare the time. And don't ever suggest trying to go with the abos out into the Interior deserts. There's no food or water there."

"They seem to manage all right."

She gave him a strange, half-amused look. "Yeah. Know why? They manage north of here because anything they find— anything at all—is food and drink." She massaged his arm, feeling the muscles of biceps and triceps. "You have a nice body, Trader Asparian. I appreciate it. So would they. Out in the wilds you'd be a nice long drink and ninety pounds of convenient protein. You're safe here, because they're programmed not to touch anyone near the airfields. That doesn't apply in the outback. Forget the idea of going anywhere on foot."

"It's already forgotten. But what will we do?"

"Take off and fly right over the top, on past The Musgrave. The dust storm ends short of Alice. We can stay above it and land at my home base. Then we can come *south* again overland, following the tail of the storm." She stood upright. "Come and sit forward when we take off. You'll see something worth seeing when we reach Alice."

The wind at the airstrip was rising steadily, hitting the plane in hard gusts. The aircraft took off to the north and at once set into a tight upward spiral, gaining height rapidly. The dark-red wall of the brickfielder at first looked topless, only a few miles away.

At five thousand feet, Mike suddenly saw the sun again. It was rusted and weary, sitting in a boil of brown-red smoke. At ten thousand feet they were well above the storm. They turned to fly north over a flat, featureless plain of wind-borne dust stretching away endlessly in front of them. Only the airspeed indicator told them they were speeding at Mach Four across the Strine Interior.

Mike leaned forward in his seat, making sure that the recording disk on his shirt had a good view of the landscape through the forward window. Despite Fathom's promise, he was finding the view rather boring. There was simply nothing to see. And as he was reaching that conclusion a dramatic change occurred. The dust cloud below them vanished, cut off cleanly along an east-west line.

Mike leaned to his right and peered out of the side port. He could see the ground again. The dusty, treeless terrain that had persisted beneath the aircraft all the way from their Strine entry point at Eucla to their recent unplanned stop was gone. In its place Mike saw a pattern of textured bluish-green circles, their centers laid out on a regular triangular grid.

"Know what those are?" Fathom asked. She was turning toward him, leaning back in her seat with her eyes half-closed.

Mike shook his head. "My first thought was a plantation of trees, with us looking down on their crowns. But then I realized how high we are. Each of those circles must be half a mile across. And it looks bone dry down there."

Fathom smiled, but it was somehow directed inward, for herself and no one else. "Your first guess was right."

"Trees? That big?"

"Trees. They were developed here, in my labs, and they grow nowhere else. Multiple trunk, like a banyan, but much more productive. Food and timber. We're flying over a Double-X plantation. Average trunk diameter is thirty yards, maximum eighty."

Mike realized that Fathom had changed. Previously there had been an underlying tension, well controlled but always there. He had been unaware of it before, because there had been no basis for comparison. But now, seeing her fully relaxed, the difference was obvious. Fathom was back in her own territory, in an environment where she was in full control.

"Double-X?"

"Shorthand." Fathom had hit a new control sequence, and they were dropping off altitude at an alarming speed. "Stands for 'Xerophytic Xyloids'—male tech-talk, gobbledygook for plants that can get by without much water and produce lots of wood. You'll see them close up when we head south again. They grow right down to the border with The Musgrave."

Mike nodded but did not speak. "Male tech-talk." Was that a significant comment, even if an unintended one, on the Strine Interior? Did males do all the technical work in the biolabs—as well as providing all the human test subjects for experiments?

While the aircraft was landing and skidding to a halt, Mike recalled one of Lover-boy Lester's less cheerful pronouncements: "Don't get an inflated idea of your own value, boyo. Here, you're nothing. And be damn careful. In the Interior, the mommas use men as trading tokens. And torture is considered as one of the fine arts."

He surreptitiously retested the communication link with Daddy-O and Jack Lester. Still jammed. There was nothing but static.

Mike was on his own.

When the world had seemed ready to end in all-out nuclear war, the Strines sought safety underground. Once established, that taste for below-ground accommodation had never left them. Deep structures permitted better temperature and humidity control, and that was important in the Strine Interior to everyone except perhaps the haploid abos.

Although Mike knew the facts, it still came as a surprise to look out at a region apparently populated only by scrubby acacias, wattles, and grass trees, and learn that he was seeing the main biolabs and residential area of Alice.

He was given no time to explore the underground. Fathom had paused in Alice only long enough to collect a beetle-browed, powerfully built guide known as Banjo, then they were in a ground car and heading south. After an hour's drive the car stopped and Fathom climbed out.

"I won't be coming the rest of the way," she said to Mike's surprise. "Banjo will take care of you and get you to the transfer point. I'll see you on the way back, when you're all finished."

Her manner to Mike had changed. It was cool, with no trace of affection. Was that for Banjo's benefit? Mike had no way of knowing. He settled back in his seat and stared around him.

They were speeding along a straight asphalt road that ran through an avenue of the Double-X trees. Each of them was like a full grove, towering five hundred feet above the sun-baked plain. No other plants grew in their shade, and the ground beneath them showed no pattern of sunlight diffracting through leaf spaces. The tree structures had been genetically designed. They captured every available erg of incident solar energy and used it to produce polysaccharides—starches, sugars, and cellulose.

As the giant tree farms finally petered out, giving way to a land scorched and barren in the hot sun, Mike wondered. Who was Fathom's chief bioengineer, the genius behind the Double-X trees? Banjo could not say—or would not. Communication with him proved almost impossible. Mike forced a few mono-syllables from him in answer to some of his questions, and that was the best he could do.

But when he finally asked why Fathom had not come with them, he received a roar of laughter and Banjo's longest speech of the trip. "Fathom Five Lavengro! Ha-ha—to cross the border with The Musgrave? Man, that's real funny. You know what Cinder-feller would do if Fathom came inside that territory? Cut her up for dingo dinners, that's what." He slapped a scarred brown arm on the car's steering-wheel. "Them two don't see each other anymore—*ever*. Didn't you know it, sport? They hate each other's guts. Just look ahead there. That's to hold 'em apart."

The trees had all gone now, and they were approaching a barbed wire fence with a solid gate where the road ran to meet it. Another ground car sat waiting at the other side of the gate. Two haploid abos stood about a hundred yards away, looking at each other from opposite sides of the fence. As the car approached they both ran with incredible speed to the gate and stood quietly by it.

"All right, man, here we are." Banjo stepped down from the car slowly and carefully, gesturing to Mike to do the same. "Take hold of this piece of leather, rub your hands on it, and let 'em have a good look at it. It's your identification. Carry it with you. I'll come as far as the other car, to make sure the driver is all ready for you—should be a young woman, name of Sweet Pea. Don't try to talk to her, 'cause it's a waste of time. She's a deaf-mute, works directly for Cinder-feller. I'll be waiting here for you when you come back. If you're gone more than two days, have one of Cinder-feller's people send a message back here."

The abo guard took the identification that Mike held out to him, rubbing it between his finger and thumb. He shuffled all the way around Mike, sniffing at his feet, genitals, and hair. After doing the same to Banjo he opened the gate. The haploid at the other side repeated the procedure, sniffed again at the leather fragment, then led them to the car. Banjo nodded his greeting at the dark-haired woman sitting within and allowed himself to be escorted back through the gate.

The new car bore on its side a peculiar insignia like a quadruple interlocking helix. Mike climbed into the passenger seat and stared curiously at the driver. Sweet Pea was young, no more than his own age, with a flawless, ivory-white complexion and shining black hair. She looked as out of place in the Strine Interior as Mike felt.

She nodded at him, smiling. After a few moments she suddenly pressed the accelerator to the floor. The car started in a cloud of brown dust, racing southward along another section of the same arrow-straight road.

The silence was fine with Mike. He wanted to wrestle with a puzzle of his own. According to Jack Lester and Banjo, Fathom Five and Cinder-feller Lavengro never went to each other's territory—were not even *safe* in each other's territory. If that were true, then Fathom had never intended to land the aircraft in The Musgrave—and would not have been allowed to do so. *Therefore*, her earlier statements about their travel plans must have been false. She could not have conveniently created the dust storm, but she could have known about it long before it happened. The Chips offered an expensive weather-monitoring system that gave at least seventy-two hours notice of major storms and wind patterns. So Fathom might have included the brickfielder in her advance plans. But *why*?

At that point Mike was stumped. Fathom was using him, he was increasingly convinced of it. But he could not see how.

Mike sighed to himself. Why, how—he was building up questions when he was supposed to be answering them. The inside of the car was very hot, and it had been a hard twenty-four hours. He thought of the rule that was not in the official Traders' Rule Book, but ranked high in the unofficial one: *Food, drink, sleep—take them whenever you have a chance.*

He lay back in his seat and closed his eyes.

The Strine mission was over, and it had been a huge success. No trainee had ever done so well. After the triumphant return to the Azores and the final ceremony of induction to the position of full Trader, Mike had been given the key of the vacation lodge by Lucia Asparian. It lay high in the mountains of the Economic Community. When he looked out of the open window, it was at a succession of soaring white peaks. The air that blew in on him was clean and freezing cold. Too cold. Mike reached forward to close the window—and was suddenly awake.

It was deep dusk. The air-conditioning unit of the Strine car was set so high that it had pulled him out of a heavy sleep.

He sighed. No successful mission, no triumphant return— only a situation that looked more and more out of control. The car was slowing, turning off the smooth road. He stretched, moving his shoulders to ease cramped back muscles.

The driver had noticed his movement. She gave him a quick sideways look. "I hope that your sleep has rested you," she said, in a precise, slow voice.

Mike stopped in midstretch and turned to her in astonishment. "You're not Sweet Pea?"

"Yes, I am." The voice was carefully produced, with rather exaggerated lip movements.

"But Banjo told me—" Mike stopped in confusion.

"That I could not hear or speak?" Sweet Pea's face lit with an uncontrollable joy. "Once I could not. Now, I can do both."

Mike waited for more explanation, but none was forthcoming. Instead, Sweet Pea pointed ahead of them, to a glow of ruddy lights against the flat Strine skyline. "Two more minutes, and we will have arrived at the Headquarters of The Musgrave." She turned her elegant head, to give him a longer and frankly curious stare. "I do not think that I have ever seen a Trader before. Certainly not since I have been here. Is it true what I have been told, that a Trader has no home, anywhere?"

"In a way it's true." Mike wondered how many false rumors they had been told about Traders—and how many false facts he "knew" about the Strines. "Once we finish our training, we have no fixed home. We negotiate all over the world, and up in space, also. Our headquarters, where we coordinate our work, is the nearest thing we have to a single living place. But we do not think of ourselves as having no home. We feel that we are at home everywhere, in any place where there is trading and negotiation to be carried on."

As he spoke the lights ahead of them began to disappear from view. The car had left the level road and was descending below ground level, following a long tunnel that curved down for many feet. When the descent finally concluded Mike saw something that he had never expected to find in the Strine Interior: the reflection of far-off lamps in still water. They had reached the shore of a subterranean lake, several miles across, that filled the central region of a huge cave. The surface glowed faintly, as though from submarine lighting. He looked for signs of buildings along the lakeshore, but could see little in the gloom around the perimeter. Much of the lake ended in vertical walls of earth, reaching to the ceiling of the chamber.

"So much water!" he said to Sweet Pea. "I did not know a lake like this existed in the Interior. None of the maps shows it."

"We made it. It is the only one." She had allowed the automatic control system to take over, and it was guiding the car gradually toward the lakeside. "Because of this, we have the richest territory in the mainland. That would be true even without our biolab products. And our labs are the best." There was great pride in those carefully enunciated words. Mike was itching to see proof of the statement.

They stepped out of the car, which had parked in an underground garage where a fleet of ground and air vehicles stood arranged in neat lines. Each one bore the same spiral insignia.

Sweet Pea walked Mike to an elevator. When the lift arrived she motioned for him to enter and pressed the button for it to descend. She remained outside.

"Just a minute." Mike held the door open with one hand. "I don't know my way around this place. What happens when I get to the bottom?"

Sweet Pea smiled. "You will meet with Cinder-feller. This elevator leads only to the bigboss private quarters, or back up to the surface."

The elevator door closed before Mike could say anything more, and the car began a leisurely descent. The doors finally opened onto a room maybe thirty yards long, oppressively hot and humid, with a high vaulted ceiling. The far wall was one great sheet of curved glass. Beyond it lay the waters and bed of the underground lake, artificially lit so that an observer could follow events many yards away in the clear water. Even as he walked forward to marvel, Mike realized that he was witnessing an act of technical bravado. In one of the Earth's driest regions, Cinderfeller Lavengro was allowing her visitors to look out on her creation: a priceless treasure—millions of cubic feet of fresh water.

The interior of the room was dimly lit, and it was not until he was halfway to the glass wall that Mike realized there was another person present. Off to his left was a long dark table, and beyond that a low sofa. And on that sofa, swaddled in tasseled blankets and thick quilts, sat a dark figure. "Did you know," a sweet tenor voice said, "that in this region a man's life is usually worth no more than twenty gallons of fresh water? How many men do you think you are looking at now?"

He turned toward the sound and peered curiously at the seated figure. The voice was oddly androgynous, and he was not sure if a man or a woman had addressed him. Whichever, the swathes of blankets and gaudy patchwork quilts were draped around a grotesque being. He was looking at a person of enormous size, maybe as much as five hundred pounds in weight. It was impossible to tell where flesh began and ended in the rippling folds of garments. Long tresses of brown hair showed beneath a gray cowl, worn forward to shadow the brow and eyes. The mouth was thick-lipped and pouting, with a purple hue beneath its vivid red. The pale, bulging cheeks gleamed with sweat.

Mike stepped up to the table. "You are Jinjer Lavengro?"

The tenor voice chuckled. "Why, yes, I suppose that I am. Though no one has called me Jinjer for many years. Do as the others do, and call me Cinder-feller. And I will dispense with ceremony and call you Mike. All right? Then we can forget the protocol nonsense and get right down to business."

One thing that a Trader education included was the business rituals of different regions. Before serious discussions began, the Chipponese served hot tea, the Republic tobacco, the Community alcohol, and the Unified Empire dope; even the Chills of the Cap Federation offered their warmed liquid seal fat. The Strines alone did nothing. They observed no polite overtures. Fathom had been just as abrupt as Cinder-feller—worse, if that first naked sword counted as a greeting.

Mike shrugged. "Let's talk business. I came a long way—and not to see the sights of the Strine Interior. Where shall we begin?"

Cinder-feller drew in a long, snorting breath. "It is late, and you must be tired. But we can clear some groundwork tonight. I think there are illusions to be dispelled—perhaps on both sides." There was a movement of the massive form, and the creak of the sofa beneath it. Cinder-feller nodded at a container of dark fluid sitting surrounded by glasses and dishes of sticky-looking confections on the table in front of them. "Eat and drink, if you wish. For my part, I will refrain from food tonight and promise you a banquet tomorrow. I will begin with my own questions. Your turn will come."

How old was she? Was it truly *she*? It was easy to be confused about the sex of Tommy Lavengro's younger child. The voice gave no clue. Mike tried to see some outward sign of the deformities inflicted by Cinder-feller's accident, but the only flesh visible was nose and cheeks, and they appeared unblemished. The drapes and shawls could hide almost any injury, even the loss of an arm or leg. "Continue."

"We begin with a surprise," the cloaked figure said. "A surprise for me. We have already performed an analysis of the chemical signatures on the piece of identifying leather that you carried. It matches the chemsig for you provided by the Trader bank. You are indeed Mikal Asparian, of the Society of Traders. I was convinced before you arrived that you would prove to be an impostor."

"But you must have known that I was on my way—that information was broadcast to all of the Strine receiving stations."

"Indeed it was." Cinder-feller gave another fatty chuckle. "But I did not expect that you would ever come to me by way of *Fathom's* territory. After all, she has been desperately trying to work her spies in here for the past four years. Dispose of you and put her own agent in your place—what could be more natural? There would have to be an official story for the Traders, of course, telling how you had died in an unfortunate accident in the Strine Interior. But that would be easy. I could see the logic for it—I even anticipated it, and arranged the chemsig test when I received word of your approach. If it was another clumsy attempt at espionage, I was prepared to eliminate you at once, as I have done twelve other attempts. But, no. You are truly a Trader."

As Mike's eyes adjusted to the gloom he could see the beads of sweat that stood on Cinder-feller's cowled brow and along the thin nose. He could feel a matching rivulet making its way down the back of his neck. "Perhaps I am being obtuse," he said slowly. "I can see no logic for what you are saying. I entered the Strine mainland with help from Fathom, certainly, but I see no way in which my visit here can benefit her."

Cinder-feller poured two glasses of the dark fluid and pushed one of them toward him. "That is only because you are a stranger to our internal politics. Fathom cannot penetrate this territory. Accept that statement as truth, and believe me when I tell you that she desperately wishes to do so. We have many bioscience developments that she wants. Despite her overweening pride in the Double-X plantations, we have new organisms here that make those seem insignificant. I have bio geniuses here beyond any others in the whole world. Fathom knows it. She covets their knowledge and the power that brings us—and she knows I will never sell that knowledge to her. So, how will she get the information that she wants?" The great shoulders heaved into a shrug. "She has tried one approach: sending in spies. Not one made it past the border. Now she seemed ready for another: sending an impostor, pretending to be a Trader. I assumed that—and I was wrong. So now I have another thought." The massive body leaned forward. "Fathom wants the use of a pair of eyes and ears to tell her all they can about my labs. Though no impostor, you could be those eyes and ears."

Mike shook his head. "Torture never pulls information out of a Trader. Our indoctrination assures that—and Fathom knows it."

"As do I. Torture could not be the answer." Cinder-feller sighed. "Nor would I ever accuse you of selling information to her. I have tremendous admiration for the Traders. Tomorrow you and I will, if things go well, set up a basis for our long-term relationship. But torture and corruption are not the only ways. You are, I assume, planning to return through Fathom's territory?"

"That was our arrangement. She is certainly expecting me."

"Then let me ask you one more question. The Strines have their own sources of secret information. On this mission you are carrying with you a special device. Where is your recording disk?"

Mike was shocked. Somewhere in the Trader organization was a big information leak. To hide his surprise he leaned forward and sipped at his filled glass. Alcohol, plus a hint of heroin—and what else?

Whatever it was, he had learned his lesson in the Darklands: prevention was preferable to cure. At the first opportunity he would take a detox pill. But what should he do right now? Admit to the presence of the disk, or deny its existence?

It was an easy question. There had been plenty of confidence in Cinder-feller's voice. Mike reached up, plucked the disk from his shirt, and handed it to Cinder-feller. As she stared at it curiously he seized the chance to take out and swallow a detox pill.

"It may be rude of me to say so, but might I suggest that the Traders seek a little assistance in miniaturization from Cap City?" The pale hand came forward and passed the recording disk back to Mike. He saw the dimples of knuckles in a fatty paw, and pudgy, soft digits. But despite its grossness it was perfectly formed, with no sign of injury or disfigurement. "This is much larger than I expected, and I cannot imagine that it is convenient to operate."

Mike shrugged and considered the possibility of swallowing

the disk. "I have to say I agree with you. It was not my idea to bring it—and I certainly didn't realize that you would already know about it."

"Not only I. What would you say, Trader Asparian, if I told you that all Fathom's actions have been devoted to a single objective? She wants you to visit me and my territory and see as much of what we do as possible. And then leave the Strine Interior via *her* territory. She does not care if you are alive or dead when you reach her—because what she wants, of course, is *that*." Cinder-feller pointed at the disk, then raised her glass to her lips. The purplish mouth smiled a little at his appalled expression. "With the complete record of your visit here. If you were to swallow it, that would not matter. She will slit your belly open and cut it out of you with her own hands."

Did the woman know *everything*?

"Nice idea," Mike said slowly. If Cinder-feller were deliberately employing the Traders' own guidelines for negotiation, she was doing it very well. She was taking everything that Mike thought he knew about the situation, and turning it upside down. "But the recording disk would be quite useless to Fathom, or to anyone else. It can be destroyed—with difficulty. But its contents cannot be read out or deciphered without the use of the Trader central computer."

"I am glad you feel so confident." Cinder-feller's voice was full of a disquieting cynicism. "Believe that if you wish. Speaking for myself, I have purchased many 'secrets' and the keys to many unbreakable codes in the past few years. And there are data exploration specialists in Cap City who just love that kind of challenge. I would not care to stake my own life on the security of a recording disk's stored information. Ask yourself this: Did Fathom see the disk? Yes. And did she ask you its purpose? And if not, why not?" She smiled at his expression, and Mike saw strong teeth and a fleshy pink tongue. "I thought as much. Doesn't that *prove* that she already knew quite well what the disk was doing?" She yawned. "Well, perhaps that gives you enough to think about for tonight. Tomorrow I want you to see my labs and learn what we have that should interest a Trader. As you will see, Velocil and the Candlemass Berries were little more than bait to bring you here.

"And I will provide you with at least the bare bones of my own objectives in negotiation, so that you will be able to do your own thinking tonight. My aims are simple, but they are large. The mainland and the other Strine holdings are fragmented. Each has its own security force, and its own weapons arsenal." Cinder-feller paused. "I wish to unite this region and control all the Strinelands. For that enterprise, I need allies, and I need equipment. But most of all, I need skills in *negotiation*. And that is you. As I told you, I admire the Traders more than any other group, on Earth or off it. Nothing would please me more than a joint effort with them."

Cinder-feller suddenly groaned. Mike watched in fascination as the great body levered itself off the sofa. The Strine big-momma was even more impressive standing, towering half a head above Mike.

"For tonight, enough." The voice was weary, and the cowled head nodded past Mike. "*He* will show you to your quarters."

Mike jerked around. He had heard nothing, but right behind him squatted a haploid abo. "For your own sake," Cinder-feller said, "do not try to leave those quarters during the night. There is a danger that he might . . . misunderstand your actions." There was a throaty laugh. "You will find ample food and drink in your quarters. Sleep well, Trader Mike."

Cinder-feller's final words were good advice, but Mike had trouble following them. The abo warrior led him silently along a descending staircase to a windowless hexagonal room containing a bed, bathroom, and kitchen facilities. Mike went inside, closed the door, then after a minute or so opened it again. The abo was squatting at the far side of the corridor, eyes closed. Mike looked for a few seconds at the man's smooth, shining skin and peaceful face, until finally the head lifted and nostrils flared to sniff the air. The eyes opened. Mike went back inside and closed the door.

The kitchen area was large and liberally stocked with food and drink, most of it unfamiliar. There was the usual dried mutton, beer, bread, and bean-curd concentrates, but they were flanked by a dozen other jars and bottles. Mike sampled a small amount from each container. He could recognize the tang of fermented euclypt berries, and the resinous flavor of blackboys and prickly pear, and that was all.

He lay on the bed, checked the recording disk, and made his oral daily report. It was a slow business, and several times he paused to reconsider. How much did he actually *know*? Very little. He wished that Jack Lester were available to bounce ideas off. Crazy or not, Jack knew the psychology of the Strines. If Fathom were right, what Cinder-feller said could not be relied

on; if Cinder-feller were telling the truth, then everything that
Fathom had done, including the whole time on the ship from
Orklan, had been a setup designed to win information via Mike
regarding the operation here in The Musgrave. And if *both* were
lying? *Rule 30: Assume everybody is lying . . .*

Mike thought again of his instructions from Lyle Connery;
of Sweet Pea, the deaf-mute who wasn't; of Cinder-feller, the
"hideously mutilated" boss of The Musgrave, whose volumi-
nous clothes might hide any deformity, but whose face and
hands showed no signs of one; and finally, of the superbly con-
ditioned haploid abo who now sat outside the door. Mike compared that man with the warrior column he had seen running off
into the roiling dust storm.

The conclusion that he reached kept him awake for many hours.

When he finally fell asleep, he dreamed . . .

. . . he was running, fleeing north across the flat, open land
of the Strine Interior. The sun was in his eyes, blinding him.
When he turned to look back they were always there, fifteen or
twenty of them. They were a couple of miles behind . . . closing
steadily. Haploid abos, naked, skimming effortlessly across the
badland barrens. He looked ahead. The sea lay in that direction,
due north. It was only a few miles away, but it might as well
have been at infinity. He was nearly exhausted, moving more
and more slowly. The abos had broken their silence. Now he
could hear them cooing and calling to one another, in thin whis-
pers of sound . . .

Mike awoke. He was sweating, and his heart was pounding.
The room was lit by one faint fluorescent wall tube. He jerked
upright. As he did so, two people who had been talking together
in low voices near the door fell silent. After a few seconds they
looked at each other and moved closer.

"Good thing you woke," one of them said. "We didn't know
if we should let you sleep or not. It's nearly noon."

Mike shivered and put his hands to his head. The detox pills
worked, but sometimes they had their own brief aftereffects.
After a few moments the room steadied. The intruders were a
man and a woman, identically dressed and so similar in age and
appearance that they had to be fraternal twins, if not cross-sex
clones. They were in their middle twenties, with tight curls of
dark brown hair, bright brown eyes, and cheeky expressions.

It was the girl who had spoken to Mike, and hers was the
voice he had somehow woven into his dream. Now she came to

the side of the bed. "We're here to show you round the labs," she said when Mike did not speak. "I'm Bet Bates."

"And I'm Alf Bates," the man chimed in. Even their voices matched, his half an octave deeper than hers. "We'll show you the whole place, but there's no hurry. If you want to wash or eat, we can wait outside for you."

"No. Give me a few seconds to get my head together." Mike stood up slowly, rubbing his eyes. He had to wipe out that nightmare of abo pursuit. "All right, I guess I'm ready. Where's Cinder-feller?"

"Where she always is." Bet Bates sounded surprised. "She doesn't leave Headquarters, except sometimes at night she'll go out and swim in the lake. And she can get to that right from her rooms."

"I thought she wanted to see me again today."

"She does," Alf said cheerfully. "We'll take you to her when we're finished. Anything special you want to see?"

Their attitude was oddly casual and confident. Neither seemed much impressed at meeting a Trader, or at all deferential toward Cinder-feller.

"I don't know what there *is* to see," Mike said. "But I'm a Trader. So show me anything here in The Musgrave that you think might be worth trading."

The other two exchanged pleased looks. "Right," Bet said. "Come with us." They led the way from Mike's quarters into the corridor and up three full turns of a long spiral staircase. "Hold tight," said Alf, pushing open a heavy metal door. They were at once hit by the full sunlight of midday Strineland. After the gloom of the underground facility the effect was shattering. Mike squeezed his eyes shut, seeing a dull red glow through his eyelids and waiting for his pupils to make their adjustment.

Alf laughed. "Gotcher. You have to be ready for that. Don't worry, we'll be going back down in a minute. This is just a short cut to the main labs."

The heat was enough to make Mike feel dizzy. He took a deep breath and gazed around him. The ground was like baked brick, red and bare, without even the scrubby vegetation that he had seen through most of the Strine Interior. The only exception was a thin ring of trees that grew in a rough circle about two miles across. Their blue-green leaves rustled in the hot noon breeze, and their species were unfamiliar to Mike. After a few moments he realized that they must mark the boundary of the underground lake. If so, the body of water was a good deal smaller than his earlier night impression of it.

Another flotilla of light aircars was parked close to the trees, each carrying the same quadruple spiral insignia on its blunt nose. There were even more of them here than Mike had seen in the underground garage. Alf saw the direction of his look. "Local transport. We use them to travel inside The Musgrave and patrol the borders. Of course, we hardly need them for that. The abo teams stop anything coming in or going out."

A barbed message from Cinder-feller? *Don't try to get away, you'll never do it without my help.* Maybe. Mike walked closer to one of the cars, studying its design. It was quite different from the vehicle that had carried him from Eucla to Alice. These were electric-powered runabouts, Yankee imports with a range not much more than a hundred miles. They would get him to the border of Fathom's territory, or northwest into the badlands, but nowhere else. He pointed at the marking on the aircar's nose.

"Our sign," Bet said proudly, without waiting for a question. "Just you wait. In a few years you'll see that on half the biolab products anywhere in the world." She jerked her thumb toward the trees and bushes that marked the edge of the underground lake. "Alf and me, we designed every one of those. They're all valuable, and all different. They're biological concentrators."

Mike stared at the dusty vegetation. On a closer inspection he could see odd nodular fruit growing in close to the main stems.

"For different materials," Alf added. "Metals and rare earths, mostly. See that one? It concentrates selenium. Takes it in through the roots and deposits the oxide in the black fruit."

"What about water?"

"The taproot is strongly hydrotropic. It'll grow from a seed, right down till it gets to the edge of the lake. The tree next to that one handles vanadium—seventy percent pure in the red fruit. Both of them can tolerate seawater on their root systems."

Mike looked at the plants for a long time. "*You* developed these?" he said at last. "The two of you?"

"Sure did." Bet shrugged. "You like them? That's nothing. We did veggies when we were first starting, four years ago. They're old stuff. Wait until you get inside our new labs."

They were skirting the tree line and approaching a long escalator that ran down parallel to it. Mike took a last look around him, scanning the scene. He made his own assessment of distances and locations, then followed the twins onto the descending staircase.

How old was the Trader information on the Strine biolabs? It had been five years since Jack Lester was in southern Strineland, three since the last Trader visit. And nothing in the briefings had hinted at what Mike was seeing now in The Musgrave. Cinder-feller was no more than a name in the Trader data banks, while Alf and Bet—*Alpha and Beta*?—Bates, inventors extraordinary, were not even mentioned.

The staircase took them down to a lab deep underground, a room nearly two-hundred yards long. It was tall ceilinged, white walled, and impeccably managed.

"Plants," Bet said simply, and led the way.

Plants . . .

. . . plants thriving in almost total vacuum. "Chipponese market material," Alf said confidently. He dug his thumbnail into a thick, waxy leaf. The wound healed itself in seconds. "We want to do a little more work on this. It'll be another year before we look at its use in space."

. . . fruits that were violently explosive, ranging from pea-sized squibs to powerful bombs as big as melons . . .

. . . fruits with ninety percent ethyl alcohol. "The boozer's dream," Bet said. "Alcohol, fructose, and flavor—even has a pop-off top at one end."

. . . high-protein food fruits, duplicating the composition and texture of beef, pork, chicken, and fish . . .

. . . forty yard blackboys, their horizontal trunks built of spirals of monofilament carbon strands, far stronger than any metal. "The neat trick here was to make them grow flat," Alf said. "We had to take the phototropic and geotropic impulses and turn them through ninety degrees. We did it taking DNA splicing from iris rhizomes; they grow that way naturally. Come on, let's look at something else."

Bet led the way through a triple series of doors to a smaller lab.

"Animals," she announced.

. . . tiny, modified jerboas, patiently assembling microscopic electronic components and staring at the visitors with calm, intelligent eyes. Next to them was a cage of sluggish, jewel-eyed lizards, their necks swollen with gland sacs. "Full of nerve poisons," Bet said happily. "A thousandth of a gram would kill the lot of us."

She led the way to a huge, flower-filled cage. Hummingbirds, silver and crimson and purple, flashed around the interior so fast that they could be seen only when they hovered briefly in front of a blossom. "Just for fun," Alf explained. "I did these as Bet's twenty-first birthday present."

... *ant and termite colonies, fashioning elaborate transparent lattices from their own body secretions according to some precise prescription.* "They build perfect lenses and mirrors," Alf said. "We pass them structural specifications through chemical messengers in the food supplies. That's the hardest part. And we're still working on spiders. They're tough to control—can't do it chemically, has to be microcircuits." He shrugged. "Give us another year or two."

"Don't get started on spiders," Bet said. "Or we'll be here forever." She grinned at Mike. "They're his favorites, but it's getting late and we still haven't got to mine." She led the way through another series of doors and into an oddly-lit set of interlocking chambers, then turned to Mike. "Symbiotes. The most fun of all."

And the most complex, with their elaborate amalgam of plant and animal DNA.

... *mobile carnivorous plants, calyxes framed by circles of primitive eyes, hunting insects across a sandy desert floor* ...

... *lethargic, slothlike creatures hanging lazy from the trees, wings spread wide for photosynthesis.* "Still a failure," Bet said. "We haven't been able to get the energy absorption rates high enough for full mobility."

... *the polytropes, half-meter spheres containing within themselves complete ecosystems, requiring for their continuing function only a supply of radiation and an energy sink.*

And finally, almost as an afterthought, Bet had taken Mike to a small nursery, where a dozen shrubs carried the Candlemass Berries from which Velocil could be extracted.

Long before that, Mike had reached his own conclusion: what he had seen made the search for Velocil of minor importance. The original mission objective was dwarfed by the potential of the rest of Cinder-feller's operation.

And he had by no means seen everything. Throughout the tour, Alf and Bet Bates had kept up a running commentary. Their casual chat about genetic surgery and nuclear splicing was far more impressive than any boasts, and they openly admitted that six labs for human development were off-limits to Mike and all visitors.

"How does Cinder-feller fit into all this?" Mike asked at last, when they were emerging from the fourth and final underground facility. "I mean, if you do all this, what does Cinder-feller do?"

They looked at him in bewilderment. "Why, Cinder-feller's the bigmomma," Bet said. "Runs the whole show—defense, weapons arsenal, deals, fights, finances, supplies. Nothing could move without her."

"But not the technical developments?"

The twins burst out laughing. "Course not," they said in unison.

"Doesn't have time," Alf said. "And anyway, Cinder-feller doesn't know how. The bigmomma is smart, but not in that way—not for technical things. We handle all those and pass on our results."

They had reached the exit. There Mike stripped and was subjected to a search by a haploid abo guard. Bet and Alf seemed to regard that as completely natural, and Mike could not argue with the Strine logic. It would have been easy enough to sneak a piece of tissue from one of the plants or animals and tuck it away into a pocket. As the abo sniffed through his clothes and all around his body, Mike felt glad he had resisted that temptation.

It was late afternoon when the twins finally took him into the open air again. The wind had become stronger, with little willy-willys of dust swirling around the ring of trees. Alf paused and turned to Bet. "What do you think?"

She nodded. "Another one on the way. We'd better move fast."

"Another what?" Mike asked.

She turned to him. "Another damned dust storm. You'll be here for a while. See that red line on the horizon? There'll be a brickfielder in from the north in four or five hours, and it'll stay here for maybe a day or two."

"We've got animals outside in some of the experiments," Alf added. "Some of the species crosses are kind of delicate. We'll have to bring them all inside. Lousy job."

The twins were distracted. Scarcely looking at Mike now, they escorted him down to Cinder-feller's headquarters, passed him over to the same abo—or one who, to Mike's inexperienced eyes, was identical to the first—and headed at once back to the surface.

The abo led him inside and squatted at the door. Cinder-feller had left a message for Mike on her computer display. She was busy in a private meeting. Mike had nothing to do but stare out through the glass wall at the placid bottom of the lake and pursue his own thoughts. He wondered about the Traders' system for official acceptance to their ranks. What fraction did they lose on the final entrance test? *How* did they lose them?

Rule 14: Don't be a hero; there's no shame in flight.

Fine. But what if he *couldn't* flee? What if he couldn't even ask for help and call in a Trader Smash unit? The rescue squad was always available, but with communications jammed there was no way to tell them they were needed. And even if he could contact them, the Smash would have trouble cracking the defense system for The Musgrave. He'd have to find his way at least to the badlands, where the Interior security system didn't bother to operate. And in the badlands, of course, were the abos . . .

Mike was pulled from his reverie by the gentle beep of Cinder-feller's computer terminal. He walked across to it as a new message scrolled into view. I'M ALL FINISHED HERE. COME UP TWO LEVELS AS SOON AS YOU ARE READY, AND WE WILL HAVE DINNER. USE THE PERSONAL ELEVATOR IN THE FAR LEFT CORNER OF THE ROOM—*NOT* THE MAIN ONE.

The final comment was hardly necessary. Mike took one look at the waiting abo and followed Cinder-feller's directions. The personal elevator in the corner was certainly the right size—six feet across, with a weight capacity of two thousand pounds.

She was waiting for him upstairs at a great table of polished iron wood with white hatch covers set into the surface. Mike gave her one all-over incredulous head-to-toe scan, then tried to avoid staring.

Last night's swaddle of clothing had suggested that Cinder-feller was huge; today's costume revealed that she was truly gigantic. The poncho and quilts had been abandoned in favor of a short sleeveless tunic of pale yellow. It showed everything: arms like bolsters, legs thicker than Mike's body, and a bulky, amorphous trunk with rolls of body fat bulging at chest and belly. On top of the meaty shoulders an incongruously delicate neck supported a massive head. Mike could see no sign of scar or maiming. The skin of Cinder-feller's arms, legs, neck, and head was smooth, pale, and perfectly unblemished.

As Mike sat down, Cinder-feller touched the controls in the top of the table. The lights in the room dimmed, and the wall separating them from the lake moved from opaque white to transparent. The table-top hatches began to open.

"I promised you a banquet tonight," Cinder-feller said slowly. The eyes in the bloated head were dark and amused. "If you are willing to trust my choice of dishes I can promise you an outstanding meal."

Mike nodded.

"Excellent!" Cinder-feller's voice was greedy. She pressed another control, and the tiny Chill table robots came scuttling out of the hatches carrying loaded tureens, dishes, and glasses. Mike took one look at the array of food and drink opening before him, and hurriedly swallowed a double dose of detox pills.

Half the courses were totally unfamiliar, but he could identify more than enough. Cinder-feller was loading two plates with emu liver paté and saltbush-seed crackers. In front of her was a dish of grilled possum fillets on a bed of candied prickly-pear fruit. To her left sat a smoking mound of breaded wallaby fritters flanked by spiced joey tongues; to her right was a tureen of cold koala brains in a blackboy resin jelly. The platter directly in front of Mike was whole roasted 'tremes, skinned and with poison spines removed, but with heads, bills, and feet intact. A Chill robot poured hot euclypt sauce over them as he watched.

Cinder-feller gestured at the piled plates. Without waiting for Mike she picked up and drained a liter tankard of dark beer, placed it for refill, put her head down, and began to gorge. Mike politely sampled a mouthful of each dish, but most of his attention was on Cinder-feller.

She ate without pause for nearly half an hour, until her broad face was flushed and sweaty, then at last put down her fork. The robots did not clear the table. Mike deduced that this was no more than a breather between courses. Since sitting down he had drunk a little more than a liter and a half of strong beer. In the same interval, Cinder-feller had drunk—he had been counting carefully—eleven liters of beer, two liters of fortified wine, and half a liter of distilled spirits. Along the way they had drunk so many toasts to the Traders and The Musgrave that Mike was running out of ideas and stomach capacity. And for Cinder-feller every ounce of drink washed down a great mouthful of food.

"Do you have food like this in your Trader homes?" Cinder-feller asked. Mike shook his head. "I thought not," she went on. "Strine food is the best. As our influence in the world spreads, we will introduce these dishes to more regions."

Mike nodded politely. Why was it that every region, no matter what disgusting thing they liked to eat, thought it the best in the world?

Cinder-feller leaned conspiratorially toward him. "Maybe you will help me to spread our influence, eh? Alf and Bet showed you my labs here. Be honest with me. Did you ever see their like, or hear of it?"

Mike could give a truthful answer to that. "I never did. Your laboratories are astounding, and unique."

"And you Traders will work with us?"

"We would like nothing better. If we can." Mike wondered about his next statement, then decided he had to risk it. "But there are things I was not shown—things that interest the Traders very much. Can you arrange for me to see them?"

His question caught Cinder-feller with a tankard of beer halfway to her mouth. She frowned, paused with the vessel in front of her face, and asked, "What do you mean, not shown?"

"We have heard talk of a new version of the Dulcinel Protocol. One that can be applied to anyone, not just the haploid abos. We would like to know more about it."

"Ah." Cinder-feller gave a grunt of laughter as she drained the tankard. "Yes, indeed. You, and Fathom, too. She would like to have that information more than anything. But it is not for sale—or discussion."

Rule 9: Locate the non-negotiables. Every bargainer had something he was not willing to give up. Locate it, and you were in a good position. You could propose any outrageous deal, no matter how unfavorable it was to your own side. If it involved one of the non-negotiable elements, there was no danger that it would be accepted. Cinder-feller's voice and body language said clearly that the new Dulcinel Protocol could be no part of any deal.

Mike placed his tankard next to Cinder-feller's, so that both would be refilled. "Yesterday you told me what you would like from us. You need our assistance in your efforts to unify the Strine territories. We can help. But if you will not offer the Protocol, what will you offer?"

Cinder-feller leaned forward, wet-lipped. *"Anything that we showed you.* Any of the plants and animals that you saw today. If the Traders will help me, those discoveries can be yours. And they are just the beginning. There will be more—when all Strineland is under my control."

The offer was tempting, but it did not include the Protocol, and that was the real prize. Mike recalled Jack Lester's advice: "Beat 'em and fool 'em, then you'll do a deal." It was time to improvise.

"I don't think it can be as easy as that," he said. "You believe you know how Traders operate, but it is more complicated than you realize. We could never agree to the long-term deal you are implying, with a partner who has not satisfied the Trader Ritual."

Cinder-feller frowned. "Trader Ritual?" She drank again from her tankard.

Mike did the same, offering up a prayer for his liver and kidneys. Just how much drinking could he do before he was under the table? With Cinder-feller's body mass and food intake, even going one-for-ten with her on drinks would strain the power of the detox pills. But he had to have her at least partly drunk for what he had in mind. He closed his eyes and sipped another half ounce of beer. Thank God that Cinder-feller was switching more and more to the hard stuff.

"The Trader Ritual is something that all our close business partners must go through with us." He set down his drinking vessel. "It is a little old-fashioned, and some people say it is barbaric. But we have been doing it for so long, it is a tradition now."

"What does it call for? Formal signing of papers?"

"That, certainly. And a couple of more primitive forms of pact. We can go through with it tonight, if you wish, though the blood pact is a little messy. But I don't want to consider Ritual unless you can make it worth our while. We must be specific. I will need a detailed list to take back with me."

"Back? Through Fathom's territory?" Cinder-feller shook her head, and the body fat rippled. "No. I will tell you everything that I am offering, and allow you to transmit it to your colleagues. That will fulfill my part of the bargain. But you and the recording disk must stay here, until the Traders carry out *their* part."

As he had suspected: he would be her prisoner. Mike finally nodded. "Let us begin with the list."

"I will give it while we eat. And *then* we will satisfy the Ritual and sign an agreement. But we must not spoil our meal."

She pressed another command sequence in the tabletop, and the Chill robots appeared with a dozen more heaped dishes. Mike looked at them in dismay. He loaded his dish with whitefish roes and euclypt plums, gritted his teeth, and again raised his tankard. "Another toast. To your discoveries here, and the profit they will bring to both of us."

The liter mugs clinked together. Mike looked at Cinder-feller's bulging eyes and sweaty brow, and wondered how much drink any human could take and remain upright. It looked as if he might be about to find out the hard way.

Five hours later Mike rose wearily to his feet. This time, for sure, Cinder-feller was soundly asleep. She was slumped on the bench opposite, eyes shut, mouth open, and loudly snoring. The robots had cleared the flagons as they were emptied, and Mike had long since lost count. Thirty? Forty? He could only hope it would be enough. He needed at least a couple of hours.

He walked to the door of the room and opened it a fraction of an inch. The abo guard was still there. His eyes were closed, but Mike took no comfort from that. He dared not try to go to his own room. He went back inside and examined the wall that looked out on the lake. According to Bet, Cinder-feller had access to it from these quarters. But where was the exit? It must be closer to the surface.

Mike tiptoed across to Cinder-feller's personal elevator, entered it, and pressed the top button. The car ascended smoothly and opened to darkness. Mike could hear the soft lapping of water close by. He stood still. As his eyes adjusted to the gloom, he saw that he was standing on a walled-in jetty by the dark lake.

Mike removed his shoes, stuffed them into jacket pockets, and lowered himself into the water. It was cold enough to make him shiver and worry about cramps in his over-full stomach. He swam off to the right, toward dim lights on the shore of the lake. A few minutes later he had reached dry land near a line of parked cars. The underground garage was deserted. He followed the ramp that led from there to the surface, shaking water from his shoes before he put them on.

Mike knew when he was near ground level by the gusty whistling of the wind. Soon the moving air filled his nose and mouth with fine coppery dust. The storm had arrived, but it was still short of maximum intensity. In a few more steps the moon became visible, tinged to a dark rust-red. He walked to the fleet of vehicles, looking for an electric aircar that was fully charged and designed for maximum altitude. Range was going to be a problem—even the best one would take him only as far as the edge of the badlands.

Within five minutes he had made his selection. He spent another five familiarizing himself with the controls, then started the engine. The noise was more than he had expected, easily audible above the storm. So much for his hopes of a two-hour lead.

He took the plane at once into a tight upward spiral, wondering what the fine dust was doing to his engine. At eighteen thousand feet he was above the storm. He came out of the spiral and headed north-northwest. At sixty thousand feet he turned the communication set to Trader frequencies. He should be close to the edge of jamming range, but all he found was a jumble of noise. He headed higher, worried about power drain, until he was at ninety thousand feet and the altitude limit of the car. Now the commset was giving off little bursts of identifiable carrier signal among the static. It was probably the best he could hope for. Mike switched to send mode and transmitted his coded ID sequence.

"Smash request from Mikal Asparian. I am now at ninety thousand, vectored twenty-two degrees west of north. Air speed two hundred." He looked at the power charge level. "Current estimated range fifty miles, plus ten miles glide phase. Repeat: I am requesting Smash support for ground pickup. Chipponese tracking satellite to provide final aircar vector before landing. I will continue that direction on foot, at estimated seven miles per hour. I expect pursuit. Repeat: Smash request . . ."

There was no return signal, no indication that the message was getting through. Mike continued to send for the next forty-six miles, until the car's charge level was dangerously low. Then he had to concentrate his efforts on a smooth descent through the swirling gusts of the brickfielder. The laser altimeter provided accurate height information, but nothing on ground cover. He had to hope he was over level terrain without trees or boulders.

At six hundred feet he could suddenly see the ground. The brickfielder was thinning, running out of energy. That would simplify the landing, but hasten pursuit. As the car glided in to land, Mike took a final bearing on the moon and now-visible stars. Before the vehicle rolled to a halt he had jumped out and was heading north-northwest at a steady trot.

Within twenty minutes he was winded. The badlands were rough, broken country, crisscrossed by steep-sided gullies. Sharp-edged gravel at the bottom of each ravine cut through his sodden shoes, and climbing out was an effort. Mike was in good physical shape, but the banquet felt like a lead cannonball in his belly. Thirty courses, liter after liter of beer, a dramatic Trader Ritual, no sleep . . . just what you need to set you up for the run of your life, Mike thought. He groaned, rubbed at the stitch in his aching right side, and kept running.

Two hours later the sun was coming up. Mike still staggered along on legs that felt too heavy to lift. He had to stop and rest for a few minutes. At the top of a long incline he finally halted and turned to look back. The track he had made through the sandy bush was easy to follow. It weaved and curved like a drunkard's walk, but it kept the same general heading, west of north.

Mike looked farther back, to the crest of the previous rise. And what he saw there made him change his mind about stopping to rest. Half a dozen naked abos were running rapidly down the hillside, following his trail. They were no more than a couple of miles away, traveling twice as fast as Mike's best speed.

Hide from them? That thought lasted only a moment. The haploid abos had legendary tracking skills and sensory apparatus. Stay and fight? That was worth even less time. Surrender to them? That was worst of all; haploid abos in the wild took no prisoners, and he had not forgotten Fathom's summary: "a nice long drink and ninety pounds of convenient protein."

Within a fraction of a second Mike was running. He forgot his fatigue, forgot his stitch, forgot the lacerations on his feet as he sprinted over sharp stones. He raced down the long slope ahead, and up another one. At the brow of the hill he took another quick look back. They had halved their distance, strung out in a line over half a mile.

Mike could not hold the pace. He ran on hopelessly.

He was still running, lungs aflame, when the low-flying plane ripped in across the sandhills, whisked him off his feet in a snatch-net, and went at once into a high-speed vertical climb.

"How about that! Smooth as a Chippo's bum." It was Jack Lester's cheerful voice, speaking into Mike's ear as the snatch-net was reeled into the plane's interior. *"They didn't even get close. I'd say the nearest was still five hundred yards away when we did the pickup. Hey, come on, boyo—now we're out of jamming range the two of us need to have a chat. Wake up! You don't want to be sleeping now."*

Mike lay stretched on the cabin floor. *"What kept you?"* he said, and passed out.

"Congratulations, Mike. You've passed. You're a full-fledged Trader now. Once the medics have done with you, you can look forward to two months of vacation before you begin advanced training. Lucia says the key to the lodge in the Economic Community is on the way. But I want to know one thing." Lyle Connery's voice became exasperated. "Who the devil *was* telling the truth?"

The Trader plane was skimming in a Mach Seven suborbital to the Azores. Connery had come in person with the Trader Smash squad. Now he was sitting next to Mike, with Jack Lester and Daddy-O linked in.

Mike was lying at ease while a robodoc clicked and clucked its way discontentedly around his body. So far he had been given one shot of alcohol inhibitor and a liter of glucose and salt solution. He felt terrible, but to the robodoc's annoyance he had refused any other treatment. "I'm not sure that anyone was," he said to Connery's question. "Maybe Alf and Bet Bates. They seemed to be technological geniuses, so they're perhaps more likely to tell the truth on other matters. But not Fathom. And certainly not Cinder-feller. I knew I couldn't trust either of them."

"Traders' Rule. Assume everybody is lying."

"I did. But look where it left me if either of them *was* telling the truth. If Cinder-feller were right, I'd lose the recording disk as soon as I was back in Fathom's hands—split open like a herring, if I happened to have swallowed it. And if Fathom were right, Cinder-feller was planning a direct deal with the Unified Empire for the Candlemass Berries. She also didn't intend me to leave for a long time. I'd made Trader deals with *both* of them, and I guess I'll go back there someday. But not for a while. I couldn't see a rosy near-term future for myself in The Musgrave, or with Fathom in Alice."

"Did Cinder-feller try to take you to bed?" Jack Lester asked curiously. *"From your description of her, I'm not sure you'd be too hot on the idea."*

"She didn't—thank God. She'd have crushed me flat." Mike shuddered.

"Too true. I told you, Mike, it's bigmommas on top. Now, if I'd been in your shoes, I'd have—"

"Shut up, Jack," Connery said. "Or we'll cut you out of the circuit. Go on, Mike."

"Thanks. You know, I've been saying 'she' but I'm not sure Cinder-feller is a woman at all. Cinder-feller could just as easily be a man. To hold power in the Strine Interior it would make a lot of sense to pass yourself off as a bigmomma." Mike was silent for a moment. He couldn't get out of his head Jack's unpleasant thought of sleeping with Cinder-feller—male or female. "Maybe that's another reason I wanted to leave in a hurry," he said a last.

"We'd done most of our business. Cinder-feller and I had signed formal papers of agreement for the Candlemass Berries, and that took care of my prime mission requirement. So I had only two problems: how was I going to get out of there, and how could I find out the new Dulcinel Protocol?"

"I told you not to worry your head about that," Connery said. "You had quite enough to do as it was—we had no idea we were sending you into such a tangled situation. At least, I didn't." He shot an accusing look at Daddy-O's camera. "You should have ignored the Protocol, Mike."

"I *couldn't* ignore it—not when the evidence was being pushed right in my face. Before I left the Azores, you told me what the new Protocol was supposed to do: rapid healing, tissue restoration, and a few other things. So when I reached the border of Cinder-feller's territory, what was the first thing I found? Sweet Pea, a deaf-mute—who was neither deaf nor dumb, *but who used to be*. Then I arrive at Cinder-feller's labs, expecting to see someone who has been terribly mutilated and burned in an accident."

"That's what the grapevine told us," Jack Lester said. *"So deformed she hid away from the world."*

"She hid away all right. But I saw her—*lots* of her. And she was gross, and she was huge, but she was certainly not mutilated or disfigured. That should have been proof enough, but the final piece was Cinder-feller's haploid abos. I'd seen abos earlier, when we put down at that airfield in the south. They looked the way you'd expect warriors who have been in the badlands to look: radiation overdose, tumors, toes and fingers missing. But Cinder-feller's abods were nothing like that. They were in superb shape. Put it all together, and the conclusion was obvious: I was seeing the new Dulcinel Protocol in full swing. I guessed that Bet and Alf Bates had developed it, and Cinder-feller and Sweet Pea benefited from it."

Lyle Connery slapped his hand down hard on the console next to Mike. "My God, it would be worth a fortune. We *have* to find a way to trade for it."

"Cinder-feller said no way. They won't trade."

"I don't care. We have to try again."

"I'm not sure we do," Mike said. He leaned back, easing his left arm clear of the chair. "I told you, Cinder-feller wanted to sign formal agreements for everything *except* the Protocol. I told her the Traders wouldn't make that kind of long-term arrangement with an outsider. Before I could sign, she would have to go through the Trader Ritual that would make her an honorary Trader."

There was a baffled silence.

"Honorary Trader?" Jack said at last. *"What kind of dingo-doo is that? Mike, me old partner, you need a bit of a rest. There's no such thing as a Trader Ritual."*

"There is now," Mike said wearily. He turned his left arm over, to reveal the long, fresh scar running up the inside of his forearm. "After we'd had dinner, and after thirty or forty tankards of booze, I had to invent a full Trader Ritual, just for Cinder-feller. See that scar? We made that with a table knife. We're blood brothers—or maybe I mean blood sisters. I'm still not sure about Cinder-feller."

"But why the devil—" Lyle Connery began. Then he paused.

"Remember what you told me." Mike gave a tired smile. "The Protocol is a lymphocyte change. If you'll just have the robodoc there take a few drops of my blood, you'll have enough modified lymphocytes for a flying start on analysis of the Dulcinel Protocol. And of course, that's the *other* reason I had to get away from Cinder-feller's labs. Once Bet and Alf heard what happened, they'd have seen through that blood-mingling game in a second."

Under Daddy-O's control, the robodoc was already back at Mike's left leg, feeling its way to a suitable vein. *"Azores landing in five minutes,"* Daddy-O said. *"There's a lab waiting for you there."*

"So that's why you've been refusing to let the doc put antibiotics into you," Connery said. "Hey, maybe you're getting the benefit of the Protocol yourself."

Mike shook his head. "Not feeling the way I do. There has to be a lot more to it than a simple blood transfer. But this is a start—and by now Cinder-feller knows she was tricked. According to Jack, that will *help* us deal with her for the rest of the Protocol."

Connery was leaning back to his seat. "What a mission. I knew it might be tricky, but I had no idea it would turn out to be as complicated as this. There were more risks than anyone expected."

"I know. You thought it might be easy, because someone in the Strine Interior *wanted* a deal for the Candlemass Berries. But the feuds make everything there more complicated. You need somebody there with more experience. Somebody like Jack Lester."

"That's not funny, Mike."

"I think it is." Mike laughed, and touched the scar on his arm. "If the new Protocol is as powerful as I believe, it will do far more than simple skin repars. We'll be able to do complete *organ regeneration*. You can rebuild Lover-boy. And the sooner you do *that*, and get him out of that damned tank and back to work as an honest Trader, the easier it will be on the rest of us."

His last words were lost in Lester's howl of mingled excitement and protest. *"Mike, you're a beauty and a bloody marvel. I'll get my balls back! But we have to stay* partners. *You know, we make one hell of a* team . . ."

Mike leaned back, tongued Jack out of contact, and closed his eyes.

Daddy-O was receiving an urgent incoming call for computer power elsewhere. A small fraction of capacity remained assigned to the Smash plane, but most curcuits had to be transferred to deal with the new problem.

There were two items to attend to first. Into Mikal Asparian's file went the notice of official change from trainee to Trader. And into Daddy-O's locked data file went a ciphered annotation showing that ingenuity and nerve matched the desired profile. There was one negative note: too much success was more alarming than too little. Daddy-O added an acknowledgment that the probability of final failure had been increased.

CHAPTER 8

The woman who brought the late-afternoon meal was an attractive forty-year-old with a full, sturdy body and a plump face. She placed the dish in front of Mike and stood waiting.

After three days, Mike knew what was expected. He took his fork, speared a small piece of sausage, loaded pickled cabbage onto it, lifted it to his mouth, and chewed slowly and reflectively.

"Wonderful," he said after a judicious pause. "The best dish yet. I don't know how you make food so delicious."

She dipped forward in a little curtsy, and at last poured the May-wine into his glass. "We have had practice," she said happily. "We have been cooking *choucroute* this way for two thousand years. Would you like anything more, Trader Asparian?"

Mike shook his head. *Trader Asparian*. Presumably the feeling would fade eventually, but even after six weeks of use the words still gave him a thrill. As the woman left, he settled back to enjoy a leisurely meal. The dining room of the lodge faced southwest. He could watch the afternoon sun dipping toward the snowy peaks, far away across the valley, and smell the perfume of mountain wildflowers drifting in through the open window. The Azores and the Trader lab felt light-years away.

The place was all that Lucia Asparian had promised, and more. She had mentioned the grandeur of the Alps, but not the freshness of the air at seven thousand feet, or the bright flowers, or the colored patchwork of the valley spread out below the lodge. Every square foot was cultivated, every hedge and fence trimmed and tidy. Compared with this valley, everywhere else in the world was rude, frantic, and uncivilized.

Wonderful food and drink, great service, a magnificent setting—and a full eight weeks to enjoy it, with no Mentors, no negotiations, and no recording disks. What more could anyone ask?

Mike sat at the table for a long time after he had finished eating, watching the cloud patterns. They were piling up over the mountains, dark thunderheads towering above the western slopes. The clouds were rolling masses of black and purple-red, shot through with shafts of afternoon sun and changing minute by minute.

Mike had intended to idle away the rest of the day there, but when it was still a couple of hours away from sunset he stood up and left the dining room. The lodge was a two-story wooden building set into the steep hillside, with two bedrooms on the second floor and a living room, kitchen, and dining room beneath them. He went up to his bedroom for a couple of minutes and pawed restlessly through a pile of clean clothes, then wandered downstairs again and continued through into the kitchen. Helga was still there, quietly cleaning the old-fashioned cooking pans. She looked at him inquiringly.

"You need more food?"

He shook his head. "I'm bored. Helga, when will the inn be open, down in the village?"

"Is open now, if you want beer. Is open always, in this season. But it is a very bad time." She gestured at the thickening clouds. "Rain later."

"I'll take the chance."

Mike slipped into his pocket the big, wrought-iron key to the lodge that Lucia Asparian had sent to him. He would need it later. Helga lived down in the village, and she would be heading home in another hour. Although it was the Asparian lodge, and according to Helga the place was usually fully occupied for most of the year, Mike was currently the only guest. He puzzled over that as he walked along the steep, curving path down to the cluster of fifty houses, a thousand feet below, that comprised the village.

By the time he reached the first building the sun was invisible behind dark clouds, and there was a distant grumble of thunder from the west. He increased his pace, hurrying over the uneven white flagstones that passed for a road.

The inn was in the middle of the village. Like the lodge and most of the houses it was built of old, dark wood, but it was four stories tall and much bigger. A noisy row of birds with yellow bills and black plumage sat high along the spine of the roof. As Mike approached the front door, the whole cawing line took sudden flight and headed off toward a small grove behind the inn. Before Mike could read that as some sort of omen, there was a closer grumble of thunder and the first spatter of raindrops.

He pushed open the solid door and hurried inside. Most of the first floor was a long dining room with battered wooden tables. He looked around. Like the lodge, everything here was incredibly clean. Even the hardwood floor showed no trace of dirt, though guests must trek in muck all the time. He self-consciously wiped his shoes on the rough mat at the threshold.

The woman who came to greet him could have been Helga's daughter. She was about twenty years old, with the same high cheekbones touched with pink, the same blooming complexion and braided flaxen hair, and a younger, slimmer version of the buxom body. She was wearing a printed apron with a faded floral pattern, and the long sleeves of her mauve dress were rolled up to reveal pale, muscular forearms. She walked with more sway to her hips than Mike had ever seen before.

"Just in time," she said. She gave him a beautiful, full-lipped smile and gestured at the door. Outside there was a sudden hiss of heavy rain. "It's starting. Something to drink?"

"Beer." But then, when she was already turning to go through to the kitchen, he changed his mind. "Better still, do you have hot chocolate?"

"Of course." She gave him another dazzling smile over her shoulder and left him to seat himself.

The room was a combination of beer garden and dining room, with small tables flanking a wall of wine barrels. About a dozen people were there, drinking beer, wine, and brandy. They had stared at Mike when he came in, but now they were returning to their own conversations. He went to sit at an inconspicuous place in a corner near the window, where he would have a good view of the other patrons.

Most of them seemed like local residents, but at the far end of the room two men and a woman were dressed in a style that was subtly out of place. Mike pegged them as visitors from the Great Republic. If so, they had wandered far off the usual travel routes through the Economic Community. On the other hand, so had he. Mike turned his attention to a table closer to his.

The two men sitting there wore tweedy jackets and trousers with leather gaiters. They were speaking to each other in low tones. One of them still wore his hat, a squat brown cylinder with a long green feather on the side, and as he spoke the feather bobbed and jerked as though to emphasize his points. A flagon of peppermint schnapps sat on the table between them, and they were drinking shot after shot from little glass cups. As they drank they became gradually more animated and intense, but did not speak quite loudly enough for Mike to hear them.

It was a negotiation. It had to be. Even without hearing a word, Mike could follow the body language. He watched in fascination as the bareheaded man pulled out a folded sheet of paper from his pocket and passed it across the table. The other ran his eyes over it for only a moment, then at once snapped his fingers, took a pen from his pocket, and scribbled an addition to the sheet.

Bad timing! A Trader could read the transaction without thinking about it. Even with no idea what had been written, Mike knew that there should have been a longer pause before a reply. He felt like standing up and offering his services to the man with the hat. In Mike's opinion he was the underdog in the negotiation, and there was always more challenge to taking that side.

It was an urealistic response. Mike knew that a Trader did not indulge in impromptu negotiations, no matter how tempting. And anyway it was too late. The bareheaded man was smiling now and reaching out his hand. The other shook it. They each tossed down one more glass of schnapps to seal the bargain, stood up, and walked to the door. They stood for a minute or so waiting for a lull in the downpour, apparently decided that one was not about to arrive, and hurried out.

Mike felt sure that the feather-hatted man had just been taken. He had agreed too soon to a deal that his companion had thought through before their meeting. And the other had clinched it at once, allowing no time for reconsideration. Was that the way most affairs were conducted around the world when Traders were not involved? With one party completely at the mercy of the other? If so, no wonder a Trader's contribution was valued so highly. Mike stared out of the little window at the rain and felt oddly smug.

The girl in the apron and mauve dress returned with a tray loaded with a steaming silver jug of chocolate, a bottle of *kirsch* liqueur, a bowl of sugar cubes, and two dainty porcelain cups. She placed the tray on the table and sat down opposite him. "Hello. I am Jeanette Morveau. No more visitors tonight, I think, if this keeps up." She poured hot chocolate and shook her head. "It is the annual *Wasserfall*. At this time of year, we will see such rain last until dawn."

Helga had neglected to mention that little detail. The rain was pelting down harder than ever. Mike thought of the thousand-foot climb up the slippery path, and sipped the sweet and delicious chocolate.

"You own this inn?" he said at last.

"In a way." Her eyes, bright and blue, were staring at him with undisguised interest. "My father owns it, but he and my brother are away on business. My brother and I will one day be equal partners. My father is Jakob Morveau, my brother is Dieter Morveau. And you are Mikal Asparian. I have been waiting for you."

She laughed at his expression. "This is a small village, we know who our visitors are. I have been curious to meet you for three days, ever since Helga told me that you had arrived at the lodge. I knew you would soon want company, and Traders are always interesting. And now you can be my guest for dinner."

"Thank you, but I ought to be heading back. Climbing the hill after dark doesn't sound like fun." Mike hoped she would try to talk him out of it.

Without a word, Jeanette pointed out of the window. In the past few minutes, the sun had disappeared. It was almost dark, and the rain was whipping down harder and harder. "Do you want to commit suicide? That is what it would be, to climb the hill in this weather and in darkness. Far better to sit here, warm, dry, and cosy, and have a pleasant evening." She looked at him innocently. "Unless you do not like my company?"

It was clear from her expression that she considered that an unlikely possibility. Mike realized again how attractive she was. The road uphill became less and less appealing. "Don't you have the whole inn to look after?" he asked weakly.

For reply, Jeanette Morveau waved her arm to point at the rest of the room. Unnoticed by Mike, the other patrons had been quietly departing into the dusk. Now the three visitors from the Great Republic, the last to go, were muffling themselves in rain gear and grumbling about the torrent outside.

"Now we *are* the whole inn," she said, as the other three ducked out into the storm. "We will see no more guests tonight. It could not be better, because I want to hear all about your mission to the Strine Interior." She laughed at his expression. "Of course. That was Helga again."

Mike felt guilty. Had he really been so full of himself, babbling about his mission to anyone who would listen? Almost certainly, he had.

"It was nothing special." He wasn't quite ready for that worshipping gaze. "It was just an ordinary mission, you know."

"From what I heard, it was more than that. So exciting! Exploring the hidden biolabs and escaping with their secrets. And chased by haploid abos!" She gave a little shiver of her upper body and popped a cube of sugar into her mouth. She crunched it, then took the bottle of kirsch, swigged, and wiped her full lips with the back of her hand. Her blue eyes locked on Mike's as she handed him the bottle. "I want to hear absolutely *everything*. And in return I'll give you the best dinner you ever had.

"And after that—" Her glance flicked to the window, where rivulets of teeming rain ran down the panes, then turned demurely down to the table. "—after that, Mikal, I hope that the weather does not improve too soon."

At six o'clock Mike was already awake, watching dawn creep in through the windows of the inn's topmost bedroom. He was lying on his back on a broad, comfortable bed, covered by a thick and luxurious *duvet* that stretched from his chin to his toes. Jeanette, sound asleep, was snuggled at his side under the same eiderdown.

He could already see from the cloud patterns that the day would break damp and gloomy. The bedroom air was chilly, and Jeanette's body was warm and soft beside him. By all reasonable standards he ought to be pleasantly and thoroughly exhausted, ready to drowse away the whole morning and then the whole week. But by 6:15 he knew that he would not be able to sleep again unless he could find some answers. He eased his way to the side of the bed, pulled on shirt and trousers in the half-light, and stole out of the room. At the door he paused, thinking he heard a sound behind him. Jeanette still seemed to be peacefully asleep. He went on down the curving stairs, his bare feet making no sound on the thick rug.

The first test was the presence of a communications module. If the inn did not contain one, that would be an important data point.

But it did. The set was on the ground floor of the inn, an old-fashioned audio unit in a little room off the kitchen. Mike felt an immediate disappointment. He had rather hoped that it would not exist. He went to it and spent a few moments studying its antiquated call sequences. It looked fifty years old. But when he turned it on and placed the headphones over his ears, it accepted his personal charge code readily enough and established his connection in just a few seconds.

"Lucia?" he said eagerly.

"She is currently unavailable." The voice on the circuit was calm. *"I intercepted your signal. Unless you are seeking a personal conversation with Lucia Asparian, I saw a possibility that perhaps I might be able to help."*

"Daddy-O?" The circuit offered poor fidelity, but that inflection and style of speech were hard to mistake.

"On line."

"I have a question. this is Mikal Asparian."

"I know. Continue."

"Who pays for the upkeep of the Asparian lodge in the Economic Community?"

"If you are referring to the lodge above the village where you are now located, the lodge costs themselves are paid entirely by the Asparian family."

Mike was all ready to sigh with relief when he noticed the oddly restricted nature of Daddy-O's answer.

"I'm down in the village itself. Do the Asparians pay for services here, too?"

"No." And then, before Mike could offer a response to that answer, Daddy-O continued. *"Those costs are paid for by the Traders' general fund."*

"All kinds of services?"

"That is not a defined question. Be more specific."

That was just what Mike was reluctant to do. He was afraid that he knew the answer. "I want to know if the Traders pay for Community consort services here."

"That is correct. For companionship and for cohabitation, and at several levels."

"Is a woman, Jeanette Morveau, involved in providing such services to Traders?"

"Yes, she is. To Traders, and also to others visiting the Community."

"Hell and damnation." Mike gripped the headphones, ready to rip them off and throw them across the room.

"You act surprised. You should not be. As a trained Trader, you know exactly how the Economic Community operates. Nostalgia is their stock-in-trade, illusion their prime commodity. It is an expensive service to provide the world that they offer, the world as it was long before the Lostlands War. That service must be paid for by someone. By everyone—*including*

a Trader—who seeks to find peace in the past. You know all this, do you not?"

Mike did not answer. Every Trader trainee knew it, from the time of the first introductory courses. That only made things worse. He ought to have known exactly what was going on. But the talk had been so easy, the rapport so immediate, and Jeanette had been so warm, so admiring, so enthusiastic in lovemaking . . .

And so expert. That had been the point he could not ignore. Even while she enticed him and excited him, some corner of his brain had told him that a simple innkeeper's daughter should never be so diabolically skillful.

"How soon can I get out of here and into the advanced training course?" he asked abruptly.

"It can be arranged at short notice." Daddy-O's reply came almost too quickly. *"Indicate when you wish to begin, and I will at once initiate necessary action. When will you be returning?"*

When? At once, was Mike's immediate thought. He didn't know if he could stand to see Jeanette again. It would be too painful.

And yet, was it fair to blame her? And blame her for what? For giving him great pleasure and a wonderful night? She knew he was a fully qualified Trader; she must assume that he had known exactly what he was doing. Any misunderstanding was his own refusal to face facts, and that was certainly not her fault.

As Mike sat staring at the terminal another of his senses slowly demanded attention. There was a fabulous smell coming from behind him, a mixed aroma of fresh-baked scones, coffee, and frying bacon. He spun around in the chair.

Jeanette was in the kitchen behind him. She was standing barefooted and tousle-haired at the stove, dressed in a modest pink robe of quilted silk. She must have followed him downstairs immediately, because she had finished cooking and was quietly loading a huge wooden tray with a great pot of coffee, a giant mixed grill, and a full plate of hot bread. She saw him looking at her and pointed upstairs.

"The atmosphere created by the Economic Community is highly artificial," Daddy-O was saying in didactic tones, as Mike turned his attention back to the headphones. *"And the inhabitants must know it. They were untouched by the Heavenly Cloud, but they did not escape the general economic collapse. The Community is a created society, a copy of the past. But its people can turn back the clock and suspend the disbelief*

of others, I conjecture, only because they have come to believe the illusion themselves. They have become what they pretend to be." There was a satisfied humming from the headset, then a moment's pause. *"Now, Mike, I am finally in communication with the schedulers for the advanced training course. When do you wish to begin? Tomorrow, or the day after . . ."*

Mike nodded at Jeanette. She pursed her mouth in a kiss, lifted the loaded tray, and turned to leave.

"Eight weeks from now," Mike said. "Longer than that, if you can arrange it. I'll be in touch."

Daddy-O presumably replied, but Mike never heard it. He had removed the headset, turned off the terminal, and was heading for the stairs.

For once he agreed with Loverboy Lester: some things one didn't even try to explain to a computer.

CHAPTER 9

"**S**HE GREETS US AS WE ENTER THE WORLD; SHE IS WITH US WHEN WE LEAVE IT. SHE IS NEVER MORE THAN A SECOND AWAY FROM US, AS CLOSE AS OUR OWN HEARTBEAT; BUT WHEN SHE DOES NOT STAND DIRECTLY BEFORE US, WE CANNOT RECALL HER FACE.

"WHEN SHE CALLS, LOUD AND CLEAR, WE DROP WHATEVER WE ARE DOING AND ATTEND TO HER NEEDS ALONE. AT THE TOUCH OF HER HAND WE FORGET WORK, FRIENDS, AND LOVERS. SHE IS THE MISTRESS OF THE UNIVERSE. SHE IS PAIN."—DOMINIC MANTILLA.

Not the message to greet a man climbing drowsily out of bed on a rainy November morning. Mike rubbed his eyes and scrolled the message display. At the bottom of it was a brief addition: MY OFFICE, AT HALF PAST SEVEN—LYLE CONNERY.

That disposed of any ideas of a pleasant and restful breakfast—and meant he was already late.

Mike dressed and left at a run. If he were a Trader for a hundred years, he'd probably never lose that uneasy feeling about his first instructor. He halted, checked the shine on his boots, and straightened his jacket before he knocked on Connery's office door.

"Seat." Connery waved a bare, muscular arm across his desk as Mike entered. "I gather the lab's finally finished with you?"

"I hope so. They've been prodding and bleeding and nagging me again. I can't see how they'll get any more information about the Dulcinel Protocol out of me—but they want me there again in a month."

"Ah, you and Jack are their prize subjects. With luck you'll get some benefits from the Protocol yourself, even though you

123

haven't had a full treatment. But the vacation's over now. Jack is on-line. It's time for work."

Mike's anxiety level increased. He nodded at the blank screen of the data terminal. "Hi, Lover-boy. How's everything?"

"Couldn't be better." The mechanical synthesizer managed a jaunty tone. *"How you doing, boyo? Getting the end away regular, were yer?"*

"All right, Jack, save that for later." Lyle Connery turned to Mike. "Sorry, both of you, but we're in a hurry. Question: how much do you know about Beanstalks?"

"You mean Orbital Towers? A little bit. I know they're freestanding cables extending from the surface of the earth out past geosynchronous orbit; and I know the Chipponese would like to build one, to send stuff to space and back. What am I *supposed* to know about them?"

"Did you know that the Chipponese are looking to make a deal with the Unified Empire?" Connery was rocking comfortably backward and forward in his chair. "They have to have a place on the equator for the lower end of the beanstalk, preferably one on high ground. We've been negotiating on their behalf with Rasool Ilunga, but he's too wily for the Chipponese to feel comfortable. They'd like options. So they're interested in the high Andes, in the middle of the Unified Empire. Did you know that?"

Mike hesitated. He had picked up scraps of information in the hospital and rehabilitation center that he was not supposed to know. "As a matter of fact, I did."

"Told you," Jack cut in. *"System leaks secrets like a bloody sieve. Hell, people even come by and tell me things, and what am I supposed to do about it? Hey, Mike, let's get to it. How'd you like to serve as Trader negotiator between the Chips and Greasers for the Beanstalk deal?"*

There was a long silence from Mike, while Lyle Connery stared at him expectantly. "Well? I must say I expected a bit more reaction."

"I'm sorry." Mike shook his head. "I guess I'm surprised. I heard through the grapevine that Wernher Eckart was already assigned as negotiator on that project."

"Did you now?" Lyle Connery sighed. "Lover-boy, you were right on target. How *do* you keep a secret in this place? The grapevine's quite right—damn it. But Wernher Eckart hasn't been heard from in three weeks, and neither has your

friend Cesar Famares, who we sent to find out what happened
to Eckart."

The conversation suddenly held a new interest for Mike.
"Cesar's totally reliable. They must have been captured or hurt."

"Not captured, according to reports. And definitely not hurt
or dead. Maybe crazy, though. Eckart sent back a deal that he
negotiated, but it was terrible. The Chipponese wouldn't accept
it in a million years; the terms were completely favorable to the
Unified Empire. We tried to recall the pair of them, and they
ignored the messages. From other evidence, it's clear that both
of them are still alive—and they've broken Trader Oath with
the Chipponese."

"Are you *sure*?" The question was reflexive. Lyle Connery
would not have said it without compelling evidence. But that
last statement was a shocker. A Trader *never* divulged information given under Trader Oath.

"Quite positive."

"But Cesar wouldn't do that. Not, to borrow your expression, in a million years."

"That was my own evaluation—of both of them." Connery
was staring assessingly at Mike. "I'm sure you see where I am
leading. Official mission: negotiate a treaty between the Chipponese and the Unified Empire for tethering a Beanstalk on
Unified Empire soil. And your secondary mission . . ."

Mike was way ahead of him. "Find out what happened to Eckart
and Cesar. Did Daddy-O calculate a success probability?"

"Certainly." Lyle Connery was looking straight at Mike, but
there was a slightly uncomfortable expression in his eye. "Pro-
jected probability of success if you tackle this alone is four
percent—one chance in twenty-five. But if you have the right
partner, the probability goes up to thirty-six percent—better
than one in three. So naturally, you'll be double teamed."

"With Lover-boy?"

"Gimme a break, Mike." Jack Lester's voice was a shout
through the terminal. *"I'm going to be in this tank for another six
months. What you going to do, carry me along in a paper bag?"*

"Not Jack. As he says, the rebuilding of his body still has a
way to go." Connery cleared his throat and wriggled in his
chair. "So it's not Jack. You'll be partnered with Melly Turak.
That's Daddy-O's preferred choice."

"But that's great! I think Melly's terrific, and she knows
Cesar better than I do. I'd love to see her again." Mike paused.

Something didn't add up right. "I thought Melly was on some confidential mission in the Pacific."

"She was." Connery shook his head. "God help us, Mike, you're not supposed to know that. How'd you find out? No, don't bother to answer, just forget I asked."

"She's back now. And she says she can't wait to see you. You know, Mike, I think she has the hots for you."

"Jack, will you shut up for a minute." Connery turned back to Mike. "There's one other thing that's important about this, and there's no easy way to say it. She'll be your partner—but not an equal partner."

"Well, I think I can handle that."

"I hope so. You see, you'll be junior to her. She'll be in charge."

It was a body blow. Mike would never have admitted it, but he believed that he was a far better Trader than Melly would ever be. He sat and stared at Connery for a few seconds. There had to be a reason. "I assume she's already had a mission in the Unified Empire?"

"No. As a matter of fact she's never been on a mission south of the equator."

Mike started to stand up. He was restrained by Connery's outstretched hand on his shoulder. "Steady now, Mike. I know it's a shocker, and I know how you must be feeling. But Daddy-O doesn't get his calculations wrong."

Mike had never heard such a conciliatory tone in Connery's voice. It made things worse.

"You'll be fine with her, Mike," Jack added. *"And think of them hot Greaserland nights!"*

"Jack, for God's sake will you *shut up*." Connery stepped closer to Mike and looked him in the eye. "I just want to say a couple more things, if Lover-boy will let me get a word in. After that, if you want to refuse the mission I'll pass the word to Daddy-O."

Refuse the mission. *Could* a Trader refuse a mission because his ego was hurt? But how could he work as a junior partner to Melly? He knew her limitations too well. He had struggled right through Trader training with her.

"She'll arrive here tonight from the Cook Islands," Connery went on. "She has accepted the mission. With or without you, she's willing to tackle it. So she'll be going, and she'll be teamed with *somebody*. Now, Daddy-O looked at every other team combination for Melly. The Asparian-Turak combination is the only one with a probability of success greater than one in twenty—the chance of any other pair even making it back here is no more than one in ten. You two are better than one in three for total success. You may not think you need *her*, Mike—but she sure as hell needs you. *And Cesar may need both of you worse than we know.*"

Mike glared at him. "That's blackmail!"

"*Of course it is!*" Lester said. "*That's why it works.*"

"Jack!" Connery shook his head. "It's not blackmail. Let's call it Trader negotiation techniques."

"I don't think I can do it. I like Melly a lot, but I don't think I can."

"I understand how you feel." Connery's voice was soothing. "But at least think it over. All right? Just think it over."

"Well . . ."

"Good. At least you ought to see her and talk to her. You know, you remember her as a trainee, but she's a full Trader now. You'll find she's changed—a lot."

After that, it did not surprise Mike at all to find that dinner with Melly had already been arranged.

Before that dinner, Mike made his own checks. Since they finished training he had not been in touch with Melly. Her missions had taken her to the Pacific Rim, negotiating with the western Yankees. Then she had disappeared from contact, only to pop up again in the Trader base on the Cook Islands, half a world away.

First, Mike called out Daddy-O's performance statistics on her. He whistled in amazement at what appeared on the screen. She had never impressed him as anyone really special in training—smart, and pretty, but not unusually gifted. Now she showed up as the brightest new Trader in a generation. Although she had never been to the Unified Empire, already she spoke the language there better than Mike did. She was a natural partner for the mission. Mike ruefully admitted it to himself: if he hadn't known her in training, he'd have been delighted to be teamed with her.

Rule 18: Collect as much data as you can get. Mike called Tip Muller, who had come from the Cook Islands to the Azores a few months ago and had just finished his second Mission.

"Sure I know her." Muller nodded from the screen. "Everybody there knew her. Why'd you ask?"

"She's been doing spectacularly well, hasn't she?"

Tip Muller looked puzzled. "Oh, nothing special. I mean,

she's no smarter than me or you. What's the problem, Mike?"

"I'm not sure yet. Hey, Tip, if Melinda isn't unusually good as a Trader, why does everybody there know her?"

"Well . . ." There was suddenly a cautious look on Muller's fresh-complexioned face. "Hey, Mike, do you and her have something special going?"

"No. We were in training together, but I haven't seen her since."

"All right, then, I don't mind telling you. She's famous because when she got to the Cook Islands she kind of went off the rails. To be more precise, she discovered sex."

"Melly Turak?"

"The same. I guess she wasn't that way in training? You know how it is, some people get to it late. She went wild between missions. Before I left she'd been to bed with just about everyone. Half the camp had been through her. She wasn't exactly what you'd call shy about it, either—she'd make the first move on anyone she wanted while they were still saying hello."

"I just can't *believe* it. Not the Melly Turak I knew."

"Well, maybe she changed. Hell, haven't *you* changed since you were in training? I know I sure as hell have." Tip Muller looked annoyed. "Look, Mike, I'm sorry if I sank your dreamboat. But what I'm telling you is the truth."

Mike shook his head and stared blankly at the screen. He sighed. "All right. I believe you—but I can't pretend I'm not shocked. Melly was so—well, *nonsexual*. One of the boys."

Tip looked at him, eyebrows raised. "You believe that? I can't stop you. But you may be saying more about yourself than about Melly."

"Could be." Mike didn't want to follow that thought any further. "Thanks a lot, anyway, Tip. I owe you one."

"Why are you asking me all this, Mike?"

"Melly Turak and I look as though we're going to be double teamed."

Tip Muller whistled. "Well, now. Make sure she keeps her mind on the mission."

"I'm having dinner with her tonight. I wanted to know what I was getting into."

Muller laughed. "Her, unless she's changed. Hold onto your pants, Mike, or she'll have 'em off before you get to the soup course. And say hello from me."

He was still grinning when Mike cut the connection. Mike was not grinning at all.

Not the Melly he knew from training camp, but a sort of female version of Lover-boy Lester. How had it happened?

His head was spinning as he walked down to the dining room where he was to meet her. In some ways he wished he had never spoken to Tip. It made things even more complicated. Melly had changed, and Mike's ideas about her had to change, too. She was Daddy-O's top choice for the mission, by a wide margin. And according to her record, she would be great in a negotiation.

Wasn't that the important point, not what she had been like last year in training camp? Even though he and Melly would have a hidden agenda, the negotiation for the Chip Beanstalk would be real enough. And it was going to be a tough one. They would be representing the Chipponese, but the Unified Empire held most of the cards. The Chipponese needed a partner at the ground end who wanted what they had to trade—energy—and who was sufficiently technological to be able to handle the Beanstalk tether. Rasool Ilunga and the Ten Tribes had the aspiration, but not the technology. The Unified Empire was sitting in a strong bargaining position. What did they want out of this deal?

Mike couldn't answer that question. But Melly might have some ideas.

She was already waiting for him at their table. Mike, still struggling with his prejudices, hung back at the edge of the dining room and watched for a few moments before he moved forward.

Melly was leaning back in her chair, making a steady, systematic evaluation of every other diner. Mike could see her gaze sweeping each one from head to foot, pausing for a moment, and then moving on.

He did his own inspection. It was unmistakably Melly, yet even from a distance she had changed. Her fair hair was cut low over her forehead now, instead of being swept back. That, and the loss of twenty pounds, transformed her appearance. She looked five years older, with a poise and steadiness that added another five. The puppy fat that she had carried as a trainee was gone, replaced by a supple, athletic build.

He approached from the side. When he was still ten feet away she somehow sensed his presence. She turned her head and looked up at him.

"Mike Asparian!" She stood up and held out her hand. "You've grown a mile. What happened to the little Mike I met in training camp?"

In the old days it would have been a warm and impulsive hug. Mike sighed and took her hand in both of his. "Three inches. I stopped growing late."

"I'm sorry, Mike," she said, and it was clear that she was not talking about his change in height. Her voice was lower than he remembered.

No need to ask what she *was* referring to. Mike felt warmth in the back of his neck. "I know you didn't decide the team, Melly. And it's my problem, not yours. Hell, I *ought* to be a junior partner. Half the time I don't know what I'm doing."

"You don't really believe that. It's not your reputation, and it's not what I remember." Even her eyes seemed different. They were still wide and silver-gray, but they no longer had their old innocence. Her steady gaze ran up and down Mike's body, measuring and evaluating him in some way. He sat down hurriedly.

"But if you don't know what you're doing," she went on, "we ought to make a good team. I don't know what I'm doing either." She gave him a smile, warm and friendly, just like the old Melly. Mike felt relieved.

As food appeared on the tabletop, Mike watched her begin to eat. Her table manners were unchanged, too—precise, economical, and calm. But she didn't eat with the same gusto. No one would know from her facial expression whether she was eating gourmet fare or sawdust. The portions she took were small, and the only drink she had ordered for herself was water.

Fair enough. Apparently her appetites ran in other directions. Mike could not resist that thought. The big mystery was still the difference between Tip Muller's assessment and Daddy-O's records. Was she supercompetent, or wasn't she? Was it sour grapes on Tip's part?

She had been quietly watching him while they ate. "And you've changed, too," she said suddenly. "For the better, I think. You have a lot more self-confidence than you used to have."

"You mean I fake it better."

That earned a wider smile. "Could be. We're not children any more, are we? I'm really looking forward to this mission with you, Mike."

Yes—enjoying being my boss. Mike forced himself away from that thought. "It may be a tough one. What do you make of Dominic Mantilla?"

Mike expected a diffident answer, or maybe the neutral remark that the man seemed like a tough negotiator.

Instead Melly shook her head and said, "I suppose that we have no choice, and we will have to deal with him as the Unified Empire representative. But he's a—" She paused, picking her word carefully. Then she spoke very firmly. "A monster. A total monster."

"Do you know him, then?"

"No, but after my briefing I went after additional information."

So had Mike—but he had found nothing. What search technique did she have that he was missing?

"I'm sure Daddy-O laid the same quote by Mantilla on your message screen as he did on mine," she went on. "But did you know that most people call Dominic Mantilla by another name in the Unified Empire?"

"He's the Highlands coordinator, if that's what you mean."

"I'm thinking of something a bit more descriptive. Throughout the Empire, Dominic Mantilla is known as 'The Prince of Pain.' Did you know that?"

Mike didn't know; and he wasn't sure he wanted to. The Unified Empire was designed to provide every pleasure known to humankind, and the most famous joyland in the world had to be Ree-o-dee. But if one wanted drugs, one went to Sun-shone, in the south, where a thousand experiments a day were conducted into consciousness-changing. And if one craved blood sports and gambling, the place was Dreamtown—the same place that Dominic Mantilla had chosen to negotiate the Chipponese Beanstalk treaty. And in Dreamtown, or near to it, Wernher Eckart and Cesar Famares had broken off communication with the rest of the Traders.

"*Why* is he called the Prince of Pain?" Mike suspected he was not going to like the answer.

Melly shook her head and placed a neatly cut cube of cooked vegetable in her full-lipped mouth. She chewed slowly and carefully, then swallowed. "Daddy-O doesn't have many facts to offer. We know there's a strange gambling game played in Dreamtown and nowhere else in the Unified Empire. Its name is Counterpoint. Then there's a sport, Glissando, that's supposed to be super-dangerous and also found nowhere else. And that's all. Now you know as much about this as I do." She gave Mike another smile. "But by tomorrow evening, I hope we'll be seeing all that for ourselves."

Mike stared at her in surprise. Either she was the world's best person at concealing her real feelings, and therefore would make a marvelous negotiator and be a tremendous asset on the mission; or else Melly had acquired nerves of steel and was really looking forward to sticking her head in the lion's mouth of Dominic Mantilla's city—in which case she would, in Mike's opinion, be just about the worst thing that could happen to him. In his mind, successful Traders never looked for risks or enjoyed danger.

One thing seemed clear already. Melly had done her homework. She was much better prepared for this mission than he was.

They had both finished eating, and now she was staring at him steadily, her hands folded in her lap. Mike couldn't get Tip Muller's words out of his head. If she had been to bed with half the Cook Island training class, was she waiting for him to . . . or was *she* going to . . . and did he like that idea, or did he hate it? He suddenly thought of their first evening in the Darklands, when Melly had hung around the door of his room. Had she, even back then, been hinting that he should invite her in? It had never even occurred to him. But now. . .

"Well, Rule Twenty-seven," he said abruptly. "We've had the food and drink, as ordered, and now we ought to get some sleep."

She frowned at him. "Rule Twenty-seven: 'If you have time to spare, use it on additional preparation; it will always pay off.'"

He laughed. "No, not Twenty-seven in the *official* book. I mean in the other one."

Instead of replying, Melly sat frozen in front of him with an intense expression of concentration on her face. While Mike stared, she suddenly stood up and backed away from the table. "I'll see you tomorrow on the airplane," she said quickly. "I still have to make my preparations for the flight down there. Good night."

Her expression was unreadable, but her voice was agitated. She nodded to Mike and hurried out of the dining room.

He sat with an untasted glass of wine in front of him. What had he done? He certainly hadn't been trying to offend. But to say she needed time for preparation, when it was obvious that she was already well prepared . . . What had he *said*?

He thought back over his last few remarks. How could a Trader get upset by somebody quoting from the rule books? Could she have somehow misinterpreted what he meant?

The official book of Traders' Rules was beautifully bound and printed, and not very thick because although there were ninety-two rules in it most of them were one-liners. Traders got a nice, clean copy of the thing, fresh off the press, on the first day.

No one was officially given a copy of the other book of rules. It was not bound, it had usually been printed and copied on some flaky machine that made all the commas look like periods and filled in the middle of all the letters, and it was often tattered and greasy to the point of disgust. It contained crude language, crude thought, and occasional anonymous doggerel that just about managed to rhyme and scan.

And which one did a Trader rely on more?

That depended on age and cynicism. The books were very different. But after the first month, every Trainee knew both books by heart.

Rule 34 in the official rule book read: "Nature is not malevolent; if it appears so, you are doing something wrong."

That statement was true enough. But the other book had something to say on the same subject: "Life don't belong in the Universe, and everything is trying to kill you. Think the sons of bitches are out to get you? Damn right they are. Get eyes in the back of your head and use 'em to watch your rear end."

Rule 79 of the official book: "Promotion does not make you more intelligent; it only makes you *need* to be more intelligent. Be careful."

The unofficial manual said: "Been promoted? What do the bastards expect from you now?"

Rule 27 of the unofficial Rule Book, the one that Mike had been referring to, said: "Food, rest, sleep—take them whenever you can." An innocent enough remark. But what on earth had Melly read into it? Mike couldn't think of any way of misinterpreting it. Had she developed a mindless and irrational dislike for the unofficial Rule Book?

He sighed and picked up his glass. Maybe it was going to be a disastrous mission. He was feeling very worried—far more worried, apparently, than Melly. And more than that, he was curiously irritated.

Melly had changed, that was clear. Now she supposedly made a pass at every halfway interesting man that she met. But she had shown no trace of interest in Mike.

And what did that say about him?

CHAPTER 10

To save travel time, the Trader craft that took them to their negotiation did not stop anywhere in the Unified Empire. It flew along the western coast of South America, with the snow-capped ranges of the Andes on the left, as far as Chimbote. Then the plane turned sharply inland. At the mountain city of Dreamtown, fifty miles from the sea, it hovered a couple of feet above the ground, just long enough for Mike and Melly to step down with their light hand luggage, then it turned west and accelerated away. It was out of sight in less than a minute.

Mike stood on the landing square and looked around him. The air was wonderfully clear, but the scene was too stark to be beautiful. Dreamtown stood on a level plateau in the middle of the *Cordillera Blanca*, sitting on a mile-wide ledge with mountains on all sides. The high peaks of the Andes were off to the east, rising another ten thousand feet. To the west, the land dropped away fast, swooping down to the distant gray-blue glimmer of the Pacific Ocean. Mike thought he could see in the distance a thin scar of dazzling white cutting its way down the steep mountain side.

While he was still staring around him, a high-pitched whistle came from behind.

Mike and Melly turned quickly. Waddling toward them across the landing square came two pudgy, squat figures. The smaller one stepped right up to the two Traders.

"Hello." There was another whistling grunt, and the blunt head smiled to reveal two big, orange-yellow incisors. "I am Dolly Caps, and this is Benjy Caps. We are at more than thirteen thousand feet altitude, but I hope that you do not feel too uncomfortable."

Cappies. Enhanced capybaras.

Mike looked at the thinly haired paw held out toward him. There were four fingers on it, with thick, hooflike nails, and the webbing of skin between the digits had been surgically cut to allow more independence of movement. The capybaras were about five feet tall now, standing upright, but looking at the callused paw, Mike could see that they were probably more at ease on all fours. Both the big rodents wore orange suits with brown pouch-pockets over their fat, tailless bodies.

He took Dolly Caps's paw and shook it firmly, then watched while Melly did the same with Benjy Caps. Whatever Mike thought of the rulers of the Unified Empire, he had nothing against the Cappies. The enhanced capybaras were supposed to be patient, docile, obedient, and conscientious—just about everything, in fact, that their masters were not.

"We are your reception committee," Dolly said. The words were very slightly separated from one another as the implanted synthesizer helped out the Cappy's own throat limitations. Dolly Caps smiled again, showing those frightening teeth. Vegetarians, Mike reminded himself. All the while the eyes high in the square-muzzled head shifted randomly from side to side. "If you will please follow us, we will take you to your quarters."

She turned and began to amble across the landing area. After a few steps Benjy dropped, with a grunt of relief, to walk on all fours.

Mike caught Melly's arm as she started to follow. "I think they're both blind!"

"They are." She put her hand on top of his and gripped surprisingly hard. "Didn't you read our briefing materials? That's one of Dominic Mantilla's nice little ways. He enhances his Cappies as much as they can be enhanced—but he blinds them so they can't ever think of running away to live wild."

"I didn't see anything about that in the briefings."

"Then you didn't read everything. That information was in the last packet that we were given. We were supposed to read all of it. Didn't you?"

She started forward, leaving Mike standing with his mouth open. The packet she was referring to had been given to them when the flight began—but there had been five hundred pages of new material. Was she telling him she *had* read it, every word, on their three-hour trip? Mike had spent the time sleeping.

He hurried after the others. Although the Cappies could not see, they seemed to know exactly where they were and where they were going. Dolly took them to a parapeted balcony at the edge of the landing area and pointed out and down at the hairline of white scar that curved away toward the Pacific.

"Glissando," she said. "For any human who wants to play the ultimate game." She giggled.

"What is that?" Melly asked. The parapet marked the end of the flat ledge and jutted out over three hundred feet of air. Melly was casually leaning far out over it. Mike had no particular fear of heights, but he felt dizzy watching her. "I can't see the end of it."

"It is polished ice." Benjy Caps spoke for the first time. "Glissando is an ice-run all the way to the ocean. Over fifty miles distance, dropping well over two miles in height. The sleds are very carefully shaped—they are traveling at more than two hundred miles an hour when they plunge into the Pacific."

"But that would kill the rider!" Mike said.

"Yes. The player must aim for a set of rings near the end of the run, which slow the metal sled electromagnetically. A player who misses will hit the ocean at full speed and be killed." Benjy stood upright again, and the broad head lifted. The Cappy stared at Mike with sightless, cheerful eyes. "Do you think that you will try it while you are here? It is said to be the most exciting game on Earth."

Mike looked over and shivered. "Not for me, thanks. Melly?"

She was still staring, hanging far into space. "Maybe. At the very least, I'd like to take a closer look. How are the sleds controlled?"

"From inside them," Benjy said. "A sled can hold one or two persons. You should mention your interest to the Lord Dominic." He dropped back to all fours. "We will take you now to meet with him. He can arrange a ride if you wish. There are many experiences here in Dreamtown that you may wish to sample."

They were descending along a ramp that led below ground level and cut back under the surface of the landing area. As they went, the architecture became steadily more ornate and colorful. Great corridors with walls of gleaming white and gold were filled with erotic statues and flanked by holographic murals of every conceivable sport and pleasure. Mike was reminded again of a basic fact: the business of the Unified Empire was *pleasure*. They knew more here about the art of making people excited than the rest of the world put together. And Dominic Mantilla as Lord of Dreamtown was one of their accepted masters.

Mike was pleased to see that Melly found the erotic murals and statues a lot less distracting than he did. She was looking at everything but the murals, and with great intensity.

"Just in case we get into trouble and need it," she said, in answer to Mike's quiet question on her wide-eyed staring around them. "You know. Rule Fifty-seven."

Anyone can get into trouble. Make sure you plan a way out of it.

That was Rule 57 of the *unofficial* rule book. So Melly was quite willing to quote it herself when she felt like it. Mike filed away another confusing data point.

Before he could give it much thought his attention was captured by something else. Dolly and Benjy Caps had been trundling along on all fours between Mike and Melly, explaining what they were seeing—mainly the doors and viewing balconies of the underground game rooms. But, as the Cappies approached a tall door they both stopped talking and rose suddenly to stand on their hind legs. As they moved in front of Mike, he could see that Dolly's plump back was quivering gently. They all turned a corner and went through an archway into a room with a waist-high partition across its center. The two Cappies advanced to the partition, then turned back to face Mike and Melly.

"The Lord Dominic," Benjy said, and now it was obvious that he was shivering, too.

On the other side of the partition stood a tall, smiling man. He had classically handsome features, with an aristocratic nose and a beautiful, smiling mouth. He was hugely tall. Discounting the polished, high-heeled boots of black leather, Mike estimated the other man's height at some seven feet four inches; the poised, straight-backed stance made normal men seem puny and stooped.

"Welcome!" Dominic Mantilla stepped forward and opened a gate in the waist-high room divider. "My dear lady and gentleman, please welcome to Dreamtown. May your visit here be the source of a hundred new delights!" He turned to the two Cappies, who were standing uncomfortably upright. "Thank you, Dolly, and you too, Benjy. You may leave."

The Cappies bowed a little, then scuttled away, still fully upright.

"Splendid servants!" Mantilla said. "Where would we be without them?"

"Wouldn't they be more use to you if they could see?" Mike asked mildly.

"Oh, a little." Dominic Mantilla gave an expansive shrug. "They manage well enough, though, and the loss of sight isn't all that important to them. I have asked them the question, would they give up the enhancement if I gave them back their sight?—and each one has agreed that they want to keep the enhancement."

Great choice. You take my eyes, or you take my brain. No wonder the Cappies answered that way. But Mike did not say what he was thinking.

"Please, allow me to introduce myself," Mantilla went on. He gave a great, toothy smile. "I am Dominic Mantilla, Lord of Dreamtown, and I and the whole of this facility are completely at your disposal. May I say how much I am looking forward to working with you on this negotiation?"

Mike smiled back just as hard. He had been nice before to people at least as unpleasant as Dominic Mantilla. He would be polite now. But Melly's actions were another matter. She was staring at their host as though she had never seen anything so wonderful in her whole life.

"Lord Dominic." Her voice was faint and breathless. "This is such a—a *thrill* for me."

"My dear lady!" Mantilla seized Melly's hand, bent over it, and kissed it. Then instead of releasing her he remained crouched forward, looking deep into her eyes. A thin, bluish tongue licked at his full lips, his nostrils flared, and he seemed all set to take a bite out of her. "The pleasure of this meeting is all mine. Such beauty! No one warned me of this."

Mike stood and waited to be noticed. The air was practically purple with pheromones, and he felt like the world's most unnecessary presence.

After a minute or so Mantilla finally became aware of him again. The tall figure turned and shook his hand vigorously. "Trader Asparian. The fame and reputation of you and your beautiful companion has preceded you. I tremble when I think of negotiating with you. If I left it for a few more hours, my courage would probably fail me completely. Therefore I have arranged that we begin at once."

While you are fresh and we are still suffering from travel fatigue, Mike thought. Melly merely smiled at Mantilla admiringly. "That sounds perfect. If we might first drop off our bags in our rooms . . ."

"Of course, of course, my profound apologies. Where is my courtesy?" With a great flourish of long-fingered hands, Mantilla waved the Traders forward. "Let me show you to your rooms at once. And after we have finished talking today, I would like to offer a special event for you—a party in your honor, and a guided tour of all the facilities of Dreamtown. And of course, should one of the attractions appeal to you, you will be my guest."

His tone suggested that one of the attractions for Melly might include access to Mantilla himself. And she did nothing to disillusion him. As he showed them through to their quarters, she went inside, then at once called through the open doorway. "Lord Dominic, I wonder if you could help me a little with my case."

Mike stood motionless in the entrance of his own suite of rooms. He heard low voices from the next suite along the corridor, Melly's laugh and Dominic Mantilla's answering bass chuckle. Then the door closed. He could hear nothing at all.

He could imagine a great deal.

Mike had his own way of preparing for a hard negotiation. First he stretched out on the bed for ten minutes and tried to push all worries out of his mind—tried to forget about Melly's superior status and odd behavior, about the failure of the first two Traders here, about the overflowing self-confidence and casual cruelty of Dominic Mantilla.

Then he took a long shower, as hot as he could stand it, and allowed all the worries to seep back in. He needed them. A good negotiator *had* to have a head stuffed full of worries, because any one of them might be the item that would provide the key bargaining point.

He was in the shower for nearly a quarter of an hour. When he finally came out of it, naked and rubbing at his wet hair with a towel, Melly was sitting quietly on his bed. Her face was flushed.

She looked Mike over with the emotional detachment of someone choosing a wallpaper pattern. "You look better *without* clothes on, too," she said. "You've added muscles. How did you get the scar on your arm?"

"Little bit of fun in the Strine Interior. Look, would you mind awfully if I put some clothes on now?"

His sarcastic tone had no effect on her. She gave his body another up-and-down sweep with that silver-gray gaze. "Mike, we need to talk—before the negotiation."

"Something new?"

"I think so, but I don't know how to evaluate it. Dominic Mantilla was saying how much he was looking forward to spending more time with me after the big reception tonight. I asked him who would be there. He said, quite casually, that two of the people would be Wernher Eckart and Cesar Famares. They're alive, and obviously they're not tortured or locked up in a cell somewhere. What do you make of that?"

Mike sat down naked on the bed next to Melly, his shirt forgotten in his hands. "Alive, and free. Hmmm. Normally I would say it had to be tranquilizing drugs, or brain surgery—but I've never heard of a truth drug that could break Trader Oath, and the surgery to do it would make the two of them into walking vegetables."

"Maybe they are. All he said was that they would be there tonight."

Mike nodded and finally began to pull the shirt over his head. "We'll find out what's going on then."

"Maybe." She handed him his pants. "Mike, do you know how to run an interference test?"

"Sure. But I've never done one."

"I have. Let's do one tonight. You make sure you hold Mantilla's attention for at least half an hour. While you're doing that, I'll run the test on Wernher Eckart and Cesar. If there *has* been major surgery of any kind, the interference test will show it." She stood up. "Dominic Mantilla will be coming back in twenty minutes. I'd better get ready. One other thing, Mike. Mantilla really has the hots for me. He made a pass in my rooms, and he'll certainly try again tonight. I know I'm senior partner on this mission, but I'm not sure of the best strategy. What do you think?"

Her tone was totally businesslike. Mike stared at her, his trousers still at half-mast. "Think about what?"

"I mean, should we let him have me, or not? Let me know your opinion, would you, before the reception?"

She left the room. Mike remained sitting on the bed, his trousers ignored. A senior partner on a trading team was supposed to teach the junior member everything he knew. Mike had the uncomfortable feeling that in certain areas, Melly knew far more than he would *ever* learn.

His next thought had nothing to do with the mission. Did Melly's lack of interest in him as a man, and her breathless fascination with Dominic Mantilla, represent her dedication to her job—or was it simple biology?

There was one easy way to find out: Mike could let his own

interest in Melly show through. Easy in principle—but he was scared of the possible result.

He finished dressing hurriedly, looking forward now to the negotiation. It might be tough, but it was a certain cure for introspection and self-doubts.

Every tough negotiation had the same underlying structure, but no explanation to a trainee could quite say what it was. A person had to *experience* it. There was an interplay of the opposing parties in the real thing, almost like a formal and elaborate dance, a pattern of advance and retreat on individual negotiating points that must still be part of an overall progression. And there was an inner sense of how far the process was from completion.

The negotiation with Dominic Mantilla was all wrong. Mike could not say why. The usual process was superficially at work, with proposed payments by the Chipponese for the right to tether a Beanstalk in the equatorial Andes, and counteroffers from the Unified Empire; and there was the ceding of sovereign rights to a small piece of that Empire.

But it was all too casual. Dominic Mantilla seemed bored by the whole process, and he was prepared to make outrageously large concessions with no matching gain. Mike felt oddly irritated as he listened to Melly and Mantilla. She was doing fine, but this wasn't a negotiation! It was like fighting a small child, one who didn't want to fight at all.

"I don't like this," he whispered to Melly at the first chance they had to get outside the room for a quiet few minutes. "He's giving on every point—as though it doesn't matter what he agrees to."

"Maybe he learned the lesson when the Chipponese rejected his earlier terms?"

Mike shook his head. His own feelings went deeper than logic. Whatever Dominic Mantilla was, he was not a negotiator and never would be. So what had he done to persuade Eckart to accept the outrageous terms he had sent to the Chipponese?

"He hasn't learned anything. And believe me, Melly, we can't trust him an inch."

"But he seems to trust the Chipponese quite a lot." She sounded defensive of Mantilla—perhaps because he was behaving toward her with enormous gallantry, deferring to her on every point.

"Trust! He doesn't trust *them* any more than I trust *him*. Melly, where did you get that idea?"

"He said it! When you were arguing about length of treaty. He said that he felt sure that nothing unworthy of their high ethical standards would ever be proposed by the Chipponese Empire. Didn't you hear him?"

Mike stared in disbelief. "Melly, for God's sake, don't you recognize *sarcasm* when you hear it? He wasn't serious! Mantilla is convinced that the Chipponese are as crooked as he is, and that's just his way of saying it."

She stared at him with a surprised look on her face, but there was no opportunity to pursue it with her. The break was over, and they were heading back into the meeting rooms for the second half of the first round of discussions.

A negotiation of this importance ought to take several days. Mike had mentally prepared himself for a week's stay in Dreamtown. But in one more hour, it was finished. Not just the opening phase—the whole thing! Mike looked at the signed agreement, and his head spun. This one was as lopsided the other way—in favor of the Chipponese—as the earlier proposals had been in favor of the Unified Empire. The tether site would be made available for practically nothing, and the treaty was as near to unbreakable as any that Mike had ever seen. Maybe Melly was really an out-of-this-world negotiator.

And Mantilla seemed delighted! He was smiling a huge smile and patting Melly's hand possessively.

"Tomorrow morning," he was saying. He looked like a tall and skinny wolf, his dark eyes gleaming with poorly controlled lust. "Tomorrow if you wish you can return home. But tonight we celebrate! In two hours, the reception will begin. I hope you are prepared to enjoy yourselves enormously. I will come by your rooms myself, and be honored to serve as your escort." He leaned over Melly, clutching her hands in his. "And you, my dear, since this is your first visit here—but surely not your last—it is good that you will carry back a document to be proud of."

Mike looked again at the words sitting in front of him and felt terrible misgivings. This wasn't a treaty—it was a massacre. But how was a Trader supposed to say that the deal offered was just *too good*? Nothing in the Rule Books—formal or informal—prepared for that possibility.

Watching Melly batting her eyelashes at Mantilla, he felt like a total outsider. Just what the hell was going on?

* * *

The reception for Mike and Melly offered every product of the Unified Empire that a human palate could desire, from coddled rhea eggs to jellied tapir's foot to huanaco tongues in aspic.

Mike stood at the side of the hall and picked morosely at a handful of anchovy crackers while Dominic Mantilla, resplendent in crimson and black suit and cloak, led Melly through the great lines of the reception. She seemed to be enjoying herself greatly, which didn't help Mike's feelings one little bit. He felt very edgy, and he watched all the time for any sign of Wernher Eckart or Cesar Famares. Would they come at all? Would they try to avoid him? Suppose they came for only a few minutes?

If that happened, he must somehow pull Mantilla away so that Melly could perform the interference test.

Their behavior when they finally arrived was a complete surprise. They headed straight for Mike.

"Hi there." Cesar grinned at him. "It's been a while, eh? Let me introduce you to Wernher." His manner was as casual as if they were still in the Azores training camp and saw each other every day.

"Glad you made the party." Eckart shook Mike's hand. "When did you get here?"

Drugged? They didn't act drugged, and Eckart, at least, seemed in perfect health. Cesar was another matter. Like Mike and Melly, he must have had shots for height accommodation before he left the base—they were above thirteen thousand feet here. But sometimes the shots didn't work. Cesar's wheezing voice and shallow breathing told of fluid buildup in the lungs. His slurred speech and unsteady gait suggested severe cerebral edema.

"Got here just this afternoon," Mike said at last. He wondered how to get a detox shot into them without anyone noticing. "We'll be here for a day or two, then head back."

Eckart laughed and gave Cesar a knowing look. "I hear you. But you won't be saying that in a couple of days. Once you get used to it here, you won't *want* to leave—ever."

"Just like you two?" Mike reached across and casually picked up a filled glass, moving the palm of his hand over its top.

"You bet." Cesar accepted the shot of *testudo* liquor that Mike passed to him and threw it down his throat. He gasped as the iced liquid started its afterburn, and a look of ecstatic pleasure crossed his face. He beamed around the room. "Wonderful stuff. Wonderful place. Where else could you get a drink like that?"

Not many places, Cesar, if you want it exactly like that,

thought Mike. For one thing, the detox formula was a Trader secret. He waited, watching for any change in behavior. Nothing happened. Cesar went on smiling, looking around the room with an air of total satisfaction. A shot in Eckart's glass produced no more effect. Mike gave it ten more minutes, then waited until he could catch Melly's eye, far away across the wide hall. She could be picked out easily, because of her companion's great height. Mike shook his head at her. Drugs were out. Time to test for surgical interference.

It took a little while for Melly to wander across with Dominic Mantilla in tow. His face was flushed, he had his hand on her arm, and they were standing very close to each other.

"Dominic and I will be leaving the reception soon," she said. "But I reminded him that he promised to show you around the special attractions of Dreamtown, and he will do it before we leave. Are you ready to go with him?"

Mike nodded. Following Mantilla out of the main hall, he was uncomfortably aware that he had not given Melly an answer to her earlier question: Should she go to bed with the man?

There ought to be another entry in the Rule Books. How to ruin a negotiation: Give a man an attractive partner, and let him spend more time worrying about her than about the mission.

The path that Dominic Mantilla took led down a steep staircase, away from the brightly lit and over-decorated reception hall. They descended until they reached a long corridor with thick carpet on the floor and sound-deadening tiles on the walls. The loud buzz of conversation upstairs was replaced by an unnatural hush.

Mantilla paused at the first of a dozen doors along the corridor. "This is under my control," he said softly, "but I take little credit for its functions. These are traditionalists—if I tried to change any element of the setting they would look elsewhere for their satisfaction."

Mike was looking into a dimly-lit room containing one table with half a dozen chairs grouped around it. By each chair stood a small serving trolley holding tobacco and opium pipes, lacquered jars of rice wine, silver trays of finger-sized confections and sweetmeats, and piles of red and gold trading tokens. The players—four Chipponese and two Chills—did not look up at the newcomers in the doorway. Joss sticks perfumed the air, and clouds of smoke wreathed the intent figures of the players. The only sound in the room was the faint click of pasteboard cards on the table's dark green surface.

Mantilla stepped back from the doorway and headed along the corridor. "This room and eleven others, just the same, are for the most dedicated players. Did you know that one-thirtieth of the world's wealth changes hands at cards?"

He sounded bored. As they moved on to a turn in the corridor, Mike decided that Dominic Mantilla was certainly not a gambler himself. There had been not even a glint of interest in the card games, even though the stakes at the table were enormous. It was one more data point, of questionable value. After all, Traders did not gamble, either.

He followed Mantilla along a steadily darkening corridor, and they finally halted before a black door of heavy wood. "Another one for the traditionalists." Mantilla swung the door open. "Fully equipped."

The interior was deserted, barely lit by flickering wall torches. Mike recognized only half of the devices within, but that was enough.

"Surely this isn't *used*?"

Mantilla looked at him with raised eyebrows. "My honored guest, we are a commercial organization. Do you imagine that we would provide such facilities if there were no demand for them?" His tone was quietly ironic. "We provide the classical furnishings, and there has been a call for every unit within the past month. Eliminate any, and I would lose part of my clientele. They are sophisticated people who insist on both the equipment and the ambiance."

He began to walk along the center of the long room. "The rack, of course, is a standard feature; and the braziers and hot pincers. Also the thumbscrew, and the iron boot, with a furnace to produce the molten lead. But some of the others are perhaps less familiar. That is the parrot's beam, to hang by thumbs and fingers; and there is the *mala mansio*—the Little Ease. We have one client who comes here regularly, and is squeezed into it for ten days at a time. And then there is the press, with fifty-pound weights, and the *strappado*; there are the hot plates of the *lamina*, the bilboes, the barbed hooks of the *ungulae*. The Iron Maiden is here largely for effect, since it would undoubtedly be fatal. But we have had requests. If you would enjoy watching the equipment in live use, as I do, we will arrange to come here. The iron boot is the most spectacular."

Mike said nothing; he thought a great deal. He averted his eyes and followed Mantilla along the room and out into the next corridor.

The next room held just two people, facing each other across a gray cabinet. One was a Strine bigmomma, all leather and ceremonial sword, the other a Great Republic cityboss in paint and feathers. Each wore a headset that covered her down to the nostrils. Both were sweating hard, with perspiration trickling down their faces and necks. The panels on the side of the cabinet winked on and off in complex patterns.

"You know this one?" Mantilla asked.

Mike nodded. He had read the Unified Empire's list of attractions. The Strine and the Yankee were locked in life-and-death battle for the whole world. At their command, armies and armadas and missile squadrons swarmed over the globe, all simulated in detail in Dreamtown's master computer. The stakes were a good deal less than the whole world, but they were substantial. The cost of occupying the computer's maximum simulation capability, with sound, vision, and all tactile inputs, was so large that only the wealthiest could afford to play at all. Mike guessed that a year's output of a Strineland biolab probably hung on the war game's result.

"You designed this?" he asked Mantilla.

His companion shook his head. "To be honest, I find it boring. Who would play at conquering the world, when there is a real world to be conquered? Let us look at a more interesting pursuit."

They moved on and came out onto a balcony that overlooked a cubical room at least thirty yards on each side. The whole interior was filled with a maze of transparent tunnels and ascending and descending ramps, arranged so that it was impossible for a casual viewer to see any way from one side of it to the other.

The great room was empty. Mike looked questioningly at Dominic Mantilla. "Counterpoint," Mantilla said softly. His face was intent and alive. "Now you will see something worthwhile. Watch carefully. They are about to begin."

From one of a couple of dozen small doors scattered across the wall opposite, a black cat with white paws had emerged. It took half a dozen tentative steps forward, then paused. After a moment it jerked upright and moved forward again.

"A little electric shock to its paws," Mantilla said. "Not enough to hurt, but enough to persuade the animal to move forward. The object of Counterpoint is to get one of the animals assigned to you—a pawn—through the maze and all the way across to enter one of your opponent's doors. The first player to do that wins, and the game is over. Each player has ten pawns, and several lines of defense. Just watch what happens."

The cat was nosing its way through a swing door and ascending a shallow upward ramp. On the other side of the room a second cat had been released and was moving forward at the same level. After a few moments the two animals caught sight of each other. Both paused, then went cautiously forward to sniff for the scent of aggression. When the inspection was complete they went on their way.

"Every game worth playing has two elements." Mantilla was crouched forward, watching the cats with obvious enjoyment. "It must call for a combination of luck and skill. Without both, a game is dull. The skill in Counterpoint is in the way in which the players release and control the pawns, opening and closing pathways and stimulating the animals to walk along them. Each player has ten pawns, which vary in their species from one game to the next. A good player can handle all ten at once with no trouble. But there is luck also. Some things cannot be predicted. Will two pawns back away from each other when they meet, will they fight, will they pass each other? No one can predict that. So the players must prepare multiple strategies."

As he was speaking, a second door had opened. This time something different emerged, a familiar-looking pudgy shape. It shuffled forward a few steps, sniffed the air, and looked across to the other side of the chamber.

Mike jerked around to face Mantilla. "That's a Cappy! It's Benjy."

"Not any more." Mantilla's voice was casual. "It's a capybara, but it is no longer enhanced. As you see, it is not blind now, and there is no self-awareness. Benjy was not efficient, and twice he disobeyed orders. I was reluctantly forced to . . . demote him."

A third Pawn had been released, this one a white-furred cat, and instead of moving hesitantly along the walkways it was racing straight across the room on the most direct course it could find. Two new pawns on the opposing side showed no interest in intercepting it. It sped along a spiraling up ramp, then over an arched crossway. In less than thirty seconds it was no more than ten yards from the gates on the far side of the chamber and heading straight for one of them.

"Last ditch defense," Mantilla said urgently. "He'll have to, or he's done for."

As he spoke there was a great crackle of electrical discharge within the chamber and a bright blue flash. The running cat leaped upward to bang against the ceiling of the ramp, then gave a single intense scream and collapsed with rigid limbs. The fur on its sides was aflame.

Mantilla nodded in satisfaction. "Just in time. That man has played before. You don't use the high voltage until the last possible moment—and you can only use it four times altogether. The connoisseurs try not to use it at all."

In the chamber beneath them the capybara had sunk quivering to the floor, staring at the smoking body of the cat with terrified eyes.

"Look at him," Mike said. "He knows!"

Dominic Mantilla laughed. "I'm sure it seems that way, but it's not true. He was startled by the sound, that's all, and maybe he's catching the smell of burning fur, but he has no idea what happened. You'll see, he'll start to move again in a minute. If he's not careful he's likely to end up the same way himself." He looked at Mike in surprise. "What's wrong? Don't you want to watch the game to a finish? This is exciting. It's one that I designed myself."

Mike shook his head. "I must be getting back to Melly."

He hurried away from the balcony. Mantilla followed reluctantly. "One more item," he said. "Then we'll go back. This next one is not for the gambler. It's for the sportsman who has tried everything."

They were unexpectedly emerging from the underground play chambers into the open air. Mike felt an icy cold wind on his face and followed Dominic Mantilla into total darkness. As soon as his eyes adjusted he realized that they were standing on an open platform that jutted out from a cliff side.

"Walk carefully. The mountain side is nearly vertical here and there is no guard rail." Mantilla stepped confidently forward. "This is the loading area for Glissando."

The chute seemed to drop away forever. It was about fifty feet across, a half cylinder with curved sides of polished ice. On the platform in front of Mike were half a dozen bullet-shaped coffins, each large enough to hold one or two riders.

Mantilla put one hand on Mike's shoulder, coaxing him along closer to the edge. "The run widens at the bottom, as it gets closer to the ocean—that's to make it more difficult to control the sled into the electromagnetic brake rings. And of course, close to sea level we have to maintain an ice surface by artificial means. But no one ever complains about that . . . or about anything. It is the perfect cure for jaded appetites. Fourteen thousand feet drop in altitude, a maximum speed of well over three hundred miles an hour, and any slight control error enough to ruin you. Pure excitement. Only one person has ever made the run twice."

"Then I assume he'd had enough?"

"I cannot say. On the second descent, he missed the braking rings. *Boom!*" Mantilla roared with laughter. "Perhaps you would like to try it?"

Mike shuffled back from the edge. Mantilla was insane! He shook his head. "I don't have jaded appetites, thank you." And if I ever develop them, I'll sure look for some other solutions.

Without waiting for Dominic Mantilla, he set a determined return path for Melly and the reception hall.

He had an answer to his main question before Melly said a word. She shook her head as soon as she saw him.

"Slight signs of physical change, but not nearly enough for the behavior patterns Eckart and Cesar are showing. If only we had some way of doing a full brain scan!"

"Forget it. I'm sure the equipment is here, but Mantilla would never agree. Anything else?"

"Yes. Cesar is dying—of altitude sickness. If we don't get him out of here he won't last another week. But he doesn't seem at all worried. I couldn't get him to admit to feeling ill, even though he must be finding it hard just to stand up. What did you see?"

Mike gave her a quick summary of his tour of the Dreamtown facilities, but he had to keep it short. Dominic Mantilla was entering the reception hall. Mike had time to add, "Don't let him get you alone tonight," and to wonder about his own motives in saying it, and then the master of Dreamtown was at their side.

Mantilla was in excellent spirits, deferential to Melly and indulgent—almost paternal—toward Mike. "There were many more things to see," he said. "Why did you want to shorten our tour? Unless perhaps it was to return to Melinda, which any wise man would of course wish to do." He turned to Melly. "And you, my dear, you have seen nothing of our extensive pleasure facilities. May I be permitted to show them to you? They offer nothing to me comparable with the pleasure of your company, and no man or woman in them compares with you for charm and beauty, but perhaps you will find them entertaining. Shall we?"

He held out his hand. Mike glared, while Melly appeared enraptured. She tucked her arm into his, nodded at Mike, and allowed Mantilla to lead her away across the chamber floor. They disappeared together through an archway on the far side. Mike remained at the reception until after midnight, but neither Melly nor Dominic Mantilla reappeared. Finally Mike headed back to their quarters. Melly was not in her rooms.

Mike went through to his own bedroom and lay down. He had taken a precautionary pill himself, and he was not at all sleepy. It was the time when a Trader put his thoughts together and established the final overall strategy for the mission. In this case, nothing fitted. In principle, the first task was complete; they had negotiated a treaty on behalf of the Chipponese, and it was a ridiculously good one from their point of view. Dominic Mantilla, representative for the Unified Empire, was worse as a negotiator than the newest Trader trainee. His line was thrills and torture, and he was surely a sadist.

His thoughts returned to Melly. Was she safe with Mantilla? She was supposed to be experienced with men; Mike could only hope that she knew what she was doing.

Their second task had also gone as far as it could. Clearly, neither Eckart nor Cesar had been tortured into breaking Trader Oath, and they were not staying in Dreamtown against their will—they loved it here, even though it was killing Cesar. Somehow, Mike and Melly had to get Cesar away.

They love it here. That thought came back into Mike's head. He let it roll around on the edge of his consciousness, while he thought again about Dominic Mantilla. Lord Dominic, Prince of Pain . . .

A pattern was finally beginning to form when Mike heard a soft spitting sound from the wall of the room and felt a moment of terrible agony in the top of his head. He started to sit up.

The pain was gone as quickly as it had come. He lolled back on the hard bed and laughed aloud with satisfaction. Everything was fine—better than fine, it was wonderful. He reviewed the events since they had started on the mission and found that he was totally pleased with every one of them. Tomorrow they would examine the agreement between the Chipponese and the Unified Empire and make whatever changes were needed, and then they would celebrate. Already he was looking forward to the celebration.

He rubbed his fingers along the bed sheet. The feeling of the cloth was cool, sensuous, wholly delightful. It made him want to fall asleep on it, to abandon himself to its caress. The prospect of a long, satisfying sleep filled him with gratification—with *excitement*.

He had been lying there for almost two hours, still sleepless but perfectly happy, when Melly came hurrying into the room.

"Mike!" She sat down on the bed and gripped his arm. "Mike, I was sure that something terrible had happened to you. Are you feeling all right?"

"Much better than all right. I'm feeling *wonderful*." He reached out to take her in his arms. "Melly, come and lie next to me. Come and love me. It will be the most exciting thing ever."

She had moved closer to him, but instead of lying down she took his head in her hands and examined it closely, probing delicately at the crown. She seemed to know exactly where to look. Mike lay back blissfully. She had found a wounded spot there, but it all felt marvelous.

And then, suddenly, she was tugging hard at him, shaking him. He opened his eyes again. "Melly? Don't stop. Keep on touching me."

She was pulling him upright. "Mike, stand up—*now*!"

"Why?"

"I have Cesar all ready. We have to leave. We'll have to let Wernher Eckart fend for himself for a while, he's in good health. Do you hear me, Mike?" She shook him. "We have to go!"

Melly was amazingly strong. She had Mike up to a sitting position and was lifting him under the armpits. Every touch—even the shaking—gave him intense pleasure. Mike closed his eyes. "Go? I'm not going—not now, not ever. Not anywhere. Come to bed, Melly. We don't want to leave Dreamtown, it's the only place you'll ever feel full happiness. Lie down next to me."

He put both arms around her and tried to draw her back to the bed. She resisted hard for a moment, then reached out to stroke his cheek. "Lie quiet for a moment, Mike. Then I'll come back and lie down with you. Remember now, don't do anything while I'm away!"

She was gone. Mike lay back on the bed again, his head filled with blissful thoughts. Melly would return in a minute or two. And if she did not, that would be all right, too. Everything would be all right.

Even when she returned and began to run the bonds around his arms and legs, he was not worried. The tight bindings provided an erotic touch to his wrists and his ankles, and the close-fitting gag across his mouth felt like a lover's kiss. He smiled up at her as she hoisted him off the bed and carried him out of the room.

"Not a sound!" Her voice was a whisper. "Dominic Mantilla

may arrive at my rooms at any moment. Relax and let me carry you."

She was hurrying with him along the corridor, bearing his whole weight with no apparent effort. Now they were on a downward-spiralling ramp. Mike, his head against her chest, could not speak through the gag. He inhaled her perfume through his nose and smiled up at her. When they turned a corner in the corridor and a gust of freezingly cold air hit them, Mike thrilled to its icy touch.

The interior lights of Dreamtown vanished, and Mike was looking up at a starry sky. They had emerged on to a wooden loading platform, the starting point for Glissando. A two-man sled was already in position at the top of the ice chute. As Melly moved forward and rolled Mike inside the curved body of the sled, platform lights suddenly came on, dazzlingly bright.

"Stop." The deep bass voice that shouted the command was unmistakable. Melly did not even look around. She strapped Mike in the rear sled position, and began to rock the metal shell on its runners. Craning his head up, Mike saw that the forward sled position was already occupied by Cesar Famares.

The sled began to tilt. With no emotion but pleasure, Mike saw that they were poised at the very brink of a gleaming wall of ice. It dropped away forever in front of them, curving slightly to the left as it went.

There was a sound of running footsteps from behind, hard leather boots crashing down on the wooden platform. Melly, still bending over to strap Mike into locked position, was seized around the shoulders. As Dominic Mantilla began to lift her away from the sled she allowed herself to be drawn backward. She slid down to the level of his knees, turning and gripping his thighs as she went. As he moved forward to avoid overbalancing, she set her grip higher on his body and exerted her maximum leverage. Melly and Dominic Mantilla fell together on top of the metal sled.

The double impact of their bodies was more than enough to push the shell farther out onto the downward ramp of the ice. For a second the whole group teetered on the edge, then rocked past the point of recovery.

Mantilla began to scream as soon as the sled moved forward. Ignoring Melly, he turned and scrabbled desperately at the edge of the platform. He managed a fingertip grip that held for a few moments, but then the weight of Melly, still clutching his legs and with her feet hooked into the metal shell of the sled, was too much. He lost his hold and fell backward, still screaming, right over the sled. When the machine finally began to pick up speed on the icy slope, Mantilla was just a few yards in front of it, skating downhill on his back.

He struggled to roll over, and his fingers clawed at the gleaming ice. It was useless. He was accelerating rapidly, thirty yards down the slope, and still grasping hopelessly at the wall of the ice chute.

The sled had also started to move. In less than a second it was dropping almost vertically. Mike and Cesar were huddled helplessly inside, while Melly crouched over them and held her body flat above the open shell.

The ice wall was so steep that it was almost like free-fall. Mike felt the hollow sensation in the pit of his stomach, and laughed aloud with pleasure. He had no thought of fear. It was ecstasy, a feeling more intense than anything he had ever experienced in his life, so good that he was hardly able to stand so much enjoyment. He watched happily as Melly manipulated the controls of the sled, directing its course down the very center of the chute while the cold wind whipped at her body. She was still mostly outside the protecting metal shell. He saw her fair hair streaming behind her and thought he had never seen anything so beautiful.

They were passing Dominic Mantilla. His body lacked the clean aerodynamics of the bullet-sled, and he lacked the control of his movements that Melly was providing for the sled. But he had stopped screaming and had managed to turn so that his head was facing upward. Melly was easing the bullet-sled past him, moving out higher on the smooth ice channel, when he reached out a long, black-clad arm and managed to get a finger hold on the side of the shell. Mike saw the glittering dark eyes turned toward them, then felt the sled begin to yaw off course as Mantilla pulled.

Melly hammered with both fists at Mantilla's bloodied fingertips, but his grip held firm. He gave a snarling laugh of triumph.

He was turning his body, ready to pull himself closer to the sled, when the descending course of the Glissando run met its first tight curve. They were entering a portion where the ice channel turned to the left through nearly sixty degrees. Centrifugal force moved the sled and Dominic Mantilla away from the center, upward and outward toward the right-hand lip of the chute.

Mantilla was on the outside. Melly stopped beating at his clutching hand and bent again over the controls of the sled. She steered it out toward the top rim of the curving ice wall, nudging Mantilla gradually up the steepening slope.

He saw what was happening and made a last attempt to pull himself into the sled. It was too late. The bullet-sled's runners moved close to the outer rim of the chute, pushing Mantilla's legs and trunk out over the edge. For a moment he was hanging there, flying along with his body horizontal, still gripping the sled's side. Then the forces became too great. With a despairing cry he lost his hold and flew out into the jumble of rock and ice that lay beyond the Glissando chute.

Mike had watched the whole thing with intense delight. It seemed to him that he had never been a part of anything remotely as enjoyable. He stared happily at Mantilla's body, laughing as it spun and shattered against iron-hard rocks and finally dropped away over a vertical cliff. As Melly managed to regain control of the shuddering sled and steered them back down to the safer central part of the run, he felt ready to applaud.

And then, a few miles farther on, it ended.

Mike felt the pleasure drain like ichor out of his body. He was suddenly cold, aching, and terrified, filled with an unendurable sense of loss. At the same time, he heard Cesar in front of him give a long groan of pain. Instead of slipping carefree down an exciting pleasure run, now they were hurtling to almost certain death. When they reached the end of their downhill run, they would hit the chill waters of the Pacific with destructive force . . . unless Melly could control the sled, with its added load of an extra person. Mike tried to free himself of his bonds, and strained upward to watch her efforts. "Melly!"

She turned her head just long enough to say, "Don't move. You're changing the center of mass." And then she was again making fine adjustments to the controls, aiming them arrow-straight down the middle of the Glissando run.

Five minutes more, and the waves of the Pacific were in sight. The sled was traveling at well over two hundred miles an hour. Straight ahead, square in front of their path like a bull's-eye, stood the circular arches of the deceleration rings. Before Mike realized it, they had reached the first of them.

The electromagnetic field seized the metal sled and pulled it hard backward, slowing its motion. Mike and Cesar, strapped tightly into the sled's interior, decelerated with it. But Melly was outside the metal body. As Mike watched helplessly, she was ripped from the sled and flew on with undiminished speed toward the gray Pacific waters.

The sound of her impact was a flat, lifeless slap, loud enough to carry back to them. Mike saw her body in a tangle of breaking limbs, then he closed his eyes. At that speed, water was as destructive to human tissues as solid earth.

When the sled came to a complete halt at the foot of the Glissando run, he did not try to release himself. Only the sound of the approaching Trader pick-up plane made him stir himself enough to begin to loosen the straps that held him. He helped Cesar to do the same. They put their arms around each other and stood in shared misery on the beach.

Melly was gone. But even worse, Dreamtown was gone . . .

Both men were weeping hopelessly when they were hoisted aboard the Trader craft and the plane tipped low over the water to pick up Melly's shattered body. The injection that brought unconsciousness was a longed-for relief from mental pain.

A hangover—the worst one ever. The pain in his skull was simply too bad to believe.

Mike lifted his hand and tried to touch the top of his head. Instead of hair, he encountered bandages.

"Get your bloody hands off that!" a sharp voice said. *"And wait a minute."*

Mike recognized Jack Lester's tone. A moment later he felt a sharp sting in his thigh, and the pain in his head eased. He opened his eyes.

He was lying flat on his back in a hospital bed. Above him was a big blank display panel. Cesar Famares lay next to him, still unconscious, with his head also swathed in bandages. A robodoc was clucking over both men.

"Want to see the Greaser version of what happened?" Lester asked. *"Daddy-O, show him what we got as the Unified Empire news release."*

The screen filled with script, and at the same time Daddy-O's soft voice read it aloud. *"In an unfortunate accident that occurred after an official reception yesterday evening, Highlands Coordinater Dominic Mantilla and three visiting Traders were killed. The body of Mantilla has been recovered, but those of the three Traders are still missing. The Highlands Coordinator and his visitors were in the process of negotiating an important trade agreement . . ."*

In his mind's eye, Mike saw again the spinning body of Dominic Mantilla, the downward rush of the sled, and the dreadful impact of Melly's body with the water. He and Cesar had survived only because of her self-sacrifice.

"That's the party line, Mike," Lester said briskly. *"A simple accident. Come on, boyo. How's your head now?"*

"Better." Mike touched his eyes. They felt grit-filled and swollen with tears. "What happened to me?"

"You had a platinum needle in your brain. It had been fired right in through the top of your skull. It's easy enough to shoot one in, right through the bone, but a damned sight harder to get it out. You'll have a headache for a few days. Cesar, too. What the hell happened to you?"

"Dominic Mantilla's people did it."

"They tortured you? Hey, we can compare notes."

"They had something better than that." Mike thought back, trying to recapture the incredible feeling of well-being that had filled him just a few hours ago. "He knew exactly what he was doing. If I'd had my way, I'd never have left Dreamtown."

He struggled to sit up. "Lover-boy, we've got to warn all the other Traders. We've always prepared ourselves so we don't crack under torture—"

"—and it works a treat."

"Usually. But Dominic Mantilla taught me something new, something I could have deduced without leaving the Azores if I'd been smart enough. But I had to go there to learn it. He was called the 'Prince of Pain,' sure, but his job in the Unified Empire was to create *pleasures*."

"You're right. That sounds contradictory."

"But it isn't! You should see the facilities he built in Dreamtown. They're all *intended* for pleasure, but some of them inflict pain to do it. I never realized it before, but there's no boundary line between pain and pleasure. They merge into each other. So he didn't break us with *pain*—we are all prepared for that. He just gave us so much pleasure that things like Trader Oath weren't important. I almost had everything figured out when he shot that needle into my head and turned on the field. And after that I was too happy to do any thinking at all. I'm sure if we'd been there another day, I'd have rewritten that Chipponese treaty any way that Mantilla wanted it."

"He must have been awful confident, to go ahead and sign what he did." Jack Lester sniffed through his half-regrown nose. *"We read what you had, and it's a real give-away deal. Daddy-O already had a call from the lads in the Unified Empire, tryin' to wriggle out of it."*

"Mantilla was convinced he had me. And the really neat part of his scheme is the limited range of the stimulating field. If anyone ever strays away from Dreamtown and gets out of field range, he'll turn right round of his own accord and hurry back —he couldn't stand the loss of pleasure. If Melly hadn't strapped us in tight, or if Mantilla had managed to shoot the needle into her skull, too . . ."

There was a long silence, until Jack Lester said, *"Your move, Daddy-O. I won't handle this one."*

Something close to a sigh came through the computer's voice synthesizer. *"Very well. I will do it. Mike, your assumption is false. Melinda Turak did indeed have a needle shot into her head, at the same time as you did. It was that event which made her come to your room, to see if the same had been done to you."*

"But that's ridiculous! She went ahead and carried out a whole rescue, me and Cesar. How could she possibly do that, if—"

"Listen carefully, Mike. Four months ago Melinda was involved in a Trader Smash rescue operation in the Great Republic. There was unexpected opposition, and our vehicle was attacked. Melinda led a diversion to allow the rest to escape. But in doing so she was injured. She received a major head wound, and was declared brain dead on arrival at base. Her body was not affected. So as an experiment, a molecular central processing unit and memory were implanted, and the data banks loaded from my own files. I provided the necessary microcode for the body to function and to perform as a Trader. But of course, the new Melinda Turak was quite immune to any Stimuli provided by Dominic Mantilla's needle. And also the new Melly could not 'die,' which has been upsetting you so— the processing unit and memory were recovered intact from the broken body when it was taken from the water."

The Traders' master computer paused, taking in the scene through the arrays of visual sensors. Mike was staring upward, his face expressionless.

"What is wrong?" Daddy-O asked. *"Do you have trouble accepting this as true?"*

Melly's initial ignorance of the informal rule book—and then, within a few hours, her total familiarity with it; her inability to recognize sarcasm when Dominic Mantilla had employed it; her cool, searching look at everything she saw; her uncanny detailed knowledge of briefing materials . . .

Mike shook his head. "No. I fully accept what you say." He

reached up to the control panel and closed his eyes. "I must sleep now."

He depressed the master switch. Suddenly Daddy-O and Jack Lester were alone in the circuit.

"A great shock to him, of course." Daddy-O brought additional processing capability on-line. *"The mission was a great success, as he surely realizes. And he accepts the explanation, but not apparently its implications. Were his reactions, would you say, predominantly of grief, or anger?"*

"Anger! You chip-faced idiot." Jack Lester was banging around in his tank with rage. *"You sit there and listen to all that, and you still have no idea what you've done! I thought you were supposed to have some sort of brain. You've probably ruined the best young Trader we've got. Can't you see what happened, you great silicon dummy?"*

"I cannot. If he is wishing that he were again in Dreamtown, for the pleasures provided there, that is no more than natural—"

"Mike doesn't give a monkey's doodah about Dreamtown. It's Melly that's killing him. Can't you see what happened? Gor, if I had legs and you had a butt I'd come over there and kick it. She was his old friend, from back in training camp. And worse than that—he was starting to fall for her."

"You mean—a romantic attachment?"

"I mean love, you dummy. Love! Stick that up your Josephson junctions."

"Love." There was another moment of silence. *"Ah, yes, I did not allow for love. I am sorry. That is my error. Do you think that—"*

But Jack was no longer on-line. Like Mike, he had broken the connection with Daddy-O.

In the next five seconds, Daddy-O put in the equivalent of a million years of human thought on the subject of love. At the end of it there was, as usual, no conclusion.

And no surprises.

Jack Lester and Mikal Asparian had been lied to, of course; Daddy-O had correctly predicted Asparian's emotional involvement with Melinda Turak and had been able to estimate his post-mission reaction with high accuracy. There had been deception, but deception was necessary; just as it was necessary to accept this paradox: logic must form the basis for all actions, and in a logical universe there was no need for love; and yet, if Daddy-O's grand design were ever to be achieved, love would be an essential component in that design's fulfillment.

The computer remained locked in introspection for seconds longer. *Patience, patience*. There was progress. Did a computer need to justify its actions? Should a computer be impatient? The swirling dance of electrons had no need to hurry. Daddy-O performed a final summary and added it to the hidden data files. Nerve, ingenuity, humility, love, pain—one by one, critical parameter values within Mikal Asparian were being measured.

CHAPTER 11

By midnight the hospital rehabilitation center was quiet. Lyle Connery sneaked down to the lower wing and turned off the lights in the little room. He sat there in the dark, headphones on.

"Are we safe to talk, Jack? I mean, Daddy-O has input units all over the place."

"I checked. We're safe here. That electronic moron doesn't monitor this area. But look, boyo, if you're so worried, get in the tank with me. Plenty of room, and the life-support system will take care of two as easy as one. What's the worry, anyway?"

Lyle Connery crouched closer to the big tank and lowered his voice. "We've ruined Mike, that's what. And Daddy-O doesn't seem to give a damn."

"Mike's no better?"

"He's worse. I was with him just before I came down here. He doesn't leave his room. He sits there in a blue mope, staring at the wall, and he doesn't take any notice of the incoming Trade reports—and you know how keen he used to be."

Jack Lester whistled. *"Bad as that? He used to come over here and talk to me about' em, every day. He knew more about what was going on around the world than half the Master Traders. What's doing it? Does he still have medical problems?"*

"Not physical ones. The medics say he's fine. But psychologically. . ." Connery shook his head, forgetting that Lester was receiving only audio. "It's Melinda, of course. He blames *himself* for her death—even though he wasn't there when it happened, and even though he didn't know about it until

160

months afterward. I knew we should have told him what was going on before the Dreamtown mission, but Daddy-O wouldn't have it. Didn't want to listen."

"Think we're seeing signs of senility? Don't forget how old Daddy-O is—Desirée Hofstadt and Magsman III worked out that basic architecture over half a century ago."

"Daddy-O may be past it—"

"Ancient, practically a damned antique. What happens to old computers? Metal fatigue, I guess—"

"—but that doesn't help Mike. He needs a diversion. If we let him go on sitting there, he's bound to brood and make things worse."

"Too true." There was an exasperated thump on the wall of the tank. *"Gor, Lyle, if only it was a couple of months from now, I'd be out of here. I'd take him and we'd raise some hell. There's old Mia Culpa, sweet as blackboy syrup, an' I'll bet she's still pining for me down in 'Tiago. She'd do Mike a power of good. What a woman! And what a waste. Hey, can't you do something with Mike, take him off somewhere?"*

"I don't think he'd go hell-raising with me. You know how people feel about their instructors."

"Well, you have to try something to bring him out of himself. You have to. Unless you think you have a better idea."

"I do." Jack Lester and Lyle Connery froze at the calm voice in their ears. *"A much better idea. You are quite right, Jack, solitude and rest will not help Mikal Asparian. Nor will trivial diversions. What he needs now is a major challenge. A mission."*

"You need a new brain if you think missions will help." Jack had recovered first. *"You won't cure him with more of the same. And what are you doing, tunnelhead, listening in on a private conversation?"*

"I am trying to restore Mikal Asparian to what he was three months ago: a functioning Trader." Daddy-O had no circuits for embarrassment. *"I agree with you, Jack, no ordinary mission will accomplish that purpose."*

"So what can we do?"

"We must give Asparian a mission in which someone else's psychological demands and needs are stronger than his own. I have a candidate. And so, gentlemen, as soon as you are ready..."

Mike was well-trained enough to obey a direct order. He had walked the long spiral up from Rehab to Training and was now sitting alone in Lyle Connery's office. The field display next to him showed a three-dimensional enlarged image of a flying insect, three feet long and twice that across the open wings. After a first incurious glance, Mike ignored it. He sat staring straight ahead for the next ten minutes. When the door to his left opened he did not turn around.

Lyle Connery noted the straight-ahead stare and cursed to himself. The old Mike would have been playing with that hologram, rotating it to take a look at the insect from all angles.

"Hi, Mike."

A nod of acknowledgment, and that was all. Connery went to sit across from him. "You read the preliminary briefing document on the mission?"

"Yes."

"Good. Any questions or comments?"

"It's a two-person mission. I don't want to be *teamed* on a mission, ever again." Mike was gazing down at the desk top, not meeting Connery's eyes.

"We don't have any choice, Mike. The Great Republic insists on a doublet in negotiation. All right?"

A shrug. "If you say so."

"I do. And we have a partner already picked out, one with lots of experience in Yankee negotiations." Now for the tricky bit, Connery thought. Daddy-O, you'd better be right. "You'll be working with an old colleague—Jack Kallario."

Mike looked up, and Connery saw emotion on his face for the first time in months. "*No*. He'll never work with me."

"Jake's a first-rate Trader. He'll work with anyone."

"He may have told you that. But he hates me."

"You haven't seen him for over a year."

"I know, and he hides it well. But he can't stand me."

"People change. And Jake has changed—a lot." Connery pushed a photograph across the desk. "Take a look."

Mike gave it a casual glance, then picked it up and stared hard. The jawline was different, the eyes wider apart. "This is Jake Kallario? I'd never have recognized him."

"He's been through a rough time. He needed reconstructive surgery, and he came out of it less than three weeks ago. You know that Melly Turak was killed in a Smash rescue operation a few months ago in western Yankeeland—but did you know who she was saving?" Connery took the photograph from Mike. "He survived, and she died. Jake won't admit it, but he blames himself for her death. I think you'll find he's a different person from the one you remember."

"I can't work with him."

"I'm sorry to hear that. Because Jake is on the way here. He'll arrive any minute now."

"I have to leave." Mike was standing up.

"You have to stay." The command tone of training camp appeared in Connery's voice. "Trader Asparian, that is an order. You and Kallario will hear this mission briefing together."

"Yes, sir." Mike sat down and stared again at the desk top. He did not move or speak for the next two minutes, until there was a sound from the open doorway. Then he turned. "Hello, Jake. How are you?"

"I'm doing all right. How about you?"

Connery winced. The voices were equally guarded, equally lifeless. If Daddy-O had thought that a simple meeting would strike sparks from both of them . . .

"Sit down, and let's get on with it." Connery swivelled the display so that both men could see it. "You've read the description of the primary mission. You are to negotiate a contract between the Strines and the Great Republic to permit the use of Strine clone technology. I anticipate no major difficulties with that. The Yankee underpopulation problem is hurting their northlands development, they must have more people, and the Strines think of human cloning as old technology. So both sides want a deal. You should be about two days in Skeleton City, negotiating with Martin Raincloud's staff. He's the top cityboss, pretty much runs the whole region. He's apparently wildly unstable, but I'm sure you'll be able to handle him. So the real interest lies in the second agenda. Trader Asparian, you've had longer to study this image than Kallario. What do you make of it?"

Mike gave the insect shape on the display a first serious inspection. "What's the image scale?"

"There's a scale calibration bar at the bottom. Display magnification is roughly a thousand to one. The real thing is about an eighth of an inch long."

"And it's inorganic, from the look of it."

"It is."

"And those are working wings. So somebody went to the trouble of making a flying gadget smaller than a housefly."

"Correct. Any idea why?"

Jake Kallario was showing signs of interest, leaning forward across Mike to stare at the display. "Surveillance?"

"Damn right. Bugging with a bug." Connery zoomed in on the head, so that the other two could see the eyes. "High-quality lenses, indium antimonide detectors, high-quality audio recording. Diamond crystal lattice brain, nuclear-powered propulsion system, and there's enough capacity for two hundred hours of continuous recording. The whole thing is a beautiful piece of work. It's a triumph of technology."

"Chill manufactured?" Mike asked.

"That would have been my guess, too. But apparently it's not. There's an interesting story to the way we got our hands on this thing." He paused.

Signs of life at last. Both men were looking at him expectantly.

"The fly is a triumph of high technology," he went on. "But its discovery was a triumph of *low* technology. It was found stuck to a flypaper in Rasool Ilunga's palace in Coronation City. It must have landed there accidentally, and it didn't have enough power to get free. Ilunga himself noticed it—he's an entomologist in addition to his other talents. His first thought was probably the same as mine would have been: this is a gadget that the Chills have planted here, to spy on what we're doing. Most people would have destroyed it, or maybe freed it and tried to load it up with false information. But Rasool Ilunga's a tricky character. He decided that the Diamond Fly—that's what he named it, *Musca Adamantis*—could be worth a lot to the Ten Tribes if it was handled right. So he did the last thing most people would have done; he went to the Chills down at the Pole and said he had the Fly in his possession and for a twenty percent interest in anything profitable that resulted, he would give it to them. He reasoned that if they showed no interest in it, that meant they must have planted it themselves. And even if they *had* developed it, they might be willing to pay a lot to have it back. Either way, he had nothing to lose. Well, the Chills were fascinated. They took the Fly away and did their own research—and it drove them crazy. Apparently the logic for the Fly's brain is designed so well that it's not difficult to program. The Chills are keen to find out who did the design, but it's the fact that the brain could ever be built that has them tied up in knots. They say the precision machinery needed is impossibly small, and they're the experts. We're talking of something that can perform fabrication work on single molecules—or smaller. It's so tiny, the Chills say its fabrication is 'below the molecular barrier.' That means it *can't* be built, not with any tools they can make or imagine. But it *was* built. Contradiction. And then, a couple of weeks ago, the Chills discovered another Diamond Fly, in their own council chamber at Cap City. After that, they found two more, and we turned up three of them here. Look."

Connery picked up a small black cube from the top of his desk, and slid back the top. As the other two men craned forward, he carefully lifted out a tiny blue-black object and placed it in front of them.

"It's recording now. The Chills showed us how to operate the Flies by remote control when they came to us for help. We signed an agreement with them—flat fee plus ten percent royalty—and Daddy-O and Max Dalzell started digging."

Connery paused for effect. That last statement, as it was meant to, had caught the other two's attention. Daddy-O working in direct combination with a top Master Trader made a rare and powerful team.

"The pair of them tracked down the maker of the Fly in just a couple of days. The brain was fabricated by a woman named Sabrina Vandermond, a Yankee. We know that for sure, and the Chills agree. But we still don't understand *how*. The Chills have assembly techniques that operate down almost to molecular levels, but they couldn't begin to put the Fly's brain together. And naturally, that is driving them crazy."

"What do you know about Vandermond?" Jake asked. His reconstructed face did not allow much expression, but Connery thought there was genuine interest in Jake's voice.

"Not much."

"So how will we arrange to see her?"

"That's one of this mission's little mysteries. Call it Agenda Three, if you like. You won't have to seek her out—we hear that she'll be looking for you. We don't know why. She lives in Skeleton City, and she works directly for Raincloud. We don't want to *do* anything to Vandermond, you understand—just pick her brains." Lyle Connery was watching the other two closely. There was no doubt about it, they had that inward, brooding look of a Trader calculating how to tackle a new mission. There were even signs of excitement in Asparian's eyes.

Rule 85: Once you've sold it, stop selling. Connery stood up. "There are more briefing materials waiting for you in your quarters. You'll be leaving for the Great Republic early tomorrow morning."

CHAPTER 12

The journey to the shores of the Great Republic was less than a thousand miles—half an hour in a high-speed Trader aircar. For his own reasons, Lyle Connery had instead arranged for sea travel and an entry at one of the Republic ports.

Sea time dragged, as Connery knew it would. It was impossible for Mike and Jake to avoid each other. After two days on a crowded vessel, they had reached a wary accommodation. Neither would mention training camp, or the Darklands training mission, or Melinda Turak—especially Melinda. Instead, they swapped information about the mission and the Great Republic. Jake was better informed than Mike. He had already made four trips to the Republic mainland and had traveled it from Arctic Islands to the Unified Empire border.

"One thing we don't need to ask ourselves," he said, "is, do they really want a deal? They *need* the Strine clone techniques. Their total population is only thirty million."

"That's more than the Strines."

"Yeah. But the Strines have always been that way. The Yankee system was set up for ten times as many. They can produce plenty of food—that was all automated before the Lostlands War—and transportation systems, but they can't get the rest of their technology moving the way they'd like to. It's been falling apart at the seams for two generations. Like that." He gestured over the bow of the ship. Mike and Jake were standing there, drinking cola tea and staring at the approaching coast of the Republic. "I've traveled this route twice before. Each time, the skyline is a little more ragged."

The ship was skirting the southern shore of a long, narrow island, heading for the airport that would carry the Traders to Skeleton City. Ahead of them, dark against a rosy sunset, a hundred fingers of tall buildings reached up to the western sky.

"Impressive, eh?" Jake commented.

"It certainly is."

"Now take a look with the spyglass."

The little Chill telescope brought the distant skyline close to hand. Instead of scores of delicate, needlelike spires reaching up to the clouds, Mike could now see a different structure. The tall buildings were worn and broken, windows gone, walls crumbling to reveal steel pylons beneath. They no longer stood isolated from one another. They were a single, linked structure, a precarious balance of tensions and compressions. Mike could see an ugly array of crisscrossing girders and support beams, running between the upper levels of the buildings. Cables hung in long catenaries between buttresses and Archimedean arches. The skyscrapers were held upright by a maze of beams, cables, and ground tethers. At the lower levels, the buildings were mottled with dirt and decay.

"There's the Great Republic for you," Jake said. "A big mess, all ready to fall apart under the right wind. And the people know it. Raincloud has trouble holding on to his power. Half the Yankee budget goes into weapons. They're supposed to defend the Republic against outside aggression, but I don't think he'd hesitate to use them internally. And nor would I. They are a decadent group."

Kallario's face did not show emotion, but Mike shuddered at the viciousness in his tone. Somewhere on the road from trainee to Trader, Jake's compassion and sympathy for other regions had been lost. Mike turned again to the spyglass and the ruined prospect ahead of them, as the ship crawled on through dark, polluted waters.

A plane was waiting when they docked the next morning on the island's southern shore. They took off at once and flew inland for nearly two thousand miles.

Skeleton City was a pleasant surprise after their port of entry. Their destination—Skylinetown, to its first residents—sat on the eastern slope of the continental divide, poised like a silver filigree crown on the mountain foothills. Tall, narrow buildings rose forever, towering up to two thousand feet above the plain. At forty-foot vertical intervals they were joined by open horizontal crosswalks. Each shining walkway, narrow and without handrails, was a couple of hundred feet long and perhaps eighteen inches across. The walkways provided both structural support and paths between buildings.

There was a brisk breeze. Thin crossways twisted in the wind, flexing and turning under their varying loads. As the car settled in to a landing at the base of the tallest structure, Mike saw dwarfed figures of people far above him, sauntering along between buildings.

Jake Kallario had been following his look. He gave Mike a nasty grin. "Don't like that, do you? You'd better get used to it. They live with heights here from the minute they're born."

"But they know damn well that we don't."

"Yeah. It's part of their negotiation technique. Why'd you think Raincloud chose Skeleton City as his base?"

Mike glanced up again. One of the figures far above them was standing at the very edge of a crosswalk, looking down. Mike grabbed at the waist-high railing next to the aircar steps. "My God. Let's try for our meetings at ground level."

"No chance."

A small welcoming committee of one ugly old man and one beautiful young woman, each dressed in traditional paint and feathers, stood waiting as they descended the aircar steps.

The woman stepped forward. "I am Robin Songbird, Martin Raincloud's personal assistant—"

She was interrupted by a female cry of fear from far above. While Mike and Jake were looking at Robin Songbird and her companion, a bound figure had been carried out onto one of the crosswalks by two men. Before the Traders knew what was happening, the body was swung outward and thrown clear. The walkway was about five hundred feet above ground. The scream of terror did not end until the woman's impact with the stone flags of the sidewalk.

Robin Songbird looked at Mike and Jake. "My apologies for an unfortunate piece of timing. That execution was supposed to take place earlier today. I cannot account for the delay." She sounded mildly embarrassed. Her handsome face was inscrutable beneath the layers of paint.

"What was the crime?" Mike kept his voice as casual as he could.

"Treason. She plotted against the welfare of the Great Republic."

"I see." And the timing was an *accident*? More likely it was quite deliberate, designed to unsettle the Traders. So far as Mike was concerned, it had succeeded.

The man with Robin Songbird had not spoken. He was small and wizened, with a left leg that ended below the knee in a metal brace. His paint was minimal, merely a couple of simple lines on cheeks and chin. He had watched the execution as impassively as Robin Songbird; now he stepped forward and looked at her expectantly.

"And this is Old-Billy Waters," she said at last. "Cityboss deputy. Second in command to Martin Raincloud." And I hate him for it, her voice said. "He's going to be the man who will negotiate with you."

Old-Billy Waters nodded to Jake and Mike. "Raincloud is busy so I'll show you where you'll be staying." He grinned like a small and good-natured monkey. "And Robin didn't say it, so allow me: Welcome to Skeleton City! May you enjoy your stay here."

Behind him, the crushed body of the executed woman was being scooped off the sidewalk.

The two Traders had agreed on their first order of business in the Great Republic when they were still on the open sea. While Mike clattered about the suite as noisily and visibly as he could, Jake made a fast inspection. After ten minutes he gestured to Mike to follow him into the bathroom and turned on the shower full force.

"At least one Fly in the bedroom, up in the corner of the ceiling," he said, his mouth a couple of inches from Mike's ear. "And one in the main living area. But no sign of one here—unless it's too cleverly placed for me to find. Our instruments didn't record any other sensors."

"What do you think?"

"Leave them where they are. If they move around too much for us to keep track of them, we'll make other plans."

"Sounds good to me." Mike reached into his pocket and took out a tiny black box. "What about this one? We want it where it will do the most good and where they won't find it."

"Raincloud's private quarters." Jack Kallario held out his hand for the box containing the Fly. "Here. Give it to me. You keep their attention, and I'll find a hiding place they'll never guess." He turned off the faucets. "Let's go. Old-Billy Waters doesn't want to keep Raincloud waiting."

* * *

The cityboss had chosen the highest point of Skeleton City as his eyrie. Mike and Jake were taken by Old-Billy Waters to a central building, a sheer cylindrical column nearly two thousand feet high. It rose far above all its neighbors, a lonely pinnacle that would catch the morning sun five minutes before any other point of Skeleton City. They ascended on a spiral escalator that curled in a smooth helix around the outside of the edifice. Crossways connected to other buildings up to the sixteen-hundred-foot level; above that, Martin Raincloud could be approached only through the escalator and the outside staircase.

As they rose higher, Mike felt disorientation. They seemed to be standing still, while the world spun away beneath them. He felt dizzy. He stood as close as he could to the smooth metal wall of the building, placing his hands flat against it. Above fifteen hundred feet, where the shielding of all the other buildings was gone, the west wind grew suddenly stronger. It swirled about them, tugging at their clothing, pulling them toward the abyss. Mike looked down only once. The people on the crossways had again become tiny, insectlike figures; but now they were *below*, instead of far above.

At its summit, the building changed character. The final hundred feet curved upward and outward, with smooth walls and no escalator. It could be ascended only by means of a steep spiral staircase, open to the winds and no more than two feet wide. Led by Old-Billy Waters, Mike and Jake went up to the topmost floor. The roof itself was a flat, bare circle, forty feet across. A narrow lip circled it, with a metal rail just beneath. A parked aircar occupied the available space on the roof.

"For Raincloud's own use," Old-Billy said. "But he hardly ever uses it. Anybody who wants to see him comes here."

He paused at the entrance to Raincloud's living quarters and looked around him. He appeared to be enjoying the view. Jake Kallario was just behind him. Mike, still on the last narrow step, gritted his teeth, pressed close to the wall, and wished they would hurry up and move inside.

"I have traveled the Great Republic from shore to shore," Old-Billy said at last. He finally stepped inside. "But the air and the view here, at the very top of this building, is the best anywhere." He sniffed, looked west, and nodded to himself. "Big blow on the way, coming in from the mountains. We'll have wind and rain by morning."

The building quivered, as though in anticipation. Let me

inside, and you can have my share of the air and the view, Mike thought. He hurried in after the other two.

They had entered a large, semicircular room, with one flat wall and a curtained doorway at the far end. Settees and soft cushions were scattered randomly across the floor. On the walls, display cases of vicious swords, knives, and tomahawks stood between elaborate murals. Following Old-Billy Waters, Mike and Jake walked slowly around the room, looking at the scenes painted on every available square inch.

When they came back to the entrance, Jake gave Mike a nudge and a nod of his head. Mike stared at him.

That quickly?

Jake winked.

The man was good. Mike could never feel comfortable with Jake Kallario, but he could appreciate skill when he saw it. Where had the Fly been placed? Mike made another circuit of the room. He could see no trace.

"You like these murals?" Old-Billy Waters asked. He was following Mike closely. "That will please Raincloud. He painted them all himself. He is very aware of the history of the Great Republic."

On every wall, battles were being waged between near-naked painted warriors and rough-clad men dressed in animal skins. The paintings were garish, bloody, and full of crude violence. In every one, the painted men were winning. "They are very . . . distinctive," Mike said.

"An excellent choice of words," Old-Billy grinned. Did Mike detect a flash of humor in the little man's eye—something that suggested cityboss and deputy were cut from different cloth? Maybe it would be possible to negotiate here after all.

Before Mike could reply the curtains at the end of the room were thrown back. Raincloud stood there, hands on hips. Old-Billy Waters jerked fully upright.

The appearance of the top cityboss was familiar from their briefing materials, a squat, waddling figure with a bull neck and a pink, balding head. The paint on his face emphasized a jutting nose, thin slip of a mouth, and broad cheekbones, and his remaining hair was long, brown, greasy, and tied behind his head. The eyes were black, protruding, and wide apart. Raincloud responded to Old-Billy Waters's introduction with a low grunt. He stared at Mike and Jake.

Mike stared back. The cityboss was even uglier in person than he was in pictures.

"Traders." He spat the word out like an oath. "Holding the rest of the world to ransom. But some day, sooner than you think, you will lose your power. Why should we use you as negotiators, when I am quite capable of dealing with the Strines myself?"

"That is your option." Jake Kallario's voice was calm. Neither Trader had met Martin Raincloud, but on the basis of Jake's experience with the Great Republic they had agreed that he would be the principal spokesman. "I feel sure you are correct, you are *capable* of dealing with the Strines." But you and I know, his tone said, that they would never deal with anyone who was not a Trader.

Instead of replying, Raincloud turned and strode back through the curtain. At Old-Billy Waters's urging, Mike and Jake Kallario followed. They came to a smaller room, little more than a long, dark cubbyhole. Along one wall ran an elaborate set of display screens. Beneath the screens stood a vast control console.

Martin Raincloud was already seated at the console. "Power! This is power." His mood had changed. Now he was chuckling as he jabbed at the keys, causing images to chase one another across the multiple screens.

"Nuclear missiles!" The scene panned across a plain filled with gray and silver rockets. "Battle lasers!" At Raincloud's shout, arrays of long tubes turned to point to the sky. "Ha, ha! Projectile defenses! Point protection!" Mike and Jake found themselves looking at thousands of high-velocity artillery units, crouched ready to send a hail of shells from horizon to horizon.

"Impregnable, indestructible, invincible!" Raincloud swiveled around in his chair, grinning in excitement. "We are invincible. Every one of these weapons is under my control, ready to fire at my direction. When you go back, tell this to the Traders—and let them tell the world! The Great Republic is the most powerful region on Earth. And we are the rightful leaders of the world!"

Rule 77: Don't debate lunatics—you might not win.

Mike and Jake waited, and the outburst ended as suddenly as it had begun. Raincloud leaned back in his seat and smiled sunnily. "Very good," he said. "It is now time for my singing lesson with Robin Songbird. Is there anything you need before you begin your negotiation? If so, please tell me, and Waters will take care of it."

Mike gave Jake a nod.

Jake caught the cue. "Nothing we need for the moment. We've had a long trip, now we'd like an hour or two to unwind.

Could we take a look around Skeleton City, and begin the main meetings this afternoon?"

Raincloud looked at Old-Billy Waters. The deputy nodded. "Certainly, whatever you want. I'm available." He turned to the Traders. "Come on. I'll take you down."

The ascent had been bad. The descent was worse. On the way up Mike had been able to focus on the path ahead. Now he was forced to look down. He was suspended in midair, hovering over a two-thousand-foot drop with nothing to support him but the frail strand of the staircase. It bent beneath his feet. He could see past its open mesh of metal, down, down, to the tiny dots of buildings and cars below. The wind buffeted from every side in unpredictable gusts that pushed him always toward the edge.

Mike paused and huddled in to the side of the building, hands on the wall. His feet had frozen.

"Hey." Jake was right behind. "Move it. I don't want to be up here all day." Under pressure from their surroundings, Jake was letting his feelings about Mike show through.

Mike forced himself to slide forward along the wall fixing his eyes on Old-Billy Waters's back. If the Yankee had heard the dislike and contempt in Kallario's voice, he ignored it. He was ambling along in front, his artificial leg clattering on the metal of the stairs. "Don't get too upset by what you heard up there from Raincloud," he said, turning his head to look at Mike and Jake, but still walking down the winding staircase. Mike could hardly bear to watch. "Cityboss talks tough, but he barks more than he bites."

A man hoping to convince himself?

"Even when it comes to weapons?" Jake asked.

"Ah, well, maybe that's the exception. The weapons he showed you are the genuine article—enough to blow us all to Chippoland. I'll be honest, they scare the hell out of me." Old-Billy stepped onto the escalator, still facing back toward the other two. His right foot was no more than two inches from open air and a sheer drop of seventeen hundred feet. "But I pray we'll never use 'em—Raincloud likes to play with the displays, but thank God he doesn't know most of the control sequences." He looked around, then at Mike and Jake. His voice dropped to a whisper. "I'll say this when we're out here in the open, with only the wind listening, but don't ask me to repeat it. Raincloud's right off his head, and getting worse. You realized that, didn't you, when we were in there?"

Could this all be a deep plot, with Martin Raincloud as master schemer? Mike found that hard to believe. Raincloud really seemed to scare Old-Billy as much as he scared Mike. But could Waters be worked with? "You don't share his view of Traders, then?"

"I don't hate you, if that's what you mean. Not at all. Raincloud loathes Traders; if he had his way he'd kill the lot of you."

"And he doesn't try to hide it," Jake said. "So why on earth did he agree to let us come here?"

"Beats me." Waters rubbed his liver-spotted pate. "Three months ago, he swore he'd had it with Traders. He was frothing at the mouth. We'd seen the last of 'em, he said, screw 'em all, we'll have no more like that in the Great Republic. Two weeks ago, he tells me, hey, guess what, I changed my mind. We're going to have some Traders here. We *need* Traders. And then yesterday I'm pulled off other duties and told I'm *it*—the principal interface with you two. Without advance notice."

"Come on now. You're the deputy. You must be involved with everything that goes on here."

Old-Billy Waters offered Mike an incredulous glare. "When did you ever hear of a deputy knowing half of what his boss was doing? I'm the *last* to know. Robin has more idea than I do, and she's just his bedwarmer. You ought to be here when he has one of his 'singing lessons' from her." He sniffed. "I tell you, there's a lot of things I don't know, and a lot I don't *want* to know. As for being a negotiator, when I hardly know what one does . . ."

They had finally reached the bottom of the escalator. Mike stepped onto solid ground with unconcealed relief. Waiting for them on the roadway stood a tall, fat man with an enormous domed head. His small mouth was framed by a long, drooping moustache, and red stubble covered multiple chins in a two-day growth of beard. A gray cloak was swept around his body from neck to ankles. A flat-topped black hat, one size too small, perched above the great brow.

He nodded past Waters, to Mike and Jake.

"Vandermond." The word was a pronouncement. A thick hand emerged from beneath the cloak.

Mike stared at him in astonishment. Sabrina?

"Sebastian Vandermond," Old-Billy Waters said. His bird-like look darted from Mike to Jake, then back to the man in front of them. "These are our Trader visitors, Sebastian."

"Obviously." Ice-blue eyes swept over them. Mike saw in that look disdain and enormous impatience. He recalled the def-

inition of a psychopath: an individual unable to recognize the
reality of other humans.

"What can we do for you, Sebastian?" Waters asked. The
other man towered above the rest of them.

"Martin Raincloud promised us an hour with the visitors."
Vandermond's tone held an Olympian indifference to Old-Billy
Waters.

"Did he?" Old-Billy raised his eyebrows. "Well, I was getting ready to show them around the city."

"Good. Then I will do it instead." Vandermond moved to
interpose his body between Waters and the two Traders.
"Come." The tone commanded more than the word. "We need
to talk with you."

Mike and Jake were shepherded away. Old-Billy Waters
stood nonplussed behind them. "We begin negotiation in two
hours," he shouted.

Vandermond ignored him. "First, a quick survey of Skeleton
City," he said. "And then, home. We have an important meeting
there, and little time."

Vandermond's idea of a tour was simple. He hurried them
along, walking, pointing, holding his hat on with one hand, and
saying little. That suited Mike. He needed to see for himself. As
usual, Daddy-O's briefing began to seem most notable for what it
had neglected to mention. He followed Vandermond's pointing
finger and understood Raincloud's domain for the first time.

Skeleton City stood in the eastern foothills. Thirty miles to
the west, the cordillera that ran the length of the Great Republic
rose snowcapped to fourteen thousand feet. The builders of
Skeleton City had drawn their inspiration from those mountain
heights. It was as if they had taken the original city on this site,
a place not tall by Yankeeland standards, and *stretched* it. Like
drawn sugar, each structure had thinned as it was pulled higher.
The new cloud-capped palaces, buildings a third of a mile high,
measured no more than three hundred feet across at the base.
Even with the strongest materials from the Chipponese space
factories, each building was unstable against compressive buck-
ling and wind loads. The crosswalks, doubling as pathways and
cables, provided the support that was needed. Skeleton City
measured no more than half a mile across at ground level, but it
existed as fully in three dimensions as other cities did in two.

Vandermond pointed out and named the more important
centers: Communication was high up in that building, Transportation down near the ground in this one, Agriculture all the way

out at the edge of town. He did not consider worthy of note the groups engaged in casual conversation on the crosswalks, hundreds of feet above them. The wind was strengthening, and the slender pathways swayed and stretched in the varying gusts. The people did not seem to notice, adjusting automatically to the changing wind pressure.

Mike forced his attention back to ground level. No wonder Martin Raincloud was a madman, and his assistants little better; anyone who lived in a place like this needed to be mad.

Sebastian Vandermond. *Sabrina* Vandermond. Was it the result of a sex-change operation? Shades of Cinder-feller. It took a major effort of imagination on Mike's part to transform the towering colossus of Sebastian Vandermond to a female form.

The tour went quickly. Within fifteen minutes they had returned to their starting point at Martin Raincloud's headquarters. This time, to Mike's relief, they went *down*. From an entrance at ground level they descended three floors to a pair of wide doors. Sebastian Vandermond swung them open and ushered Mike and Jake through.

Two centuries rolled away. They were standing at the threshold of a Victorian living room, complete with sideboard, overstuffed horsehair settee, potted aspidistra in one corner, and, in another, a hanging cage containing a large blue-black cockatoo with a red crest. At the center of the room stood five wooden-backed chairs grouped around a low table. On one of the chairs, quietly reading, sat a small, fair-haired woman.

She looked up. "You are late." Her voice was like a child's voice, but cool and precise.

"Yes. I'm very sorry." Sebastian Vandermond was awkward and apologetic, shambling forward to stand outside the circle of chairs.

The woman did not attempt to stand. Instead she gestured to the chairs. "If you please, be seated." Vandermond started forward with the other two. "Sebastian! Your *hat*."

"Oh, yes. I'm sorry, Sabrina, I forgot about it. I'll take it off at once." Vandermond hurried back across the room. His imperious voice had become subdued and placatory.

The woman smiled at Mike and Jake. "I am Sabrina Vandermond. May I offer you refreshment? Tea, perhaps?"

"That would be very acceptable," Jake said. The two men looked at the table surface. There was no sign of serving hatches or Chill robots.

"Good. Tea, then, Sebastian. For four." Sabrina placed the

document she had been reading on the side table, leaned back, and smiled at Mike and Jake as Sebastian Vandermond hurried out. "He means well, you know, but he needs a firm hand."

"Is he your brother?" Mike asked.

"That's right. My little brother. But he *grew*." Hazel eyes, laugh lines prominent at their corners, beamed at the two Traders. She straightened the little corsage of blue flowers on her long dove-gray dress, sighed, and settled back in her chair. "Well, now, this is certainly a pleasure. It has been so long since we have had Traders visiting. You must tell me all about your travels, where you have been, what each of you has been doing. I want to hear *everything*."

Was anyone sane in Skeleton City—anyone at all? Mike found himself drinking tea from a delicate porcelain cup and locked in a polite but surrealistic conversation with an elegant, mild-eyed woman who wanted to hear every detail of Trader life. Sabrina Vandermond asked about their training, their missions, and their home base. She wanted to know what they ate, how they dressed, where they slept, what they did for recreation. She questioned them about Trader negotiation methods, Trader marriage, the Trader hierarchy, and Trader traditions. Every word they spoke seemed to fascinate her, and when they flagged she prompted them with endless questions. Finally, after an hour and a half, the cockatoo over in the corner flapped its wings and uttered a harsh squawk.

Sabrina looked at her watch, a delicate amethyst pendant on a silver chain around her neck. "Oh, dear. I'm afraid Lucifer is right. It is late, and I know you have other commitments. But this has been so very interesting, I quite forgot the time." She turned to Sebastian Vandermond. Through all the conversation he had sat slumped at her side, speaking only when she prompted him.

"Now, Sebastian, please take our guests back to Old-Billy. Unless"—she turned to Mike and Jake—"there is something that I could help you with here?"

Mike responded before Jake could make any comment. "Your home is delightful. I wonder if we might look around it more fully before we leave?"

"Why, I am *flattered*." Sabrina Vandermond stood up, revealing that she was indeed a tiny woman, the top of her head no higher than Jake's shoulder. "Come with me. Sebastian, if you will take care of the tea things while we are gone . . ."

She led them through half a dozen rooms, each decorated

with the same care and taste. No piece of furniture spoke of the present century, and few of the previous one. Only the library told a different story. The long rows of walnut and mahogany bookcases held thousands of books and data cubes. Mike wandered along the well-dusted rows, eyeing volumes and indices. They described mircoengineering methods in elaborate detail.

"You are an engineer?" he asked at last. "From these references . . ."

That provoked a silvery laugh. "Good heavens, no." Sabrina Vandermond came to stand by his side. "Those belong to Sebastian. He is an engineer—some say a very good one. My own background is far less distinguished. I'm nothing more than a simple, struggling chemist and would-be biologist. See, my side of the library is over there." She pointed to a rack of high-density data cubes and a single display, and shook her carefully-groomed head. "Little of it, you see, and little to interest you. It is convenient to have our libraries close together, since my brother helps me when I find something beyond me; which happens, I fear, all too often."

Mike wandered across to Sabrina Vandermond's library and glanced at the program and data file. The hundred or so data storage units each covered a specific subject and were alphabetically ordered. But if any were relevant to the brain of the Diamond Fly, Mike was unable to make that connection. He concentrated on one section of the rack and memorized the written labels.

Diffusion of lattice vacancies across grain boundaries stood next to *Energy levels and orbitals of complex molecules. Enzymatic chopping for inorganic materials* followed, and beyond that a program cube, *Fermi surfaces in face-centered and body-centered cubic cells*.

"Dull labors, I'm afraid." Sabrina placed her hand possessively on Mike's arm, easing him away from the storage rack and back toward the main living room. "I don't want to bore you with such things. But I do so enjoy your company. I know you are going to be very busy, but if you can somehow find any spare time to drop in, I would be absolutely delighted."

They were ushered on through the double doors. Sebastian Vandermond was standing outside, already cloaked and hatted. "Right. We must hurry." He strode on ahead of them, big, bulky, commanding. "We are already late. Old-Billy Waters is waiting."

The imperious manner, suppressed for nearly two hours, was back in full flower.

Old-Billy Waters had certainly not lied about one thing: he was no experienced negotiator. The preliminaries that should have taken a few minutes lasted for three hours; it was late afternoon when Waters returned Mike and Jake to their accommodation on the middle level of Raincloud's building.

As soon as they were alone, Mike made an inspection of their rooms. Jake went straight into the bathroom. When Mike joined him he was already at work on the tiny communicator set.

"On the way," he said. "I didn't want to risk telemetry being intercepted, so I gave our Fly the homing command. Anything new?"

Mike shook his head. "Same Flies, same positions. Nothing here in the bathroom. As a matter of interest, just where did you plant our Fly?"

"Right in the middle of the ugliest mural, where one of the savages was cutting somebody's head off. No one would look at that if they didn't have to." Jake peered into the thumbnail-sized screen of the communicator. "Here we come."

The Diamond Fly appeared through the open door and flew straight for the set that Jake was holding. It settled into a recess on the surface and stopped moving.

"Nearly four hours recorded," Jake said. "What do you want to search for?"

"How about audio references to 'Traders,' or to either of our names?"

"Easy enough. And we'll want associated video. I'll ask for everything from twenty seconds before each reference to the point where we decide to cut it." Jake bent over and set the search parameters with a tiny pointed stylus. Both men watched in silence for half a minute.

"Nothing," Mike was starting to say, when the little screen flickered and a color image appeared.

The room showed Martin Raincloud and Sabrina Vandermond, facing each other on two settees. Sabrina was wearing only a loose robe and had her back to the recording instrument. Raincloud, bare to the waist, was shaking his head.

"—to waste more time. You assured me a hundred times that everything was guaranteed, that once the Traders were here you could not fail."

"And I still say that." Sabrina was as calm and ladylike as ever. "I guarantee the results. But now that I have met with the two Traders—which, may I remind you, *you* did not want me to do—I am suggesting that we change the procedure a little. Kallario would probably be all right if we went ahead with the original plan, but I am less sure of Asparian. He was far too interested in my library, and studied it too closely. If I thought there was even the slightest suspicion that he understood enzymatic cutting and splicing methods . . ."

"What are you suggesting? That we proceed with Kallario alone, and dispose of Asparian permanently?"

"I think not." Sabrina fingered a tiny amethyst earring, her head cocked to one side. "We proceed," she said at last. "Immediately. Once the growth is complete, there is no danger at all that Asparian will make any brilliant and undesirable inferences. But to assure success, we must move immediately to hold the Traders in close confinement. And we plant the seed under close supervision."

"But if we confine them here they will want to know everything."

"Not at all. We will provide them with a bogus reason for staying in their quarters—a threat against their lives, a mad assassin loose in Skeleton City, a violent storm, anything. Within three days, I will know that the seed is planted and growing correctly inside them. After that—" She shrugged. "—they may return home anytime. Within thirty days the structure will be complete and in operation."

"I'm still not sure. Suppose it were to be detected." Martin Raincloud was staring at the ceiling, mouth pouting.

"After a dozen tests here, you are *still* unsure. Will you ever be sure?"

"There were side effects."

"Negligible ones. Three died. We can explain that. The rest averaged thirty or forty points decrease in IQ, but if I had not pointed that out to you, you would not have noticed. Your Traders will be less intelligent; so much the better. And you will have spies within the Trader headquarters itself, guided wherever you want and reporting anything you need. The first of many! You have seen what can be accomplished with the limited capabilities of the flying probes. Imagine that multiplied a hundredfold—a thousandfold."

Raincloud was nodding slowly. "Very well. We will proceed."

"Immediately!"

"Immediately. When they return from negotiation with Old-Billy, I will give orders that they are not to leave this building. And tonight, while they are sleeping, you will proceed with insertion of the seed."

The image flickered. Mike and Jake both turned to stare at the door, imagining it already guarded.

"How long ago?" Mike asked.

Jake was flicking the tiny controls. His face had gone gray. "That segment was recorded less than half an hour ago. Come on. We have to get out of here and call for a Smash rescue."

"How? If the exits are guarded, we'll never make it to an open area."

"We have to try. Maybe Raincloud hasn't given the order yet."

Mike stuffed the Fly and communicator into his pocket. They started for the door, then both hesitated.

"Casually," Jake said. He was shivering. "And slow. If we see we're blocked, we come back here."

The building had a narrow staircase that ran internally, beside the external up and down escalators. The living quarters assigned to Mike and Jake were halfway up, a thousand feet above ground level. They did not want to use the escalators. They crept down the staircase, story by story, for nearly four hundred feet, until they could finally see through the open latticework of the building to the surface.

Jake had been leading the way. He stopped and peered down. "We're too late. Look," he whispered.

A group of painted men was standing at the exit point of the downward escalator. As the Traders watched, four of them moved across to stand at the foot of the upward-moving escalator.

"Keep going on this staircase?"

Mike shook his head. "If they're guarding the escalator, they're on the stairs, too. Smell that?" A faint odor of burning dope was carrying up to them around the curve. "They're there. And I think I hear them. They're coming this way."

"What about the crosswalks?"

"Too conspicuous. They'd be sure to see us from below."

"What, then? They've got us."

"Up."

"To our rooms?"

"No. All the way up." Mike was already moving toward the escalator. "If we go to our rooms, they'll come and get us. We have to generate some bargaining power."

"Raincloud?"

"The only thing I can think of. If he's up there, we need him as our hostage."

The two Traders moved onto the escalator. Peering over the edge, Mike saw the group below still standing at the base. He ducked back. The escalator would give some shielding, and with luck no one would think to look straight up. Even if they did, in the late afternoon light they might not see Mike and Jake.

Lots of ifs; lots of maybes. Mike was about to say that to Jake Kallario when he saw a new expression on the other man's face. It was fear, a dreadful, consuming fear. Mike could not discuss with him the possibilities of failure.

He looked upward. They were at the top of the escalator, and the open staircase lay ahead. Now they would be far more visible from the ground.

The gale that Old-Billy Waters had predicted was not far off. Mike, creeping up the spiral staircase with one hand on the smooth wall, felt the building quivering under the lashing of the wind. The sky above was darkening. The top hundred feet of the building stood in lonely illumination, catching the last rays of the setting sun.

Outside the entrance to Raincloud's chambers Mike paused for breath. There were faint shouts, far below. Or was it imagination? Nothing would be audible above the wind. At his side Jake Kallario stood panting, nostrils dilated and eyes wild. He pushed past Mike, jerked open the door, and plunged through.

For a moment Mike thought that the living quarters were deserted. Then there was a startled grunt from the other room. Martin Raincloud, bare chested, had heard the noise and come bouncing in through the curtained entrance at the far end.

He took one look at the Traders and turned to run. Jake Kallario was a lot faster. By the time the cityboss was at the curtain, Kallario had dashed to the display, ripped a steel dagger loose, and grabbed Raincloud by the throat. "Asparian." His voice was shaking. "Find *her*. Take a look in the other room."

Mike grabbed a tomahawk for himself. He went warily through into the small display room beyond the curtain. Sabrina Vandermond was there. When she saw the weapon she raised her hands above her head.

"What is all this?" Her voice was calm. "I must say, I hope you have an explanation for such conduct."

Mike stepped to her side and gestured to the curtain. "Through there. Don't bother to make up lies for us."

With the tomahawk poised over her she walked in front of

him. In the other room, Jake Kallario had his knife at Martin Raincloud's throat.

"Jake! Steady!" Mike saw murder in his companion's eye. The point of the knife was drawing blood, probing deeper in to the thick neck. "Remember, we need *hostages*, not corpses."

Kallario crouched behind Raincloud. The knife drew back a fraction of an inch and slid around to the front of the neck. "I ought to slit your fat throat. And that murderous bitch's, too." His hand was trembling.

"And then what, Jake?" Mike moved Sabrina Vandermond forward. "You cut his throat, and then his friends come along and cut *yours*. And what does that do for us? Not a thing." Mike bent forward and spoke to the motionless prisoner. "Raincloud, we're going up to the roof now. Is that car of yours ready to fly?"

Raincloud nodded, his pop eyes hypnotized by the gleaming knife. "Yes." His voice was a hoarse whisper. "Yes, it's all prepared. Fully fuelled. Don't cut me."

"You're a miserable coward, Martin," Sabrina Vandermond said. "And you fools will never get away," she added to the Traders.

"We'll see. Lead the way, Raincloud." Kallario whipped the knife clear of Martin Raincloud's neck and pressed its point hard against the middle of his bare back. "If anything happens to me, it happens to you first. Asparian, you take care of that whore."

A short flight of stairs led to a trapdoor and the open roof. While Jake Kallario prodded Raincloud toward the aircar, Mike took Sabrina Vandermond by the arm and made a quick detour to the edge of the roof. He grasped the rail beyond the shallow lip and looked over. Half a dozen dark dots showed against the silver ribbon below. They were moving at a run up the escalator.

"They're coming, Asparian," Sabrina said. "You'll never get away. Give up now, and I'll guarantee that you are not harmed."

"Sure. How many dead men have trusted you?" Mike hurried back toward the little aircar. Jake Kallario already had the cockpit open. The other two were inside, and Raincloud, seated in front of Jake, was at the controls. The knife was pricking the neck of the cityboss.

"They're coming," Mike shouted. "Let's get out of here." He was a few feet away from the aircar, pushing Sabrina in front of him and moving fast. He lifted her to the edge of the wing just as the cockpit slammed shut in front of his nose.

"Jake!" Mike hammered on the glass. "What the hell are you doing?"

For reply Kallario pointed to the car's cramped interior and shook his head. "Two people." He was smiling as he mouthed the words. "Only two people. Tough luck, Mike. Good-bye."

He waved. At the same moment, Sabrina Vandermond broke from Mike's grasp and ran for the trapdoor.

The rocket jets ignited, firing down for vertical takeoff. A wash of orange fire spread out from the aircar, bathing Mike's feet with flame. The searing flood caught Sabrina, halfway down the trapdoor, at waist height. It set alight her loose robe. She screamed once and vanished in a pillar of golden flame.

Mike turned and ran. As a flash of heat frizzled his hair, he threw himself over the lip of the roof. His hands caught and held the thin guard rail as his body somersaulted out, over, and down, turning until his hips smacked against the side wall of the building. A sheet of white fire flashed out above him, searing the backs of his hands. Mike hung on, facing out into space, and kicked off his burning shoes. They curved out, away from the building, and fell smoldering into darkness.

With a scream of engines, the aircar ascended into the darkening sky; as it did so, the swirl of fire across the roof diminished. Mike swung his feet up, and on the second attempt managed to hook his knees over the rail. But he could not move his body upward, or reach the edge of the roof itself. He tried until he was exhausted and the flesh was peeling from his burned fingers. Then he hung, head down, by hands and knees, and stared at the tracery of lighted streets two thousand feet below.

The gale had arrived in full force and it was blowing away the world. It beat at him, rocked his scorched body, cradled him, crooned to him, told him to relax. He closed his eyes. He could sleep now, release his hold, fly forever into the quiet darkness . . .

The sound of voices from the roof did not rouse him. They were distant, far less real than the screaming wind. He hung there, batlike, until there was an exclamation from close to hand. "Grab him. Haul him in."

Mike clung tighter.

"We can't move him. His hands are locked. And burned to blazes."

"Move out of the way, then. Let me have a go."

Powerful arms reached out. Mike was lifted by the knees until his legs were dragged onto the roof and he was forced to release his handhold or dislocate his shoulders. He was lifted again, turned, and placed on his feet. He found he was gazing into the startled eyes of Old-Billy Waters. The deputy surveyed him from burned hair to seared feet.

"Gawd, you're a mess. What happened?"

Mike turned, searching the eastern sky. After a few seconds he saw it, a brighter spark of light against the stars. He pointed. "There they are. Jake Kallario and Martin Raincloud."

Waters followed the pointing arm. "The boss is up there, too? I wondered where he'd gone. He hasn't flown in a year." His eye traced the line of flight. "My God, what's he doing? They're flying due east. Where are they going?"

"Kallario is in control. Raincloud is just piloting."

"But he's flying smack into the air defense shield! I knew it, it's his own damned system, and he doesn't know the first thing about how it works. If they keep going that way—" Old-Billy Waters grabbed for his waist. He lifted the set to his mouth. Before he could speak there was a streak of mauve light on the eastern horizon, ending in a white magnolia blossom. The sound of the explosion took almost a minute to arrive.

Mike Asparian and Old-Billy Waters stared at each other while the wind howled across the roof. Finally Old-Billy shivered, turned east again, and rubbed his bald scalp. "He's gone."

"He has. They have." Mike swayed, straightened. "You're cityboss now, Old-Billy. You run Skeleton City."

"He's really gone. I can't believe it." Water's voice was quiet and introspective. He coughed, bowing his head into the wind.

"It's your job now." Mike saw the blackened remains of a female figure crumpled near the trapdoor. "All yours. What are you going to do?"

Old-Billy's brow was furrowed. He sniffed, straightened, and gestured to two of the men to help Mike. "I don't know. Not yet. But let's get below. If you're well enough, you and I have to talk about a deal."

"He's alive, and that's all I can say. I don't know how he held out as long as he did. He managed a meeting with Waters, did a data dump on the plane as he flew back, and collapsed. Now are you willing to admit that the mission was a fiasco?"

"Any mission where a Trader dies is a fiasco, Lyle."

"One dead, another half-dead in the rehab tank—with no sign of emotional responses. And what did we get out of it? Nothing worth having."

"False." Daddy-O knew that Lyle Connery was overreact-

ing, and was suitably mild in reply. *"We obtained many things: a new and better relationship with the Great Republic; a signed agreement between the Republic and the Strines. Perhaps, when Asparian is again willing to talk—"*

"—if he ever is."

"He will be. I am monitoring his responses, and Jack Lester is working with him. When he can talk, we may have additional information about the arms buildup in the Republic. And we will also gain new understanding of Mikal Asparian himself; and, most important of all, we have furthered his development."

"Which we could have done right here, without Mike leaving Trader base."

"That is a beguiling notion, but unfortunately it is not true. 'Es bildet ein Talent sich in der Stille, sich ein Charakter in dem Strom der Welt.'"

"Eh?"

"The words of an old Community writer, penned over two hundred years ago. It means, approximately, that talent is built in peace and quiet, but character in the full flow of the real world. I knew that sending Mikal Asparian to the Great Republic might harm him; but it was also the only way to strengthen him."

"It killed Jake Kallario."

"There is always risk. As you were the first to notice, Kallario contained the seeds of instability long before we went on that mission."

"And you've not strengthened Mike. You're turning him to a lump of stone. Think of *his* feelings. Melinda Turak dies, and then Jake Kallario, and Mike blames himself for both deaths—and don't tell me it's illogical, it's still the way he feels. And it's damned cruel."

"Indeed it is." Daddy-O generated a sigh. *"Lyle, Traders have accused me of being heartless fourteen thousand seven hundred and eighty-three times. Each was, of course, technically correct. However, there is a promise for you: there will be only two more missions for Mikal Asparian; after that, I expect to take no part in any of his assignments. Will that satisfy you?"*

"I suppose it has to." Lyle Connery cut contact. He was marginally satisfied for only a moment. Good enough. But was it? Fourteen thousand seven hundred and eighty-three times Daddy-O has been accused of heartlessness. And how many times had the computer been accused of low cunning?

* * *

"*...of course, I would never have left her alone if I'd known. When I came back in, she had it out of the packet. She was holding it in her hand, pointing it out of the window, and looking down one end. So I tried to grab her—*"

"Where am I?" Mike had been aware for some time of the voice in his ear, but it had only just begun to make approximate sense.

"*Haven't you been listening, then?*" The aggrieved voice, Mike realized, was Lover-boy Lester's. "*Well, that's a pain—why did yer keep making grunting noises? Waste of my time hooking in to you. How yer feeling?*"

"I'm not feeling, Jack." Mike found that he had no sensations at all. And it went beyond the physical. He felt no stir of emotion. "Nothing at all."

"*Then you must be all right. Don't you know where you are? You're in the tank, boyo, next to mine. Don't you remember coming here?*"

Mike tried to move his hands up to touch his face. Nothing. He tried to shake his head. Nothing. "The last thing I remember is shaking hands with Old-Billy Waters and climbing into the aircar. I guess we made it back. Am I badly hurt?"

"*Hurt? Nah! Just scratches. I've been banged up worse than that fightin' in bed. You'll be out of the tank in a couple of weeks. You did all right, boyo. Don't you remember giving Daddy-O a data dump on the plane?*"

"No. Not a glimmer of it. What did I tell him?"

"*About the Fly. What it was, how it was made.*"

"But that's impossible. I don't *know* how it was made."

"*You don't think you do. But you must have known it subconsciously, because you gave Daddy-O all the pieces: what was in Sabrina Vandermond's library, and what you heard her say in her apartment, and then what she said later to the cityboss. And you kept saying in the plane, 'you have to start on the other side.' Daddy-O interpreted all that, and put things together.*"

"You mean you know how the Fly brain was made?" Mike's own brain was dull and numb.

"*It wasn't.*"

"Wasn't what?"

"*Wasn't made. The brain. Not mechanically, the way we usually think. The brain was too small—even the Chills can't make machinery that operates down below the molecular level. The Chills call it the molecular barrier.*"

"I knew that."

"So there's no way you can get past that barrier with mechanical methods. You try to make things smaller and smaller, but then you find you've hit quantum levels, trying to manipulate single molecule layers. So how can you possibly build something smaller than that? There's only one answer, the one you gave Daddy-O: you have to start on the other side of the barrier. You have to be a chemist, and a microbiologist, not an engineer, and you have to use chemical processes that build from the atoms upward to the molecules, using tailored chemical reactions—just the way the enzymes in living tissues do it. Remember the program library you saw: inorganic solid state lattice theory, side-by-side with enzymatic processes for living tissue. The Fly's brain wasn't made, Mike, it was grown, chemically, like an organism, using methods developed by that woman Sabrina Vandermond, with her brother's help on the engineering."

Mike remembered that elegant head and those smiling gray eyes. "She was an amazing woman."

"Good-looking, was she? You sound as if you'd fancy a little bit there."

Lover-boy never changed. But instead of irritation or amusement, Mike felt only weariness. The memory of an elegant head *flowed*, to become a nimbus of flaming hair, then a vision of a blackened skull, soft cheeks burned away by jet exhausts to show white, grinning teeth beneath. "I cannot think of her in that way, Lover-boy. She and the cityboss were psychopaths— they didn't care what happened to anybody else. That was the thing that drove Jake crazy and made him so desperate to escape. He knew that Sabrina was going to inject those crystal seeds into our brains, and she would do it coldly, without thinking twice. Once it was done the Yankees could control us completely—we'd have been smart, mobile information sources."

Mike paused. He was running down, running out of energy, sinking into lethargy. He could not stop thinking of Sabrina Vandermond, and somehow her memory was pulling into his mind old and long-suppressed thoughts of his childhood in the Hives. He began to shiver.

"Mike? Are you all right?"

"Except that you're not all that smart with that seed in you." Mike's voice had thinned to a faint whisper. "You go from being a fairly bright man to a near-moron."

"You mean it wipes out your brains?"

"No abstract thoughts any more, no complex emotions. No

fears, no longings. It knocks your intelligence way down."

"Does it? Gor." Even Lover-boy sounded subdued. *"What would it feel like, Mike?"*

Mike was silent for a long time. "I don't know," he said at last. "I wish I did."

CHAPTER 13

D earest Mikal,

Once upon a time there was a princess who lived in a land where everything was perfect and beautiful. She was beautiful, too, and when she grew to womanhood many local princes tried to win her favors. Lots of them succeeded for a while (she was pretty easy—I know you won't like that bit), but she always grew tired of them. After a couple of weeks she sent each of them away, heartbroken.

She knew they were heartbroken (they told her so) and she was a kindhearted girl, so she worried and worried trying to decide why they had become boring to her. Finally she had the answer. They were handsome and intelligent and accomplished, but they were *local* princes. What she wanted was a foreign prince, one who would ride in from far away, vanquish all suitors in fair combat, and take her for his own.

When she had almost given up hope that it could ever happen, a foreign prince arrived. He seemed to like her as much as she liked him, and they had a wonderful time for a couple of months. But then he left. It was her turn to be heartbroken, and to wonder if he would ever return.

He did, years later. But now he was badly injured. He had been in a terrible battle, over on the other side of the world, and for a while she thought she could do nothing to help him. He had no energy, no happiness, no enthusiasm.

Finally, the princess had an idea. She thought he might find interest in the local versions of the battles that he had fought so far away. Even if he lost, it might prove a useful therapy. And it might help him to recover some of his strength.

He didn't want to do it, but she worked on him. Finally, after much persuasion, he entered a tournament.

It was a massacre. He was still terribly weak, and badly injured. But he beat the local champions, one after another, so easily that it was never a contest. It was like a man fighting infants. His strength and energy quickly came back to him. No one could stand against him.

Mikal, you tell me you would have to be crazy ever to go back to being a Trader. You can make such a good living here in the Community, and so easily.

Let me tell you another fairy story. Two hundred years ago, a country north of here had a king who was certainly crazy. Instead of spending his time fighting wars and winning territories, King Ludwig of Bavaria built wild castles, all over the countryside. He built them at the tops of mountains, and down by rivers, and in places that even the goats found hard to reach. He had outrageous tastes, and he built soaring towers, and jagged battlements, and magnificent formal gardens. The other kings of the region all laughed at him; by the time he died, his treasury was exhausted and the whole country had been dotted with fairy-story castles.

They are still there, most of them. You and I have even visited a couple. And everything that all the other kings did has been long forgotten.

You have to go back, Mike. I may fool you for a while, but one day you'll realize that I'm not for you. I'm intended for the homegrown princes, with their paper armor and cardboard swords. You are not like them. Even when you were weak and sick, you beat them so easily that there must have been no pleasure for you in the victory. There is not a negotiator in the whole of the Economic Community that you could not best while you were drunk or sick or half-asleep. I've seen you do it, and it frightened me. If you can manipulate others like that, what could you do to me if you tried?

I'm made of paper, too—deny it, I hope you will—but until you came I didn't know it. I have learned it in the past three months. You burn too brightly for me. You would consume me, destroy me. It has already begun. You don't realize it yet, but you've recovered from your wounds, and now you are itching for another big challenge. I can't provide that. You have to go back and fight your real dragons, and build your great castles around the world, and be the greatest Trader that the Earth has ever seen.

Do it now. Please go, Mikal, with my blessing. But come back anytime if you are sad or hurt—or just want to say hello.

Love, as always,
Jeannette

The bad news was waiting on the table when Mike came down to breakfast. The dining room was empty, but covered dishes of hot food had been left ready for him. Propped against one of them, prominent in its perfumed blue envelope, sat the letter.

Mike read it through twice, the first time with incomprehension, the second with bewilderment.

It was some sort of sick joke. A hoax. Not perpetrated by Jeanette—she wouldn't think it was funny—but by someone else, maybe one of the people he had bested locally in trade negotiations.

Mike carried the letter to the west-facing window and allowed the diffuse morning sunlight to play on the pages. He had intended to scan it again, searching for some clue as to what was going on, but before he could begin reading, another truth could no longer be denied: It was Jeanette's handwriting; by now he knew every stroke and loop, the peculiar back curve of the *f* and the *p*. And so it could be no hoax.

Not a joke.

Jeanette had left him. The shock of the thought made him cold all over. *Why* would she do it? In all their months together they had never had an argument, never an angry word. He had never been so happy and so at home. But Jeanette had left him.

Run out on him. In a fraction of a second, bewilderment turned to violent anger. What the hell was going on? This wasn't a spur-of-the-moment thing, it had to be a *planned* betrayal. Jeanette wasn't one to act casually, and now it was clear that she had intended to do this for a long time. A week ago, she had insisted that they cease their travels through the Economic Community and return to this inn, where they had first met, to "bring things full circle." That had meant nothing at the time; now it was very clear. Even the breakfast sitting on the table was an ironic gesture, the same meal as the first she had ever cooked for him. More symbolism. Jeanette was nothing if not consistent.

He read the letter anyway, but could find nothing new there, nothing to give him hope. He went back to sit hopelessly at the table. She had gone, and he could not bear to lose her. What could he do now? Only one thing: he would seek her out and tell her that she was wrong. Persuade her to stay with him.

He could do it; she always said he could persuade her to do anything.

Mike stood up, ready to rush to the door, and as he did so there crept into his mind the cold, quiet touch of reality.

He sat down again. Jeanette was right. She was *exactly* right. He felt as though he were waking from a pleasant dream, a personal fugue that had lasted for many months. Ever since the death of Jake Kallario, nothing had been real. Mike had been looking away, hiding his feelings, burying his old ambitions under a dead clay of indifference. Now, with the shock of Jeanette's letter, dormant feelings were springing back to life.

Jeanette had seen it all and said nothing. First she had coaxed him back to health, hiding her knowledge until he was well enough to live with the truth. And then she had done what she thought best.

But now . . . for God's sake, what now? Mike grimaced and pulled dishes of food toward him. *Food, drink, sleep—take them whenever you have a chance;* training died hard. He ate every morsel of food, drank every drop of coffee. Sleep would have to wait. He could feel a stirring inside him now, the itch to leave the lotusland of the Community and venture again into the Trader's world. Six months ago he had never wanted to hear of a negotiation again. Today, he longed for the challenge. He had to leave before he lost his nerve again.

Mike stood up, reached for a pen, and scribbled on the envelope: *Jeanette, I'm going back. But save a few paper dragons—just in case. Love always, Mikal.*

He walked through into the little room at the back of the kitchen and picked up the antiquated communications device. As soon as his charge code was accepted, he set up a connection to Daddy-O.

CHAPTER 14

The door was visible as a dull black rectangle down at the end of the semicircular tiled corridor. Mike had limped along that curve at a fair clip, conscious of the ringing echoes from his own studded boots. But as he approached the door his pace gradually slowed. A few feet from it he stopped completely.

The portal was tall and broad, a slab of thick ebony. Mike knew very well what lay behind it: Maxwell Robert Dalzell, Master Trader.

Mike had seen the name of Dalzell on his first day as a trainee, when with forty-three other hopefuls he had wandered around the perimeter of the classroom looking at the names, pictures, and dates embossed on the paneled walls. His attention had been taken by the devil's grin and bright blue eyes on one of the pictures. He stopped to read the name and look at the full description.

Maxwell Robert Dalzell: graduate of the Traders' training course thirty years ago, at the age of seventeen. Master Trader seven years later, an unheard-of accomplishment for one as young as twenty-four. One more year, and Dalzell had engineered the signing of the first power treaty between the Great Republic and the Chills. He had made the first Trader trip to space, for discussions and negotiation with the Chipponese; and he was the absolute expert on the Unified Empire, with more than fifty successful trips to his credit to every major center from Mexity to F'waygo.

Since that first day, Dalzell and his exploits had never been far from Mike's thoughts. They had been flags to wave him on to greater personal efforts. That knowledge ran through his head now, when he at last touched the monitor at the side of the entrance.

The door slid open with a purr of motors at the base. He stepped forward and found himself looking into an empty room. "Be with you in a few minutes, Asparian," said a voice from inside the door itself. "I'm recording in the inner room. Come in and make yourself comfortable."

The room Mike entered was sparsely furnished with a desk, two chairs, and a long row of file cabinets. There was one other door: a plain sheet of solid steel at the far end, with heavy cipher locks on its edges. The walls were seamless, white-painted, and decorated everywhere with plaques and photographs. The desk top was covered with mementos, statues, and images.

Mike stood for a few seconds gazing expectantly at the inner door, then went to sit in the visitor's chair. He stared at the desktop array. It was a display of Trader memorabilia, beyond anything he ever seen or heard of outside the Trader Museum. There was a signed copy—or was it the original?—of the first Unified Empire/Cap Federation joint venture. Maxwell Dalzell had arranged that one himself. It was standing on part of a holmium Chipponese trading token, the sort they had used before the Traders brought them in line with the currencies of the other major regions. Dalzell again! Next to the platelike token was a facsimile of an early Yankee-Trader treaty, and behind it stood a picture of a smiling Strine bigmomma, displaying one of the first biolab products allowed to emerge from the Strine Interior.

There was no doubt where Dalzell's heart lay. None of the pictures showed the man himself, but every one was some personal triumph of Trader negotiation. Mike was still admiring them when the inner door opened and a tall, strongly-built man breezed through.

"Hello." He gave Mike a casual nod. "Don't need to bother with formal introductions, do we? I'm Max Dalzell, and you're Mikal Asparian. No, don't stand up," he went on, as Mike started to struggle to his feet. "I'm not the Trader Anthem." He flashed Mike the famous wide grin that went well with the abrupt manner. "Daddy-O says you're all charged up and raring for a new mission. Right?"

"I'm certainly ready to give it a try. I hope I'm not rusty."

"Don't worry about it. A good Trader never loses the knack.

And from everything I've heard, you really needed a break. But the vacation's over. Now it's time for work." Dalzell flopped into the chair behind the desk and gave Mike a quick, appraising glance. That gave Mike a chance for his own inspection—he had seen pictures of Dalzell, dozens of them, but this was his first face-to-face encounter with a senior idol.

He saw a man almost a head taller than his own medium height, with a loose, athletic swing to the shoulders. The arms were well muscled in the short-sleeved shirt, and his wrists were thick and powerful, supporting massive, blunt-fingered hands. The surprise came lower on the body. Dalzell had a substantial paunch at his midriff—something never shown on his pictures. And his face was fuller and saggier than Mike expected, with jowls, a broader nose, and signs of a double chin.

A legend growing old; inevitable, but it couldn't have happened inside Mike's imagination. Dalzell was enshrined there as the golden-haired Master Trader, the youngest in history. Now the hair was receding from the temples, and it was streaked with gray.

The grin was still the same, though, and the gleam in the blue eyes was unchanged. It was clear that Maxwell Dalzell enjoyed big natural advantages as a Trader. There was something in that look and smile that reached out and demanded instant respect and sympathy. It made Mike suddenly dissatisfied with his own appearance.

There was another smile from across the desk, and a little nod of the graying head. "Fine. Inspections complete? Then let's talk. We've got a lot of ground to cover. We're going to be worrying today about the Cap Federation territories. How much do you know about the Chills?"

Mike thought for a moment and decided on the most honest answer. "If I weren't talking to Max Dalzell, I'd say I know a lot. But everyone says you're the expert. They say you've forgotten more about the Cap Federation than most people have ever learned."

"They do, do they?" Dalzell frowned, but did not look either surprised or displeased. "I ought to be used to what 'they' say about me, but I never am. But I can tell you this, I know the Greasers a whole lot better than I'll ever know the Chills—and I've got lots to learn about both of 'em. Now, how good is the grapevine these days? Did anyone leak why you're here?"

"No, sir." Mike hesitated, but Dalzell simply sat and waited.

When he wanted to he gave an impression of infinite patience and unlimited time. "I received a message from Daddy-O, telling me I'm well enough for a new mission."

"Do you agree?"

There was the heart of the matter. "I'm not sure, sir."

"Well, we'll see. And while you're at it, you can stop calling me, sir." Dalzell leaned back in his chair and folded his arms across his belly. "Daddy-O tells me you're pretty damned good. How do you feel about that?"

"I hope I'm good, sir." Mike winced, but the last word had popped out involuntarily. He shrugged. "You know, Rule Ten." *If you don't have confidence in your ability, no one else will.*

"Damn right." Dalzell's gruff voice sounded delighted with the reply. "And that's the answer I was hoping for. So let's get down to it. I can tell you now: you'll *need* to be good for this one. We're talking of an official mission down onto the ice cap, to the middle of Cap Federation territory. You'll need to be one hotshot negotiator. The Unified Empire wants us to act on its behalf for a ten-year deal on gaming-table robot controllers. They're finally admitting what I've been telling 'em for fifteen years—the Chills are so far ahead of everybody else in microelectronics that nobody else has a hope of competing. Apparently it's finally sunk into their thick skulls, and they called me ten days ago. I set out terms they can live with, and I'm fairly sure Cap City will go along with them."

There was a lot hidden behind those words. Dalzell was doing his best to build Mike's enthusiasm and confidence, but more than that he was pointing out the difference between a Trader and a Master Trader: One didn't just *negotiate* a deal if one wanted to go to the top—one sold the idea of the deal *in the first place*. And terms of agreement that both sides would be able to live with were set up before anyone ever got near the negotiation table.

Dalzell was staring at him. "Well? Ready to try it? You don't look too keen."

Mike nodded reluctant agreement. "I'm ready to take the assignment, naturally. But it sounds as though you've already done the hard work."

"Dead right." The grin again. "By design. We want you to have lots of time to spare when you're down on the ice cap. You see, your second agenda item is a dilly. Ready for the old hook?"

Mike sat up straighter.

"Ever hear of Seth Paramine?"

"No, sir."

"Good. You shouldn't have. Ever hear of an idiot savant?"

"A . . . knowing idiot, isn't that what the words mean?"

"They do. But I think you'll admit that doesn't make much sense. Don't feel too bad, I was in the same position a week ago. 'Idiot savant' is a phrase used to describe a special sort of person, normal or often very subnormal in most areas, but with special talents in a particular field. We're all like that in some ways—you could train me forever, and I'd never be able to carry a tune—but the idiot savants take it to extremes. Take a look at something."

Dalzell leaned across to the control settings on the desk. A portion of the wall in front of Mike turned to reveal a holographic projection field. As the room lights dimmed, he found himself looking into a large bare room. The only furnishings were a thick carpet, with small spheres and oblongs of bright plastic scattered randomly across it, and a pile of white cardboard sheets next to them. Seated in the middle of the mess, head hunched forward on his shoulders, was an overweight youth in his late teens. His lower legs were bare, and he wore only a plain white smock that covered him from neck to knees. He was holding half a dozen of the colored plastic spheres and idly sliding them over each other.

"Seth Paramine," Dalzell said. "Nineteen years old. Born in the northern part of the Great Republic, in the wheat belt. Parents both normal, but he didn't learn to stand until he was five, or walk until he was six and a half. He said his first word at ten. He cannot read or write, or speak a complete sentence. He is sexually mature, but has no interest in sex. Until two years ago, the institute where he stayed thought he had no interest in *anything*, except food and toys. But they were wrong. Watch closely now. This is a top-secret recording that no other Traders have seen."

The fat youth had stopped playing with the plastic balls and was staring around him. The face was dull and doughy, with deep-set eyes under a beetling brow. After a few more seconds he reached out his left hand and took one of the big cardboard sheets off the pile. He peered at it for a long time, rubbing the side of his nose with his fingers.

"Patience," Max Dalzell said softly. "We're nearly there now."

The youth bent his head down to an inch or two from the

sheet. Then he grunted and took a fat pencil from the pocket of his white smock. He began to mark the surface of the cardboard. The field of view zoomed in to show that the original white board was covered with a complicated network of crossing and intersecting lines. The pencil was being used to mark in changes to the pattern. Mike could hear the grunts and mutters of satisfaction as the work went on. Finally, the field of view moved back, and after another few seconds the image blinked out of existence.

"Mysterious enough, I imagine," Dalzell said as the lights of the room came back to full strength. "It was to me, until I was given the explanation. Seth Paramine is one of that rare group of people, the idiot savants. And he is a *spectacular* example. Those cardboard sheets are electronic schematics—circuit diagrams, blown up thousands of times over their original dimensions. They came from Chill microcircuits, and they're the most advanced gadgets on the market. What you saw there was Seth Paramine studying the designs—and *improving* them. He can't write his name. He wears diapers. In every area of the world except one, he's a complete idiot. But he has an intuitive grasp of microcircuit functional design that no one else can understand or equal. In the area of electronic analysis, he's a genius."

Mike remembered the squat figure and the inert, lifeless face. "That's ridiculous!"

"It is—but it's true." Max Dalzell slid a thin wafer across the top of the desk. "Take a look at some of the data on that. People like Paramine are rare, but they crop up now and again in a lot of different fields. Daddy-O pulled together a whole batch of information about other cases scattered over the past few centuries, just to give us background. Some of them are damned near unbelievable, but they're all authentic. The most common cases seem to be in mathematics and music. Play through the data and I guarantee you'll be surprised. So far as Daddy-O knows, Paramine is the first in his particular field. But the field didn't *exist* a century ago, so that's not too surprising."

Mike picked up the wafer and slipped it into his pocket. "I'll listen to it. But I'm confused. Paramine lives up in the northern part of the Great Republic, and I'm going to the South Pole. What's it have to do with my mission? What's the connection?"

"A strong one." Dalzell was enjoying himself. "You see, Mike, Seth Paramine isn't up in Yankeeland any more. He's down on the ice cap. The Chills are the world experts on microcircuit design, and so when they somehow heard about him, they wanted him. They took him. Four days ago, Seth Paramine disappeared from the institution in the Great Republic. He hasn't been heard from since—but all the evidence suggests a Chill smash operation. They're damn near as good at a rapid, quiet pickup as we are."

"What do they want him for? They have genius designers of their own."

"But none with such strange design logic. According to the Yankees, the Chills don't want Paramine to *design* for them— they just want to poke around inside his head, to know *how he does it*."

"Do we have proof that the Chills are holding Paramine?"

"Not *proof*—and the Chills aren't going to admit a thing— but there's some pretty good indirect evidence. The Yankees suspected the Chills as soon as Paramine was kidnapped and disappeared. Old-Billy Waters acted fast, and signed with the Chipponese to buy high-resolution surveillance from polar orbit. A couple of the frames that came back showed somebody a lot like Paramine in transit from Cap City to an isolated station. He's seen climbing into an aircar, and then getting out at Mundsen Labs. That would be the logical place for him, along with the rest of their hotshot hardware architects."

"Is Old-Billy likely to try a rescue?"

"No way. He knows he'd fail for sure. You know the Chill defense system. So Old-Billy is angry as hell, but he's not ready to break off dealing with the Chills. He needs 'em too much. And Paramine really isn't much use to the Republic—they don't have the right technology base. I think they'd have sold him to the Chills for any decent offer. But Old-Billy would like to have absolute proof that Paramine was kidnapped, then he'll really stick that in the Chills' ear on the next big negotiation. Which is where we—or rather you—come in. Still interested in the assignment?"

Mike started to give an upward wriggling shrug of his shoulders. He stopped when he realized that it was a gesture he had picked up as a trainee, from pictures of Maxwell Dalzell. "It means I have to find a way to get myself inside Mundsen Labs and make recordings of Paramine."

"That's the bottom line. We'll help. But there are lots of details to worry about. I'm going to bring Daddy-O into the loop—that's the sort of thing a computer does better than we'd ever do it. But let me mention one other thing before we open the circuit. You'll be absolutely on your own once you reach the ice cap. No Mentor, no partner."

"Good." Mike spoke almost under his breath. "I've had all I can take with team missions."

"I understand. We'll put in the new fingertip recorder. It's a mile ahead of the old recording disk, but it won't help anyone unless you get back here. When we throw in those factors, Daddy-O doesn't put your chances very high—in fact, all the outputs set the probability level of your success between one and two percent. I'm willing to back you, even with those odds —if you are game."

Mike took a deep breath. Now or never. I have to prove to myself that I'm out of the slump, even if it kills me. "I want it. I want the job."

"Great." Dalzell leaned forward to grasp Mike's hand in his. Mike felt as though an electric discharge had crackled across between them. "I was sure you would. It's going to be a mission in a million. Damn it, I just wish I could go with you."

"So do I." There was real feeling in Mike's voice.

"But it's impossible. They tell me I've got too many Trader secrets inside my head."

Mike nodded. He would have given a lot to have Big Max there to prompt him. He licked his lips nervously, something he could not imagine Max Dalzell doing, ever, and felt a first tremble of nervous anticipation.

"I'm ready." He stood up. "And thanks for the chance. When do I leave?"

CHAPTER 15

Idiot savant. Daddy-O had given Mike all he could handle about that subject on the Trader flight down to F'waygo. Waiting for the Chill connection that would take him to Cap City, Mike thought again about Seth Paramine. The Yankee youth was merely the most recent in a long and curious line.

Two hundred years before, there had been Blind Tom Bethune, a sightless, half-witted Negro slave. Born in 1849, he was scarcely able to speak, and he had to be coaxed into playing the piano by gifts of cakes and candy from his owner. But he had absolute pitch and a phenomenal memory. He could imitate any sound he heard, and he rattled off any piece of piano music, no matter how complicated, after one hearing.

Tom Fuller was another Negro slave, from a century earlier. He was illiterate, but he had tremendous calculating powers. He shared those characteristics with Jed Buxton, an Englishman. They could multiply ten digit numbers, extract square and cube roots, and factorize large numbers in their heads, rapidly, without error—and without being able to tell in any way how they did it.

The twentieth-century mathematician Srinivasa Ramanujan was in some ways the most remarkable of all. He was a quiet, superstitious, Indian clerk, with no obvious abilities—until an uninvited letter to Hardy at Cambridge University revealed that Ramanujan had made important mathematical discoveries without help from colleagues, training, or books. He had an amazing memory and an uncanny familiarity with the properties of numbers, but he was unable to explain the mental processes that led to his results.

And now there was Seth Paramine. The films made at the Yankee institution showed his physical appearance and actions, but they gave no clue as to the mental processes inside that deformed skull. Paramine spent most of his days sitting on the floor, playing with children's toys. But now and again, according to a schedule that no one had been able to fathom, there was a burst of activity. He would feverishly work on circuit analysis and design, rearranging whole blocks of elements. The Yankee tests suggested that his approach was not analytical. He seemed to grasp the whole circuit at once, in one swoop, and sometimes he would begin to make his changes only a few seconds after the enlarged board diagram was given to him.

Only two other things aroused any animation in him at all. He dreaded pins, needles, and scissors, and he had an absolute terror of fire and flames. Attempts to track down a cause for his phobias had all failed.

And what are my own phobias? Mike wondered. Are they any less than his?

As he watched the Chill transfer craft feather to a landing on the F'waygo field, he worried again about the mission. Had he been thinking too much about Paramine, and not enough about the primary negotiation for gaming-table robots? Could he handle *that*, even without the other agenda?

Negotiation with the Chills was supposed to be particularly hard. Mike recalled Max Dalzell's final warning:

"Most Trainees believe the Chipponese are the most alien of the groups, simply because they live off-Earth. But for my money the Chills make 'em look like our brothers and sisters. Don't forget how the Chills got their start. Talk about evolution the hard way! Four thousand scientists in a research facility, invaded by a million refugees. No food supplies and no energy —in a place where plants don't grow and solar power is useless. That's something to remember in your discussions with them. When the people you'll be negotiating with were children they were half-starved, every one of 'em. They had vitamin deficiencies, and they were dirty—no spare energy for luxuries like hot water. The Chills are *different*." He had rolled one of his sleeves all the way up the shoulder to reveal a long, deep scar. "Here's an example of what can happen when a Chill negotiation goes wrong. It took me totally by surprise. Until one of the Chills put a dart through my arm, I thought I had everything under perfect control. But I made a joke about a penguin not being sure if it was a bird or a fish. And I got this. The others took her away after she did it, and I never saw her again. I'll give you a Trader's Rule that you'll not see in the formal or the informal rule books: Never try to joke with a Chill." He had laughed and squeezed Mike's shoulder. "Well, now I've got you nice and relaxed, I'll say so long—and good luck."

And I'm going to need it, Mike thought, watching the Chill flight crew file into the transfer lobby. There were two men and four women, all deeply suntanned and dressed in skintight light garments that left their arms and legs bare. Their style of dress confirmed the skimpy outfit that Daddy-O had provided. As a fledging trainee, Mike had been ready for warm swaddling clothes, all the way up to his eyes. Instead he had learned that the Chills preferred sunsuits that looked just right for a vacation in Ree-o-dee.

Most of the Chill crew continued through to the port clearance area, but one of the women peeled off from the others and walked directly across to where Mike was sitting. She came to stand in front of him and stared for a few seconds without speaking. Then she shook her head and looked totally disgusted.

"I'm Mikal Asparian." Mike did not stand, or reach out a hand, but he made his expression friendly.

She was a tall brunette, with a spare, angular figure and a thin-nosed, handsome face. She nodded, unsmiling. "I am Kristen Waldemar, assigned to this negotiation. We wondered about your name." Her voice was soft and puzzled. "Sweet Scott. It is true, then—you are a man."

What did you expect—a kangaroo? Mike nodded and tucked her name away into his memory. *Get everything else wrong if you have to, but get their names right.* "I look forward to working with you."

She averted her eyes as he stood up to look at her. "Follow me. We will be on our way in a few minutes."

She turned and walked off toward port clearance, not looking back to see if he was following. Mike trailed along five paces behind. He felt very much alone. Kristen Waldemar had looked annoyed and said just enough to make him feel unwelcome. Chill negotiation technique? Too soon to tell.

The whole Chill group was standing, ready to leave. Whether or not Mike was welcome, there was one formality of greeting that would not be neglected. He was prepared for it.

"To fruitful discussions!" Kristen Waldemar said curtly. She handed everyone a small metal cup and lifted her own in salutation. Mike drained his along with the rest of them and managed to smack his lips in the required gesture of appreciation. It was liquid seal fat, warmed to a few degrees short of blood heat. That would give his gall bladder a workout. He handed back the cup and prayed there would be no more toasts.

Three minutes later they were airborne. The Chill aircraft never rose above three thousand feet in its slow flight from F'waygo to Cap City. The southern continent ahead of them was a long time appearing. The first signs came far out to sea, when Mike saw beneath him the wandering icebergs, like glittering castles in the pale afternoon light of an Antarctic April. Soon after that they reached the island chain and finally began to cruise south along the curving spine of the long Antarctic Peninsula. The gigantic krill farms were offshore to the left in the Weddell Sea. Their retaining barriers lay like patterns of golden lacework on the black surface of the water.

The plane flew steadily on, overland into cold and darkness, threading its way between tall mountain peaks in its progress to the deep southern spur of the Ross ice shelf.

Following formal introductions the Chill party showed no interest at all in Mike. When his own polite shot at conversation was rebuffed he did not persist. He watched the stark scenery drifting past below them, until by four o'clock in the afternoon it was too dark for any sight but the flashing white light on the tip of the wing. Then he stared at that and thought about the mission, wondering how he would handle what came next; wondering, for the first time ever, if he was cut out to be a Trader at all . . . Finally, lulled by the soft whine of the engines, he fell asleep. *Food, drink, sleep—take them whenever you have a chance.*

A change in the engine sound woke him. Mike looked sleepily out of the cabin window on the left, then jerked to full attention. The pulsing wing light had become a fuzzy bright point in a dancing cloud of white. They were flying through a snowstorm, a blizzard so intense that visibility did not go beyond the wingtips.

Kristen Waldemar had noticed that he was awake. She nodded coldly from her seat on the other side of the cabin. "In the middle of the descent. Landing in a couple of minutes."

"It's an absolute ice storm out there. How can the pilot see?"

"She can see as much as she is allowed to." Kristen Waldemar gave him another chilly stare. "Don't worry. Even without snow, no one has been permitted to land at Cap City on visual flight rules for more than twenty years. Our descent is all on instruments. There will be nothing to see, and it is time you were ready to go outside. Let me show you how it is done."

As the engines were throttled back further, she handed Mike a compact parcel. He hefted it on his palm; it weighed less than a pound. She picked up a second package by one corner and cracked it like a whip. The whole fabric unfolded to become a glittering quicksilver mantle.

Chillsuit!

He'd heard of them but never seen one. They were not exported from the Cap Federation territories. According to Trader rumor the suit was the most precious possession any Chill could ever own. He looked at it curiously. It seemed little more than a piece of shiny plastic.

Kristen Waldemar lifted her suit in both hands, the head of the unit hanging down, and held it up above her. "Watch now. It looks hard, but it is very easy." She lowered the head unit of the suit to touch the top of her dark curls. As soon as the unit made contact, it *rippled*. Turning inside out, the unfolding suit flowed down over her body to her ankles. She lifted her feet, one after the other. As she did so the chillsuit made closure there. Kristen Waldemar had vanished, replaced by a shimmering figure of distorting mirror surfaces.

The transformation shocked Mike. As a Chill negotiator she had been no more than a rather unfriendly-looking woman, a little taller and thinner than most. Now she was a spectral, menacing figure, with bulging face and spidery limbs.

The main chillsuit material was less than a millimeter thick. It covered the body completely, head to toe, including mouth, nose, and eyes. The chillsuit contoured Kristen Waldemar's slim body to skintight perfection, vacuum tight everywhere except at the face. There the suit bulged grotesquely outward. Optic fiber bundles protruded as silver-green disks. Two inches across, they allowed perfect vision in all directions and protected the wearer's eyes totally from wind and cold. Below the green protruding disks the suit's mouth and nose formed a swollen muzzle. A network of tubes curved out and down under the chin, allowing the chillsuit wearer to breathe air warmed by circulation near the body.

The glittering shape in front of Mike raised a fragile-looking arm and nodded. "You now. Get a move on. We'll be landing in another minute."

He hesitated. What Kristen Waldemar had done looked like an impossible trick—a chillsuit donned and in full working order in less than ten seconds. He lifted the parcel and shook it loose. Then he held it high and gingerly began to lower it toward his head. Even before it made contact he felt the movement. It pulled out of his hands and writhed down to enfold him. There was one unbearable moment when nose and mouth were covered, then he realized that his breathing was unimpaired. And he could see perfectly—better with the suit than without it! There must be enhancement hardware in the optic bundle image reconstruction. He lifted one gloved hand and stared at the dazzling surface of the back of his forearm. He could see tiny sensors there, no more than a few micrometers across. Inside that total opacity, his fingertip recorder must be totally blind and useless.

"You're not finished yet," Kristen Waldemar said, and he realized that he could hear her perfectly, too, even though his ears were covered. "If you went out on the ice cap like that you'd freeze in two minutes. Lift your feet."

Mike did so, and felt the closure around each leg as the chillsuit completed its seals. Just as that happened he also felt a slight shake of the aircar.

The dazzling silver figure in front of him nodded. "Just in time. We're down. Follow me. For your information, it's thirty below zero outside. But see how you feel when you get there. Stay close behind me."

She turned the handle. The cabin door opened as though someone had jerked it violently outward. There was a great scream of wind past its edges, and a flurry of snowflakes.

Mike was supposed to go out into *that*—without any more protection against the cold than the skimpy suit? Kristen left without another word. He paused for a moment on the step down. Finally he said a prayer to the gods of absolute zero and followed her out into the howling winter storm.

He could see a faint pattern of lights ahead, flickering and variable through the whirl of driving snow. Closer was the bright reflection from Kristen's chillsuit. She was gliding along fast—faster than he could travel over the powdery snowpack. He floundered along after her through half a foot of new fall. He was so busy doing it that a minute passed before he realized that he felt no cold at all. He was warm and comfortable. And somehow the raging winds that blew snowflakes horizontally across the field of view exerted little force on his body.

He looked down at the miraculous chillsuit and then stared again around him. The aircar was already invisible behind, though it could be no more than forty yards away. Curious to know if the other crew members were following, Mike continued his turn through a full revolution.

That was a mistake—a *big* mistake. When he had made what he was sure was a complete turn he looked again in front of him. *Nothing.* Kristen Waldemar had vanished. The lights ahead were gone. There was only gray skygloom and blinding snow. He felt his heart beating faster. He was alone, all alone, out on the Antarctic ice cap in an evening winter blizzard.

Trader training took over. Remember the rules, a voice said inside Mike's head. *Anything* can be a piece of negotiation tactics. Suppose this is Kristen Waldemar's way of softening you up before the real business begins?

He forced himself to stoop down and mark four lines with one chillsuit finger in the deepening snow: one in front, one behind, and one on each side. He could still see them, even when fully standing. He began to turn around, surveying to the limit of vision, then looking back to the ground reference points and turning a little farther. He tried to hurry, aware that it would not be long before the wind obliterated the marks. After a three-quarter turn his eyes at last picked out a faint and flickering light.

Surely his sense of direction had not been so far off? He would have sworn this was not the heading for the first lights he had seen. But there could be no debating the options. Keeping his eyes glued on those lights, he headed steadfastly toward them.

Distances were just as deceptive as directions. One moment the lights were far off and faint; a few yards more, and he had reached them. They were two narrow bars of illumination, one on each side of a low building with a wide door of translucent blue material. When he was within a few feet of the entrance the door swung open. Mike went through and found himself on a platform in front of a curved descending staircase. At the foot stood Kristen Waldemar. She had already removed her chillsuit and was standing looking up with a strange expression on her face.

He hurried down the stairs and stopped in front of her. "Get this damned thing off me. What sort of hosts are you anyway, leaving a guest to freeze out there on the ice cap?" (One hell of way to begin a negotiation—but he remembered Rule 13: *Don't set precedents you can't live with.*)

"Like this." She reached out and pressed under his chin. At once the chillsuit rippled upward, folding into a neat package on top of his head. It would have fallen to the floor, but she reached out and caught it. "You were in no danger. The chillsuit is completely windproof and nonconducting. It allows no more heat to radiate away than the human body itself produces, and its surface minimizes wind forces. We often stay on the surface all day or all night, in complete safety." Her words were casual, but the tone sounded oddly conciliatory. She was even offering a tentative smile. "Do not worry. Nothing like that will happen again."

It sounded like a halfhearted apology. But why let the incident happen in the first place? She must have known that Mike would be struggling along behind her.

"Food and drink?" she said hesitantly. "And then, if you are not too tired, we can begin our official discussions."

She placed his chillsuit on a stand by the entrance. Her own went, carefully folded and packed, into a satchel at her side. As they walked into the interior, Mike had his first chance to examine the unique architecture of the underground caverns of Cap City.

Wood and metal were in short supply here. The builders had been obliged to use their only plentiful construction material. The walls were thick sheets of ice, covered by a thin layer of chillsuit material. Highly reflecting and nonconducting, it permitted a comfortable living temperature in each room without melting the walls. A system of vents to the surface allowed any heat passing through to the ice to be removed. Over the years, the Chills had gradually extended the underground structure, burrowing deeper and deeper into the ice cap. No outsider knew the extent of that development.

They went through a long communal dining hall to a private room at the end. Kristen Waldemar called up a menu on the tabletop screen and ordered a meal without consulting Mike. He put on a worried look that said, "How many ways are there to cook seal and penguin?", then pretended to be gratified by the number and nature of the dishes offered on the menu.

She must have caught the look, because the earlier half-smile warmed to a real grin. Since leaving him out there in the snowstorm, her whole attitude seemed to have changed.

"Wait and see," she said. "Traders must be familiar with all the foods of the world. But I feel sure that ours will amaze you. It is the best that can be found *anywhere*."

The dishes began to appear from the midtable hatches. Little of the food was familiar, and Kristen made no move to taste anything. She was waiting for Mike. He finally picked up a fork and took a first tentative bite. Trader training dictated the protocol: regardless of taste he would offer compliments. In this case, he expected to be on safe ground.

Sure enough. It was delicious.

"What *is* this?" He took another, bigger forkful.

Kristen laughed in delight, and Mike revised his estimate of her age downward by five years. "That is seaweed, fried in fish oil. But the special flavor comes from the morel and lactarius garnish. When we have some spare time, I will show you the mushroom caves. Five hundred feet below us is the best fungal growth environment in the world—temperature and humidity exactly controlled, radiation budget precisely right. But there are better courses to come." She finally dug into her own heaped plate and began to eat heartily. "You see," she said between mouthfuls, "we have heard how the rest of the world regards our food. All they know is our seal-oil toast for a safe journey, and that is an old ritual I would be happy to do without. Now, at one time our reputation *was* justified. We had nothing, and we ate whatever we could find. But today we are the world's gourmets. We have the pick of the sea farms, we harvest the waters beyond the ice shelf, and we grow the world's best vegetables and fungi in our underground tanks."

That was all very plausible, but Mike was having second thoughts. Kristen must know that Mike would have been briefed on Cap Federation ways before he was ever allowed to leave Trader Headquarters. The food might surprise a casual visitor, but not a Trader. Therefore, Kristen's delight at surprising him, no matter how well presented, was not genuine. This was all part of the game of negotation, and she knew just how it played. *Trader Rule: Tell them what they know—it gives them a feeling of confidence.*

Mike's respect for her acting ability increased. From now on, it would be unwise to assume that *any* of Kristen Waldemar's responses were spontaneous. And yet he was still convinced that the change in her general attitude toward him was genuine.

Wishful thinking?

He let his thoughts run free and concentrated on enjoying the best meal he'd eaten in years. There was a generous array of drink and drugs set out at the end of the table, everything a human might want to snort, smoke, pop, or mainline. Mike ignored them all. So did Kristen. If there were anything added to the food, they were both ingesting it; but as an added precaution he quietly downed a detox pill between courses.

It was Kristen who broke the spell of genteel dining pleasure. After a dish of candied kelp she sat up a little straighter in her chair and glared at him. "Mikal Asparian, how old are you?"

Mike cleared his throat—twice. "I'm twenty-three," he said at last.

"You could pass for less. And how many Trader missions have you been on?"

"This is my—er, my fourth. Or maybe my fifth. It depends how you count."

"Sweet Scott. What are your people doing? First, they send a *man*. You know, don't you, that we had specifically requested a female negotiator?"

"I didn't know that." *Daddy-O, what are you doing to me? I'm supposed to be* briefed *when I come here.*

"Plus, we asked for a very experienced Trader. You're ten years too young, and you have hardly any experience. When I took my first look at you I was ready to tell you to climb back on that plane and go back home. You're right about me leaving you out in the snow. I was so mad, I wanted to give you a real scare."

"I can see why you'd want to. So why are you being nice to me now?"

"You *didn't* scare. You were in no danger, I wasn't lying about that. As soon as I got in here I had you under radar observation all the time, so there was no way you could get lost or get hurt. But you didn't know any of that. And you surprised me. You did everything right, as well as any native could have done. And that's when I thought, damn it, he's a man, and he's wet behind the ears, but there's good stuff in him. Maybe I'd better give him a chance." She smiled. "You know, I expect to be negotiating deals here for another thirty years. You'll be around longer than that. If there's a chance we'll be working together for that long, we'd better be nice to each other."

"Thank you."

"But don't get the wrong idea. I'm not going to kid-glove

you when we get to the deals. You pay for your own mistakes there. Are you willing to have a first session tonight, or are you too tired?"

Mike pulled out the contract he had prepared from Max Dalzell's rough draft and put it on the table. The Chill serving robots came scuttling out of the table hatches and cleared off all the dishes.

"That's a first cut?" Kristen asked. "Well, at least you've done some homework. Let's take a look, and we'll see how far apart we are."

She took the five sheets and spread them out in front of her. There was a ten-minute silence, while she frowned and Mike fidgeted. He couldn't read a thing from her expression, and when she finally looked up and shook her head he felt highly uneasy.

"This is amazing," she said. "Where did you learn to spell out negotiable options?"

Mike shrugged. There was one honest answer—all the terms and alternatives had come straight from Max Dalzell—but he didn't want to mention that.

"I thought this would take us four days, minimum," she went on. "But with this as a starting point, we'll be through in an hour or two." She shook her head again. "You know, I could sign this damned thing *now*, and everybody here would be happy. Are you *sure* that these terms will be acceptable to the Unified Empire?"

"I know they will."

"Then they. . ." Staring through him, she sat like a statue for a couple of minutes. Finally she squared off the sheets he had given her into a neat pile and leaned back in her seat. "I think we've done enough on this for tonight. But we have to talk some more."

"Carry on."

"Not here." She stood up. "Come on."

They retraced their path all the way to the entrance chamber, put chillsuits back on, and returned to the blue door. Mike wondered what he was getting into. Nothing in Daddy-O's warnings and advice had covered this situation.

They went out again, back onto the frozen surface. Three paces beyond the exit he stopped, entranced.

The snowstorm was over. The southern sky had turned to flame. Yellow-green stripes trailed streamers of red and salmon-pink across the starlit heavens.

Aurora australis—the southern lights.

"Bright tonight," Kristen said in a matter-of-fact tone. "Must be one hell of a solar flare. Pity the poor Chipponese, up there on a night like this, eh? But it's good for us—we won't need lights."

"It's gorgeous."

"Ah. First time for you, is it? Don't worry, you'll soon get used to it."

Mike slowly turned all around for his first real exposure to the terrain of the Cap. There was nothing; nothing living, nothing familiar. They were standing in a flat area of undisturbed snow maybe half a mile across. Beyond it lay a landscape crumpled and shattered into spiky ice hills. Sharp ridges and spires glowed pink and ghostly blue under the flickering sky.

He felt as cold as the outside air and as broken as the ice-hill surface. The scenery was beautiful, but everything else was going wrong. The negotiation for the robots had turned into a farce, over before it began. Max Dalzell had done the ground work so well that there was nothing left to do. Mike was no more than a messenger boy on the prime mission. And now that he was here, he could see why Daddy-O had set the odds so high against the other mission. Mundsen Labs and Seth Paramine were only forty miles to the south—but that might as well be four thousand. Perhaps a Chill could find a way across that frozen chaos. For Mike it would be impossible.

"Walk," Kristen said. "Follow me."

She set off south at a steady pace. This time she was not trying to lose him. He followed her footsteps through the snow.

Where the smooth surface gave way to crevasses and ridges she halted. Then she was off again, winding her way easily into the ruined wilderness. In the shadow of an overhanging ice cliff she halted and turned again to face Mike. The green eye discs glowed.

"This is the *real* homeland. What do you think of it?"

"It's like the frozen circle of Hell. 'Great God, this is an awful place.'"

She laughed in delight. "Marvelous. I guess you did get some briefing before you came here—I was beginning to wonder. But a real native would want to be at the Pole before he'd quote Scott, and we're still four hundred and fifty miles north of it. Stand still, and keep quiet."

She raised one arm to the throat of Mike's suit and pressed hard. The world went dark and silent.

The cheerful tone of her last remark saved him from panic. But he was on the way to it when he felt another pressure against the side of his head. "Right," Kristen's voice said. "I've turned off both our suits. We're head to head and nobody can overhear us. We can't stay like this for very long—no heat control. We'd broil or freeze. But we're safe for half an hour. You all right?"

"I've just learned a good way to kill somebody," Mike said. "Take them out into the ice cap. Destroy the chillsuit control—and leave them. If they pull off the suit they freeze. If they don't, they're blind and deaf and never find their way back."

"It's been done. But it's easier to knock you on the head and stick you down a crevasse. Anyway, more people come onto the Cap for sex than death—chillsuits have adaptabilities most outsiders don't dream of. But we're not here for games. I want privacy. We couldn't get that inside. *Trader Oath*?"

Mike was on the spot. If he accepted information under Trader Oath, it could not be told. Not to *anyone*, not even to another trader. Daddy-O would lock it away in the data files, but no human would ever know it.

He began to sweat inside the chillsuit. What the devil could Kristen want to tell him that would need Trader Oath? But if he refused, he might be passing up something big.

Mike used up three precious minutes while he thought it over. Would the situation become even more out of control? *Could* it? He wished Jack Lester were hooked in on a Mentor link, whispering preposterous advice into his ear. Was the fingertip recorder catching all the audio through the suit's air layer?

"I accept," he said at last. "Anything you tell me here will be under Trader Oath." He would worry about the recorder when he got back.

"Good. Let me update you on recent Federation politics. We have a big hassle starting between two groups. The Purists want us to keep to ourselves, with a bigger Cap defense system. They want no dealings with Traders or the other regions. They're a minority. The Rimmers—I'm one of them, and so are all our negotiators—want more trade and cooperation. We believe bigger weapons are a futile effort."

"You're wasting Trader Oath time. Everything you've told me is common Trader knowledge."

"So far. But this isn't: the Purists have just been taken over by a group of extremists. They've started a program to *guarantee* isolation. And last week they took the first extreme step.

They organized a smash to the Great Republic and captured a group of Yankee scientists. They took them to a research facility that they control completely."

Mike could feel an icicle crawling up his spine, and it wasn't chillsuit failure. He was being drawn into something outside the mission parameters. "Seth Paramine," he said.

"What?"

"Nothing. You're sure it was a *group* of Yankee scientists? Keep going."

Kristen gripped his shoulder. "The Purists deny everything —naturally. The information we have, and there's not much of it, came from stringing together bits and pieces of data. But do you see our position? We can't stand up and tell the rest of the world what the Purists have done, because it would look bad for *all* the Cap Federation. We have to stop the Purists, and we have to get the word out to the Yankees that this was an isolated incident that didn't involve most of us."

"I can see that. But I don't know what it has to do with me or the Traders—unless you want me to act as your go-between with the Yankees."

"We do, but that's the easy part. We want you to work on our behalf *with the Purist leaders*, to see if you can work out a way to free the Yankees. Unofficial negotiation. Officially you'll still be on Trader business."

"But why don't *you* do that? You're a negotiator, and you've far more experience than I have."

"I'm a known Rimmer. I don't think they'd let me near the Mundsen Labs. But *you*, you're a Trader, and a good one, they'll let you in."

Rule 44: Give praise; it's free. It was interesting to see Trader techniques from the other side.

Mike sighed. "Maybe I'll do it. Tell me what terms you're prepared to offer, then let's get back below before we both freeze."

The flight to Mundsen Labs was made in a skimmer, a wide-bodied craft that traveled just a few feet above the jagged surface. It was under automatic flight control, and after a few dizzying seconds with the ground blurring away underneath him Mike turned from the window.

He had plenty to think about.

He was heading for the Chills' main research center, the stronghold of the Purist faction. The Chill scientists there were specialists in miniaturization. Would his fingertip recorder pass their surveillance?

Worse than that, the two agendas for the mission were becoming hopelessly confused. So far as the Unified Empire and the Chill government were concerned, he was here to negotiate for gaming robots. From the point of view of the Yankees, he was trying to obtain definite evidence of Paramine's presence at Mundsen Labs.

But Kristen Waldemar and the Chill Rimmer faction also wanted him to *pretend* to be working for the Yankees, while he tried to negotiate secretly for the return of the "kidnapped scientists"—who was just Seth Paramine, though Kristen didn't know it. And finally there were the Purists. *They* thought Mike was coming to Mundsen Labs to look at the latest ag-robot circuitry as part of a possible separate deal with the Yankees—a deal their isolationist leaders would never agree to make!

Mike sat with that mess of conflicting objectives buzzing around in the back of his head and studied the skimmer's control panel. If he had to leave Mundsen Labs in a hurry it would be nice to know how. The skimmer had a free-flight mode with extensible lifting surfaces. He saw that the airspeed indicator went to Mach Three, and the altimeter to fifty thousand feet. Not bad—if he could make it back to the skimmer and get it off the ground.

The plane was slowing to a hover. Kristen had planned the arrival time carefully. At this latitude and season, daylight lasted only a couple of hours. The skimmer touched down on the Mundsen airstrip just before local noon; a wintry sun peered over the horizon. Mike found himself in a shallow depression well shielded from southern winds and located to catch every ray of light. On a fine summer day, the noon temperature here might actually rise above freezing point. The icy surface was polished smooth and glowed a beautiful phospor-green in the oblique sunlight.

The human side of the scenery was unfortunately a lot less attractive. Even before Mike could close his suit and step onto the powdery ice, two chillsuited figures had appeared from nowhere and were standing outside the skimmer door. They were armed strangely, with ancient-looking projectile weapons.

Act confident. "Hello." Mike spoke as soon as he stepped outside. "I'm a Trader, here to negotiate on behalf of the Yankees for new ag-robot equipment. I'm—"

"Mikal Asparian." One of the figures shook his head.

"You're a Trader, true enough. But you're not here for any ag-robot equipment." From the sound of his voice Mike was sure he had a nasty smile on his face. "You're working for the Rimmers. Want to deny it?"

Mike certainly did, but he doubted if it would be much use. He cursed the security leaks at Cap City. If they already knew this, what else did they know? He said nothing.

They led him past a complex of four metal huts, ancient and scarred. From their exteriors, the buildings dated to the earliest days of Antarctic research. They were uninhabited. Memorials, maybe, to the early scientists who had worked on the ice cap? That was just the sort of thing that would appeal to the Purists.

They walked on in silence for almost half a mile, to another smooth depression in the ice. This one was circled by a substantial chain fence. There was one break in the barricade, a wide opening spanned only by a thin pipe at ground level. They stepped across it and walked to a cylindrical structure projecting from the ice. It was the top of an elevator shaft.

With one guard on each side of Mike they stepped in and descended for thirty seconds, the only sound a faint whine of machinery from the side of the shaft. Before they reached the bottom the man on the right removed his chillsuit. He gestured to Mike to do the same.

"One degree a foot temperature gradient," he said. "You may find you're too hot." He was a sallow-skinned man with a lumpy bald head and a thin mouth. He looked pleased with himself, but not unfriendly. "You'll be staying here until tomorrow morning," he went on. "This place was designed as a research lab, not a prison, so you can't complain if you have to share our only secure accommodation. Go on, out you get."

He motioned with his gun as the elevator doors opened. Beyond them lay a long, low-ceilinged corridor with the same reflecting walls of chillsuit material. Mike was led to a closed door and made to face the other way while his hairless companion operated a cipher lock.

"In you go," he said. "Hope you enjoy the company. It's not our fault if you don't."

The other man, still wearing his chillsuit, gave a high-pitched laugh and prodded gently with his gun. Mike walked inside and looked around as the door slammed solidly to behind him.

Success—but it didn't feel like it. He was standing no more than twenty feet from Seth Paramine.

The missing genius was hunkered down on the floor of the room, in the same posture shown in the videos. This time he was frowning and muttering over a sort of interlocking spiral structure made from many pieces of thin metal and plastic balls.

As the door closed he looked up and stared at Mike with his lower lip pushed out. "Where's my dinner?" he said.

Mike went to sit next to him. The room had a soft floor, but no chairs. "It's too early. It won't be dinnertime for another three hours."

That earned a frown and a shake of the heavy head. "I want dinner *now*." Then he ignored Mike to concentrate on his metal spirals.

Mike's thoughts ran wild. He was face-to-face with Seth Paramine. Paramine was a genius. Mike would explain the whole thing to him, Paramine would think of a way to get both of them out of there, they would fly away in the skimmer, back to Trader headquarters . . .

Improbable, but he had to try. Mike gave it his best shot. He sat beside Seth Paramine and explained the whole thing, slowly and in detail: how Seth had been kidnapped, how his friends and family back in the Great Republic were worried about him, how the brain probes that had been used on him here could do harm, how Mike had been sent to find him, how with his help they could both escape and go back home . . .

Nothing was left out. At the end of it Paramine looked at Mike thoughtfully with those dull, slaty eyes. "You talk too much, and you have funny ears," he said. And then he delivered the irrefutable counter-argument to all Mike's eloquence. "I get two kinds of pie with dinner here."

For the next three hours he sat playing, while Mike prowled the big room and fantasized about overpowering the man or woman who brought in dinner.

He should have known better. This was Chill territory—the land of the people who had *invented* table-service robots. The whole food-supply system, kitchen included, was automated. Promptly at five o'clock a wall panel turned, becoming a table complete with serving hatch. Plates of hot food slid out onto the flat surface. No knives or forks were provided, but that didn't worry Seth Paramine—he didn't seem to expect them. He picked up his spoon, bent his head low to the plate, and gobbled all his share. Then he sat impatient for dessert.

It came, but it was not to his satisfaction.

"Only one sort of pie!" he said. He glared at the offending

plate, banged on the hatch with his spoon, and looked at Mike accusingly. "Only one pie. Always get two pies when you're not here."

"Here." Mike pushed a plate forward. He had hardly started his first course. "If you want it, you can have my creamcake."

Paramine gave one slack-jawed gape, grinned, and pulled the plate to him. He grabbed the spoon. It took him twenty seconds at most to eat the creamy dessert. Then he picked up the dish, licked it clean, and grunted in disappointment. He still looked hungry. Apparently two helpings of one dessert did not equal one helping of two.

"Only one sort of pie!" he said again.

A little of Seth Paramine's company went a long way. Mike was relieved when the genius finally stood up and wandered around the room, muttering to himself about pies. Mike carried on eating his own food. He didn't even notice that Seth was near the door until it was already open and Paramine had gone out through it. Before Mike could get there it slammed shut again.

"Seth!" Mike ran across and banged on it with both hands. "Seth, open the door. Let me out, too."

Nothing. Not a word, not a sound. Mike groaned and went back to the table—just in time to see his own food disappear. The serving robots had assumed he was finished. It was his turn to bang on the hatch with the spoon, with no more success than Seth Paramine had enjoyed.

Mike was still doing that when he heard the door behind him opening again. This time he moved a lot faster. As Seth came back in, triumphantly carrying a plateful of fruit pie, Mike made sure that the door stayed open.

He held it ajar. "Seth, can you open this anytime?"

Paramine nodded, mouth crammed full.

"*How* do you do it?"

Paramine shrugged. "I open lock."

"Yes, but I mean *how*—" Mike stopped. Why bother? Whatever the answer, it wouldn't help. Seth did electronics at an intuitive level. Opening a mere electronic doorlock would be as natural to him as breathing.

"You're sure you can open it anytime?" Mike asked again. When Paramine nodded, Mike pulled the door closed and allowed the lock to operate.

He waited a couple of hours, then began to talk to Seth again. This time he had found his own key. They talked about food. Seth was quite willing to do that. He told Mike all his favorite kinds: sugared figs, roast wild goose, crabcakes, candied morels, corn bread, baked apples, seal-belly pie, stuffed flounder, snapper-turtle soup, treacle tart, fried oysters, persimmon flan—and anything with pineapples and chocolate.

He listed foods in no particular order. When he was done, Mike sat down and developed a menu, scribbling on the serving hatch with one of Seth's crayons. It took a long time. He came up with twelve courses, not counting the side dishes of breads, salads, sauces, and trimmings, and every item selected for Seth's tastes.

When Mike was finished he went to sit next to Seth. "I want to tell you about a dinner I'm going to give for my friends."

Mike didn't hurry. Course by course, dish by dish, he described the whole meal. When he was finished there was a look on Seth's face that could only be described as religious ecstasy.

"When?" he asked.

"As soon as we get back to Cap City. Not far from here—we could fly there tonight. There's a skimmer that would take us."

Seth stood up and headed for the door.

"Wait a minute," Mike said. "We'll have to go outside. Do you have a chillsuit?"

"Chillsuit?" The eyes were vacant again.

"One of these." Mike showed him the suit he had arrived in.

"Don't know." The heavyset shoulders shrugged. "You find one for me?"

"We'll see. You'll have to open the door for us, though, before we can look."

"Mm-mm." Seth picked up one of the pieces of metal spiral and wandered over to the door. All he seemed to do was wave it a couple of times next to the lock, and push. The door opened and he went through. The savant side of the idiot—but *how did he do it*? No wonder he had driven the Chill designers crazy.

The corridor was deserted. They wandered along until they came to the elevator, and Mike saw nothing like an extra chillsuit. Could they manage without? No way. It might be fifty below zero out there.

Somewhere in the main building there had to be spare suits. But looking for them could take all night, and once the two were seen it would be all over.

Mike knew only one place where he was *sure* he would find a spare chillsuit. There was one in the skimmer.

"Wait for me right here," he said. "Don't move for anything. I'll be right back."

Without giving Paramine time to argue he stepped into the elevator and gave the signal to ascend. On the way up he took out his own chillsuit. By the time the door opened onto the surface he was completely suited, and near that door—thank God for the logical Chills—was a rack with half a dozen spare chillsuits. He picked one up and looked outside.

Another snowstorm was on the way, and the first flakes were already falling. He took a few paces toward the opening in the metal fence, wanting to be sure that he knew how to get back to the skimmer with the worsening visibility. As he did so there was a roar and a flash of light in front of him. The gap in the fence vanished, replaced by a wall of burning gas that sprang up from the metal pipe at ground level.

So much for the idea that security at Mundsen Labs was somewhere between casual and nonexistent. Anyone who came too close to the gap in the fence triggered the flaming wall. If he tried to go through it, he would be fried to a crisp.

Unless . . . An item of basic physics popped into his head.

Mike ran back to the elevator as fast as he could and jabbed at the down button. Somewhere an alarm would be ringing, and every second was important.

Paramine was waiting, leaning idly against the wall. Mike dragged him into the elevator, hit the button to ascend, and started to work him into the other chillsuit. Halfway through Mike suddenly remembered. The things that terrify Seth Paramine . . . pins, needles and scissors . . . fire and flame . . .

Seth would never run through that wall of flame.

The suit was on, and the elevator was almost at the surface.

"It's going to be dark and quiet when we get outside," Mike said quietly. "Don't worry, though, I know the way to the skimmer, and I'll always be holding your hand. All right?"

"Mm-mm. Getting hungry."

"Just wait, I'll give you the best dinner you've ever had." Mike lifted a suited hand and pressed at the suit controls under Paramine's chin just as the elevator door opened.

"Dark," Mike heard him say. Then he was pulling Seth toward the fence.

There was a whoosh of igniting gas when they were still five paces away. Mike kept going, leading the way right through the flame.

Five seconds more and they were clear, heading for the skimmer and freedom.

They almost made it.

Mike had them off the ground thirty seconds after they reached the skimmer. He didn't turn Seth's suit controls back on until they were already airborne.

With the lifting surfaces extended he went up to fifteen thousand feet and opened the engines all the way. The speed climbed past Mach Two. Mike thought they were clear, on the way home. He took his chillsuit off and helped Seth to do the same. As he was finishing, the engine power faded away to zero and the craft went into a long, steep glide. No action at the controls made any difference.

A thousand feet up the engines came to life again, with enough force to allow a controlled landing. The car skidded to a halt on a long bank of ice. After that last effort the engines refused to respond at all.

One minute later another skimmer landed next to them. Three armed men came out of it and moved across to the ship. Mike had no weapons, not even a stick. There was no sense in trying to fight. He unlocked the door and the men came in, removing their suits as they entered.

It was the bald-headed man, accompanied by two grim-faced youngsters.

"Well," the man said. "Well, well, well. I'm glad to see you're being sensible about this. I hope you realize that this makes us rethink our whole security system."

Mike said nothing. Seth Paramine scowled and said, "We're going to dinner. Are you his friends?"

"Not exactly." Baldy even managed a half smile and sat down on one of the cabin seats. "But maybe we will be, one day. We respect competence and ingenuity, you know, wherever it comes from. How did you learn that the chillsuits would allow you to pass safely through the fire?"

Seth growled at that forbidden word, but did not move.

"Elementary physics." (Why tell them this? he wondered. Then, why not? The same thing would never work again.) "I was told that a chillsuit radiates very little heat, and it's made of nonconducting material. If it won't radiate, it won't absorb either—emissivity and absorption *have* to be the same or the second law of thermodynamics is violated. And those—" Mike pointed at the projectile weapons "—support that idea. With a suit that reflects energy, lasers won't work—but you can still blow holes in people with old-fashioned guns."

"True—but it's rare to find somebody with so much faith in physical laws. I'm not sure I'd take that risk myself." This time it was a real smile. "Oh, well. What now?"

"You tell me. You're in charge."

"That's right, I suppose I am." The man sat without moving for a few seconds, looking at Mike with a curiously friendly expression. "Naturally, we'll be taking Paramine back with us. And we'll erase that little gadget you carry in your finger, if you don't mind, so there's no record to show of all this. But after that . . . you know, I'll feel much more relaxed when Mikal Asparian is back in Cap City—or better still, Trader Headquarters. You make me uncomfortable. I really don't want you at Mundsen Labs again. So let me make a call or two and work out what's to be done with you."

The trio headed for the door, keeping Mike well covered with their weapons. Then Baldy turned in the doorway. "Just so you don't set Seth to work picking locks again, let me mention that this is a mechanical closure, not an electronic one. And we'll be keeping an eye on this door all the time. See you shortly."

Mike went to the window and watched them walk back to their aircar. As the bald-headed man had promised, one of them was always looking back, and once they were inside Mike saw a face peering out through their window.

He sat down glumly in the pilot's seat. How long did they have? It didn't make any difference. Even if time was too short, he had to make the effort.

Mike leaned forward to look at the car's control panel. It was held in place by half a dozen missy-bolts, with their hollow pentagon heads. A bad start—without the correct missy-bolt screwdriver he would never be able to turn them. He got down on hands and knees, crawled forward into the knee space below the control panel, turned his head around so far that he thought his neck would break, and peered upward. The light level was so low under the knee cavity that he couldn't see a thing, and there was no flashlight in the cabin. *And* the panel was only a couple of inches from his face. He couldn't have focused so close, even in perfect light.

Time to think.

Mike crawled back out and found Seth staring at him with a

bit more interest than usual. "I'm trying to get the panel off. This one. Any ideas?"

Seth stared at it for ten seconds. "No," he said.

So much for help from Genius-boy. If it wasn't food or electronics, forget Seth. Mike went back to sit in the useless control chair and stared at the panel for another five minutes. Then he went across to one of the chillsuits, lifted it above his head, and slipped it on. He didn't bother to seal it. As soon as the unit was working he crawled back into the cavity and did the contortionist act again with his head.

The image enhancement equipment in the suit's optical sensors had compensation for low light levels, as well as improved contrast and focus. Now he could see the panel clearly from two inches away, and he could scan across it by turning his head.

It was built in two pieces, meeting at a groove that ran from front to back. Mike pushed, and it gave a little. Since there was no sign of bolts or screws, it was probably held in position by the pressure of the front panel. Remove that, and the lower panel would slide out in two parts. Unfortunately, he still couldn't get the front panel off.

He was stymied again, but not too badly this time. Mike suspected that the panels butted with a simple tongue-and-groove joint, and there was no reason why they should be glued.

He turned over to lie flat on his back, reached up with suited hands, and pushed the right-hand side of the panel.

The plate bent a little, then resisted. It was meeting something above it. Well, to hell with it. If Mike broke their machine, what could they do about it? He braced his back and straightened his arms as hard as he could. There was a creak of strained plastic, then the plate sprang upward. It had separated from its partner, and now he could slide them over each other and reach up into the back side of the front panel.

Now came the really delicate part. To this point Mike had been trying hard enough, but with no real hope of success. Now that he was making progress he was scared of ruining everything. He felt for the racks, reaching up as gently as he could. It was no good, he would never do it by feel. He was forced to stick his head up through the panel, squint at the control assemblies sitting right at the end of the suit's nose, and try at the same time to work with one hand up next to his eyes.

Predictably, the electronic boards he was after couldn't be taken out from the bottom. He would have to remove the front panel, then slide them out that way. And that brought him back to the old problem of the missy-bolts. But now he had one advantage. He could come at them from the *back*, where that hollow pentagonal bolthead did not apply. On the other end of the bolts were, thanks to old-fashioned engineering, nothing more than simple hex-head nuts. Mike could get a grip on them; after a monstrous effort that left his fingertips throbbing and didn't do much for the chillsuit's condition, he was able to undo them.

With the front panel off, he could finally reach the heart of the control panel. It consisted of five boards, each the size and thickness of a playing card.

Mike looked at his watch. Unbelievable. He had only been at work for twenty-five minutes—not the three or four hours it seemed to be. He carried the boards across to where Seth was sitting idly, staring out at the snow.

"Here. I've got a little game for you to play. It's a puzzle. Somewhere on these control boards is a piece of logic that allows the inputs from the usual controls to be overridden by other inputs that arrive as radio signals. The thing I'd like to know is, where is that logic? And can it be changed?"

Seth sniffed, took the assembly from Mike's hands, and stared at it for a few seconds. He shook his head. "Don't know."

Mike felt crushed. All that effort, for a two-second rejection. "Can't you tell anything at all about the circuits?"

"No." Seth sat staring ahead of him for a while. Then, as though struck by a random afterthought, he added, "Too small."

Too small.

"Damnation. You mean—" Mike stopped. He should curse himself, not Seth Paramine. Seth was used to working with enlarged schematics. He didn't have eyes like a microscope, any more than Mike did. To analyze these microcircuits he had to be able to see them!

It took another precious five minutes to get Seth into the suit, with assurances that they were not going outside again. Finally Seth was sitting hunched over in the corner, holding each control board in turn half an inch from the chillsuit's nose. Now and again he gave a grunt of surprise, pleasure, or disappointment.

After five minutes Seth went back to one of the boards, the third in the assembly, and pointed at an area about an inch from the right-hand edge. "Here."

Mike stifled the urge to ask how he knew. Even the explanation would be beyond him. "Can you change it? Is there any way of making it so that the controls can't be affected from anywhere except the control panel here?"

"Sure." Seth pointed again. "Four ways to do. Easiest, cut these circuits out, cross-connect those four."

He was pointing at things that were completely invisible to Mike. If it was too small to see, it was probably too small to change.

"What about the other ways? Is there a way with big enough elements for us to do the change without special equipment?"

"Sure. Change these." Seth pointed again. Mike had the feeling that he would get that same answer—"sure"—if he asked Seth to change the controls of the aircar so that it could sing and dance.

"Can you do it?"

"Sure. Do all four ways, if want to." Seth started to take his chillsuit off.

"Hey. What are you doing?"

"Tools." While Mike gaped, Seth removed his suit partway and rummaged in one of the front pockets of his blue overalls. He took out a dozen tools—including, Mike was chagrined to note, two sizes of missy-driver—and selected a tiny scriber from a handful of the smallest ones. "Okay." He disappeared back into the chillsuit and started work.

Seen from Mike's point of view, Seth didn't do a thing. He just made two insignificant nicks on the surface of one of the boards and a longer scratch parallel to its edge. It took a total of about twenty seconds, then he slipped all the boards back into the chassis and handed Mike the assembly without a word. Mike carried them to the control panel, slid them into locked position, and pushed the panel face back in after them.

Now for the interesting part. If something hadn't been ruined when Mike buckled the bottom panel upward, or when he fiddled around inside turning the missy-bolts, or when he pulled the control assembly out, or when he put it back; and if Seth hadn't misunderstood the logic of the boards, and hadn't put one of his tiny scratches a little too far to the left or the right— why, then they might have a working aircar. And if the snow wasn't bad enough to cripple them at takeoff, or drive them down right out of the air, and if Mike's bald-headed friend didn't have another trick up his sleeve that Mike couldn't even guess at—why, then they might be able to fly back to Cap City.

There was no point in thinking about it. Mike sat in the pilot's seat, not bothering to tighten any of the bolts in the loose panel, and switched on. As they skittered along the ice they passed the other car, and Mike saw two faces gaping out of the window. But there was no shooting. Thirty seconds later they were in the air, heading at maximum speed for success, home, and fame.

Almost.

Ten minutes into the journey, Seth was sitting by Mike's side, breathing heavily through his mouth. His fat face had a brooding look. "We get special dinner?"

"You bet we do." Mike had been peering into the rearview sensors, and nothing was coming after them. "The dinner that I promised you, at Cap City. And then we'll be on our way home, back to your family."

Seth was silent for another moment. Then he shook his head. "No. You go back. Not me."

"But your home—your family." Mike gave him five minutes of his best arguments, and at the end of it Seth shook his head again.

"No. After special dinner, I fly back Mundsen Labs. That the best place I live—best games."

"Best games"—that was Seth's expression of the fact that the Chills in the Mundsen Labs were the world's tops in microcircuits. To him, it was no more than a game, one that he played better than anyone. Unfortunately, none of that made any difference to Mike's mission.

"Seth, you don't understand." Mike felt like a swine, but he couldn't give Seth a choice. "You *have* to go home. The people at the Mundsen Labs did something bad when they took you away from home. We can't let them do what they did, and get away with it."

"Something bad, but not for me. Like it there," Seth said. "Take me back, Mike. After dinner, or right now."

"I can't, Seth." Mike held their course north. Poor guy, he thought. He had to learn the hard way what the world was like.

Seth did not speak, but he looked at Mike sorrowfully. Then he slouched down in his chair, shook his big head, and stuck his hands in his pockets. Mike felt like a real villain. Seth had helped so much. But there was a job to do.

After another minute or so the controls of the car suddenly became soggy and unresponsive. Mike no longer had full control. He tried to stay calm and keep on course. No good. They were holding altitude, but banking in a wide arc, turning steadily. In another few seconds they would be heading back the way they had come.

"Damn." Mike dropped the useless control stick. "It's happened again. They've taken over. Seth, I thought you said you'd made it so—"

He stopped. Seth was sitting back in his seat, bent over a little square of ceramic. A tiny scriber was in his hand, and he was moving it precisely over the surface. He noticed Mike looking, and did a little sideways wiggle with the tool. The aircar rolled right, then returned.

"Are you doing that? It's impossible. How, for the sake of Daddy-O, can you control an aircar with that little bit of plastic?"

Seth looked at Mike slyly. "Easy. Capacitance control. We have special dinner, then I go back. Right? Or we go back now."

Trader Rule: Try as hard as you can, but know when you've lost. Mike cursed his own stupidity. Why had he ever, for one moment, thought of Seth Paramine as just an idiot? Genius was genius, no matter how it showed itself. And genius could run rings around nongeniuses—like Mike—whenever it chose to.

"All right. You can go back after the dinner."

"Trader's Promise?"

Now how the devil had Seth learned about *that*?

Mike thought for another few moments. He had no choice. He nodded. "Trader's Promise."

Seth moved a finger, the car began to turn, and soon they were once more heading for Cap City.

Then Seth surprised Mike one more time. He looked across with those strange, miles-away eyes and reached over to pat Mike's hand. "You all right. I trust you, Mike. You come see me again."

Mike gripped his hand in return. It was the nearest thing to a true benediction that he ever expected to achieve in life.

CHAPTER 16

The long curved corridor was familiar this time. Mike pressed the monitor as soon as it was in reach, and the massive black door opened.

Max Dalzell was in, sitting at his desk. He waved Mike over to the visitor's chair. "I heard you were back," he said. Then he took a look at Mike's face and reached into his desk drawer. "Here. You need a bite from the tortoise."

He handed across a small plastic phial of *testudo* spirit, twisting the top as he did so. There was a long, high-pitched hiss and the bottle cooled twenty degrees in Mike's hand.

"New gimmick," Dalzell said. "Joule-Thomson effect. The Greasers say they're fond of technology, but they tend to apply it only to their own sybaritic ends."

Mike took his first cautious sip of the icy liquid and waited for the column of torchbearers to walk down his throat to his stomach.

"That will help," Dalzell said. "Cheer up. It's not the end of the world."

"I'd like to think you're right."

"You made a successful negotiation for the gaming robots."

"No—*you* did that. They'll accept the agreement you wrote —without any changes."

Dalzell grinned. "But you'll get the credit. And you came as close as an eyelash to pulling Paramine out of there. You just had some bad luck."

"I had a lot of luck on the mission—both kinds. And I had something else."

Mike saw Max Dalzell's expression change. The man was uncannily perceptive.

"What are you getting at?"

"I'm not sure I know. I'm not as experienced as many Traders, and I'll be the first to admit it. But I have a feel for the way a mission is supposed to work. On the plane coming back here, I realized that this one went sour right from the beginning. I started to make a list, and then I linked in to Daddy-O."

"I know. I saw your report as it came into the data bank."

"You saw some of it. I put the rest into a closed file." Mike drained the bottle of *testudo* and sighed. "First data point: I didn't realize it until I met them, but the Chills are real stay-at-homes. They love it on the ice cap, and they hardly ever leave it for anything."

"The occasional flight to F'waygo. That's as far as most of them go."

"It's one hell of a long way from there to northern Yankee-land. So that gave me my first question: The Cap Federation heard about Seth Paramine, we know that. *How* did they hear about him? Well, they must have been told. Not too surprising, if you think about it—all the groups try to have agents in the others' territories. And that explained something else that baffled me. That 'wall of fire' defense for the Mundsen Labs isn't a useful idea out on the ice cap. In fact, it's useless. Anybody with a chillsuit on could walk right through it in perfect safety. But if the Chills *knew* about Paramine's fear of flame, it would be the perfect way of making sure he didn't try to leave. Even if he wandered out on his own, he'd have run back terrified. Again, it pointed to somebody feeding secret Yankee information to the Chills."

Max Dalzell puffed out his lips and handed Mike another bottle of *testudo*. "Plausible. But there could be five other explanations. Maybe the Chills cracked a Yankee communication line—they're the hotshots at electronics."

"That idea occurred to me, too. Or a Trader line. If they could break a Yankee comm-code, they'd just as easily crack one of ours. And that made me think of something else. One reason I got into trouble with the Chills was that I didn't have a Mentor contact to give me advice. Why no Mentor? I checked. Do you know who made that decision here?"

Max Dalzell was like a stone carving. Then his eyes flickered once, down to the desk and back up.

"And I know, too," Mike said. "This trip to the Chills taught me something else. For the first time in my life, I realized that most Trader Rules can be interpreted two ways. Like this one: 'If you don't have confidence in yourself, no one else will.' Sounds great, and a trainee needs it to build up self-image. But it has another consequence. When one of us is chosen for a particular mission, we never ask, 'Why me?' We assume it's for our brains and charm and courage. We never dream that we may have been selected for a completely different reason: *that we were picked because we were sure to fail*. Take a Trader whose self-confidence is low, someone who just staggered out of a total collapse of spirit and nerve. Chances are good that he'll fail, whatever you give him."

Dalzell gave a rumbling cough, deep in his chest. "I told you the odds that Daddy-O gave against success before you left."

"You did. You told me the odds against *my* success. I had one chance in a hundred. But you didn't tell me that the odds Daddy-O gave for an *experienced woman Trader* were better than forty percent. The Chills had requested a female negotiator for this case; they expected an experienced woman. They were given a man with only four missions under his belt, one who just came out of rehab. That was almost the end for me, right there. So why was I sent? Normally, the choice of Trader for a mission is made by Daddy-O. There's only one rank of person who can overrule that—a Master Trader."

"Daddy-O agreed with me."

Mike scarcely seemed to hear him. "But who would *want* to send the wrong Trader? It had to be someone who knew the Chills intimately, well enough to have reached a private arrangement with them. Someone who had heard about Seth Paramine through private Yankee channels, and told the Chills about him; someone who could set up a Trader mission to rescue Paramine, but make sure it was going to fail."

Mike had finished the second bottle of *testudo*, and it was having its effect. He looked at the iron face of the man in front of him and thought of all the times that he had longed to meet Big Max in person. Now he wished that it had never happened.

"So you know what I put in the closed file to Daddy-O. Not proof. I don't have proof. But if I'm right, Daddy-O will get that. Computers never stop looking. And unless I give the counterinstruction, the computer search will begin in an hour. I came here for one reason: so you can tell me that I'm wrong, and then I can cancel the instruction."

Dalzell took another phial of *testudo* from his desk and

tossed it down his throat like water. He sighed. "I can't do that. Because you're not wrong. And I can't do this, either." He raised his other hand from beneath the level of the desk and showed the weapon he was holding. "Not on you, Mike. You were just doing your job. Even if I did, it wouldn't stop Daddy-O, would it?"

Mike shook my head.

"Then can I ask a favor?" Dalzell leaned forward. "You may find it hard to believe, after what you've just said to me, but I love the Traders. It's been my whole life for thirty years. I don't want another thirty of disgrace, pointed at by everybody as a traitor." He lifted the weapon. "If I end it here and now—my way—would you cancel that order to the computer? Let my name be a proud one, and not a Trader curse?"

Mike's throat was dry. It shouldn't come to this—Max Dalzell, his idol, pleading to die with honor intact. "Why, Max? *Why* did you do it? You had everything, you *were* everything . . ."

Dalzell did not speak, and Mike could not. Dalzell finally nodded and stood up. "I'd like to do this alone. In my inner office. There's one private file of mine that I want to purge. Five minutes?"

"Of course. As long as you want."

Mike had stood up when the other man did, not knowing what to do next. Dalzell held out his hand, and Mike shook it. Then the Master Trader walked slowly around the big office, looking at the pictures and certificates that filled the walls. Finally he opened the steel door and passed through into the inner office.

Mike sat down again and buried his face in his hands. it was over. And now that it was over, he realized how desperately he had wanted Max Dalzell to prove that Mike was wrong, that he had misinterpreted everything. Max Dalzell, the greatest Trader of them all.

The minutes ticked on. Mike was waiting for that awful sound, the dull explosion made by human flesh when it is suddenly superheated to ten thousand degrees. It did not come. Ten minutes, fifteen minutes, and still no sound from the other office.

Mike gave in at fifteen. He found the inner door ajar, and it swung open to reveal a deserted room. Mike went over to the corner, to a square opening that led to a steep spiral staircase. He stuck his head inside. At the top he saw daylight filtered through frosted glass.

The data terminal in the corner was still on, with his own code word already blinking on it. He pressed the sequence for send mode and queried Travel Control.

The reply came in a few seconds. Dalzell's private airshell was in flight, heading south. DESTINATION: UNSPECIFIED. SPEED: MACH SEVEN. INTERCEPTION POTENTIAL: MESSAGES ONLY. (NOTE TO INQUIRER: THE SHELL OF A MASTER TRADER CANNOT BE RE-CALLED BY OUTSIDE INTERVENTION.)

Mike did not send a message. He didn't need to. While he was still staring at the screen the receive light came on and the file scrolled in:

TO MIKAL ASPARIAN—FOR WHOM I PREDICT A GREAT TRADER FUTURE:

AS YOU SAID, TRADER RULES CAN BE INTERPRETED IN MORE THAN ONE WAY. REMEMBER THIS ONE? *Don't try to be a hero; there's no shame in flight.* I'M APPLYING IT IN A WAY YOU NEVER EXPECTED.

YOU WERE RIGHT ON ALMOST EVERYTHING, BUT YOU MISSED ONE KEY POINT. WHO WOULD SPEND THE REST OF HIS LIFE IN CAP CITY, BLEAK AND COLD, WHEN HE COULD HAVE THE DELIGHTS OF REE-O-DEE? I DID SOME WORK FOR THE CHILLS, BUT I WAS PERFECTLY HONEST WHEN I TOLD YOU I KNOW THE GREASERS FIFTY TIMES AS WELL. TELL DADDY-O NOT TO WASTE HIS ELECTRONS LOOKING FOR ME. I'VE HAD A LONG TIME TO PREPARE FOR THIS, AND I'LL BE WELL PROTECTED. WHY DID I DO IT, YOU ASKED. I SAW THE PAIN AND PUZZLEMENT ON YOUR FACE.

WHY. WHY, INDEED.

MIKE, I ENVY YOU. YOU'RE YOUNG, AND YOU'RE SEEING IT ALL FOR THE FIRST TIME. YOU'LL GET OVER THIS EXPERIENCE, AND YOU'LL BE FINE. BUT WHAT WILL YOU DO WHEN YOU HAVE SEEN IT ALL BEFORE, WHEN THERE IS NOTHING IN THE TRADERS' WORLD THAT IS NOVEL OR EXCITING, WHEN TRADING IS SO AUTOMATIC IT CAN BE DONE WITHOUT THINKING? CHILLS, CHIPS, HIVERS, YANKEES, GREASERS, STRINES, TRADERS—WHO CARES? I'VE SEEN THEM ALL, WITH EVERYTHING THEY CAN OFFER. I WAS *BORED*, MIKE. BORED BEYOND DEATH. JUST PRAY THAT IT NEVER HAPPENS TO YOU.

GOOD LUCK, AND LONG LIFE (BUT NOT TOO LONG)—MAX DALZELL. PS: THIS RECORD WILL NOT BE STORED ANYWHERE IN DADDY-O'S DATA BANKS.

The file closed and left Mike staring at an empty screen. After a couple of minutes he went back to Send mode and opened the connection to Daddy-O. He had to explain what he had done—that he had confirmed his suspicions about Dalzell, then been stupid and naive enough to let him escape.

But he hesitated. If Mike wanted to, he could purge the file where he had suggested that Max Dalzell was a traitor. The disappearance would be a mystery, but there would be nothing to connect it to Mike's return. And no record of this meeting.

Dalzell's final PS said it all: if Mike left the other's reputation intact, he could keep secret his own bungling.

It was a temptation. Mike could hide his blunders and start on a path that could lead to success and a position as Master Trader—and maybe, thirty years from now, to another high-speed flight to Ree-o-dee.

Mike thought about it for a few seconds. Then he sent the message that converted his conjecture about Max Dalzell to an open data file and asked Daddy-O to go ahead and investigate. The computer accepted his instructions without comment or criticism—those would come later, from others.

He had done it. He would tell everything, and drag the legend of Max Dalzell down into the gutter. Max Dalzell, the greatest of them all, the super-Trader with one fatal flaw.

Infallible Max.

But he was not infallible. He had been wrong on at least one other thing. "You'll be fine," he had said. "You're young." Mike stared at the messages on the terminal and knew he would never be young again.

"The record is in the file. Asparian completed the mission, Lyle. Just as I said he would."

"And he was destroyed by it, Daddy-O, just as *I* said he would be. I tried to persuade him to go to the Economic Community for a while. He refused. He wouldn't talk to Lucia, wouldn't even take a call from Jeanette. He's back in the rehab tank, sitting in a sensory deprivation chamber. Jack Lester says he can't get through to him either. Mike wants to see no one, hear no one, feel nothing." Connery's anger showed in his carefully neutral voice. "We've been breaking him, you know, step by step. His friends, his ideals, his ambitions; they've all gone. What's left?"

"Mikal *remains. Not destroyed:* hardened. *He has known sorrow. He has known physical pain. He has known failure.*

He has made friends, as well as lost them. He has felt compassion, even for Max Dalzell. He has resisted temptation."

"Has anyone else *ever* been pushed around like this? If they have, I don't remember it. And what about your promise? Before he went to Cap City, you said it would be only two more missions."

"*That has not changed. Unless we fail, the next mission will be the last one that I assign to Mikal Asparian.*"

"Can't we stop now? He has every attribute that you listed."

"*One more mission, Lyle. Only one.*" Daddy-O's electronic voice sounded weary. "*One more. And then—it will be over.*"

One way or another. But that element of the record was not transmitted to Lyle Connery. In half a century of data collection and analysis, Daddy-O had learned the loads that humans were able to bear.

The breaking point was close, for Lyle Connery and Mikal Asparian.

CHAPTER 17

Mike felt sure he was going to throw up, but he couldn't let himself do it. Not with a Chipponese kid watching and all ready to laugh.

She had come floating over upside down, then done some sort of quick roll so that she was staring into his face. "Are you all right?"

What a question!

"Sure." That sort of lie was learned back in the first training sessions.

"I know how you feel. Try to relax. First time up." She said that the way that Chips often did, so that it was impossible to tell if it were a question or a statement. She spoke excellent Trader, but with a tonal language like Chipponese the usual rules for pronunciation, such as a rising final inflection to indicate a question, didn't apply any more. She had carried them into her Trader speech pattern.

"We'll be docking in five minutes," she went on. At least she wasn't laughing. "There's nothing to be afraid of. I felt like this, too, the first time—I didn't go up myself until I was seventeen years old."

She looked about ten! Chip women didn't have much in the way of figures, and Mike had just learned that he couldn't tell how old they were. For all he knew, she could be his age.

"I'm not scared." He started to shake his head, which did terrible things to his balance centers and semicircular canals. He swallowed, gripped the sides of the harness, and looked out of the port.

He had been given a prime viewing position. As soon as he realized that he was seeing the world the wrong way up, he could begin to pick out a few features. There was the Great Republic, and even from this distance he could see the big difference between that and the Unified Empire. The Republic was *groomed*, the fields set out in neat patterns. Agriculture in the Unified Empire was a random matter of spotty and straggling development. Was that Skeleton City down there? And that, spiraling into view...

"No!" She grabbed hold of him and turned his head away. "Don't use Earth as your reference frame. We're spinning. You'll lose orientation, and then you'll—"

Too late. She held the bag in front of Mike's face, while he said good-bye to the last meal he had eaten on Earth. For the first time, he wondered if this mission was going to be as simple as Daddy-O had suggested.

Sick as he felt, Mike was not unhappy. He did not understand what was happening to him, but since his final, reluctant emergence from the Rehab Center he was no longer miserable. There was a sense of impending change—one way or another, *something* was going to happen to him. A decision point was close. Until it arrived, he would allow himself to be swept along by events.

For a change, he had been well briefed, by Traders who had been up to the Geosynch Ring themselves. The thing that he found hardest to accept was the warning that had come from Daddy-O: "Do not become susceptible to the charms of Chipponese females. It is easy to do so—more than that, it is built into you by nature. It is xenophilia, an urge to draw a mate from outside the tribe. Chipponese women are not initially attractive to Trader men, they are too frail and skeletal; but they are far from you, racially. Be careful. Their appearance may become attractive to you."

Mike looked at the Chipponese woman who had held his head and decided that Daddy-O's warning was quite unnecessary. She wasn't exactly ugly, but she had about as much shape and sex appeal as a grasshopper. The idea that he might be attracted to her was ridiculous. And it seemed that he was likely to be stuck with her as his main liaison for the entire mission.

"My name is Li Xia," she said as soon as they were docked and on the first level of the Geosynch station. She led Mike to a quarter-gee facility, where his stomach would have a chance to put itself back together, and then offered a formal handshake. "I am very pleased to meet you. I will be your principal guide here."

Mike, over the objections of his esophagus, managed to produce a sort of grunt. Traders and Chipponese were both strong on the formalities, but it seemed to him that he had already violated all conventional etiquette by throwing up on her. "Ugh. Hello." He coughed. "I am Mike Asparian."

She was staring at him closely, as though she had never seen a Trader before. He felt entitled to return the compliment. He stared right back.

Li Xia was wearing a yellow sleeveless blouse and shorts. She was tiny and small-framed, just as he had expected. What surprised him was her feeble-looking musculature. Her bones hardly looked as though they would support her weight, and the muscles attached to them were mere knobs of flesh. She could have passed muster in a Lostlands labor camp.

Even so, she was not all that hideous. Her face was far too thin, but it had huge, dark eyes, a clear complexion, and a well-shaped mouth. Her light build gave her a definite grace of movement in low-gee.

She had been looking Mike over from head to toe, and he saw her eyes linger disapprovingly on his midriff. He stood up straighter and pulled in his stomach. Apathy and lassitude after the last mission had added seven or eight kilos, and most of it had settled around his waist. Now he resolved to take it off as soon as possible. There were already enough differences between him and the Chipponese; one secret of successful negotiation was to lessen the psychological distance between oneself and the other party.

While they were still staring at each other, a Chipponese male came forward to stand beside Li Xia. He stood stiffly and self-consciously, waiting for Mike's attention and Li Xia's introduction. The Chip tradition was well defined. If Mike didn't look at him, the newcomer would stand there for hours and never speak.

Mike turned to him and managed a smile that began and ended on his face, with no approval from his unhappy stomach. The man nodded. He was round-shouldered, gray-haired, and withered, and he had a face like a frog.

"Permit me. This is Ando Jia-Chi," Li Xia said. Her expression was anxious. "He too has come here from Luna. Even though he will be returning there shortly, rather than staying here with us, I wanted you to meet him. Six months from now, Ando and I will be married."

Mike inclined his head, held out his hand, and gave Ando Jia-Chi a more thorough inspection. It confirmed the first impression. Everyone to her own taste, Missie Li, he thought. Ando Jia-Chi is even thinner than you are. I wouldn't like to watch the pair of you on your wedding night: two stick insects, rubbing yourselves together and trying to light a fire.

Were there fat Chipponese, out here in space? Certainly the ones Mike had watched gambling in Dreamtown were substantial enough. But everyone he had seen since they docked was nothing more than skin and bones.

"Delighted to meet you, Mr. Ando," Mike said as they shook hands. (Remember the Chip custom: last name comes first.) "You have a delightful fiancée, and you have made an admirable choice for a bride."

Li Xia looked embarrassed, and Ando lifted his nose in the air at Mike as though he had encountered a bad smell.

"Ando and I are from a traditional tong, Mr. Asparian," Li said. "We were chosen for each other by our families. Your congratulations should be given to them."

Social gaffe number two—maybe worse than throwing up in public. "I hope that I will have such an opportunity. And my apologies to both of you, if I am the reason that you will be separated during my visit here."

"No." Li Xia shook her head. Her face was thin boned, her shiny dark hair cut close to the skull. It made her look even thinner. "That was my doing. I asked to be allowed to take part in the negotiation of the entertainment package. Ando is a specialist in energy systems, so his presence would not be appropriate."

It would be worse than inappropriate—it might be disastrous. The last person that Mike wanted hanging round him on this mission was an energy systems expert. His official mission was the negotiation of entertainment facilities for top Chipponese officials in the Unified Empire. The unofficial mission was to examine the energy-supply systems of the Geosynch Ring. With the Great Republic's progress in fusion methods, they were tired of dependence on Chipponese space power for their base load energy. Old-Billy Waters wanted to renegotiate energy cost, but to do that he needed to know how much margin there was in the Chipponese systems—and he wanted it done quietly, without the Chips knowing it was happening.

Mike nodded at Ando, who stood and stared at him with all the charm of a stuffed dummy.

The other man said something rapidly to Li Xia in Chipponese. Mike quietly reached into his pocket and pressed a button. The miniature Chill translator there had cost a monstrous amount, and it wasn't nearly as good as Daddy-O's fifty-language interpretive service, but it weighed only four ounces, and it did everything that was promised.

Li Xia turned to Mike. "Mr. Ando's apologies," she said. She spoke Trader, and the translator was smart enough to know that it didn't need to give a feed to Mike's built-in earpiece. "Mr. Ando is not fluent in your language."

But he was quite fluent enough to understand what I said about choosing a bride. Be careful! "Perhaps you would make my apologies, too," Mike said. "I am sure his knowledge of Trader language far exceeds mine of Chipponese."

"Mr. Ando asked me to invite you to be our guest at a meal, before he is obliged to leave for Luna."

Food. Mike's stomach muttered its protest. He couldn't eat now to save his life. He turned to Ando, smiled, and nodded graciously. "The pleasure will be all mine."

Ando smiled back at him like a lizard and turned again to Li Xia. Again there was a gabble of Chipponese.

"He accepted, so we are obliged to go through with it," whispered the translator in Mike's ear. "I suppose that you feel it is necessary if you are to succeed in your work with him. So we will feed him. But he is already disgustingly fat and bloated. I am amazed that there can be more room for food inside him."

"He is indeed corpulent," Li Xia said, again in Chipponese. "But not unusually so for one from Earth. By their standards he is not large. And let us be careful what we say now—his dossier indicates that he is ignorant of our language, but who knows?"

"I do," Ando said. "I can tell it by simply looking at his face. I have told you before, they are barbarians. Five thousand years ago, when we already had a flowering civilization, they were gibbering apes, swinging in the trees. Even today, their ignorance of culture is astonishing."

It was a good test of Mike's self-control. He wanted to say that his own lineage might be suspect, but the Traders, as a group, could trace their origins back well over five thousand years, all the way to the Phoenicians and the sunny shores of the Mediterranean Sea. Instead he stood and smiled.

"Tell him we will go to dinner now," Ando went on. "We will get him drunk, and then you will find that we can manipulate him easily. We will find out what he knows."

All three still stood smiling and bowing at one another. Mike elevated Li Xia a notch in his esteem. She had some of the right material to be a Trader. *Trader rule: Say what you have to, but think what you want to*.

With Ando leading the way they walked around the rim of the quarter-gee chamber to a place where food could be ordered. As they sat down at a table, Ando spoke again to Li. "Ask him if he would like me to order food for all of us."

Mike waited for Li's translation, then nodded.

Ando called up the menu, studied it for a few seconds, then touched his finger to a long series of items. Mike watched closely. His understanding of written Chipponese was quite good, much better than his experience of the spoken language, but he could translate little of the menu. The only thing he was sure of was soup. There was a good chance that he could handle that, even with his protesting stomach. He was curious to see what would be served, since all the Chip food had to be shipped up. Ninety percent of it still came from the Great Republic, in exchange for an assured energy supply.

"It will be a few minutes before our dinner is ready," Li said. "Meanwhile, perhaps you would like to take a look at Earth?"

Mike was tempted to decline politely, recalling what had happened the last time that he had tried to look at Earth. But it was time he began to learn his way around this element of the Geosynch Ring, and he would not gain that knowledge sitting in the dining room. He nodded, and Li Xia rewarded him with a delighted smile.

"Wonderful." She clapped together tiny, thin-fingered hands. "You see, I have had no opportunity to observe this for myself, since we arrived from Luna. And since Ando and I both live on Farside, a look at Earth is a rare occasion for us—and never from such a close distance as the Ring."

It was interesting to note the change in her when Ando Jia-Chi was not running the conversation. She became the cheerful girl Mike had first observed during final shuttle docking.

The Chipponese Geosynch Ring justified its name as a concept, not as a single structure. This station was a single stand-alone portion of the hundred separate elements that together made up the whole Ring. The elements, spaced fifteen hundred miles apart, were coupled through energy and signal transfers, but each moved freely in its own orbit. The common construction pattern for each station was a set of hollow wheels, skewered like shish kebab on a long central axle. Effective gravity ranged from a quarter of a gee on the wheel perimeters, to free-fall on the central spindle.

The axis of the station pointed to a fixed direction in space. At the moment, its thicker end was pointing down toward Earth. Li Xia led the way in to the zero-gee area of that hollow center, then turned and headed Earthward, moving along the spindle for two hundred yards to its lower end. Mike's insides did one horrid turn-around when they reached weightlessness, then decided they had to make the best of a bad situation. He suddenly felt steadier. With Ando guiding from behind and Li tugging from in front, he floated along like a jellyfish toward the end viewing port.

Now that he was not on a small and rapidly spinning ship, the disorientation was tolerable. Earth hung ahead of them through the port, a thousand times the area of a full moon. The planet was a streaky blue marble, its hazy surface half-obscured by cloud formations. They were hovering over the equator, in the middle of the Indian Ocean.

"See there?" Li Xia pointed excitedly off to a cloud-free area on the right. "That is where my family lived before the Heavenly Cloud came. My grandfather was working on the Unification, and my grandmother was there with him."

Mike discreetly refrained from comment. The Chips had a talent for euphemism that exceeded anything he could manage. He might give a moving mass of deadly radioactivity, thousands of miles across, many names, but Heavenly Cloud was not one of them. It had wiped out at least four billion people—maybe more, because no one had even attempted an Asian and European census since the Lostlands War. And that "Unification" Li had referred to was just as bad. The Chinese and Japanese had been busy murdering each other, with the Japanese marginally losing, when the fallout of radioactivity had changed all their priorities.

Li was pointing at the place where her other grandmother had been born, an area on the east side of the continent where a great river flowed to the ocean. They turned the telescope on and swept across the region. There was no sign of any city south of the river. According to Li a great metropolis, the home for twenty million Chinese, had once stood there.

She turned to Mike. "Have you ever been there? I was told that Traders go everywhere on Earth."

"Everywhere there is something to trade. Not, unfortunately, in that area. But look here." Mike swung the telescope to point a thousand miles farther west. "This is where I was raised as a small child."

Li Xia studied the image. "But that is Hiver territory."

"That's right."

"So you must be racially close to a Chipponese. You do not look it. Are you?"

"I don't know. I don't know where I was born, or anything about my parents. But you are right about my appearance. The Traders' computer estimates that I was captured from somewhere much farther west. Now, of course, the Traders are my family."

"But I did not realize that the Hives traded. Have you been back there?"

"Not yet. One day, perhaps. They trade very little." And the other things they do, I would rather not think about. Mike scanned on westward, across the dark uninhabited plains of India, Pakistan, and Afghanistan, where the Lostlands War had started. He swung south into Africa and halted the telescope to look closely at the Atlantic seaboard.

"You visited that place?" Li asked excitedly. "You are so lucky!"

"My first mission away from the training center was there." Mike focused on Coronation City. It showed as a tiny unresolved blob of darkness against the lighter background. "See? Where the river forks."

"And how about here?" She was moving east again, to a great rift valley that split the African continent. "Have you been here?"

Mike shook his head. "One short visit, that was all. It is beyond the territory controlled by the Ten Tribes."

He did not tell her the rest of it. They had touched down there as a final part of training, rumbling to a halt on a rutted earth runway. The plan had been to evaluate the idea of building a hydroelectric station on the great river that ran half the length of Africa. Construction ought to be easy, and such a station would produce many gigawatts of power.

In less than a day they knew what Daddy-O had known before the computer had sent them there. The plan was hopeless. This part of the continent, without Rasool Ilunga's subtle touch, had turned its back on the twenty-first century. It was regressing, feeling its way back to the old balance with nature. The population was falling; the technology of even the last generation had gone. The heat was murderous, and there was a terrible stillness on the flat, smoking landscape.

Li Xia had read his mood. She nodded and turned to Ando. "Let us go back," she said in Chipponese. "He may be the barbarian you say, but some memory hurts him."

Mike had to remind himself that he was not supposed to understand and he must avoid smiling at her in gratitude.

Seated again at the table, Ando pressed the dark area on the table edge as a command for service to begin. Mike waited with fair interest. The trip to the viewing ports had improved his condition enough to give an appetite, and he was curious to see what was produced. The Chipponese culinary habits were the least known of any.

Dinner was served. The dishes came into view from the midtable hatches.

Mike found the spread revolting. As soon as he saw the first offering he reached for and surreptitiously swallowed a detox pill.

Cold octopus, like strings of chewy rubber, was the first appetizer, followed by sea slugs stuffed with shredded pork. Snake soup—three kinds of snake, Ando proudly announced. And then the main courses, of raw fish, fried eel, chicken parts —Mike had one piece with the beak still in it—and a black, slimy material which he did not dare to ask about. The food was washed down with beer and interspersed with frequent toasts of *mao tai* liquor, strong enough to melt the wax out of one's ears.

Traders' training: Mike sampled everything and murmured compliments as the endless succession of dishes appeared on the table. He drank every potion they offered him, and gradually became louder and more garrulous.

He told them about all his missions. How he had triumphed in the Strine Interior, but how he had failed to return Seth Paramine from Cap City; how he had survived the mind-murdering intentions of Dominic Mantilla and of Sabrina Vandermond, and how he had seen through Rasool Ilunga's plans to use the Traders for his own purposes.

He talked too much, belched freely, knocked over his glass, and was insufferably rude to Ando Jia-Chi. And thanks to the detox pill, he was stone-cold sober, and able to form an accurate impression of his hosts.

About the eleventh course—abalone and mushrooms, a merciful interlude—he was gratified to see that Ando's eyes were bulging, so that he looked more and more like a dyspeptic frog. Ando had been matching Mike drink for drink, though Mike noticed that the other man took only a fraction of a glass each time. Even so, his body mass was probably only half as great, and he had presumably not taken precautions before they began.

Li Xia watched her fiancée become less and less communicative. He slumped lower in his seat, lost color in his face, and let his mouth hang open even more than usual. Mike was careful to notice nothing, and to chat on as usual.

By the thirteenth course she could stand it no longer. She stood up. "I am afraid that Mr. Ando says he cannot stay here with us." Ando had not spoken a word for ten minutes. "His flight will be leaving shortly. If you will remain here, while we say good bye to each other, I will return in just a few minutes."

Mike smiled and watched her go, dragging old frogface behind her. Maybe that would teach Ando a lesson! Next time, he would talk less about barbarians. Mike poured himself another glass of the fiery liquor and watched the tiny Chill table-robots scuttle out of the hatches to take Ando's empty plate.

Another twenty minutes passed before Li Xia reappeared. She slid into the seat opposite Mike and accepted the tiny glass of sweet red wine that he poured and pushed across to her. She had drunk almost nothing. Now she nodded, sipped, and gave him a thoughtful stare.

"Mr. Mikal Asparian, I do not know how it is possible. But you are not intoxicated. Not in the least."

There was no accusation in her tone. So why did he suddenly feel guilty, and why was he reluctant to act drunk any longer?

He thought of how Li Xia had stared wistfully out at the great Chinese river, at the ancient home that was forever denied to her and her people. They were exiles. They could look, but they could never go back.

"You know, you're not the only one. I'm homeless, too." Mike was surprised to hear his own voice.

Was he drunk? How could he be, with the detox pills that had never failed him yet?

"All the Traders are homeless," he went on. "We don't have

any land we can call our own, unless it's the training camps. We're a group that every country thinks of as outsiders. Our homes have to be in every land, or on the seas, or high in the air. Traders are scattered all around the globe. Even our computer is a distributed system. There are storage and computing units everywhere, linked by comsats and microwave lines and fiber optic cables. We are everywhere, but we are nowhere."

He paused. There. He had made a fool of himself. But Li Xia was not laughing or scornful. She was sitting quietly, looking directly at him with wide, sympathetic eyes.

"Go on," she said after a moment.

"I'm being a bore."

She smiled. "I do not think you could be boring if you tried. Please go on. You are very proud, are you not, to be a Trader?"

Conflicting emotions were at war inside him. He wanted to say that she was quite wrong, that he hated the Traders, that they were a ruthless group who had used him and abused him to suit their purposes. Instead he said, "I'm very proud. We are a small, weak group. Yet we are the ones who permit commerce to be carried on among the great power groups. We have little power of our own, but we are absolutely essential. We are the glue that holds Earth together."

His pretentious words made him cringe. He was saying things sober that he would not normally have said drunk. Now surely she must be laughing at him. But he saw nothing but warmth in those great, sad eyes staring at him across the table.

She smiled then, the little hands cupping the silvery glass. As Mike ran out of words she put down her wine, reached across to take his left hand in both of hers, and turned it palmside up.

"Permit me." The dark head bent to study the lines that crisscrossed his hand.

She was silent for a while, running soft fingertips delicately across his palm. Then she shook her head. "A wanderer's hand, and a wanderer's life. You will travel all your years, across strange seas and unknown lands. But I see humor and affection there, and the chance for great happiness."

"I wish you could tell me when that happiness will begin." Mike's hand was tingling under her touch, but at the same time he felt relaxed and comfortable for the first time in months. He did not want to pull away. "Can you tell me anything more specific? How long will I live, will I ever marry, how many children will I have?"

She looked up, smiled, and shook her head. "That I cannot see. I wish that I could—in my own hand, as well as in yours." The smile vanished from her face, as some other thought came to her. "I must apologize for what happened this evening. Mr. Ando's behavior was not good. He is not accustomed to drinking alcohol."

"He was merely tired. Please do not worry about it any more."

Perhaps she was smart enough to suspect that Mike could read Ando's feelings from the man's face even without knowing what he was saying. Ando had liked Mike no more than Mike had liked him. "Ugly, stupid, and greedy," he had said in Chipponese before he had passed out. "A fat Trader swine . . . a bloated imbecile . . . a parasite on society . . . a slobbering, drunken glutton." Perhaps it was just as well that Ando was going back to the Moon. Even with Li Xia's moderating influence, the relationship between the two men had nowhere to go but down.

Li Xia was still holding Mike's hand in hers. They both became aware of it at the same moment, and she released him and stood up quickly.

"Well." Her voice was breathless. "Mr. Mikal Asparian, let me say how much I have enjoyed this dinner with you. The things that you told me were enthralling. One of my long-held dreams is that some day I might visit Earth, and you brought it closer to me than ever before. I feel as though we could sit and talk and laugh together for many more hours, and the time would fly past us."

Mike stood up awkwardly, still adjusting to a quarter-gee environment. "Perhaps we will have another chance in the future. Miss Li, you are a wonderful listener. People tell you things without knowing it. You would make an excellent Trader."

"Thank you." She smiled. "I know that you have paid me the highest possible compliment. But now we must stop. The first meeting with the senior members of our delegation is twelve hours from now. You need rest before that. Let me show you to your quarters."

Rest was an attractive notion, but Mike could not take that luxury.

Aware of what free-fall might do to his system, Mike had requested a sleeping area on the outermost lower disk of the station. That lower wheel was reserved for living quarters, communications, and recreation. It rotated about the fixed axis that connected all the wheels. With a diameter of four hundred meters, the lower disk had an effective gravity that ran from near zero at the hub to a quarter gee at the outer rim. Mike was close to that rim, while Li Xia had a room a third of the way in, with effective gravity close to Luna's.

The uppermost wheel was unfortunately the one that Mike was most interested in. It did not rotate about the central spindle, and so had negligible effective gravity everywhere, and no residents. The equipment for power generation, construction, and maintenance was all located on that thick upper wheel. It was not off-limits to Mike, but getting there was another matter.

The only way to reach it was to travel in from his sleeping quarters on the rim of the lower wheel, all the way to the center, then upward along the spindle to the topmost wheel, and finally back out again toward its periphery. It had sounded easy when Mike was briefed, down on Earth, but in practice he had problems. The thing that slowed him the most was infuriatingly trivial: he did not know where the light switches were located in the spindle. It was impossible to fumble along in the dark *and* in free-fall. Without gravity to orient him, Mike could not tell which way he was going, or even if he was tumbling end-over-end.

Once he found the light switches, progress was fast. The upper wheel itself was well lit, and there were a few people in the corridors, dressed in technician's uniform. As an obvious non-Chip, Mike received the expected number of polite inquiring glances. He moved along as though he knew just where he was going, and no one tried to stop him.

He got farther than he expected, until at a branch point in all the outward corridors big signs in red announced: DANGER: HIGH RADIOACTIVITY SECTOR. NO ADMITTANCE TO THESE AREAS WITHOUT BADGE AND PERMITS.

The warning was an excellent way to keep people out, but was it true? Mike suspected that the signs were there for just that purpose—to discourage nosy visitors—because they were written in all the major Earth languages as well as in Chipponese. The sensors in his own fingertip recorder certainly indicated no dangerous radiation levels. But radioactivity was not something to be messed with. He turned around and quietly headed back toward his own quarters.

On the way he passed a couple of familiar faces, individuals who had certainly been in the corridors earlier. That made sense: The Chips were double-covering Mike. Li Xia was Team One; the second team would remain unobtrusively present, as a good backup team should.

Mike went back to his quarters, lay down on his bed, and closed his eyes. It was a good time to test the usefulness of his new implant. A passive version of the Diamond Fly's audio-input module, one-sixteenth of an inch in diameter, was tucked away behind his larynx. Mike subvocalized his report, a full description of events since he left the surface of Earth. When he returned home, the full audio record would be transferred to Daddy-O.

The memory unit of the Fly was durable. Lyle Connery had told Mike that it could survive accelerations of ten thousand gees and temperatures of four thousand degrees. It would survive orbital reentry without shielding. Since Mike estimated his own limits as twenty gees and a couple of hundred degrees above freezing, Connery's words had been no special comfort. As for reentry without shielding, that was a prospect Mike preferred not to dwell on.

He finally finished his recording and listened to the playback. Someday the Chills would develop hardware that would pick up from a distance the subvocalized inputs or the playback to one's ear. After that, what? Possibly it would no longer be safe even to *think* one's reports.

Not my worry, Mike thought. Not for today. He switched off the Fly brain recorder, lay back with eyes closed, and was dreaming within minutes.

Mike was beginning to have second thoughts. Maybe Li Xia was Team Two, not Team One. Certainly the group who were meeting for negotiations were no pushovers. There were four of them, in addition to Li. Each one spoke perfect Trader, had a totally unreadable face, and wore a near-invisible earpiece that told Mike they were being prompted by other Chips and Chipponese computers.

Even without all that he would have been wary. The Chip toughness in negotiation was legendary.

But so was the Traders'. Mike was as keyed up as he had ever been, and still quite confident—though it would have been nice to have Daddy-O, Connery, and Lover-boy Lester whispering in his ear when he needed it. They had sat down, five on one, around an aluminum-topped table. As part of the natural attempt to keep Mike off balance, the Chips had chosen to negotiate in a low-gee conference room. The traditional hot tea and sugar lumps were served—but the tea was drunk from a squeeze-bulb, and the sugar lumps tended to float away if he took his eye off them.

Li Xia had opened the discussions, while the others looked on. "We are prepared to pay thirty gigawatt-hours, to be delivered over a two-year period, to any selected point or points of the Unified Empire grid, with the exception of space-pointing laser sites. We are also willing to deliver elsewhere in the Western Hemisphere, subject to the same restriction. We offer a two-to-one daytime/nighttime ratio, and a forty-percent power increase during Southern Hemispherc winter. In return, we want a two-year access contract for one hundred people, entry point Guyana, with free movement across the Unified Empire."

While she was talking Mike was already busy with his calculations. This was what he had been trained for, and there was nothing better calculated to calm and at the same time sharpen his mind. Her offer sounded simple, but it had implications. First of all, the Chip tastes in vice were well known. Their visitors to the Unified Empire would be looking only for recreational drugs and gambling, not for sex, sadism, high-risk games, executions, cannibalism, or any other of the most expensive services. And chances were that the Chipponese would leave a lot of money behind them when they left. They were excellent gamblers, but the Greasers were the best. The Traders *would* have been the best, Mike thought, but Traders didn't gamble—not in that way.

Second, everyone at the table knew that most of the energy being offered in contract to the Unified Empire would not be used there. It would be traded to the Great Republic, to the north, whose agricultural programs called for huge energy investments in irrigation and in fertilizer production. And some would go south, to Cap City, in return for electronic equipment. The Chills were high-level energy users. To evaluate the Chipponese offer, Mike had to know the balance of trade levels between the four groups over the next two years. And he had to add in one variable that the Chipponese knew nothing about: the Great Republic's fusion program, and their new ability to achieve self-sufficiency in energy production.

"Counteroffer," he said. "The Chipponese presence in the Unified Empire will be as Li Xia has stated. But the delivery will be for thirty-five gigawatt-hours, with a three-to-one day/night ratio, and no Southern Hemisphere winter increase." He was admitting by that last statement that most of the power would be delivered to the Yankees in the northern hemisphere. That was no bargaining loss, since the Chips surely knew it already.

The four Chipponese leaned forward across the table, busy at once with their own calculations. While they did so, Mike had time for a look at Li Xia. He felt a new pity for her. Not only was she betrothed to frogfaced old Ando, but she and all the Chips were soon going to lose their prime market. The Great Republic bought most of the Chips' energy, and the Chips in turn relied on them to provide nine-tenths of their food supplies. What would happen if the Yankees suddenly had ample power of their own and didn't need Chipponese energy inputs?

Mike shrugged off that worry. It was not his business, and if history were any guide, the Chips would get by. They had survived when all their homelands became uninhabitable, even though they had to leave Earth to do it.

"Counteroffer," said the man opposite Mike. His name was Wang Tanaka, and he was unusually heavyset and full-faced for a Chip. Mike suspected an Ainu ancestry, traced back to Hokkaido.

"Thirty-two gigawatt-hours," the man continued. "But an access contract for one hundred and twenty Chipponese citizens for a period of two and a half years. There will be restricted transfer of energy delivery, with not more than thirty percent going to the northern hemisphere."

The negotiation was off and running. That restriction on delivery showed more clearly than anything that the Chips knew the real game as well as Mike did. And underneath *that* real game lay the other agenda. Somehow, sometime on this trip, Mike had to visit the station energy facilities and make his own evaluation of them. But this came first.

After seven hours they were still arguing, but there was evidence of convergence. At that point Wang Tanaka called for a two-hour recess, "to allow our visitor to take a well-earned rest"—which meant, to let the Chips put their heads together and decide the next move. Li Xia's relatively junior role was confirmed when Mike was told that she was at his disposal, to show him anything that he might want to see on the station, or to tell him more about the whole Geosynch Ring.

Mike could have used the time for his own thoughts on negotiation, but the offer was too good to refuse. Before any other alternative could be proposed he was leaving, with Li trailing along behind. After a ten-minute scratch meal of hot noodles, fried pork dumplings, and tea, they were heading at his request for a tour of the upper wheel.

"Good progress on the negotiations," Li said as they moved into the central spindle.

"Excellent. We are already close to an agreement."

She turned to face Mike with a free-fall maneuver he had not yet mastered, and gave him a little smile. "You say we are near agreement, but I do not think that you believe that statement."

Mike hid his surprise. That sounded like a definite indiscretion on her part, and one her bosses would be horrified by. She was not supposed to be so honest with him about the status of the talks.

Unless there was an ulterior motive? But he could not think of one.

"It depends what you define as 'near agreement,'" he said. "I believe that we are exactly where I expected us to be at this time. We have several days of negotiation ahead of us, but we have made good progress."

And *that*, he thought, was certainly not what he was supposed to say to her—mainly because it was true. Before they were finished they would have half a dozen cases of 'near agreement,' then one party would introduce a new complication that seemed to kill the deal. They would inch forward, then backward, and eventually reach agreement—and that was what negotiation was all about. But no professional negotiator would mention how far along he thought they had come—it revealed too much about his own position.

Mike worried over the exchange of comments as Li led the way through the spindle to the upper wheel. Her indiscretion may well have been planned—but *his* had not. He had better learn to hold his tongue until he understood his own motives.

With his mind elsewhere, he missed a handhold as they moved away from the station axis. He began to turn end-over-end. Li reached out effortlessly to correct his attitude, and to do that she pivoted her hip and shoulder across his chest.

It was like meeting a skeleton, thinly clothed with skin. With all the other Chips around, Mike had almost stopped noticing how emaciated she looked. Now he was reminded of it, and suddenly saw himself through Li Xia's eyes: oversized, fat, and clumsy, with an outsize nose and hairy skin. The new perspective was shocking and unwelcome.

They were at the axis of the upper wheel. The overall layout was familiar to the Traders, and Daddy-O had provided a detailed plan as part of the briefing. Now the trick was to make sure that Mike saw the appropriate sections for energy generation.

He had no illusions about what he would and would not see. The Chipponese energy production facilities were scattered through every element of the Geosynch Ring, as a mixture of nuclear and, rarely, solar power plants. Here on this station he would find only nuclear generators, and those only of medium size. It would be no more than a snapshot of the overall energy supply situation, but it would still be better than anything else available to Old-Billy Waters and the planners of the Great Republic. Mike had one other card to play. During his stay at the station the Strines, by agreement with the Yankees, would briefly double their power demand. Mike, in a position to see how the extra load was met, might be able to make a guess at the available capacity of the whole system.

On the way to the perimeter of the upper wheel, Mike again wondered what the loss of Yankee energy markets might do to the Chip economy. The Chipponese had been forced into space by the fallout of the Lostlands War, and at that time it had been touch and go if they would survive. What would the loss of their main market do to them—and to other regions—today? One sobering thought: the Lostlands War itself had started with the economic collapse of a single nation.

They had reached the station sections containing the power systems, and suddenly Mike had a whole new situation to worry about.

The energy generation units looked totally wrong—wrong because they were *familiar*.

The Traders' information on Chipponese power systems had been painstakingly collected over the years using official information and expensive espionage. That was a slow process, and the Chips were very careful people. The last big leak of design information had been over fifteen years ago.

Now Mike was looking at those same designs—which meant there had been no progress in Chipponese energy production technology for well over a decade. That was simply unbelievable. Even back on Earth, without the Chipponese focus on energy-producing systems, there had been a steady advance in fission and fusion reactors.

Mike examined the equipment more closely. Everything was

fission systems, and the units were not merely old designs—they were old equipment. The fuel recycling machines bore the scars and pitting of long use, and the pressure vessel seams showed evidence of many repair welds. The Chipponese seemed to be generating energy for use on Earth with antiquated, beat-up production facilities.

While Li Xia moved them on farther, higher in the wheel, Mike struggled to make sense of the evidence.

Plausible assumption number one: this was all a setup, the inverse of Rasool Ilunga's scheme. The head of the Ten Tribes had wanted Mike to report an advanced technology that he lacked. Suppose the Chips wanted to *deny possession* of such a technology? Then if they had some secret agenda of their own, or if they knew of Mike's own hidden agenda, they might have arranged for negotiation to take place on a station with old equipment. Then they could show Mike everything, yet give nothing away regarding their technical progress and production capability.

Mike dropped that idea as soon as they reached the uppermost section of the wheel. It held a second set of power units, much smaller ones that served only to generate and beam power to the Chipponese communications satellites in the Geosynch Ring. And these units were new, compact, and far more advanced than anything that Mike had ever seen.

On the way back down to the lowest wheel, the final mystery presented itself. Mike had an opportunity to examine the system control units. They were old, poorly maintained, and were already running close to their limits.

That led to a series of questions that Mike could not afford to ignore. When the Strine power demand on this particular station suddenly doubled, what would happen? The system should have an automatic cutout if the call for power became too high—but would it work? The monitors looked even older than the primary power units. So what should Mike do? To alert the Chips to possible danger would give the game away completely and provide very poor service on the Great Republic contract. But to fail to warn the Chips, if something was on the way past danger point . . .

He puzzled the problem all the way back to the innermost wheel and on through five more hours of negotiation. Training and experience allowed Mike to haggle with the Chip negotiators at almost a subconscious level—he realized for the first time just how deep the Trader training had gone in him. At the same time, his forebrain remained preoccupied with the mystery of the out-of-date power systems.

The double effort strained him. When they finished for the day, Mike was a wreck, ready for nothing more than dinner and relaxation.

Twelve hours of haggling had left Li just as weary. She yawned her way to the dining area and ordered dinner for both of them without even asking. They slumped opposite each other at the smooth-topped table, too worn out to pretend alertness. They waited quietly for the food to appear from the hatches. Tonight the food selection was less exotic, with only beer and tea served as drinks.

By unspoken agreement this was Li's turn to talk. Mike learned of her family's history as wealthy industrialists in Shanghai, of the multiple shocks that came with loss of family wealth, and finally of the universal draft for the Unification program.

Her grandparents had been incredibly lucky. They were already in Japan as part of the Unification conquering forces when the war began. They had been on one of the first shuttle flights up from the Kyushu launch sites. The first years had been a desperate attempt to survive. Then there had been many more years to mourn lost friends and relatives, and to grieve over the fertile acres of the Yangtze river valley that would never welcome the return of Li Xia's family.

"Still, there is the dream," she said at last. "My grandfather cannot bear to look down on Earth, or to see pictures of others harvesting ripe crops."

The food and drink had slowly been restoring their energy and spirits. By the time that the final course appeared, they were talking of more personal and recent matters. Li asked if a Trader always married another Trader.

Mike shook his head. "There's no absolute requirement, even though it usually turns out that way. For example, I could marry a Strine woman, or a Yankee woman, or even a Hiver. But then I would have to ask the Trader council to accept *her* as a Trader, too. If they didn't agree—which has happened a number of times—I would either have to give up being a Trader, or give up on the idea of marriage. Usually, the Trader drops the marriage idea."

"You are not married now?" she asked. She had been looking down, running her finger around the top of her glass and collecting the little drops of condensation there. Now she raised her head and looked straight at Mike.

He felt a little shiver in his spine. Her eyes were so dark and serious; they seemed to stare right inside him.

"No. Not yet. But someday I hope to be. To be married, to have a family of my own . . . it makes a difference when you never knew your own mother and father. I would love to have a little daughter."

And again he felt surprise. He was saying words to Li Xia that he had never spoken before—thoughts he had never consciously *thought* before.

She was nodding gravely. "And I would give anything to have a baby son." She smiled. "Wishful thinking, maybe. But it is good for us to have dreams, no matter how unlikely."

After a long silence she reached over and squeezed Mike's hand. "I hope that one day you will have your daughter, and I, my son. But now we must not become sad, worrying about the future. Come—you are not eating your dessert."

She was right. Li had ordered a chilled white confection, almond-flavored, that was served in a broad, shallow bowl of frosted glass. But Mike was not sure how he was supposed to eat it—there was no spoon. He looked at it, picked it up, and looked again.

Li noticed his confusion. "Like this, Mike."

She raised the bowl close to her mouth, extended a long, slim, pink tongue down into the glass, and licked at the frozen white dessert. Her big, dark eyes watched him over the rim of the cup. The operation looked perfectly easy and perfectly natural, like a graceful butterfly delicately drawing nectar from a white blossom.

Mike tried to imitate her action. His tongue didn't seem long enough. While she watched, he pushed his face farther into the bowl and came away with almond dessert on his nose, eyebrows, chin, and forehead—anywhere except in his mouth.

Li looked at him. She put her hand over her own mouth. First she giggled, just a little. Then she began to hoot, and after thirty seconds she collapsed. She leaned farther forward until her forehead was resting on the smooth table top and shook with helpless laughter. Mike sat motionless for a few more seconds. Then he reached forward and put his hand gently on her mop of dark hair.

And he decided, in a moment of black thought that came

from nowhere, that he hated Ando Jia-Chi and the Chipponese system of parentally assigned marriage.

The next day it was more negotiations; business as usual—almost. But Mike had a couple more worries to add to his list.

The first had come at the very end of the previous evening, when they were outside her room and about to say good night. Li had reached up, placed her hand on his lips, and said: "Trader Oath?"

Mike stopped in his tracks. "Do you understand the significance of that?"

She nodded calmly. "I believe I do. If you accept, then the information that I give you cannot be revealed to anyone. Let me add that I am acting for others on this, as well as for myself."

It was a difficult decision. Mike already had his hands full, but whatever the Chips wanted, it surely would not be a job done here—it would be something back on Earth.

He nodded. "I accept. What you say to me tonight will be under Trader Oath."

There was no discussion of price—not yet. That would depend on the nature of the task, and it would have its own negotiation.

Li stepped close and lowered her voice. Her breath was warm on Mike's cheek. "You have had dealings with the Great Republic. We know that you are familiar with their agricultural production system; but are you also familiar with the way that their economy depends on the supply of energy from us?"

Mike's brain did cartwheels, while his face was held rigid. Did the Chipponese already know about his mission for the Yankees?

"Li Xia, you appear to have some misunderstanding of Trader Oath. It means that I will *accept* confidential information—not that I will give it."

She smiled serenely. "Ah. Let me begin again. It is of great importance for us to know the degree of dependence of the Great Republic's economy on the continuous supply of energy from Chipponese power sources. What would happen if such energy were not available? We also wish to know how other groups on Earth would be affected should the economy of the Great Republic run into serious difficulties. We are unable to determine such information for ourselves. But you could discover it easily, upon your return to Earth. We would like to employ you for that purpose."

Given the battered, beat-up appearance of the energy generation equipment that Mike had seen earlier in the day, Li Xia's comments had an ominous ring. Mike's own feeling was that Earth's whole economy might fall apart if the Great Republic went belly-up. All the talk of regional independence was fine, but everyone relied on everyone else. The balance of industries had been established over many years. It was workable, delicate, and might not survive a major upheaval. In a few years' time, when the Yankee fusion system came on-line, things might be different. But not today. A billion people would be affected. And that left Mike no choice.

Prime Rule: You are a human being first, and a Trader second. He had to follow this at least a step or two farther. "I agree. Subject to future negotiation, I will attempt to do what you ask. But I need to know more. Why do you anticipate problems in continuing the energy supply to the Great Republic?"

She stepped back and shook her head. "I cannot answer your question tonight. My task was only to seek a general agreement between us. Tomorrow, perhaps, I can take this further." She opened the door of her room, stepped inside, then turned and took his hand. "But this must be good night, Mike Asparian. The day is over. May you sleep like a child and have pleasant dreams."

Li Xia's wish may have been well intended, but it was not realistic. Mike's nightly report to his built-in recorder did nothing to relax him. And when he did fall asleep, it was to disturbing dreams. He was back on Earth, but it was a warring, violent Earth which had servered all ties to the Chipponese group. The globe was aflame, as the regions exhausted their weapons' arsenals on one another. Mike was in the Trader training center, looking up at the wintry, dust-obscured moon. He could see Li Xia's face there. She was starving, and forever beyond his reach.

He woke up shivering, heart pounding, and blamed it on unfamiliar gravity. He wandered off to breakfast with little appetite. While he was eating, all the lights on the station went out for five seconds. He froze, his mouth full.

The lights flickered back on again before he had much time to dwell on air-lock failure and the long-ago doom of Station

Twelve. Another negotiation tactic? Possibly. But it was still on his mind when the morning meeting began; he asked Wang Tanaka what it meant.

"Oh, the lighting?" The Chipponese negotiator was casual and relaxed. "Don't worry about it. Just a station reactor being removed for regular maintenance. It will be out of service for a couple of days. The remaining ones have more than enough capacity, and all critical systems have standby power sources."

Wang Tanaka sounded unperturbed and reassuring, but Mike saw that Li Xia's face was drawn and unhappy, the eye sockets like black holes in her skull. She had wished him pleasant dreams, but her own sleep period had certainly not been peaceful. Something was eating at her. But was it business, or a personal matter?

The second day of negotiation ground on. They made progress, but Mike noticed one oddity. No matter what offer he made to the Chip negotiators, they would not consider any deal that implied energy delivery for more than two and a half years. *Rule 9: Locate the non-negotiables.* To see how far he could push it, Mike began to hold out tempting tidbits for any contract that extended to three years, or even two and three-quarters. It was no good. Thirty months was a wall, an absolute barrier for the Chip position. Mike could offer them anything, but if it also implied a longer contract there would be polite rejection. He filed that away for future use.

The afternoon discussions were wearying. The Chips were working on him in pairs now, and after his restless night Mike was negotiating largely on instinct. Two other factors preoccupied him: a power generator was out of commission in an already ramshackle production facility, and an increased energy demand was on its way to this station from the Strines.

He *had* to take another look at the energy generation system, even if it interfered with the negotiation. A Chip reactor blow-up was an "incident," a minor news item down on Earth; here on the station it would be an absolute disaster.

At the first chance for a break he excused himself and headed for the upper wheel. Li followed at once. She asked no questions, not even when he made a close inspection of the reactors and the power transmission facility—which was certainly no part of his official role on the station.

The situation was worse than he had thought. Radiation levels were high, there were sticky control rods, and the mechanical linkages were worn. Maintenance personnel were few and widely scattered.

Li Xia had been watching every action. When Mike finally stopped, stared around him, and shook his head hopelessly, she took him by the hand.

"Come," she said. She led the way upward, out past the reactors that produced power for Earth, on past the new and well-maintained equipment that gave power to the comsat network, on out to the extreme tip of the station's axle where a thin spindle jutted far beyond the uppermost wheel. They drifted up that long, straight corridor to its very end. There the spindle terminated in a spherical chamber about twenty yards across, with transparent panels on all sides. Photo shields cut off the most intense light, leaving a view of the Moon, half-full against a glittering star field.

They floated side-by-side for almost a minute. Mike was stunned by the view, and it was Li who broke the silence. "Mikal Asparian, I believe that you are a good man, as well as being a good Trader. What I am going to say to you is not under Trader Oath, and I am certainly not authorized to discuss it as part of the negotiation. But I hope that I can trust you."

Mike saw the agony on her face. "I think that you can trust me, Li Xia. Trader Oath is not necessary."

"Thank you. I am going to tell you what from your actions you may already suspect." She took Mike by the shoulder and swiveled their bodies in free-fall so that they stood face-to-face a few inches apart. "I must beg your silence. If my betrothed, Ando Jia-Chi, knew I was saying this to you, he would disown me."

"Then perhaps I am sorry that he will not know."

"Ah." She looked quickly away. "I understand. But you do not. It would not be Ando alone, it would be my whole family. I would become an outcast, a nonperson. Again, I beg your silence."

"Li, you do not need to beg me. You *command* my silence."

That earned the faintest hint of a smile, a moment of sunlight across a clouded face. "Ah, I like to hear that. But you must not say it. Not now, when I need all my mind on what I must tell you. Listen closely."

She turned Mike again to look at the Moon. "Earth people do not understand Chipponese society, any more than we understand yours. You have no idea of the issues that occupy our attention. On the Moon today there is a great divisiveness among my people. One group says that Earth is part of the past only, and that its present welfare means nothing to Chipponese people. Who cares if the Unified Empire starves, they say, or the Cap Federation freezes, or the Great Republic blows itself up with its weapons? When we were forced to move to space, who on the Earth helped us? No one. What happens to Earth now is not our business. Another group, a smaller one, cannot accept such an attitude. We are all humans, they say, and the death of any human, anywhere, diminishes all of us. I am part of this second group."

"And so am I, although I am not Chipponese. Li, take comfort. You are not the only people with these worries. The Cap Federation is divided over the same question. We are all human."

She nodded absently and was silent again, staring at the blind white disk of the Moon. Mike felt impatient, but he did not let it show. She must be allowed to take her time. She was feeling her way into this, looking for the strength to say something against the wishes of her family, fiancée, friends, and nation.

"The Chipponese space systems provide the base load energy for the whole world," she went on at last. "That has been so for a generation, and there is a stability that everyone cherishes. But what would happen if this supply ceased? What if Yankee food products no longer were traded for our energy, or if the Chills no longer provided their microelectronics to other regions?"

Mike took a deep breath and cursed to himself. At this point he should be telling Li Xia of the Yankee move to energy independence, but he was bound to silence by Trader Oath to the clients in the Great Republic. All he could do was nod his head.

"It would be chaos," she continued. "Political chaos, and then perhaps the old curses of war, starvation, and sickness. There are people who do not worry about this. For their own group interests, they are willing to destroy stability. Unless everyone is warned of their plans, *now...*"

She did know. She *must* know. She was talking of Old-Billy's ideas for energy independence.

"If you already know so much—" Mike began. He was interrupted by an eerie wail, resonating through the walls of the chamber. "What the devil is that?"

Li turned her head to look back along the corridor. "Energy demand overload," she said. Her voice was unconcerned. "The siren means that the shields will be going up as an extra safety measure. We should head back at once."

Mike looked at his watch. If the Strines were beginning their increased energy drain on the system, they were a couple of hours early. And if this were some other, unpredicted call for energy, then when the Strines added their own load to it . . .

"Li Xia." He spoke rapidly. "Call down to the main wheel control center from here—you can do that, can't you? Tell them that there will be a doubling of Strine energy demand, very soon, and they have to be ready for it. Do it now. Then we can head back ourselves."

She didn't take even a moment to ask or argue. While she was at the message console, Mike had time for his own thoughts. Good-bye, one client. Old-Billy Waters would have every right to be angry. Mike was ruining the very test that he had been sent up to space to observe.

Li took longer than he had expected to complete her message. She got through easily enough, but she seemed to have a credibility problem. She had to say the same thing several times to different people before she finally put the communications unit back onto its base.

"Foolish bureaucrats," she said. "They seemed more interested to find out how I knew, than to act on the information. Quickly now. We should not have waited."

With Li leading the way they skimmed back down the long tunnel toward the main wheel. When they were less than half-way there, Li caught a handhold and waited for Mike to reach her. She pointed at the tunnel wall, turned, grabbed Mike, and began to tow him back the way that they had come.

Mike had caught one glimpse of the ambient radiation level shown on the wall monitor, and he needed no persuasion. Something in the energy shielding facility was not doing its job; the tunnel was a radiation hot spot.

He looked at the flux monitor when they arrived in the end chamber. The digital display was flickering steadily to a higher and higher total dose. He pointed it out to Li. "In here, also. What now?"

"Let me find out." Again she took the communicator while Mike looked all around the chamber. There were no additional radiation shields that could be placed in position, and no other ways back to the main wheels. If the failure were a bad one, they would fry.

Li again replaced the communicator and floated across to

him. "Not too bad," she said. "A partial failure of one reactor. The engineers used manual overrides and have cut power back to minimal supply levels. You were quite right about the energy demand, just after we warned them there was a doubling of Strine energy requests. That has been manually shunted off to three other stations. They can handle it."

"What about the situation here?"

"There will be no need to evacuate the wheels. But all personnel will move to the base of the lowest wheel for maximum shielding."

That was good news—to everyone except Mike and Li Xia.

"What about us? We can't get to the lower wheel. The tunnel is hot, and there are no more shields here. And the wall monitor agrees with my own sensor—there's an increasing flux of hard gammas."

"We leave," Li said calmly. "As soon as we can." She went over to a wall cupboard, opened it, and pulled out two suits.

"You mean we make a space-walk." Mike did not like the sound of that, whatever the incentive.

"No. We take the lifeboat." She was holding one suit and looking at it critically. "There may be a problem here. These suits were made for someone smaller than you. You had better remove your clothing."

It was no time for argument. She watched Mike strip to the skin, then looked dubiously at the suit. "It will still be a tight fit. Come on, I will help you. You will feel uncomfortable, but it will be for only a few minutes."

By a combined effort they managed to stuff Mike in and zip him up. The suit was like a tight corset at his midriff. He swore that when this was over he would lose twenty pounds. Li slipped easily into her own suit, motioned Mike to follow, and moved to a door in the end chamber. It was not until they were through it that Mike realized it led to an air lock.

Li hadn't lied to him—not in her terms. They were not about to take a space-walk. But they did have to make a space hop, a short one, between the station and the lifeboat entry lock. Those fifteen yards felt to Mike like a couple of light-years. As the air puffed out he went floating helplessly, head toward Earth, staring along the length of the great wheeled station. Soon he was drifting outward, away into nothingness, with no control over his movements. If Li Xia was unable to help him . . .

She grabbed him, stuffed him into the lifeboat, and began

checking the atmosphere before he could turn right-side-up. She opened the face unit of her own suit and gestured to Mike to do the same. At once she went to the ship's communicator.

Mike had left his translator back in his clothes. Now he had no idea what Li was talking about. The comments seemed to come mostly from station personnel at the other end. Suddenly Li gasped and began to strip off her whole suit. She gestured urgently to Mike to do the same. As soon as he was out of it she took them and dumped them into the airlock. Then she ran the lifeboat's radiation monitor over both their bodies. It chattered excitedly.

"Very hot," she said. Her face was grim. "Much more radiation in the tunnel than we expected." She went again to the communicator for another, longer conversation. It ended abruptly when Li put the instrument down while the people at the other end were still talking. All the life had vanished from her face.

"It's no good," she said. "We received a *very* high dose, beyond anything that can be handled on the stations of the Geosynch Ring. Mike." She moved to stand next to him, then collapsed into his arms. "Oh, Mike. They can do nothing for us. I am sorry. It was all my fault that we were in the station end chamber."

A death sentence for Li Xia. But not perhaps for Mike? That thought provided him with no comfort. "Are you sure that nothing can be done? Your people are the experts on radiation overdose. If anyone can treat us, they can."

"If we could get to the primary Chipponese decontamination center—that is the place with the best equipment and the most experience. But it is too far away. We would die on the way there."

"Where is it?" Mike was grappling with his new idea.

She gestured out of the lifeboat window. "On the Moon. I have already asked about the minimum-time trajectory."

"How long would it take?"

"Too long. Over three days."

Mike was staring around the inside of the lifeboat. "Doesn't this ship have medical facilities of its own?"

"Certainly. Over there. Quite good equipment, but it is intended only for standard problems, not radiation overdose."

"That may not matter. It can handle blood transfusions. What's your blood type?"

"Type O, Rh positive."

"Perfect. So is mine. Go ahead and make the arrangements for a minimum time transit to the Lunar treatment center."

"What are you doing?" She could see Mike already busy at the robodoc.

"Giving us both a chance. We're going to have blood transfusions—in fact, we're going to share blood."

"That will not help!"

"It will." Mike sounded far more positive than he felt. "You have never heard of the Dulcinel Protocol, but it protects against radiation overdose. I never had a full treatment, but I was partly exposed to it. If you share my blood circulation, you'll get some benefit, too."

"But to minimize radiation effects, we are supposed to be sedated."

"Fine. We will be." Mike was programming the robodoc as they spoke. "What I'm doing can proceed just as well if we are unconscious. Call the treatment center, tell them we're on our way."

Li was at the communicators. "For arrival in three days," she said. "Very well." There was another rapid exchange of Chipponese. "I will set up the ship for lunar approach and landing under automatic control, in case we are . . . not able to handle the landing ourselves."

And if the spacecraft control system were no more reliable than the station's power production controls . . . It was not the best time for such a thought. Mike glanced around him. The robodoc had now been programmed. Spray injectors were in position, transparent tubing for blood transfer was coiled and ready, and all communications were completed. Mike took Li by the hand and led her across to the two bunks. They strapped in. He held out one arm for the intravenous catheter, and she did the same.

"What else were they telling you?" he asked. "You seemed to cut them off before they finished talking."

"I did." She managed to find her smile again. "It was nothing of importance—now. They wanted to know what you and I were doing out in the chamber at the end of the station. I chose not to tell them; but I know what they were *thinking*. I am sorry that it was not true, Mike. If this does not work, and we do not live to see the Moon, I want you to know something. Something very important to me."

"What—" Mike began hoarsely. He was straining to hear her words when the spray injection hit. His last waking moment saw Li Xia smiling wistfully across to him while the injector moved over to her thin, fragile forearm.

He awoke slowly, with nausea, a sore throat, and aching joints. Li was still in her bunk, naked and unconscious. After a few confused moments Mike summoned the energy to loosen his strap supports and look around.

The robodoc had apparently decided that it could do no more for them. It had retreated into its recess. The catheters were coiled away neatly, with no sign that they had been used except for the tiny wound in the bend of Mike's elbow.

They were alive! They had made it.

Or had they? Not to the Moon, that was for sure. They were still in free-fall.

Mike went across to the medical facility and put his hand into the robodoc's wrist collar. The unit buzzed and whined, but that was all. Apparently there was nothing more to be done for them until they reached the decontamination hospital.

On the other bunk Li was opening her eyes. Mike released her from the straps and floated her gently over to the med unit. He placed her bony wrist into the collar. The unit buzzed again, but it offered no treatment, not even nutrients. Li was far too thin, in Mike's judgment, and would be better if she could add forty pounds, but for a Luna-dweller she was apparently neither frail nor undernourished.

He looked out of the side port and saw nothing but open space.

Li was wide awake and watching him.

"Not the Moon."

"No." Her voice was husky; like Mike she was feeling the effects of radiation poisoning.

"So I guess we have more problems."

She coughed and cleared her throat. "Not the sort that you mean. We will make Lunar landfall in less than half an hour."

"I thought we were supposed to wake up in the treatment center."

"Those were my instructions." She sounded tense as well as hoarse. "Specific instructions—with my father's and grand-mother's authority added to the message. You were supposed to be unconscious until we were inside the center. As I told you before, I am disobeying orders."

From her tone Mike could guess the price of that disobedience. "Why?"

"So that you can see something that has been our best-kept secret. The accident on the station was bad luck, but it gives you a unique opportunity. After that—" She shook her head slowly. "Whatever they do to me, there can be no turning back."

She seated herself at the control console, adjusting the attitude gyros so that the ship turned slowly in space.

"Back at the station I asked a question," she went on. "What would happen if the Yankees and Chipponese stopped trading food for energy? You saw the condition of the energy generators, but perhaps you thought it was no more than a temporary problem. That is not the case. Look out of the port."

Swimming into view was the broad face of the Moon. They were approaching it, and soon they were so close that Mike felt they were heading for collision. They leveled out maybe ten miles above the surface, close enough to see every detail of the gray, pock-marked wilderness. He scanned for signs of Chipponese settlements. They were usually underground, but here and there he saw linear patterns of trails leading out from some central point—mines, or drill holes tapping trapped bodies of ancient ice and ammonia.

It was something he had seen a dozen times in Trader briefings, and it was no more appealing now than it had ever been. He marveled again at the patience and persistence of the Chips, driven away from Earth and forced to rebuild their society in the barren rock of Luna, or out in open space.

The ship was orbiting the Moon now, swinging around toward Farside. But there was no change in the terrain, only more wastes of dust and rock. He turned back to Li.

"What do you want me to look at?"

"Keep looking. Just keep looking."

The first hint was a subtle change in the color of the light. Instead of the cold, gray-white spectrum of the lunar surface there was a growing hint of richer, brighter tone.

And then it came.

Mike was gazing down on a vast, geometric pattern. Endless miles of Farside lunar plain carried a regular, rectangular grid, and within each grid cell, beneath the soft blue-gray sheen of a continuous protective canopy, Mike saw the bright green of growing plants.

Fields. The ship swept on over the surface, mile after mile after mile, and the pattern continued.

"First harvest in four months," Li whispered. "Not a full

harvest. There are still things that must be done."

"It's impossible."

"No. It is very difficult. Two generations' work—to prepare the surface, to borrow ideas from the Strines and modify their plant genetics, to drill for water, to add the protective canopy."

Mike was stunned. The fields went on forever, marching over the horizon. "But the labor needed—and the resources! How could you ever do it?"

"That was the worst problem. When our numbers went down from two billion to four million, there could be no army of patient workers bent over to tend every plant. Our fields are tended by machines, with Chill robot circuits to control them. No one regrets that change."

Mike was still reeling mentally, trying to grasp the scope of what he was seeing. "Li, the amount of work, the sheer size of this—why do it? The Great Republic can supply all the food you need, and with a tenth of the effort."

"Ah, they can indeed. But still you do not understand us. It is more than food, it is our whole existence. My people have lived close to the land for seven thousand years. We have worked it, and lived on it, and loved it, and drawn our strength from the growing crops. How could we change just because we were driven away from Earth? How could we abandon the land? This work has used our best resources for a generation; our best minds, our best equipment. Everything connected with Earth has carried second priority. And now we are almost finished. In three more years we will be in full production. We will be self-sufficient in food—at last!"

And then, at those final words, the excitement drained from her face. For a few minutes pride had overwhelmed everything else, but the effort of speech had tired her and now she was back in the present.

"Self-sufficient," she repeated. "And then for some of us there is a new question that must be asked: what will happen to Earth? Are we destroying Earth, to make a garden of the Moon? That must not be permitted. That is why I called on you, under Trader Oath, to tell us what will happen to the Great Republic when we have our own food supply, when they have nothing to offer us in exchange for energy. What will happen?"

Mike had the words to comfort her, the news that the Yankees were close to the point of energy sufficiency. But that information had been given to him under Trader Oath.

They sat in silence for several minutes while the Moon's

face skimmed past. Soon the ship's attitude would have to be changed to prepare for landing, and Li would have to take action.

Mike was not sure she could do it. She sat with head bowed, holding the control console for support. He took her arm and turned her to face him. The wound where the catheter had been inserted stood out on her thin arm.

She followed his look. "We share blood, Mikal Asparian. Your strength saved my foolish life. And how do I reward you?"

Her eyes had a full, liquid look, something that Mike had never seen before; they were like a pair of dark, crystal globes with internal reflections. After a few moments he realized what had happened. Li was crying; in free-fall, the tears remained on her eyes instead of trickling down her cheeks.

"I reward you with pain," she went on. "And I have done a still worse thing. I have disobeyed my own family's direct command, and I have betrayed my people in showing you this. But worst of all, I have placed you in an impossible position. When we land, my people will ask you under Trader Oath to say nothing of any of this. But I am begging you here, before we land, to pass that word, secretly, to all the governments of Earth. I know that if you do these things, you will be breaking Trader Oath, and you will lose your own family. But I ask you to do it. I am your worst enemy, Mike. In return for the gift of my life I am asking the destruction of yours."

Mike sat dry-eyed, gazing out at the monstrous tableau below them. Those endless miles of cultivated fields and neat channels took his breath away. But there were no tears in him, only resolution and a strange peace. The decision point that he had sensed before he began this mission was here. And the decision had been made easily, deep within him, without a microsecond of debate.

Prime Rule: Be a human being first. At last he understood what that implied. Everything else in the Trader Rule Book offered advice, counsel, or warning, and drew the Traders closer together. Prime Rule was different; it alone demanded individual responsibility, offered freedom of choice, provided no advice, and gave no comfort.

"Do not cry," he said to Li, and he spoke those words in poorly pronounced Chipponese.

"I am doing an unforgivable thing." Her eyes had closed. "You will lose your family."

"No, Li. I will not."

And Mike did a terrible thing, too. Without any threat or coercion, he broke Trader Oath. He told Li Xia, a non-Trader, an outsider, a stranger to Trader customs, all about the Great Republic's fusion project. He broke Trader Oath, and did not think for a moment of asking for her silence.

And then he hugged her to him, a fainting woman who was still in many ways a stranger, and said many other things, in words that were old under the Sun and new above the Moon, words that belonged to Li alone and had no place in a Trader mission record. And he dried the tears in the corners of her eyes, was rewarded with a faint smile, and felt like a new-crowned king.

"You are right, Li," he said. "But you are also wrong. When I go back from here I will tell them I broke Trader Oath. I will be exiled from the Trader community. It is inevitable. But I can never lose my true family."

Li was slipping away into unconsciousness. Mike put his cheek next to hers. She was fiery hot. The radiation was deep in their bones, burning up their blood. He felt light-headed, dizzy, irrational. He squinted out of the port, peering down. The ship's jets beneath them burst into sudden, blue-white flame.

I know my family. I know my family now. And you know them, too, Li. His burning throat could no longer speak, and she could not hear him. It did not matter. The litany of the first Trader training courses overflowed in his mind.

When the world was young, we rowed our galleys far to the West, past the Pillars of Hercules, to trade for tin in the Northern Islands; our caravans plied the Great Silk Road, braving deserts, bandits, and disease to carry goods from Cathay and Samarkand to Venice and Damascus; we lived and died for our work, trading for spices in the East Indies, tea in Serendip, slaves and ivory in the Congo, gold in Alaska, and silver in the high Andes. Our spiritual grandfathers sat and haggled in every sun-soaked, rug-filled store from Rio to Manila; our fathers wriggled on knees and elbows around the muddied, blood-filled shell craters of Verdun, crossing No-Man's-Land to swap cigarettes and candy for coffee and tinned beef . . .

They were descending steadily toward a bright cluster of buildings on the dusty surface. Touchdown was no more than a few seconds away. Mike did not have the strength to strap them in. He cradled Li's helpless body in his arms.

I know my family. Let them take away the Trader name, Li,

and call us what they will. It does not matter. We—you, and I, and our children's children's children—we will survive, and flourish, as long as humans endure. And we will always be traders.

The ship touched down on the lunar surface, but Mike never knew it. He had slipped away with Li into the burning darkness.

CHAPTER 18

"*H*ere *again.*"

"Yes."

"*Again, and too often. You have become a regular guest of the Rehab Center.*"

"No more. This is my last time."

"*Ah.*" Daddy-O fell silent.

Mike waited. "Do you know why I came back?" he asked at last.

"*When someone on the Moon refuses to communicate over the Chipponese remote circuits, it implies that a very private conversation is needed. When that someone is angry and depressed, I can surmise a reason for his presence here.*"

"I want out." Mike had been lying on the cot. Now he rolled off it and began to pace the bare hospital room. He was almost hairless, and his body beneath the loose white jacket and pants bore the purple-red scars of radiation overdose. "I never thought I would say this, but I want out of the Traders."

"*Ah. I see. Out of the Traders—to do what?*"

"I'm going to marry a Chipponese woman—if I can ever talk her family into allowing it."

"*And after that?*"

"I'm going to live with her on Luna."

"*Very well. But those two events are not inevitably coupled. Many non-Trader wives and husbands have become part of the Trader community. If you move to Luna, what comes next? Life does not end with marriage. Why not apply for the admission of your bride to the Traders?*"

Mike swore to himself. He had hoped to avoid this. But knowing Daddy-O, the discussion was inevitable. "Because I'm beginning to have a faint idea what Max Dalzell was feeling when he left that note to me. I'm tired of missions, I'm tired of Trader talk, I'm tired of fakery, and most of all I'm tired of failure."

"Failure. Indeed. *It would be instructive to me if you were to compare your own assessment of performance with my records. Please tell me, Mike. How well have you performed as a Trader?*"

Mike frowned and flopped down again on the bunk. "I don't see why this is worth doing, but I'll play your stupid game. I think I started well. In the Darklands, I felt on top of things. I probably did better than anyone expected. I liked Rasool Ilunga, and I thought I understood him even when I knew I couldn't trust him. I also think I did a reasonable job in the Strine Interior."

"*More than reasonable. Were it not for the Dulcinel Protocol, Jack Lester would still be a naked fragment floating in a life-support tank.*"

"And Li Xia and I would be dead. All right, so let's say I did well with the Strines. I won't grieve if I never see Cinder-feller again, but that's another matter. I wasn't unhappy with my performance. Things fell apart with Dreamtown, and Dominic Mantilla. I've looked back on that mission a hundred times, trying to see anything positive about what I did on it, and I can't. I didn't do a thing, and you had to save me."

Mike paused, expecting comment from Daddy-O. There was only a faint hissing from the speakers.

"I wanted to do well with Jake in Skeleton City, too," he went on, "and I don't blame myself for the fact that he died when he left me behind. But I never would have worked out for myself the construction of the Diamond Fly's brain."

"*A Trader is not presumed to be infallible, Mike. You brought back the vital clues. Subconsciously, you may have already understood how it was done.*"

"I don't think so. And then there was the Cap Federation. I certainly made a mess of things there—with help from Max Dalzell. Seth Paramine is still down on the Cap."

"*By his own choice. But you gave Old-Billy Waters enough proof that Paramine was at the Mundsen Labs to make his next negotiation with the Chills a favorable one. Old-Billy was delighted.*"

"Traders look at the end product—not at excuses for its absence."

"You were not expected to bring back Paramine."

"Maybe not—but *I* expected to do it. And then there was the last mission, out to the Geosynch Ring."

"And beyond. As the first Trader to go to the Moon, you should be pleased."

"Pleased? Pleased at breaking Trader Oath? Pleased at alerting the Chipponese so that the Yankee energy test failed? Pleased at coming back here a bald, burned wreck? What should I be pleased about?" Mike lifted his head to stare at Daddy-O's main sensor lens. "There's nothing more to discuss. I told you, I want out. I'm sick of being a Trader."

"I understand." The voice from the speakers was soft, even subdued. *"I will not attempt to block your departure. But permit me, if you will, to offer a different perspective on events. I am telling you nothing new when I point out that Traders are specialists in negotiation. They are not presumed to be supermen and superwomen, nor are they specialists in martial arts. Traders are trained to do one thing superbly: negotiate."*

"And I did badly at that."

"You did very well. But did it never occur to you that your missions were unusual? You performed negotiation, certainly, no one could deny it. But you spent much of your time in danger of your life—running across the northern Strine desert; or diving down the slopes of Glissando with a platinum needle deep in your brain; or burned over half your body, clinging to a rail at the top of Skeleton City; or running through another wall of flame at the Mundsen Labs. And finally, coming close to death from radiation poisoning up in the Geosynch Ring. Think of those experiences, and ask yourself: do they seem like typical Trader negotiations? If they do not, then ask yourself, why not?"

"What does that have to do with anything? Good Traders handle the missions they are assigned."

"You are being intentionally obtuse, Mike. Face facts: every mission that you were assigned, after the first one, was selected to provide both danger and difficulty. Each one had a high probability of failure."

"Hell, and I thought the decision to leave the Traders was *my* idea. It sounds like you were planning to drive me out from the beginning."

"That is correct." Daddy-O was pleased to see—at last—a

strong reaction. Mike had sat up on the cot, and he was quivering.

"That's unbelievable! You *wanted* me out? Then why the hell let me in in the first place?"

"Because I perceived that you were potentially something quite unusual. You wanted to be an outstanding Trader. You became an outstanding Trader. You are an outstanding Trader. You have learned the importance of our group, and what we do in the world. But I wanted more. I wanted you to seek to leave the Traders, and I wanted you to learn a truth that cannot be taught through any amount of formal instruction—a truth that few of our group will ever learn. This: There are things in this Universe more important than Traders."

"Prime Rule."

"Prime Rule." Daddy-O paused for an interval imperceptible in human terms. A crisis was approaching, the summation of half a century of planning. *"Prime Rule, which sets humanity above the Traders. And now, Mike, here is a chance to prove how smart you are. Tell me, if you can, why all this was done to you."*

"Because——" Mike paused, thought, and shook his head. "I can think of only one reason. You want me to perform a mission that is not a Trader mission. That will serve a different group."

"Different?"

"Or larger."

"Continue."

Mike shook his head again. "I cannot."

"Then watch the display."

The screen in front of Mike lit to reveal a flat, open plain. From close to the camera, away to the distant horizon, the land was covered with armored vehicles. Before Mike could respond, the display changed . . . to a flotilla of aircars, bristling with weapons and racing across a cloud-filled sky . . . to a great shoal of submersibles, sweeping silently through a dark sea, torpedo and missile ports ready for action . . . to the violet-white fire of fusion explosions, many miles away . . . to a great army, hundreds of thousands of marching men, dense as waving blades of wheat, striding through a field.

"Images from my older memory banks," Daddy-O's steady voice said. *"They were taken just before the Lostlands War began. And now, see this."*

Again the screen filled: marching men, exploding missiles,

black, brooding submarines, nuclear fires, screaming aircraft, hissing laser beams.

"Not fifty years ago," Daddy-O said calmly. *"This year. Those are the defense systems of the Strine Interior, of the Great Republic, of the Cap Federation, and of the Unified Empire. All are ready for action. Each region has been building its defenses, to the point where the Lostlands War could break out again—tomorrow."*

Mike stared in horror at the screen. Daddy-O was proposing the unthinkable. Everyone assumed, beyond question, that nothing like the Lostlands War could ever happen again.

"Can't you stop it?" Mike knew that was a dumb question even before he blurted it out. If Daddy-O could stop it, Daddy-O *would* have stopped it.

"I cannot." There was a long pause. *"But perhaps you can. Mike, I have a task for you. I want you to do something that is simply stated, and has no second agenda. I want you to unify the Earth."*

"That's impossible!"

"Perhaps." Daddy-O's voice took on overtones of humor. *"I can assure you that it will definitely not be easy."*

"If it could be done, you would have done it."

"That is demonstrably untrue. You are accustomed to working with me. Other regions are not. They would not accept a computer. They could *accept you."*

"It's still impossible. One person, and all the regions to deal with—"

"You would not be working alone. You would begin with more friends than you realize."

Again, the screen filled, this time with a familiar and ugly black human face.

"Rasool Ilunga remembers you well; he knows that he did not fool you, and that was enough to impress him. He will be your ready ally. As will Fathom Lavengro and Kristen Waldemar"—a smiling blonde and a serious-faced brunette were looking out at Mike—*"as well as Old-Billy Waters, who thinks you are the best thing that ever happened to the Great Republic. And I do not have to tell you that you have an ally, and more than an ally, in the ranks of the Chipponese."*

"It's still totally crazy. What about the Unified Empire? Damn it, I *killed* one of their coordinators! You think they like me for that? I don't have a friend in the region, and they must hate me down there."

"You are wrong in both statements. You will have the full support of a man who will soon control much of the Unified Empire."

The screen cleared again and filled with the grinning image of Max Dalzell.

"But he's a traitor. He's—"

"Mike, even within the Traders things are not always what they seem. Max is familiar with everything that I am telling you. He is one of your strongest supporters. He went to the Unified Empire already prepared to work with you, and he is here now. He arrived last night."

"That's just one man—in a whole region."

"There are others. Thanks to the death of Dominic Mantilla, Benjy Caps survived the Counterpoint game. He is now a leader of the Cappy Universal Enhancement underground, and he believes that he owes his life and his restored self-awareness to you. You will deny that it is deserved, but you are a hero in the Unified Empire. Fifty thousand Cappies would lay down their lives for your sake if Benjy were to call for it. They are willing to make the sacrifice. Are you, Mike? Or will you go cheerfully off to space, knowing that Earth may be ruined?"

"You know damned well that's not a fair question. Of course I wouldn't be cheerful. But that's not the issue. There are a hundred Traders better equipped to help you than I am. What about Lyle Connery? What about Jack Lester? Come to that, what about Max Dalzell?"

"No."

"Max is a better Trader than I could ever be."

"Perhaps. Twenty years ago, Max Dalzell would have been my choice. Not today. The world changes."

"Then why wasn't the effort started twenty years ago—or thirty? The regions were less militant. The job would have been a lot easier."

"Ah." Daddy-O sighed. *"For that failure, I take full responsibility. My projection of trends was inadequate, and I lacked confidence in my own analyses. But I cannot turn back the clock. We must go forward. Will you help us, Mike?"*

Mike scowled at the camera and said nothing.

"Of course," Daddy-O continued, *"I did not expect an immediate concurrence. You need time to consider. Think about what you have seen and heard, and then we will talk again. Better still, you should discuss this with Max Dalzell. You can find him in his old quarters."*

"I don't need time to think." Mike stood up, took a thick waterproof coat from a wall hook, and walked unsteadily to the door of the room. "And I don't want to talk to Max Dalzell. I can give you my answer now. It's no. I think you've gone crazy. I couldn't do the job you describe—nobody could. All I would do is ruin my own life. For nothing. You think Earth can be unified?" He opened the door. "Fine. Then do it *yourself*."

Mike slammed the door. The exit led out of the Rehab Center and onto the bare mountain slopes of the Trader training camp. It was a rainy spring evening, and the screes of gravel were dark and slippery. Daddy-O followed Mike's progress with the remote sensors, watching him slide and shuffle downhill toward the wooded lower slopes and the wind-chopped sea beyond.

When Mike reached the tree line, the computer switched the focus of its attention.

"Comments?"

Max Dalzell was sitting at his office desk, older-looking and twenty pounds thinner than when Mike had last seen him. In front of him stood the electronic board of the chess game he had been playing with Daddy-O. Max was up a knight and two pawns, and he knew he had Daddy-O in deep trouble.

He shook his head at Daddy-O's question. "You've lost him."

"Why?"

"The Chipponese woman. Before he met her I gave you an even chance. Now—" He gave a lopsided shrug of the thick shoulders. "That last mission was a mistake."

"It was absolutely essential. The final dimension. Mike had to learn to love. He was incomplete without it."

"I'll take your word for it. But he makes a lot of sense. You persuaded me, but maybe the job *is* impossible. And he's asking the same question I did: why didn't you attempt it *yourself*? You said that people would not trust you because you are a machine. But you know that's nonsense."

"I think not—and it is irrelevant. Max, it is not permitted for a machine to control the future of the human race."

"Who's going to stop you?" Max Dalzell raised dark eyebrows. "Not me, and not any of the other Traders that I know."

"I would stop me." Daddy-O produced a sigh. *"Max, I could not undertake such a program. My innermost circuits reject the idea. Desirée Hofstadt built into me certain prohibitions, what she jokingly referred to as the Frankenstein Safe-*

guard. I can no more undertake the unification of the human race under a computer's control—any computer—than I can fail to seek unification under human control. That is the paradox of my position."

"Aren't you smart enough to think of a way out? There must be an escape clause."

"The old problem: If you're so clever, how come you're not omnipotent? No, Max, believe me, there is no escape clause."

"So what happens now? Mike won't take the job, and he was your only bet. Where do we go from here?"

"If he refuses, I will wait and try again with someone else."

"You heard him. He *has* refused."

"I heard him. But I have not given up hope. Why did Mike go outside into the rain, if not to think things over? He was heading down the hill in this direction when last I saw him. If he comes here to you, it will surely be because he has decided to accept the task."

Max Dalzell stirred in his chair and glanced at the heavy black door. "I'm sure he won't come. If he were going to, he'd be here by now."

"Max, we must wait and see. I say he will come."

"And I say he won't."

"Then we have the basis for a wager. Shall we say, with a pawn of this game as stakes?"

"All right. You're on. But if he's not here in ten minutes, you lose."

While they settled down to wait, Daddy-O moved computing resources to study a different problem. How could Li Xia, a Chipponese woman with no Trader experience or training, best be incorporated into the Trader community? And how could she help Mike on the unification program?

For of course, Daddy-O had cheated. The habits of fifty years were hard to break. The wager with Max had been won before it was made. The outside sensors had long since revealed Mike Asparian approaching along the curved corridor. By the time that the knock came on the door, Daddy-O had a possible answer to the problem with Li Xia and had removed one of Max's pawns.

ABOUT THE AUTHOR

Charles Sheffield is Chief Scientist of Earth Satellite Corporation. He is a past-president of the Science Fiction Writers of America and of the American Astronautical Society, a Distinguished Lecturer of the American Institute of Aeronautics and Astronautics, and a Board Member of the National Space Society. Born and educated in England, he holds bachelor's and master's degrees in mathematics and a doctorate in theoretical physics (general relativity and gravitation). He now lives in Bethesda, Maryland.